A NORTHERN LIGHT

a sweet and spicy alaskan romance

Harlow Brígh

ISBN 978-1-972589-03-8 (Paperback)

ISBN 978-1-972589-04-5 (eBook)

ISBN 978-1-972589-05-2 (Audiobook)

Any reference to historical events, real people, and real places, are used fictitiously. Other names, characters, and places are products of the author's imagination.

Cover art and design by Sonya Redman

First print edition 2026

HA! Harvick Anderson Publishing

ha-publishing.com

Dedicated to S & M— *Some people come into your life as friends and quietly become something far rarer. Family, not by blood, but by choice, by steadfastness, by the thousand small ways they show up without ever asking for recognition in return.*

This book is for you both.

For the way you proved that there is a little bit of Alpenglow everywhere. In every open door, every steady hand, every phone call, every time you showed up. You never asked for thanks, and perhaps that is why I can never properly give enough of it.

We would not have made it through this last year without you. Not through the chaos, the change, the uncertainty, or the hard days that seemed to arrive one after another. You carried pieces of the weight as though it was the most natural thing in the world, because to people like you, it is.

Much like the residents of Alpenglow, you take care of your own.

And somehow, through all of it, you reminded us that home is not always a place. Sometimes, it is simply the people who refuse to let you weather the storm alone.

A Note from the Author

Long before Alpenglow existed on paper, it existed in pieces of my real life. In the sound of rain against metal roofs. In docks that creak beneath wet boots. In the snow and the people. My family has called Alaska home for generations, and no matter where life carries me, some part of me will always belong to the mountains and the water here.

Alpenglow may be fictional, but its spirit is not.

I have seen pieces of Alpenglow all across this state. In harbors in Sitka and Seward where gulls scream over the docks and rain settles into your bones. In communities where life can be hard, isolated, and unpredictable, but people still find reasons to gather, laugh, celebrate, and take care of one another anyway.

That is the Alaska I always wanted to write about.

It's not just the mountains or glaciers or northern lights, though those deserve every bit of their wonder. But the people. The stubbornness. The humor. The generosity that appears without fanfare and disappears before anyone can properly thank it.

So if you still find yourself longing to visit Alpenglow, I hope you come north someday. Stop at the little coffee stand with too many stickers in the window. Order fresh halibut somewhere overlooking the water. Wander into a tiny grocery store where everyone somehow knows everyone else's business. Watch the tide roll in beneath a gray sky and listen to the floatplanes overhead.

You might discover that Alpenglow exists a little more than either of us expected.

With love from the Last Frontier,

Harlow

Trigger Warnings...

Before you dive in, a tiny heads-up from your friendly Alaskan author.

This book comes with a healthy amount of steam, a few colorful words, and enough chemistry to melt snow off the ground in the middle of winter. It is not sweetly fade-to-black, and the people of Alpenglow tend to love with their whole hearts and very little restraint.

That said, this story also takes place in coastal Alaska, where life revolves around the water. Boats, docks, rough seas, and the realities that come with them are woven throughout the story. There is also an autistic child whose relationship with the water becomes an important part of the plot and emotional journey.

At its heart, though, this is still a story about family, community, and finding light in even the coldest places.

So grab a blanket, maybe a cup of coffee strong enough to survive an Alaskan winter, and settle in. The happily-ever-after is waiting for you at the end of the dock.

*This book is intended for mature readers **18+***

To appreciate the beauty of a snowflake, it is necessary to stand out in the cold.

—UNKNOWN*

*(*commonly misattributed to Aristotle)*

Glossary of Alpenglow, Alaska Terms*
*Maybe not in any dictionary, but it might help!

Alpenglow: A breathtaking, rosy-pink glow that bathes Alaska's mountain peaks at dawn or dusk, when the sun is just below the horizon. This fleeting optical wonder turns snowy summits into vibrant, blushing art against a deepening sky.

Aurora (Northern Lights): Shimmering ribbons of green, blue, violet, or crimson light dancing across the northern sky, caused by charged solar particles colliding with Earth's atmosphere. Common during long Alaskan winters, the aurora can appear faint and ghostlike or blaze so brightly it feels as though the entire sky is alive. In places like Alpenglow, people still stop what they are doing to watch.

Alpenglow Town: Fictionalized coastal Alaskan Town located on the fictional island of Chiltak, somewhere in the Prince William Sound. Established in 1977 by Aksel King, modeled after the coastal Norwegian Lofoten Island's fishing villages of his homeland. Now home to the children of Aksel King and seventy other full-time residents...give or take.

Prince William Sound: Vast, island-studded embayment east of the Kenai Peninsula, ringed by steep, glaciated mountains and dense rainforest. Known for its inhabited wilderness, remote, boat-only access for most villages and towns, dramatic fjords, calving glaciers, and wildlife viewing. It's a place of isolation, resilience, and stunning natural beauty, with small communities relying on fishing, subsistence, and limited tourism.

Williwaw: Fictionalized small Alaskan town on the eastern side of the mountain pass from Alpenglow Town on Chiltak Island. It is the main connection for goods and larger items via the weekly barge and the Alaska Marine Highway ferry.

Kisa'adi: A fictionalized Alaskan Native village of Chiltak peoples, located on Chiltak Island, about 5 miles south of Alpenglow. It was historically further south but was moved after a devasting flood.

Chiltak People: Fictionalized Alaskan Native descendants of eastern Prince William Sound's blended Chugachmiut and Eyak roots, with cultural threads of Tlingit-Haida influence from ancient trade and intermarriage. Skilled mariners and fishermen who navigate fjords, coves, and open water in skin qayaqs, subsistence harvesters on sea and land, preserving traditions of ceremonial respect for land and water. The permanent villages of Chiltak peoples traditionally had one large, post-and-beam, spruce plank house in the center of the village, covered with sod, with several smaller sod-covered family houses surrounding it, allowing for both community and privacy. Around all of this were annually risen totems, chronicling the village history. In the summer, they would travel to family fishing camps.

Xtratufs: Iconic brown rubber deck boots loved by Alaskans for fishing, mud, rain, or slush. They're a staple of everyday fashion, from commercial fishermen to city folks, symbolizing tough, no-nonsense Alaskan style.

Cheechako: Someone newly arrived in Alaska, often clueless about the realities of bush life, extreme weather, and remote living. Derived from Chinook jargon meaning "just come," it's a classic label for outsiders learning the ropes (and frequently the butt of good-natured ribbing from old-timers).

Sourdough (a person, not the bread): An experienced, long-time Alaskan who's weathered multiple winters and mastered bush life. The opposite of a cheechako, the term harks back to gold rush pioneers who carried sourdough starters for bread, and is now a proud label for gritty, knowledgeable old-timers with deep roots in the land.

Oosik: A classic bit of bawdy frontier humor. Alaskan slang for a walrus penis bone (baculum), often used as good-natured teasing to question a guy's toughness, size, or experience.

Sha'aéil: A traditional Chiltak endearment, roughly meaning "my sun and sea".

Potlach: A traditional ceremonial feast where totem poles might be raised, gifts given, stories shared, and social status affirmed; still practiced in modern forms to honor events, pass down traditions, or sometimes just to share community. In Alpenglow, a potlatch is a good way to celebrate a Wednesday.

Alaskan Bush: Expansive roadless wilderness with remote forests, tundra, rivers, and Arctic lands unreachable by road, where people live off-grid in cabins or small villages, depending on bush planes and seasonal travel for supplies and connection.

Alaskan Bush plane: Tough, versatile small aircraft designed for the remote wilderness. These rugged planes land on gravel bars, riverbanks, frozen lakes, beaches, open water, or tiny clearings where no runways exist, using big tundra tires, floats, or skis depending on the season and terrain. They serve as essential transportation in a state with vast roadless areas, carrying people, supplies, mail, hunting/fishing parties, and gear to isolated areas.

Charters: Privately hired boat or bush plane trips used for transportation, sightseeing, fishing, hunting, cargo runs, or wilderness access. In remote Alaska, charter work helps keep small towns alive and usually comes with weather delays, questionable coffee, and at least one story nobody fully believes.

EPIRB: (Emergency Position-Indicating Radio Beacon) A marine emergency beacon designed to send a distress signal and GPS location to search-and-rescue satellites if a vessel sinks or someone activates it in an emergency. The kind of thing every responsible captain carries and hopes they never need.

North Slope: Alaska's vast Arctic region stretching north of the Brooks Range to the Arctic Ocean. Known for brutal winters, massive oil fields, tundra landscapes, and isolated work camps where people routinely disappear for weeks at a time to work long shifts in extreme conditions.

Snowmachine: What Alaskans call a snowmobile. Used for winter travel across frozen rivers, trails, or tundra to reach cabins, hunt, or visit neighbors, essential in places without roads.

Mushing: Traveling (and a sport) by dog sled pulled by a team of huskies or malamutes. A historic and still-practiced mode of winter transport in remote areas, still tied to the Iditarod race legacy.

Termination dust: The first light snowfall dusting mountain peaks in late summer or early fall, signaling the end of warm weather and the approach of winter. It's a bittersweet, beautiful harbinger that locals joke about as a warning to stock up or head south if you're not ready for the cold.

Plankhouse: A large traditional wooden communal dwelling historically used by coastal Alaska Native peoples. Built from heavy timber planks, plankhouses served as gathering places, homes, and centers of village life during long coastal winters.

Lake Sletta'a: A fictional lake tucked within the foothills of the mountains of Chiltak Island, known for its still water in summer, ice skating and ice fishing in winter, and historically protected for the salmon runs that return there every summer.

Bentwood boxes: Versatile, steam-bent wooden containers for storage or cooking, often decorated with symbolic designs. In Chiltak oral tradition, what Raven stole with the light.

Yøl: A traditional Scandinavian and old Norse-inspired winter celebration centered around warmth, food, storytelling, music, and gathering together during the darkest days of the year. In Alpenglow, Yøl traditions brought over by Aksel King have blended with local customs over generations, turning the holiday into a community-wide celebration filled with lanterns, evergreen garlands, bonfires, strong drinks, and the stubborn belief that light always returns after even the longest winter night.

ONE

Hyder

"I think I might be dating Ellie."

Hyder King said it the way an old man might comment on the weather. Absently, while bracing one boot against the gunwale of his 39' trawler, *The Ahnah*, and hauling a thick coil of rope out of the storage locker.

Across the deck, Tala Rivers paused mid-scrub. The rag in her hand hovered over the salt-streaked aluminum of the cabin door while she slowly lifted her head and looked at him as if he'd just admitted he was secretly raising goats in the engine compartment.

"You *might* be?"

Hyder didn't look up right away. The rope was damp and stiff with dried salt, and it took a moment to shake the loops loose before he could wind it properly.

"That's what I said," he grunted.

Tala blinked as the wind slid across the water, just strong enough to rock the boat beneath her feet. The floats of Sutton's yellow Kodiak clinked softly against the dock nearby, and somewhere down by the town pier a halyard slapped a mast with the steady metallic rhythm of a loose metronome.

She straightened slowly, pushing her braid back over one shoulder. Tala was barely five foot three on a good day, but she carried herself like someone who had never once worried about size as a disadvantage. The lower half of her head was shaved clean, the rest of her thick black hair braided down her back. The chipped front tooth she'd earned in a fight outside an Anchorage bar years ago showed when she grinned.

Which she was doing now.

"Captain Oblivious," she began mildly. It was a tone she had perfected in the thirty years they had been best friends. "How in the hell do you not know if you're dating someone or not?"

Hyder kept winding rope, leaning down to stack the coil neatly on the deck beside the cleat, tugging the end tight, and finally glanced back up at her.

"I've been thinking about it—"

"That's the problem," she interrupted.

"What is?"

"You're *thinking* about it." She tossed the rag into the bucket beside her Xtratufs and leaned one hip against the cabin wall. "You ever notice," Tala continued thoughtfully, "how people who jump out of Jayhawk choppers into the Bering Sea for fun somehow become complete idiots when women are involved?"

Hyder snorted softly. "Rescue diving was not for fun."

"You literally volunteered," she scoffed.

"The Coast Guard needed good swimmers who were used to cold balls."

"Uh-huh." The wind tugged at the loose hem of Tala's flannel as she folded her arms. "Very well, Lil' Frogger," she sighed, "walk me through this slow and careful."

Hyder rested his hands on the rail and looked out across King's Cove. The water had started to change. It wasn't rough yet, but the surface had that faint, restless texture that meant something bigger was building offshore. The incoming tide carried a sharper smell than usual, deep salt and kelp, the cold mineral scent of water that had traveled a long way before reaching the cove. Even Lenny and Squiggy, the two otters who lived in the cove, usually begging for treats, were busy feeling the water with their whiskers and chittering nervously, taking turns diving for kelp, wrapping themselves in anchors.

Storm's coming.

Behind him Tala cleared her throat loudly. "Hyder..."

"Yeah?"

"Ellie?" she reminded him.

He sighed. "Right. So I've never actually asked her out."

Silence settled over the deck as Tala stared at him for a full three seconds. Then she dragged her hand slowly down her face.

"Geez. I swear, you King men can be morons."

Hyder frowned. "What?"

"If you've never asked her out, how could you possibly be dating?"

"She keeps showing up."

Tala blinked again. "Showing up where?"

"Everywhere."

"Such as...?"

Hyder began gathering another length of rope while he thought about it.

"The Forget Me Not."

Tala snorted. "That's the only coffee shop in town, and until last month her sister worked there."

"The Raven," Hyder continued, ignoring her.

"That's literally the only bar in town and the only good grub. We all go there. Practically every night."

"She was at the dock yesterday, waiting, when we pulled in..." His voice trailed off.

"Oh, wow," Tala's eyes widened dramatically, "you mean she came to the dock of the Lodge where she works as the manager? You must be right. Obviously, you're a real committed couple."

Hyder hesitated, realizing how ridiculous he sounded when he said it out loud. Or rather, when Tala said it out loud.

Still. It feels intentional.

Tala watched his expression shift and started laughing. Not politely either. It came out loud enough that a seagull lifted off the nearby piling with an irritated squawk.

"She wants to come to Williwaw tomorrow when we go pick up supplies from the barge," Hyder gave one last attempt to plead his case, but even he knew it was thin.

Tala grabbed her sides as she laughed even harder. "Her parents live there, dummy. She probably just wants to go see them. Plus, we're going to lug a few casks of beer and supplies for the Merc, not having a romantic evening of dinner and dancing."

"Beer can be romantic." Hyder grinned back at her.

"Only if you're drunk," Tala retorted as she picked her rag back up. "Besides, Ellie is probably just lonely. She's hanging around us more because her sister has gone off to college. We're some of the only people in town around her age."

Hyder grunted again. "Willow and Sterling are closer to her age than we are."

Tala turned her head slowly, again giving him that look that told him he had said something unreasonable.

"Would *you* want to spend your free time with Sterling?" she deadpanned.

Hyder opened his mouth. Closed it again.

"Exactly." Tala rolled her eyes. "Your little brother only hangs around girls to bang them. Everyone knows that."

Hyder rubbed the back of his neck before admitting, "Yeah."

Sterling had always been the charming one, brilliant in ways that made most people forgive everything else. Though Hyder suspected the Stanford PhD in engineering he had earned this spring had done nothing to improve his judgment when it came to women. Or slowed him down. Still, the kid had finally graduated, and now he had a real job up on the North Slope for the winter. Hopefully, the responsibility would do him some good.

Hyder doubted it, but it would certainly be harder for him to run through women at his usual pace up there, since the Slope was a frozen, male-dominated oil patch where the nearest woman was usually a hundred miles away.

At least Willow, Sterling's twin, balanced him out. Their sister had spent the last five years transforming her greenhouse into something out of a Nordic magazine on agriculture. It was an enormous, glass-encased farm that grew fresh vegetables and herbs and supplied duck eggs for Healy's baked goods. Half the town survived on whatever Willow, along with her two best friends, their cousin Kael and his girlfriend, Sofiya, who both worked with her, decided to grow that season. He only wished she could find someone she could share it all with.

But as he could attest, it was slim pickings in Alpenglow. It wasn't like they could all be as lucky as Sutton, their eldest brother.

Sutton had his life completely sorted out.

Of course he does.

Sutton had always been the one who carried the real weight of things. The Lodge. The planes. The town. Hyder supposed it made sense he would be the first to get his shit together too. He could still remember the exact moment Sutton realized he was in love with Charlie Griffin, the schoolteacher who had arrived in Alpenglow terrified of flying and somehow ended up marrying his brother, a bush pilot.

Their wedding was a few months ago, in late July, almost a year to the day Charlie had set foot in Alpenglow. It was nothing fancy, just the town putting on a party the only way they knew how. Loud and filled with music, food, and laughter. Then the couple left on their honeymoon for two weeks, and Charlie had come back pregnant.

Gemma, Sutton's daughter, had nearly exploded with excitement when she found out she was getting a sibling, talking a mile a minute about what she would name the baby and how the baby could sleep in her room so she could read to it every night.

First grade and already practicing being a bossy sister. Hyder chuckled quietly at the thought.

Even Hope, their not-such-a-baby-anymore sister, was doing better these days. She was fifteen now, had grown a little taller over the summer, had matured some, and had two good friends in Finn and Kake who seemed to understand when she was struggling and helped pull her out of her slumps before she slid down too far. She was still questionably obsessed with Taylor Swift and was probably on her phone too much, but she was also doing better in school now that Charlie understood her ADHD better and was able to teach to her strengths.

All in all, the Kings were doing great. Even this charter season had been their best yet. Every week they'd been filled to near capacity in the Lodge, and there was now talk of building a honeymoon cabin on the cliffs up north. Hell, they were also discussing replacing one of their planes that they'd lost last year and buying another boat so they could handle all the extra clients. Right now, they were contracting out with Dutchy, one of the other locals. He was a solid fisherman, if a little gruff around the edges, but the Kings figured it was only a matter of time before he retired.

Hyder glanced over at Tala. She was tightening a bolt on the storage hatch with the focus of someone who was pretending not to listen to his loud thoughts. If they bought the second trawler, Tala would probably captain it. She'd earned it, even if she was a pain in the ass.

Yeah, life is good.

Still...something felt like it was missing. Maybe that was why he was imagining things with Ellie. He certainly had never considered dating her. Not that she wasn't attractive and perfectly nice. Sweet, really, and super organized. He just had rules about dating women in town. He only did it if he thought it might lead to something serious. He supposed he was waiting to find his person, and he always believed he would know her when he saw her. A love-at-first-sight kind of thing.

Hyder cleared his throat and pushed away from the rail.

Better not say that out loud.

Tala would roast him for a week.

The wind had strengthened another notch now, rippling the water in darker lines and slapping against the deck pilings. Out to the east, beyond the mouth of the cove, the sky was thickening into a low gray ceiling rolling in from Prince William Sound. Hyder inhaled again, slowly, deeply. The smell of the tide was getting stronger. Icy water pushing in fast. Meaning winter wasn't far behind, despite the calendar saying it was still autumn.

"Getting ugly out there," he murmured offhandedly.

Tala followed his gaze.

"Yeah."

He rubbed the back of his neck again, feeling on edge.

"Storm's coming."

Tala smiled slowly, a wicked look in her dark eyes. "Maybe more than one."

"What's that supposed to mean?" Hyder frowned.

Instead of answering, Tala nodded toward the ramp.

Hyder turned. Ellie was making her way down toward the dock. Her strawberry-blonde hair was whipping wildly around her shoulders in the rising wind. One hand held her jacket closed while the other lifted to wave at them.

Hyder scowled automatically.

"See, she's everywhere," he muttered under his breath.

Something about the way Tala was smiling beside him made him suspicious. But before he could say anything, he had to brace his legs as another gust rattled the rigging along the dock and sent the tide smacking hard against the hull of *The Ahnah*.

Storm's definitely coming.

TWO

Sola

Sutton *"Puñeta!"*

Marisol Rivera-Kelly slammed both hands onto her desk hard enough to rattle the keyboard and had to fight the powerful urge to throw her phone across the room.

"You okay, Sola?"

With a deep breath that did very little to cool the fire climbing up her spine, Sola pushed her chair back and turned to face Frieda, who sat behind the counter that separated the cramped provider workspace from the waiting room. The older woman had her glasses perched halfway down her nose and a stack of patient intake forms balanced neatly beside the jar of hard candy she guarded like a dragon over treasure.

"No," Sola muttered, her voice coming out sharper than she intended. "Not really. I hate insurance companies."

Frieda snorted.

"Ha. I know, right? They're the worst." She leaned forward slightly, curiosity bright in her eyes. "What did they deny this time?"

Sola turned back toward the glowing screen of her computer, where the email was still open like a personal insult.

"What didn't they deny?" she grumbled. "Poor Mr. Torres needs better medication for his diabetes, but they're still insisting they'll only pay for the Metformin." She rolled her eyes before continuing, her frustration bleeding into every word. "Even though it's doing *nada* to control his sugars."

Sola sighed, leaned back in her chair, and glared at the stained ceiling tiles like they might offer a solution. As much as she would love to think of her white coat as armor that allowed her to shield herself from bad prognoses and orchestrate the outcomes, she knew there were simply things out of her control. Not that it didn't eat at her.

"If we can't get a handle on it soon," she added quietly, "he's probably going to lose a foot."

Frieda clucked her tongue, shaking her head, though Sola noticed the look that crossed her face. It was the same one she always wore when patients came in with conditions she believed could be fixed with discipline and better choices. If they just tried harder. Frieda meant well, but the world she believed in was not the one Sola lived in every day, not for many of the patients that came into the East Harlem clinic where they worked.

Take Mr. Torres.

He had grown up poor and lived his whole life poor, and even though he worked two jobs for years, he'd barely kept his family hovering above the poverty line. Here he was, in his 70s, surviving on nothing but Social Security and whatever scraps of disability insurance he could get.

Worse than that, he lived in a neighborhood that was the very definition of a food desert. Fresh produce was a luxury. Whole grains were expensive. Even if he had the money, which he didn't, the closest place to buy healthy groceries was three subway stops away. The food bank helped, but only barely.

Sola pinched the bridge of her nose, trying to stave off a building headache.

"Do you suppose Doctor Rob could help?" Frieda finally suggested.

Sola's stomach twisted. She knew Frieda meant well, but the suggestion lit another spark of anger in her chest. She hadn't spent four years in college, another four in med school, and three more in residency just to run to another doctor every time she needed to advocate for one of her patients.

"Help with what?"

Speak of el diablo *and he shall arrive.*

Doctor Edelstein appeared around the corner of the hallway as if he'd been summoned by her irritation alone. His balding head glinted as he leaned casually against the counter and took a moment to pop the lid off Frieda's candy jar. Doctor Rob, as he constantly insisted everyone call him, selected a butterscotch candy and unwrapped it slowly while flashing a smile he clearly believed was irresistible.

Sola had another word for it.

Slimy.

And just subtle enough about it that no one else seemed to notice.

"Sola needs some help with the insurance company," Frieda said helpfully, smoothing a hand over her carefully coiffed, faded red hair. She actually did seem to think the man was charming.

But Frieda never had the chance to feel his roaming hands "accidentally" graze her boobs in the supply closet, and she didn't have to deal with his condescending tone every time she needed a consult. It had been like that since she'd joined the practice almost a year ago. He turned to her now and winked.

"Well," he said smoothly, "I have a patient waiting, but I can squeeze you in right after." He tilted his head toward the hallway. "If you want to meet in my office."

Sola could not think of a single thing she wanted less. Still, she forced a polite smile.

"Thanks." The word tasted like vinegar.

Doctor Edelstein sauntered away down the hall, humming to himself.

The moment he disappeared, Sola picked up her phone and began dialing the insurance company again.

She would get the medication approved herself. Even if she had to walk in her favorite Badgley Mischka heels that she had found on clearance, all the way to Manhattan and personally park herself in the insurance office lobby until someone caved to her demands.

By the time Sola climbed the narrow stairs of the third-floor walk-up in the South Bronx that evening, her feet hurt, her patience was gone, and the city had drained every last ounce of energy from her body. She had finally gotten the insurance approval, but Doctor Rob still managed to steal one of her new patients, and on her way home, someone grabbed her ass on the subway. She would have kneed the offender in the crotch, but when she turned with a scowl, the three men behind her all had looks of innocence plastered across their faces.

The moment she pushed open the door, the smell hit her. Garlic. Plantains. Something savory and spicy that made her stomach instantly growl. The rich scent of mofongo drifted down the short hallway like a warm embrace, pulling her forward into the small, rent-controlled apartment that had been home for nearly two decades.

"*Mamí*?" she called.

"In the kitchen!"

Her son lay stretched out on the carpet of their living room. The only place in their tiny apartment where he had any space. He didn't even have his own room, still sharing one with his grandmother.

August had a large sheet of paper spread in front of him, his tongue poking out slightly as he concentrated on the careful lines he was drawing. A map was forming under his pencil. Tight clusters of streets twisting around one another in patterns that only he fully understood. She looked closer and realized it was some ancient European town neither of them had ever been to.

"Hey, GusGus," Sola said softly, leaning against the doorway as she slipped off her heels, sighing and curling her toes. "I missed you today, bud."

August didn't look up. He didn't pause his drawing either. The pencil continued moving in steady, precise lines.

Sola didn't take it personally. She knew she could force eye contact if she wanted to. Make him respond in some close approximation of the way other kids did. Those not on the autism spectrum. But she had learned long ago that her Gus communicated just fine in his own ways, when he was ready.

And he was happy doing what he was doing. That mattered more than any social convention.

In the kitchen, Lucia Rivera stood at the sink rinsing an old banged-up pan that had come over from Puerto Rico with her more than thirty-five years ago. Her salt-and-pepper hair was pulled into a loose bun, and the small frame she'd passed down to her daughter was wrapped in a faded floral apron.

"You're late, Marisolita," Lucia said without turning.

Sola sighed. "I know. Long day."

Lucia turned then, wiping her hands on a towel before giving Sola a long look with her dark, serious eyes. Something else Sola had inherited. In fact, if one were to look at pictures of her mother at her age, one would think they were twins. Sola was grateful she had none of her father in her. Though she supposed she had both the Irish temper and the Latina one.

"You look tired, *mija*."

"I am tired," Sola admitted as she dropped her purse on the small kitchen table and stretched her neck from side to side. "Insurance companies tried to kill one of my patients today."

"Mmhmm," Lucia hummed softly. "Sounds about right."

Sola poured a glass of dark red wine and leaned against the counter while her mother dished food onto a plate. Sola took it and sat down. Her mother joined her, sitting in companionable silence, satisfied to see her daughter eat.

She was nearly finished, letting the comfort of familiar tastes and surroundings ease some of her tension, when her mother told her, softly, "There was...something at school today."

Sola's shoulders immediately retightened and her stomach dropped. She put down her fork, no longer hungry.

"What kind of something?"

"Some boys threw Gus's notebook away. He had a meltdown," Lucia added. "The teachers handled it, rescued his book, but it was a rough afternoon for him."

Sola closed her eyes for a moment. The exhaustion in her bones seemed to double.

She and her mother loved August fiercely, more than anything in the world, but the struggle to make sure he was safe, understood, and protected...it never stopped. She was constantly reading articles about ways schools could help, and their school definitely tried. But the bullying was getting to be a problem. And he was only nine. What would it be like once he entered middle school? Or later?

She turned toward the living room and watched August carefully shading one corner of his map.

If I could just find a way to move us somewhere a little safer, she thought. She shook her head. The idea of leaving their neighborhood seemed impossible. She was born there. August, too.

Her mother cleared her plate as Sola stood, forcing her shoulders to fall, and walked toward the single bathroom. A long shower would make everything better. She only hoped the hot water would last. They had been having problems with the heater for a few weeks and the super was taking his time fixing it.

Lucia's voice called after her. "Oh! I almost forgot."

Sola paused, her hand on the bathroom doorframe. "What?"

"A headhunter called today."

Sola groaned quietly. She'd been getting calls for the last year, ever since her residency finished. But it never amounted to anything. She had deliberately chosen to get a DO, a Doctor of Osteopathic

Medicine, rather than an MD. She liked the idea of treating the whole person. Mind, body, and spirit. Rather than just attacking symptoms with pills or procedures right away. Unfortunately, many in the medical world still looked down on DOs as lesser or practitioners of "alternative medicine," even though her training was just as rigorous and the licensing was identical in practice. The job offers usually mirrored this idea.

"Three times," her mother added, her voice eager.

That made her turn around. Lucia picked up a scrap of paper from the counter and rushed over, handing it to her.

Sola glanced down at her mother's messy handwriting.

A name. A number. And a place she had never heard of.

Alpenglow. Huh.

"It's to start up a new practice," Lucia explained animatedly, her eyes now bright. "A whole house is included. Moving expenses too. And the pay is twice what you make now."

Sola stared at the paper, acknowledging a slight tingle of excitement running up her spine. Then her mouth twisted and she looked up, meeting her mother's gaze.

"*Qué carajo*...? Where the hell is Alpenglow?"

THREE

Hyder

The thing about big families was that they were rarely quiet or calm. The Kings were no exception.

Even when the Lodge stood empty of guests, the place never really *felt* empty. Someone was always around. A sibling passing through the kitchen looking for coffee, cousins drifting in from Kisa'adi Village just to say hello, one of the Lodge staff wandering through the mudroom in search of dry gloves or a missing headlamp. There were rarely fewer than a dozen people coming and going through the main house.

It was one of the reasons he slept on his boat in the summer. Just for a chance to...

Be.

Without everyone *being* there too. Unfortunately, it was already starting to drop below freezing at night, which meant he'd soon have to move back up to his room in the Lodge, and just deal with all the noise and chaos.

There had not been any Lodge guests for more than two weeks. For years that had been the natural rhythm of things. Once moose season shut down, and the cold rolled in, the wilderness tourists usually disappeared. There was not much reason for travelers from the Outside to come all the way to a remote town on a small island in the Prince William Sound once winter settled in. The cove got icy at the shallow edges, the smaller boats were pulled out of the water, and the town folded inward for the long dark stretch until spring.

But this last year had changed things a little.

Not dramatically, not yet, but enough that the family had begun to feel cautiously hopeful about winter bookings. The hot springs up in the foothills, east of Alpenglow, had always been there, with steam curling up through the spruce trees on cold mornings like something out of a storybook. The Kings had finally done something with them, building a stone soaking pool and a pair of simple bathhouses nearby so everyone could actually enjoy the place without freezing to death in the process. Someone had suggested marketing the experience. Something about soaking in hot mineral water while the aurora moved across the sky above the valley. The idea sounded more romantic than practical, since there were certainly other options for travelers if they were so inclined. Places more established and easier to get to.

Then Hope got involved.

She had started posting short videos online about life in Alpenglow. At first, they had mostly been little slices of daily life. Sitka stealing a whole chicken from the kitchen, the cove glowing gold under the midnight sun, the alpenglow blushing across the mountains in autumn, one of her brothers doing something foolish that she could caption with devastating sarcasm. Things he supposed most teens did just for something to do.

But somewhere along the way people had started paying attention. Apparently, Hope had gathered a surprising number of followers, and those followers had begun asking questions about visiting the Lodge in winter once she showed them the hot springs. These were a different kind of tourist than they were used to. Less into hunting and fishing, and more into the *experience*.

Hyder did not pretend to understand how any of it worked, but somehow it translated into a handful of winter reservations. Not many yet. Just enough to make everyone curious about what the next few years might bring.

Still, tonight the Lodge belonged entirely to them, which meant dinner was going to be loud, rather than subdued in deference to any guests.

That was also why Ellie had come down to the dock, calling out to Hyder and Tala to say it was time to eat. Tala was now doing her absolute best not to turn the entire walk back to the Lodge into an I told you so speech, which she was mostly accomplishing through expressive looks rather than words.

Hyder noticed every single one of them, his normal grin weakening slightly as the three of them climbed the gravel path toward the Lodge. The storm he had smelled was fighting to make itself known, rustling the spruce trees and carrying the cold bite of the incoming tide up the hillside.

Beside him Tala bumped his shoulder.

"I'm not going to say it," she chortled.

Hyder shot her a look. "You already are."

Ellie walked a few steps ahead of them, one hand pushing her hair out of her face as the wind whipped it around again immediately. The twinkling path lights were on, casting a warm golden glow across the wide steps and the gravel path.

Even after nearly six years, Hyder still found himself slowing slightly whenever he approached the Lodge like this. It was solid in a way that made him proud every single time he looked at it. Thick log beams and stone foundations anchored the building into the slight slope, while the front porch and wide windows and French doors faced the cove so guests could watch the changing light across the water with the town boardwalk in the distance. It was large enough to host visitors comfortably but designed so the family had their own private spaces as well, a balance that had taken Sutton months of arguing with architects to get right.

Behind the Lodge sat the Natatorium, the pool house, whose name Hyder still found ridiculously formal even after all these years. The architect had insisted on calling it that during the design process, and Hyder had taken a certain childish pleasure in pronouncing the word whenever possible. The building itself had long since become part of the normal rhythm of life at the Lodge, a warm place to swim or soak when the weather outside turned truly bitter.

The staff cabins stretched beyond the main house, nestled neatly among the trees so they felt pleasantly separate yet never far away. Behind them lay only a small runway they rarely used, a workshop where they serviced planes and boat engines, and then nothing but dense forest for miles until the mountains rose, already covered in termination dust.

It had taken the King siblings years to build everything. Years of stubborn planning and bone-aching hard work. Yet every time Hyder looked at it, he still marveled a little at what they had managed to create from nothing but forest.

They entered the house through the mudroom, the warmth and noise from the kitchen already enveloping them. Hyder toed off his boots and lined them beside the others, noticing that the row had grown unusually long tonight.

Warm light spilled from the kitchen along with the unmistakable smell of grilled meat. Hyder's stomach answered immediately. Inside, the enormous dining table was already crowded. Overcrowded. Hyder stopped just inside the doorway when he saw it.

Only three chairs were empty. At a custom table that could easily seat twenty people.

Amos and Melodie were halfway down, speaking over one another in the animated way they always did when arguing about village news from Kisa'adi. Two other cousins from the village listened with quiet interest while Kael Attla leaned back comfortably beside Sofiya Antov, the two of them sharing a plate of fries while Sofiya laughed at something Willow had just said.

Micah sat near Sutton at the head of the table, their heads bent together. Charlie was on Sutton's other side, passing around a bowl of Willow's salad greens.

Hope and Gemma were at the other end of the table, along with a few of the younger cousins, laughing about something. Sitka was sitting carefully behind them, waiting for someone to drop a tasty morsel.

Hyder cleared his throat.

"Ladies first." He stepped aside for Ellie with exaggerated politeness.

The plan was simple. Let her sit first, then choose whichever of the remaining seats was farthest from her. Unfortunately, Ellie slid neatly into the middle chair of the three open seats. Which only left the chairs directly on either side of her.

Tala dropped into the seat on Ellie's left side and very carefully did not look at Hyder. He could still hear the suppressed laugh.

Hyder sighed and took the last seat, doing his best to scoot it as far away as possible, without being obvious.

Dinner tonight was moose burgers that Sutton had grilled outside, thick patties topped with a sharp cheese that Sofiya had made from her herd of goats. There were bowls of fries from potatoes Willow and Kael grew, scattered across the table along with big platters of burgers, buns, and all the fixings.

They had arrived in the middle of an ongoing conversation.

"...I'm telling you," Micah was proclaiming loudly as Hyder reached for a burger, "that engine is going to need work before spring. It needs to be dismantled and rebuilt."

Micah was another bush pilot who did any of the town runs that Sutton couldn't. And he was Sutton's oldest friend. Which meant he was probably one of the only people who could change his brother's mind once he had decided something. Besides Charlie, that was.

"It'll last another season," Sutton replied calmly as he took a bite of French fry and chewed thoughtfully.

"Famous last words. It's not like we can afford to be down another plane come March."

Hyder watched as Charlie stiffened and her warm brown eyes skimmed over his brother, her face tightening. He didn't blame her. Last year, his brother was on a supply run when his plane's engine had an oil line break loose. He had barely managed to survive the emergency landing on a high glacier. The plane hadn't been so lucky. What made everything worse was it had appeared that the crash was caused by some type of tampering, though they had never been able to figure out by whom or why. The mystery still aggravated them all, like some unfinished plot line in a book, just hanging there. And though the town was no longer on high alert, it still made everyone watch any visitors a little closer.

"I know, and we can do the engine on the Skywagon," Sutton answered him, though he took a moment to run a hand over Charlie's back, as though he knew, without looking, that the memory bothered her. "But we need to figure out which plane we want to buy first. I sorta want to get another Beaver, but I haven't found one in good enough condition. Marshall has one, but he's being stubborn about it. I'll wear him down though."

"Hyder," Amos called suddenly from farther down the table, "how was the water today?"

Hyder swallowed a bite of burger before answering. "Choppy. Storm rolling in from the sound."

Amos nodded as if that confirmed something he had already suspected.

The conversation rolled onward around him in the easy, overlapping way King family dinners always did. Plates moved back and forth across the table, someone asked for ketchup, Hope slipped a fry to Sitka, and Gemma interrupted three different adults to ask about whales.

"Do whales come into the cove in winter?" she finally got around to Hyder, walking halfway around the table.

"Sometimes," Hyder admitted.

"What if one gets stuck in the ice?"

"Well, the deep parts of the cove rarely ice over." He shrugged. "But if it did, then we'd help it."

"With what?"

"Chainsaws!" Micah called out.

Gemma's blue eyes went wide.

Hope didn't even look up from her plate, her platinum hair falling forward as she added dryly, "He's lying, Gems. Mostly."

"Mostly?" Gemma whispered.

Hyder glanced down, forcing a serious tone. "Just don't fall in and you won't have to find out."

Gemma gasped and walked back to her seat, her elfin face twisted in deep thought.

Then Sutton asked Willow about next season's charter calendar. Sofiya teased Kael about the story he was telling Amos, while Melodie tried, unsuccessfully, to get everyone to pass the salad bowl back her way.

The room hummed with voices and movement. Hyder felt it, and he loved it. He loved the people. But he couldn't help but still feel like he was alone, even as he was surrounded. It made no sense.

The phone rang and Willow jumped up immediately.

"I'll get it!"

She hurried across the kitchen and lifted the receiver from the wall phone.

"Hello, King Wilderness Lodge."

The rest of the table continued eating while she listened. Then her whole expression brightened.

"Oh! No worries, it's not too late," she said cheerfully. "We're four hours behind you."

Several people looked up.

"No, really," Willow continued. "I was hoping you'd call."

She paused to listen again, taking out a notepad and scribbling down something.

"Yes, of course. Can we set up a time for an interview?"

Sutton's attention sharpened instantly.

"Zoom is perfect," Willow said, pacing a little as she spoke. "It'll be me and a couple others."

Another pause.

"Friday good?" She laughed softly. "Anytime works. We'll make it work...yes, that's perfect."

When she finally hung up the phone, she turned back toward the table with unmistakable excitement, tossing her long black braid over her shoulder.

"I think I found us a doctor!"

The kitchen quieted almost immediately. Hyder glanced across the table just in time to see the look that passed between Sutton and Charlie. He knew Sutton had wanted a full-time medical professional in Alpenglow for a while. That urge had only heightened in the months since they had found out Charlie was expecting. Hyder understood. They had lost their mother from complications while giving birth to the twins. Nan had managed to deliver Willow just fine, but Sterling was breech, and after his birth, their mother had hemorrhaged and died within minutes. They were right next to her, holding her hands the whole time.

The Kings had hired a recruiting service, and the town had banded together, as they always did, quickly building a new clinic near the square. It was simple, but modern, and they'd barged in all the latest bells and whistles, all in hopes of attracting someone to take the position. They'd thought maybe a traveling nurse practitioner. Someone who would sign a year contract at least. But a real doctor would be tremendous.

Hope leaned forward eagerly. "What's their name?"

"Doctor Rivera-Kelly," Willow said, looking down at the notepad. "Marisol. She sounds great," she continued, clearly still energized from the conversation. "She has this charming Latin accent and she's from New York City."

Hyder snorted.

"A New Yorker, huh?"

Willow nodded, shooting him a wary glance that said she knew what he was going to say and wanted him to keep his mouth shut.

Hyder leaned back slightly in his chair, grinning and ignoring her.

"Does she know there's no pizza here?" he asked dryly. "And while the sun never sets in summer, our town definitely sleeps."

A few people laughed. Willow was not one of them.

Sutton rested his elbows on the table, considered before speaking.

"Well," he said at last, his tone measured but hopeful. "Let's just see how the interview goes."

He glanced around the table at the gathered family, then picked up Charlie's hand, kissing it while he met her eyes.

"Hopefully she works out."

FOUR

Sola

Sola had flown into JFK, LaGuardia, and Newark so many times over the years that she had lost count. From the sky, she could tell them apart, but the one thing they all had in common was the vast city skyline, filled with skyscrapers she knew by heart, millions of ant-like cars on the roads below, and other buildings stretching as far as the eye could see.

This...is not *that.*

The last hours had been nothing but water, a vastness of ocean as far as she could see. Then, for the last half an hour...mountains. So close, despite how high they were flying, that it felt as though she could reach out and touch the snow-covered ridges and peaks. And they went on with no end in sight. Just like the ocean had.

Then, as the plane slowed, lowered for approach, and banked, she saw the city of Anchorage. It was small, with only a few tall buildings, and all around it, almost like the sides of a shattered bowl, mountains rose higher than any skyscraper. It was awe-inspiring, but in a whole different way. Admittedly, she knew there was probably more to see, but she was sitting in the aisle seat, with her mother beside her, and her son with his face pressed up against their only window.

She was slightly surprised at how easy it had been to get August to understand they were moving. She had expected a fight or a meltdown on the day they left. Something. But he'd stood there, listening to her explain about a new school, new friends, a safer place... all the while with his gaze over her shoulder, saying nothing. Processing, she'd hoped.

Then, her mother said, simply, "There will be so many new things to make maps of, *mijo.*"

For a moment, August turned to Lucia, almost met her eyes, gave a slight smile, then replied, "Okay," and ran off to gather his notebook. As if he thought that was the only thing that mattered enough to pack for their move.

Even now his notebook was in his hands, clasped tight, ready for all his sketches of whatever he saw out of his window. It might not even be what Sola would think of, but it would matter to him. Her son had always had a keen instinct for maps and weather. It was a little eerie, but at least the one thing she had never worried about was him getting lost in their city. He always knew how to find his way home, from the minute he could walk. And he always left an umbrella out for her when he knew it was going to rain. Even on the sunniest of days. She had only made the mistake of ignoring the umbrella once, because he was always right.

The plane straightened out and lowered its gear, coming in for landing, and Sola took a deep breath. The day had been a long one. They had started early, just as the sun was rising over New York, catching an expensive cab from their apartment, loading in everything they were bringing with them. All day long, the sun followed them west. To Seattle, then their flight here. But at least they were almost done.

It was astonishing to her how easy it had all been to pack up and go once they realized they were starting a new life in a fully furnished home with three bedrooms, two whole bathrooms, and a kitchen for Lucia to cook in, with a massive table for August to draw on.

Everything, their whole lives, had fit into five large suitcases and four big, taped boxes. Even saying goodbye to the apartment that she had lived in since she was nine, that August had always lived in, was easier than she had thought. Though carrying down all those suitcases and boxes without an elevator certainly helped.

Not that Sola wasn't nervous. She was the mother to a son with autism, so she was always a little anxious. But for now, August seemed remarkably comfortable, and so was her mother, so Sola let her own excitement for their new life take the lead.

She thought back to the interview almost three weeks ago.

"It's 1,000 square feet, with two exam rooms, a small waiting room, an office, a bathroom, and a storage room." Willow King had smiled as she explained the layout of the new clinic. Then she had forwarded a list of all the equipment that was already in the clinic, along with a few pictures, and a quick note explaining that they would order anything else she needed.

It seemed almost too good to be true. Her own practice, fully funded, and no one who came had to pay for healthcare. She was going to be able to treat anyone who walked in the door to the best of her abilities. She knew there had to be a catch. It was not until the end of the interview, when the very attractive man named Sutton, who had been quiet the whole time, finally opened his mouth, that she realized what the catch was.

"Have you taken a moment to look up Alpenglow on a map or to find some pictures?" he'd asked. His incredibly deep, slightly European tone and serious eyes were unnerving.

Sola blushed and looked down. She hadn't. She had googled it the night she got the paper from her mother, right before she called to set up the interview. But she only read enough to know it was in Alaska. That alone had given her pause, because Alaska was one of those mysterious places one hardly ever thinks about. Ironically, when she was little, she had thought it was a big island, somewhere down by Mexico, since that was where it was on the map in her school. It wasn't until she was much older that she'd learned enough to know it was up north and much bigger and colder than she'd realized. As she quickly thought over his question, she realized that when she tried to bring up a picture of Alaska in her mind, she saw only igloos and polar bears. Even though, rationally, she knew that was probably not the case. Or at least not entirely the case.

But something about his stern demeanor made Sola straighten her shoulders and look him straight in the eye over her computer screen. And she lied. A great big, bold-faced lie.

"*Si*, of course. Alpenglow looks beautiful. I am very excited to live there."

Sutton stared back at her for a moment, clearly still unsure, until the pretty blonde next to him, who had earlier introduced herself as Charlie, elbowed him in the side and he winced a bit.

"What?" he grumbled under his breath to the woman while she glared at him.

"Be nice." Charlie's southern accent came out strong, and Sola watched Sutton's whole demeanor change. Suddenly he didn't look so serious, and one side of his mouth actually lifted into a slight smile.

Willow then took over, "That's great, we are so glad you think so. I think I can speak for all of us when I say that we were super impressed with your resume and would be honored if you would consider coming on board. Did you have any questions for us?"

For a moment, Sola was not sure. She did have questions. She had spent the last few days coming up with thousands of them. But they had answered many of them already and the most important to her was August.

"Well, if I did take your offer, I guess my biggest concern would be my son. His name is August, but he likes to be called Gus. He is nine. And he is..." she hated this part. Half the time people would look at her with sympathy. The other half was almost like they just didn't get it. Like she was telling them her son had two heads.

"...autistic," she finished, waiting to see which half these people would be.

Charlie ended up surprising her. Her face lit up.

"That's great," she began. "I love to get new students. Oh, I guess I should explain that I'm the teacher here. Is Gus in third or fourth grade?"

"Third..." Sola heard the shock in her voice. She was expecting the same tepid responses she'd had for the last few years from his teachers. Questions about Gus's IEP and functioning level. His behavior.

"Fantastic," Charlie beamed. "I have a great group of other boys and girls around that age. He's gonna fit right in. If you do take the job, and I really hope you do, you'll have to shoot me a quick email about some of his likes and dislikes, and how *he* learns best, so we can make the transition as easy as we can for Gus."

That was it. The moment Sola knew she was going to move to Alpenglow.

It wasn't the pictures of the beautiful red cottage or the backyard with a small tire swing. It wasn't the clinic and how well planned it was and how the town had already agreed to order every single thing on her list. It wasn't even the money, though the money was great. It was the feeling of certainty, for the first time since she'd first learned that August was wired differently, that there was someone who wouldn't look at him like he was an *other*. Someone who seemed to already think of him as just a little boy who needed to learn, and who was already thinking of ways to give him community. Sola wasn't naïve. She knew there was every possibility it might not work. August would still face struggles. They all would. But maybe, just maybe, Alpenglow might be a place where August could fit in.

Sola sent her acceptance letter the next day. She would have said it right there during the interview, but she didn't want to seem too eager.

Now, as the plane touched down, she was suddenly feeling less sure. Everything was different. There were cars on the roads, but they were widely spaced out, not bumper to bumper. There were buildings, but they had enormous parking lots and were wider than they were tall. And the colors. It was hard to explain. She was used to concrete, two-hundred-year-old brownstones, and structures so high you had to tilt your head back while the sun glinted off miles of glass. It was all a different shade than what she was seeing now.

Nature. That's what I'm seeing.

Trees that stretched even farther than the buildings in New York City ever could. But instead of the red and orange leaves she had left behind, they were already barren or the deep green of spruce. And of course, all the mountains, jagged rows upon rows, their peaks already buried and smoothed by snow. Everything felt like it was of the earth. Untamed, rather than manmade. She felt small. Which was not necessarily bad.

Just...different.

After they got off the plane, and after they'd gathered all their bags, they headed to the hotel that Willow had arranged for her. Even that felt unusual. In the lobby was an enormous brown bear in a glass case, preserved like it might reach out and eat you if you weren't careful. It hardly seemed possible that something so big and wild could exist. But there it was, standing on its hind legs, its teeth and eyes gleaming, looking alive. The three of them stood there for a moment, their heads tilted back, eyes wide.

"Kodiak Grizzly," August blurted out.

Sola smiled. It wasn't often that her son chose to speak unprompted, but when he did, it was usually with something she was slightly surprised that he knew to say.

"Yes, *mijo*. It's awfully big, right?"

August kept his eyes on the bear, but he nodded. Sola grabbed his hand and walked toward the desk to check in. They had one night there, to try and get over the long day of travel, then tomorrow morning, they would catch one more plane.

To Alpenglow.

When Sola woke, it was still early for Alaska.

2:45 a.m.

Years of getting up and out the door by seven, to make it to work by eight, were still in her system. She tiptoed across the carpet, trying not to wake her son, and gently pulled open the curtains.

"Ay bendito!" she breathed with wonder. It was snowing and clearly had been for hours. A blanket of white covered the world, softening whatever rough edges Alaska might have had. She was a New Yorker, so she'd experienced snow and cold weather her entire life. But this was different too. It was pure white, not covered in the grime of the city, and there was not a single step disturbing it.

Sola turned, reluctantly, and went to take a shower. They still had hours before they'd be picked up, but she knew she would not get back to sleep. She was too excited.

Once she was dressed, she made herself coffee, her face twisting at the offensive, watered-down mess the Keurig had spit out. In one of their suitcases was her mother's *la greca*, the battered aluminum pot that had been on their stove for as long as Sola could remember. She supposed she could manage one morning without it. But certainly not two.

Sola pulled a chair closer to the window. She would watch the quiet show while she waited for her mother and August to wake. From behind her, she heard the door that separated her room from her mother's suite and turned. Her mother was wrapped up tight in her faded robe and came shuffling over in her old slippers.

"Mamí, you're up early."

Lucia waved her hand and scoffed.

"Ah, Marisolita, it's almost seven-thirty back home. I slept in. So did you."

Sola almost said, "This is home now, *Mamí,"* but she didn't. It was too soon to say that. She wasn't even convinced herself.

August sat up, his dark brown curls a wild mess, and stared at them with owl-wide eyes for a moment, like he was trying to remember where they were. Then he threw the covers back and jumped out of the bed and rushed over. His eyes widened even more at the fat snowflakes coming down outside. Slowly, they drifted to the ground, adding to the soft carpet below.

"Dendritic snowflakes," he whispered in awe.

Sola was not sure what that meant, but she was sure he was right. She reached over and ruffled his hair. He let her, without pulling away.

"What do you say if we all get dressed and go for a walk in the snow?" Sola suggested.

A big, green SUV pulled up beneath the covered portico of the hotel. It had slowed down to tiny flakes after the sun finally rose, then stopped altogether. Surprisingly, plows had already been around, and cars were steadily driving in the streets, like it was just any other day, and the overnight snow was no big deal.

In the city, snow like this would force a near standstill. It would be hours, maybe days, before the plows got all the roads cleared. Especially in their Bronx neighborhood. In the meantime, neighbors would go out and help one another shovel parking spots and sidewalks, but driving was normally put off.

The car door opened and out came the man from her interview. Sutton King. His legs unfolded and he stood tall, his head above the roof as he came around.

"Hi there." He smiled, small but genuine, and Sola could admit it was charming in its own way. "You must be Gus."

He surprised her by going straight to her son, with his huge hand held out in a greeting. She waited a breath, ready to give an apologetic look when her son ignored him, but she was even more surprised when her son took the man's hand and shook it.

Then he turned to her mother. "And you must be Lucia." Her mother blushed. Actually blushed. Sola's mouth dropped open on its own.

"*Sí, joven*, nice to meet you. *Qué gusto.*" Her mother put her own hand out first and he took it, his smile widening before he turned again, to greet her.

"Doctor Rivera-Kelly?"

Sola smiled, nodded her head, and shook his hand as well, looking up to meet his eyes and trying not to marvel at their deep blue color.

"Yes, but you can call me Sola."

"Very well, Sola." He tilted his head toward the pile of luggage on the cart behind them. "Is that all your stuff?"

Sola followed his gaze. It still seemed surreal that everything they owned was there, in those bags and boxes. But it was. Including all the winter gear they'd been told they would need. What they weren't already wearing, that is.

"Yes, I'm sorry it's so much."

He chuckled and moved to grab the cart, pushing it over to the back of the SUV. "This is nothing. You should see it when my sisters and my wife come to Anchorage to shop. I have a hard time shoving it all into the back of even the big plane."

Sola moved to help him, lifting one of the suitcases and tossing it in. She could tell, by a small frown that crossed his face, that it bothered him for some reason, but he didn't say anything.

"Did you guys get something to eat? Because it would be good if we could get going sooner rather than later, while we still have a break in the weather." He said this while he looked up at the sky. August looked up too, as if they were both reading from the same book.

"Yes, we ate. We can go anytime."

"Great," he said as he Tetrised their last bag, shut the trunk door, and moved to the passenger side, opening both the front and the back doors wide. "Then let's go."

"*Gracias*," Lucia practically simpered as she walked past and got into the back. Sola waited as she watched her son go around the back to the left side and get in by himself. Sutton, or someone, had clearly thought about it and put in a booster seat for him, and he sat, putting on his belt without help like he'd done it a million times before. Sola was a little shocked, but she kept it to herself, got in, and even smothered her astonishment as Sutton closed first her door, then her mother's.

The small airport they pulled up to was another surprise. There were several tiny planes up on blocks for the winter and dozens more floating by long docks in a lake.

"Hey, Sutton," an older man wearing an old red flannel called from a metal door of a building marked Spenard Light Aircraft Repair. "You ready to take off? It looks like another storm is rolling from the north in a few hours. If you leave now, you should be able to outrun it."

Sutton moved to the back, pulling out their luggage.

"Yeah, Marsh," he yelled back over his shoulder. "I'm gonna load up now and be off in fifteen minutes."

"Gotcha," the man returned as he came over. "You need a hand?"

"Nah, I got it, but I'd like to introduce Sola, our new doctor," he nodded his head to her. "And this is Lucia, her mother, and Gus, her son."

"Well, well, well." The man smiled cheerfully, eyes twinkling and reminding Sola of a skinny Santa Claus. "Nice to meetcha, Doc. I'm Marshall. I taught Sutton here everything he knows about flyin', so I can tell ya, you're in great hands."

"It's nice to meet you too." Sola gave him a weak smile in return as she followed his gaze over to the plane that Sutton was busy shoving all their bags into.

She'd heard the words 'bush plane' when they'd explained to her over the interview how one got to Alpenglow. But somehow, it never really registered how small the plane would be or that it would be on floats. Not that she feared flying, but she was a little scared of the water. She could swim, and so could her mother. August was another story. They had tried to teach him at the local YMCA, because open water was always something parents of autistic children worried over. But the loud, screaming kids always had him covering his ears, rather than moving his arms. Eventually, they'd given up. Sola felt the old fear climbing over her shoulders, threatening to bring all her carefully crafted plans to a halt. She met her mother's eyes and could tell she was thinking about the same thing.

Sutton finished loading and jumped out onto the dock, the small yellow plane with a wide shark-tooth grin behind him tipping slightly back and forth.

"You guys ready?" His question was innocent, and Sola was breathing deep, doing everything in her power not to panic. She had to get inside. They all did. There was no turning back now. In the end, it was August who decided for them all. He practically ran over to the plane and even took Sutton's big hand to help him up.

"Well, Marisolita, I guess that is that," her mother whispered and followed her grandson. Sola had no choice but to join them.

FIVE

Hyder

It's getting late.

Hyder knew it, not because of the time, but because he'd seen Charlie come out onto the front porch of the Lodge at least three times in the last hour, her hand raised over her eyes, scanning the sky for a streak of yellow.

Sutton was not due for at least another half hour. But when he'd called from Anchorage, he'd said he might leave early to get ahead of the storm that had been building all day. The weather reports said it was pushing down from the north, fast and heavy.

They did not technically need the new doctor to arrive today, but the family had quietly agreed they would rather race the weather window a little than call and tell her she needed to sit in an Anchorage hotel for the next week. Or more. Nothing scared off a newcomer faster than explaining just how isolated things could get in Alpenglow.

He and Tala were down on the dock, working on *The Ahnah*, winterizing her before the worst of the winter winds arrived. The trawler rocked gently against the bumpers as the rougher wind started scraping across the cove.

A low, uneven thud echoed across the water. Both he and Tala glanced over instinctively.

Another boat was sitting at the dock behind them, its hull bumping harder than it should have against the dock. It sat lower in the water than *The Ahnah*, its paint worn thinner to dull patches of gray beneath a name stenciled across the side in peeling black letters.

Dead Reckoning.

Dutchy stood hunched over near the stern of his boat, retying a line with slow, deliberate movements that looked more like habit than care. He was all angles and ropy muscle, wiry in a way that came from years of hauling nets, too much rotgut whiskey, and not eating well enough. Salt and pepper hair stuck out beneath a battered Budweiser cap, and his shoulders carried a permanent stoop, like the weight of the sea had settled into his spine and never left.

"Storm's comin' in faster than they said," he called out without looking at them, then spat into the water. "You'd think a fancy city doctor would have the sense to wait it out."

Tala's mouth tightened, but she leaned her hip against the rail like she was not about to give him the satisfaction of a reaction.

"Or," she called back evenly, "you'd think a town would have the sense to get a doctor here before an early winter locks us in for the next month."

Dutchy snorted, the sound humorless.

"We had doctors and nurses before," he muttered, looping the line once more than necessary. "They never stay. Not when things start going wrong."

Hyder didn't respond, but his jaw ticked slightly.

Dutchy was one of those people who seemed to find pleasure in being hard. He'd been in Alpenglow longer than most. Longer than most of the buildings. He had fished the same waters as Aksel King once, back when things had been different. Before the quotas tightened and prices dropped. Before half the independent boats in the Sound had folded under the weight of it all.

Dutchy's was one of them.

Now he worked charters when he could, taking whatever runs Hyder didn't have time for or those for whom he figured Dutchy's disposition would seem like a charming caricature of Alaskan toughness. It kept him on the water.

Barely.

Dutchy straightened slowly, one hand braced against his knee before he rolled his shoulders like something in them pulled too tight.

"You ask me," he went on, eyeing the sky instead of them, "any *cheechako* dumb enough to come out here this time of year ain't gonna last long anyway."

Tala let out a soft breath through her nose. "You're just a ray of sunshine today, Dutchy."

He grunted, then started to walk off toward the Lodge.

Hyder finally spoke, his tone even. "Dock lines still look loose."

Dutchy's gaze snapped to him, irritation in his dark green eyes. "They're fine."

Hyder gave a small shrug, then turned and caught Tala's gaze, both of them doing their best to smother their grins. At least until Dutchy was gone. They both got back to work, Hyder crouching near the stern, tightening a strap over one of the deck lockers and checking that nothing had been left loose, as another soft sound drifted down the hillside above them. He looked up automatically.

Charlie again.

She stood at the porch railing, holding her head back with that same anxious tilt to her shoulders.

"Do ya think she'll ever get over it?"

Hyder glanced sideways. Tala had paused again, mid-task, a tackle box hanging from one hand while she watched the porch with quiet curiosity. He shrugged, reaching for a wrench beside him, knowing exactly what she meant.

"I don't know," he admitted as he tightened a bolt. "I hope so. It's not like he can stop flying."

His brother was not the only bush pilot in town, but he was the best one within two hundred miles. Charter guests trusted him to get to Alpenglow. Hunters trusted him to take them out in the middle of the wilderness. And the town trusted him to get all the little supplies they always needed to make life in Alpenglow easier.

Tala leaned back against the rail of the trawler, squinting up toward the Lodge again.

"Well," she said carefully, "I suppose if the person I loved had crashed onto a glacier, I might keep an eye on the sky too."

Hyder frowned. "He didn't crash. Not completely."

"He definitely crashed. The plane rolled. Hell, the Beaver is still up there in parts! And he broke half the bones in his body!"

"Yeah." Hyder looked up thoughtfully. "That part was unfortunate."

Tala grinned. "You're impossible, Coastie."

"Thank you. I try. Just for you."

She tossed the box into a storage locker and slammed it shut.

"So," she continued, rubbing her hands together to warm them up, "what do you think this doctor's gonna be like?"

Hyder shrugged. "I have no idea. You know as much as I do, other than I heard she aced the interview. To be honest, I don't have high hopes, but I am not about to tell Dutchy that. I just really want her to last at least until Charlie has the baby, or Sutton is gonna be the impossible one."

Tala tilted her head and pursed her lips.

"I'm betting she's an old granny."

Hyder blinked at her, a grin tugging at one side of his lips.

"A granny?"

"Sure," Tala answered confidently. "Gray hair. Sensible shoes. One of those big purses full of those weird candies."

"Weird candies."

"Yeah." She smiled. "You know what I mean. The kind that the traveling doc used to give out when we were kids in the village. After he gave us those shots."

Hyder barked out a laugh. "You mean lollipops."

"Exactly." Tala nodded seriously.

"Well, maybe. If she's nice, maybe she'll give me one. Without a shot."

"You're a thirty-two-year-old boat captain," Tala reminded him.

"And? That doesn't mean I don't deserve a lollipop."

Tala shot him a look that told him he was an idiot. Hyder would have been shocked if she hadn't given him one.

Just then the low rumble of an engine drifted across the water, and they both looked up at the same time.

Tala to the sky. Hyder toward the porch again.

Charlie was already there. Her arms were wrapped tightly around herself. Even from down on the dock, he could see the tension melt from her shoulders.

A moment later the Kodiak came skimming over the Lodge from due north, its bright yellow body cutting across the pale early-afternoon sky.

Hyder frowned. "He came the fast way."

Tala followed the line of the plane, adding matter-of-factly, "That shaved at least twenty minutes."

"Storm must be closer than we thought."

They both knew what that meant. Last autumn, a storm had torn through their town, knocking down trees. A huge one had smashed through the school roof, and the repairs had taken the whole town months to make. When this one came, they would deal with it, but they all hoped it would land on them a little gentler.

A hard gust of wind whipped across the cove just then, blowing Hyder's hair back and biting through his Gore-Tex. He glanced around for his gloves. The air had dropped noticeably in the last hour.

By at least five degrees.

The Kodiak circled low once, then lined up perpendicular to the mouth of the cove. The water near the entrance was already beginning to chop, the wind pushing narrow waves toward the shore.

Sutton judged it perfectly. He landed just past the rough water, the floats kissing the calmer surface with barely a splash. Smooth and perfect. Like always.

Tala was already moving. She jumped off the trawler before Hyder could, grabbing a thick rope coil as she jogged along the dock. By the time Sutton brought the Kodiak alongside, she was already braced at the dock cleat. She leaned down, wrapped the mooring line around the float, pulled it tight against the bumpers, then moved down and did the same to the back mooring cleat. Even a rough storm would not be able to tear the plane loose from one of her knots.

After shutting down the engine, Sutton popped open the cabin latch and leapt down onto the dock. He leaned back into the plane, holding his arms out and saying something Hyder could not quite hear over the wind. A small, young boy appeared in the hatchway. Eight, maybe nine. The kid jumped straight into Sutton's arms without hesitation.

Sutton laughed and set him down gently on the dock. Then he turned and lifted one hand again to help someone else climb out.

The boy turned in a slow circle, his wide eyes taking in everything around him, until his gaze snagged on *The Ahnah*. He stared at the aluminum hull like it was the most fascinating thing he had ever seen.

"Boat!" he shouted and took off running.

Behind him Hyder barely registered the woman stepping onto the dock.

"Gus! No, *mijo!*"

Hyder dropped the tool in his hand and vaulted the rail of the trawler in one smooth motion, landing on the dock just ahead of the boy.

The gap between boat and dock yawned open beside them, black water slapping quietly against the pilings and bumpers.

Hyder scooped the kid up easily.

"Hey there, partner," he said with a laugh. "You gotta be careful around the water, okay?"

The boy's hazel eyes met his for a brief moment before sliding away again. But he nodded, then wriggled impatiently to get down.

Hyder set him carefully back on the dock just as the woman caught up to them.

She dropped to her knees and pulled the boy into a tight hug.

"You can't do that, GusGus," she murmured quickly before adding in Spanish, "*No es seguro.*"

Her voice cut through the wind, soft but laced with a warm lyricism that stole his breath. Instantly he was reminded of the raw, fiery passion of *Carmen*, an opera he'd once been reluctantly dragged to in Seattle, only to emerge utterly ensnared. He still listened to it when he was out on his boat. Alone.

Hyder straightened slowly, realizing the temperature had dropped a notch, even as the wind blew harder.

Then she looked up and the world tilted.

She was small. Petite enough that the tall boots she wore, impractical designer things with narrow heels, made her look even more delicate than she probably was. Dark hair spilled over her shoulders in thick waves, catching the low light of the sun. Her eyes were deep chocolate and soulful, framed by long black lashes and perfectly arched brows that gave her face a striking intensity.

Her mouth was soft and wide and expressive. Perfect for kissing. And at the moment slightly breathless.

Hyder forgot every single thing he had been about to say.

"Hi," he finally managed.

It sounded unbelievably absurd the second it left his mouth, but it was all he had.

She blinked like she had only just realized he was standing there.

She stood up, her gaze following the line of him, from his knees, all the way up to meet his eyes.

"Hello."

For a moment neither of them moved, the air between them feeling thick and strangely charged. As if the storm was already there.

Then it hit him.

Lust.

Not the slow kind. Or the thoughtful, polite kind he was used to where he could take his time to decide if being with someone was a good idea or not.

The sudden, stupid, lightning-strike kind. Deep in his gut.

I want her. A perfect stranger.

Hyder's brain scrambled for something rational to grab on to, knowing his thoughts were insane. He didn't even know her name. He had heard it weeks ago but instantly forgot it as unimportant. It suddenly seemed vital. As though his whole life depended on knowing it. And they had spoken exactly one word. Two if hello counted.

He forced himself to breathe before he passed out.

"Hey, Hyder!" Sutton's voice cut across the dock. "Can you give us a hand?"

Hyder tore his eyes away from her, nodded quickly, and forced his feet to move. They didn't want to leave her.

"Yeah," he called back reluctantly. "Coming."

Between him, Tala, and Sutton they hauled all the luggage up the hill steps toward the Lodge. Tala grumbled the entire way.

"You know there's a perfectly good dock over by the boardwalk," she muttered. "We'd only have to carry it up one ramp over there."

Sutton shrugged. "Too windy."

"It's always windy," Tala retorted.

"Not this windy."

"You just like making us carry things."

Sutton grunted, looking serious, then a small smile broke through his stoicism. "Correct."

They loaded the suitcases and boxes into the back of the Suburban Sutton had bought that summer to hold their growing family. By the time they finished, Charlie had come down from the porch. Willow followed close behind her, with Gemma and Hope trailing in excitement.

There was a quick round of introductions. Names passed back and forth.

Sola. Her name is Sola.

Gus inspected Sitka, who sat without moving a muscle, his heterochromatic gaze meeting the boy's like some secret language was passing between them.

Then everyone climbed in the Suburban, and Sutton drove off with Charlie and Willow. And with *her* and her family.

Hyder stood beside the gravel path as the engine started. He didn't realize he hadn't moved until the Suburban rolled away down the road toward town and disappeared in a low cloud of dust.

"What the hell was that?"

Tala stood beside him, a genuinely shocked look on her face.

Hyder blinked.

"What?"

She pointed down the road.

"That. If I didn't know better," she continued slowly, "I'd swear you just fell in love with the granny doctor."

Hyder scowled at her.

"And Ellie," Tala added with a wicked grin, "is going to be super disappointed."

Hyder didn't answer. Because he didn't have one.

SIX

Sola

The ride into town was short. Perhaps a mile or two at most. But it felt longer.

Her brain, she decided, must simply be exhausted after the long days of travel yesterday and today, and the overwhelming cascade of new sights, new sounds, and new people. Because whatever had just happened on that dock made absolutely no sense to her.

She had seen handsome men before.

New York City was overflowing with them. Every possible variation of tall, short, dark, blond, charming, brooding, intellectual, artistic, athletic. And everything in between. She had dated enough of them over the years to know exactly what she liked and what she didn't, and she'd never once been under any illusion about what those relationships meant.

Sola was not a prude. Far from it. She thought of sex as something natural, healthy, and entirely separate from the emotional weight so many people insisted on attaching to it. Perhaps back in college, before August was born, she had believed love and sex belonged together, but that idea had been dashed thoroughly enough that she had never bothered to question her beliefs again.

Since then, she'd been perfectly clear with anyone she dated. She wanted physical. Nothing more. And the men never complained. It had worked well for the last nine years, allowing her world to focus on exactly three things. Her son. Her mother. And becoming the best doctor she possibly could.

Everything else, especially men, had simply slipped in the small spaces around those priorities. It was something she could control, when everything else in her life was chaotic.

Which was precisely why whatever had just happened made so little sense. She had barely spoken to the man. Yet something inside her had reacted as if a switch had been flipped.

She supposed it could be just that he was tall, dark, and handsome. A classic combination. And he had that voice. Deep, with a vaguely polished edge that she couldn't quite place.

But so did Sutton. Except Sutton didn't make her feel the same way at all. He made her nervous. Maybe even a little intimidated. He carried himself like a man who was used to responsibility and not particularly interested in explaining himself to anyone, and there was something about the steady seriousness in his deep blue eyes that made her instinctively straighten her posture when he looked at her.

Hyder, though...

Hyder had been entirely different. His blue eyes had sparkled with a warmth that felt effortless and genuine, and when he jumped off the boat to scoop Gus away from the edge of the dock he had moved with a kind of instinctive elegance that reminded her of a wild animal reacting before thought could catch up.

And the way he looked at me...

The memory made her belly tighten. He had looked at her like she might be the most interesting thing he had ever seen. Or tasted.

The thought was ridiculous.

Absolutely ridiculous.

She forced her eyes toward the truck window. Outside, the world rolled slowly past beneath a soft curtain of snow that was just beginning to fall.

Water. There was just so much of it.

When they had landed earlier, she had barely noticed anything except the enormous sweep of gray water stretching in every direction, broken only by distant shapes of white-capped mountains that rose straight out of the sea.

Now, as they rolled slowly along the narrow road toward the cluster of cottages ahead, she could see more of the town itself.

It was appealing. Almost storybook charming.

Small wooden houses, all painted a cheerful red with white trim, lined the curving boardwalk that stretched along the edge of the cove, their windows glowing warmly against the growing storm clouds while smoke twisted from chimneys. Snow had begun collecting on rooftops and railings, softening every hard line and corner.

Yet they were still on the water. All of it was on the water. And despite her attempts to stay calm, Sola could feel a familiar thread of panic creeping in.

"It's okay, Marisolita," her mother murmured quietly beside her, her voice soft enough that no one else could hear it. She reached for Sola's hand and gave it a gentle squeeze. Sola let her.

Lucia had always possessed an uncanny ability to read her daughter's emotions before Sola had fully acknowledged them herself.

Sola nodded slightly. But she knew they would both have to keep a close eye on Gus. A very close eye. Preferably with a physical hand on him whenever they were near open water. Otherwise, Sola suspected she might lose her mind entirely.

Willow, meanwhile, had been narrating their entire drive with cheerful enthusiasm.

"And that building there is the Mercantile," she was saying brightly, pointing across the cove toward a red two-story structure near the other end of the boardwalk. "It's basically our general store and where we get our mail. If you ever need anything quickly that's usually the first place to check. If they don't have it, Cheryl, she runs the Merc, will make sure to order it."

"Oh," Sola murmured politely. "I see."

She was only absorbing about half of what Willow said.

The truck slowed.

"We're almost there," Willow announced happily. "I really hope you like the cottage. It's called the Aurora," she continued. "We gave it a little spiffing up and ordered all new furniture for you guys. Luckily it all arrived last week. I was starting to worry."

She jumped out, waving to them to follow.

"It's the only three-bedroom cottage on the cove," Willow added as they climbed down. "Though one of the bedrooms is a little small," she admitted apologetically. "But it does have a fenced-in backyard."

Sola followed her along the boardwalk, the wood creaking softly beneath their boots as the snow drifted quietly around them. The cottage they stopped at stood slightly back from the water. On dry, or rather snow-covered land. Thankfully.

Like all the other cottages, it was charming and red, though it looked a little bigger than most. She felt some of the tension ease from her shoulders immediately.

When Willow pushed open the door, warm air spilled out to meet them.

"Welcome home," she grinned as she stepped back, letting them go first.

The entryway opened into a tidy mudroom where hooks lined one wall and a wide wooden bench sat beneath, to sit on while taking off boots and winter gear.

"Plenty of space for coats," Willow explained cheerfully.

They stepped inside slowly and everyone slipped off their boots. Beyond the mudroom the space opened into a kitchen that immediately felt larger than the entire apartment they had just left behind in the Bronx.

An island sat in the center, and a wooden table with four chairs filled one corner near a wide window that looked out toward the snowy yard.

"I hope you like what I picked out. But if you need anything different, just let me know," Willow explained as she flipped on another light.

They followed her, trying to take everything in.

"Refrigerator and pantry are stocked," she added. "We figured you probably wouldn't want to grocery shop tonight."

"*Gracias*," Lucia smiled warmly.

From the kitchen, the house opened into a surprisingly wide living room with polished floorboards and a thick woven rug that softened the space. A stone fireplace crackled softly against one wall, casting golden light across a comfortable couch and two oversized chairs positioned on either side of the hearth.

"*Ay, mira esto*," Lucia whispered to Sola as she ran her hand across the back of the couch. "This place is beautiful."

Sola could only nod.

On the far side of the living room, a short hallway stretched toward the bedrooms. Willow led them down it, speaking as she went.

"This one is the master." She pushed open the first door.

The room was bright and airy with large windows, a neatly made full-sized bed covered in thick blankets, and a wide dresser beside the wall with a mirror above. An attached bathroom opened from one corner with a clean white sink and a shower already stocked with fluffy towels. It smelled of lemons and basil and reminded Sola of rooms she had seen in magazines. Not something she had ever had for herself.

"Over here is the second bedroom," Willow continued as if nothing she was showing them was out of the ordinary.

Lucia stepped inside and immediately her smile widened.

The room was clearly arranged with an older occupant in mind. Another comfortable full-sized bed with a soft quilt that looked to be handmade stood pushed against the wall, and a sturdy armchair sat beside a small reading lamp near the window. A knitted throw had been folded carefully across the back of the chair, and a small table beside it held a stack of books.

"*Perfecto*," Lucia whispered.

The final room sat across the hallway, past another bathroom with a tub.

"And this is the small one," Willow said apologetically as she opened the door.

Sola stopped in the doorway in surprise. The room might have been smaller than the others, but it had been arranged with obvious care.

A twin bed sat against one wall beneath a thick duvet printed with a pattern of stars and constellations, and along the opposite side of the room, taking up the entire length of the wall, was a long desk beneath a window that looked out toward the snowy yard.

It was perfect for drawing maps. Perfect for August.

"*Ay, mira*," Lucia whispered again.

Sola was in awe, blinking as she did her best to hold back tears of joy. Her son finally had his own room.

When they returned to the living room Sutton was just coming through the front door carrying the last of the boxes.

Charlie followed behind him, reaching to move one of the suitcases out of his way.

"Nope," Sutton grunted immediately, pulling it away from her. "You shouldn't be lifting those."

Charlie snorted. "Exercise is good for me." She turned toward Sola. "Please tell him."

Sola laughed softly, the doctor in her rising automatically to the surface, thankfully taking her mind away from how close she was to crying.

"Well," she said thoughtfully, "exercise *is* good for you."

Sutton folded his arms and lowered his brow.

"But he's also right," she continued with a small smile. "Those suitcases are pretty heavy."

"See?" Sutton said triumphantly, shooting Sola a grateful look.

"Well," Willow said brightly, clapping her hands together, "we'll let you get settled."

It was clearly an argument she had heard before and did not want to hear again. At least not in front of the newcomers.

"Like I said, we stocked the fridge," she reminded them. "But the Raven makes a fantastic chowder if you feel like venturing out later."

Sola nodded, grateful and still overwhelmed.

"And if there's anything else you need," Willow continued, gesturing toward the kitchen counter, "I left instructions there on how to get hold of me or Sutton or Charlie."

She smiled warmly and came closer. It wasn't until she wrapped her arms around her that Sola realized what she was doing. Sola did her best not to stiffen, but she was not sure how to react. Luckily, Willow didn't appear to notice and she pulled back, moving on to Lucia.

Lucia immediately understood the assignment, embracing the younger woman back tightly, murmuring in her hair, "*Gracias, niña dulce.*"

Willow walked toward the front door to leave, but she stopped and turned. "I'd love to stop by tomorrow morning and take you over to the clinic and show you around town. If that's okay?"

"That would be fine." Sola cleared her throat, ducking her head as the emotion hit her once again.

The Kings gathered their coats and stepped out into the snow one by one, their voices drifting down the boardwalk as they walked away.

The house grew suddenly quiet, so different from the warm chaos that had just left.

Sola turned slowly in the living room, taking in the soft glow of the fire and the smooth floorboards beneath her feet.

Their family had always been small and quiet.

But the Kings...

They were loud. Full. Alive in a way she had not expected.

She turned once more. Then froze.

"Gus?"

Her heart jumped into her throat. She hurried down the hallway, checking each room quickly before stopping at the final door.

Inside, a small lamp glowed softly beside the desk. August sat in the chair with his notebook open in front of him, pencil already moving carefully across the page as he began sketching the shapes of the town outside.

Alpenglow was already finding its way onto August's map.

SEVEN

Hyder

Dawn came, icy and relentless. With the kind of dim Alaskan light that crept in gray and then suddenly sharpened everything into focus. Hyder lay on his bunk in the belly of *The Ahnah*, staring at the low ceiling until the decision settled like the frost that was already coating the metal.

It's time to move inside.

Last night's storm had almost been more than he could bear, tossing him from one side of his bunk to the other, and the Lodge had a perfectly good room waiting with a king-sized bed, thick quilts, and space to stretch without banging his head or feet. He told himself it was practical, even if he would miss his solitude.

But who am I kidding?

It wasn't the cold or rough water that had kept him awake last night. It was those eyes. Dark, serious, and the color of salted cedar after rain. They didn't just look at him. They saw him, peeling back layers he'd spent years stacking like cordwood, hidden carefully behind a solid grin. And the worst part? He didn't mind. He wanted her to keep looking. Which made the whole thing dangerous.

He still had his rules, and he had no intention of breaking them. There was no sense in complicating the fragile balance of a town this small. And the new doctor wasn't just any newcomer. She was essential. The town couldn't lose her. Plus, she didn't arrive alone. There was her son. And her mother. Hyder wouldn't call them baggage. That word felt cruel and dismissive. But it was weight. Real weight. The kind that changed the physics of any move he might make.

Besides, rules didn't come from nowhere. They came from watching things unravel. From knowing how quickly something small could become everyone's problem.

And his family was already circling him. Last night at dinner, he tried to casually ask about the newcomers. Whether they liked the look of the town so far. And their new home. How the clinic setup was going. Willow had answered, "Don't flirt with the new doctor," with that bright, know-it-all-little-sister smile that made his ears burn. Sutton's frown had deepened into something almost protective, the question in his eyes unmistakable. And Tala, damn her, had just sipped her coffee with that sly, cat-like expression that said she'd already read every thought he wasn't saying out loud.

Then there was Ellie. After dinner, when he and Tala slipped down to the Raven for a beer, while Nobuhiro was belting out Christina Aguilera and letting the whole town know what a girl wants, Ellie slid onto the stool beside Hyder. Close enough that her perfume, something woodsy and floral, wafted over him. Tala's smirk had been immediate. Hyder had muttered about needing the head and bolted. He knew he couldn't keep dodging her forever. But breaking things off had to be gentle. The Lodge couldn't afford to lose its manager either, not with the winter crowd coming.

He grunted as he swung his legs over the bunk, his knees creaking like old dock pilings. The cold never forgave the years he spent plunging into the Bering Sea to haul half-frozen fishermen aboard. He dressed quickly in thermals, a flannel, and heavy socks, and shoved a seabag with the few things he actually kept on the boat. A toothbrush, spare layers, a dog-eared paperback he was almost done with. Then he headed up the path to the Lodge, his breath fogging heavy in the sharp air.

A hot shower first. Then maybe he could catch Willow before she left. He'd overheard her telling one of the cousins that she was giving the new doc a tour of the town and clinic today. Maybe he could...help. Offer to carry something. Walk along for some company. Anything to be near those eyes for a few minutes more without admitting why.

The boardwalk still wore six inches of fresh snow, with sparse footprints, already melting at the edges. Hyder grabbed a shovel from the small storage locker near the end of the row and started clearing the path to Sola's door. The scrape of metal on wood echoed in the quiet morning across the cove. Willow stood on the porch steps, arms crossed, one brow arched high enough to disappear under her wool beanie.

"You know Sutton pays one of Healy's kids to do this." Her voice was dry.

Hyder didn't look up. "Qaniq's probably still asleep."

Willow snorted but said nothing else. She was always the smart one in the ways of people. Or maybe she was just waiting.

He finished, shook snow off the blade, stowed it, apparently timing it perfectly. Willow was just raising her fist to knock when the door swung open.

Lucia stood there, wearing an apron dusted white with flour, her smile broad.

"*Buenos días*! Good morning!" she called out. "You're just in time for *pan con huevos revueltos* and the coffee. Come in, come in. Don't let the heat out!"

Hyder felt the scent hit him before he even crossed the threshold. Eggs for sure. But there were also onions, peppers, maybe a whisper of garlic, and the faint sweet char of toasted bread.

Underneath it all, strong coffee. It wrapped around him like a blanket, seeping into the ache in his knees, loosening them.

They stepped inside, taking off their coats and boots. The small house glowed with morning eastern light through lace curtains, the kitchen table already set with five colorful plates, four mugs, and one juice glass before Gus, who was already waiting. Lucia waved them toward the table like they were family arriving late.

"Sit, sit. While the food is hot."

They sat just as Sola appeared from the hallway, hair still damp from a shower, wearing a simple sweater and jeans, her delicate feet bare. "*Mamí*, good morning—" She stopped short when she saw them. Her eyes flicked first to Willow, then to Hyder, where they stayed. A small flush touched her cheeks.

"Oh. Hello."

"Hi," Hyder replied. It came out rougher than he meant.

Willow kicked him under the table.

Don't flirt with the new doctor.

The reminder from their earlier conversation rang in his head. He rubbed his shin and mouthed, "What?"

I only said hi...Geez.

Willow ignored him, stood and rushed over, and pulled Sola into a quick hug. Sola stiffened, her arms barely lifting, one hand patting Willow's back awkwardly like she wasn't sure where to put it. A flash of something... panic maybe? Or discomfort?... crossed her face before she smoothed it away.

Interesting.

The new doc wasn't used to being touched. Or maybe she just wasn't used to this much easy affection. Willow could be a lot.

Lucia bustled over with loaded platters. Fluffy scrambled eggs flecked with red and green, thick slices of toasted sourdough slathered with butter, a side of sweet fried plantains still sizzling faintly. The coffee was poured into the heavy mugs. Dark, strong, and sweetened just right. Hyder took a sip and had to admit it might give Cheva's brew over at the Forget Me Not a serious run for its money.

Lucia hovered just long enough to watch him, her expression softening in approval like she'd just learned something about him.

"Eat, eat," Lucia urged, refilling mugs before they were half-empty. "You need strength for this cold."

They ate in comfortable quiet at first, broken by Lucia's gentle questions. How was the drive? Were the roads icy? Did they want more? And Willow's cheerful answers. Hyder mostly listened, stealing glances at Sola. She ate neatly, precisely, but he caught her closing her eyes for a second on the first sip of coffee, like it tasted like home. He had to force his eyes away then, because the pull was magnetic and dangerously intimate, like gravity itself had shifted toward her in that moment.

When plates were cleared and mugs drained, they thanked Lucia for the meal as they rose and headed for the mudroom, putting on their boots and shrugging into heavy coats. Willow zipped hers with a decisive tug. "We'll walk, if that's okay. It's not far."

"Of course," Sola answered softly. "Lead the way."

Hyder did his best not to close his eyes when he heard the opening strings of opera once more, a sudden, bright fanfare that demanded his undivided devotion, and his gaze dropped to her feet again as they stepped out. Different boots today. But still with heels and shiny leather instead of suede. Better. Not enough, though. He frowned, picturing her in proper Kamiks, insulated and grippy, her toes safe from frostbite. She'd still look good. Hell, better even. Grounded and ready for this place. He kept his mouth shut. Offering to buy her winter boots on day two of knowing her would definitely get another look from Willow.

And who knows what Sola would do.

As they started down the freshly shoveled boardwalk, the icy air clean around them, the contrast hit him. Last night, another noisy dinner at the Lodge. With plates clattering, the family teasing, Ellie lingering too close. Versus this. The quiet morning in a different cozy kitchen. The spicy, comforting taste still on his tongue, the company soothing. And for once, he didn't feel alone.

He shook his head and tried to focus on the present and the conversation Sola and Willow were having, just in case it was something important. Instead, all he noticed was the way Sola walked beside him, close enough that their sleeves brushed once. Then again. Warming him.

He felt it both times. Not just the physical touch, but that same electricity arcing between them. After the second time, she adjusted, just slightly, and it didn't happen again. He missed it.

There weren't really words to describe how he was feeling. He didn't need them. Some things you just felt. Despite every rule and your whole family telling you not to feel it.

EIGHT

Sola

Not since her father went back to Ireland, when she was a little younger than August was now, could Sola remember there being a man sitting comfortably in their space like that. Not one that Lucia had decided deserved feeding.

Certainly not one she seemed so excited about feeding. Not even August's dad, back when Sola still thought he was someone worth bringing home.

The kitchen had drawn her from her room that morning, smelling of garlic and olive oil, when she saw that the little table was already crowded with dishes. And people.

It had been...a lot.

Not the people. The food. Platters so full that she, her mother, and August could not eat them in days if they tried. Sola supposed it could have simply been because her mother was still on East Coast time and had been awake long before sunrise, needing something to occupy herself in a strange new place.

But the look of pure satisfaction on Lucia's face as Hyder demolished not just seconds but thirds made Sola suspicious.

"Eat, eat," Lucia had insisted cheerfully, sliding another plate toward him before he could protest.

"*Mamí*," Sola muttered.

"*Qué*...what?" her mother replied innocently.

Hyder, for his part, didn't seem inclined to refuse.

"*Señora* Rivera," he said between bites, "this might be the best breakfast I've had all year. All my life!"

Lucia beamed and Sola stared between them like they had secretly arranged this meeting behind her back.

Now, as the three of them walked along the boardwalk toward the town square, Sola did everything in her power to keep her focus firmly on Willow, who was leading the way while pointing out buildings and narrating the town like a cheerful tour guide.

It was bad enough that she had spent half the night thinking about the man currently walking beside her. And they had not been respectable thoughts.

They had been dark and carnal. Filled with sighs and heat and hands.

Even now she was doing her best not to imagine what he might look like naked. Not to imagine those strong, rough hands sliding along her body, or those powerful arms lifting her as easily as he had lifted himself over the boat rail to rescue her son.

Ay, carajo, she swore silently. *Shut up, Sola*.

They continued south along the boardwalk, the snow squeaking beneath their boots as Willow pointed toward the buildings along the cove.

"That's the Mercantile again," she said brightly, gesturing.

Next to it, at the end of the boardwalk, stood the wide two-story building painted deep green.

"And that's the Raven and the Frog," Willow continued.

Hyder snorted beside Sola.

"Everyone just calls it the Raven," he said.

"Why?" Sola asked before she could stop herself.

Hyder shrugged lazily.

"Because we're lazy."

She turned to smile at him automatically. And froze. For a split second the image in her mind returned with alarming clarity. His hands gripping the back of her thighs, lifting her easily, pulling her against him...

Carajo! She swore again to herself, more forcefully this time.

Willow was already continuing down the boardwalk, oblivious to her thoughts.

"Come on," she said with a wave. "Let's cut through the café. It's the quickest way to the square. It's also the warmest!"

They stepped into the white building with cheerful azure-blue trim and shuttered windows. Below the windows, wooden flower boxes sat empty, snow collecting in the containers where blooms would presumably return in spring.

Inside, the air smelled richly of coffee and butter, and something sugary that made Sola take notice, even though she was still full.

Conversation did not stop exactly when they entered. But it softened. Like everyone inside had silently agreed not to stare too obviously at the new arrival, even though nearly every pair of eyes drifted curiously in Sola's direction. Sola smiled, holding her head up, trying not to feel overwhelmed.

Willow clapped her hands together lightly. "Okay, everyone, since I know you're all *dying* to know...this is Doctor Rivera-Kelly."

An older woman with graying hair pulled back in a loose bun stepped forward with a genuine smile.

"I'm Cheryl," she introduced herself. "I run the Mercantile."

She shook Sola's hand firmly, her grip surprisingly strong.

"You give me a list anytime you need something, and I'll make sure it shows up on the next supply run."

"Thank you," Sola said sincerely.

Though truthfully the cottage already seemed stocked with more food than they could eat in a week. Maybe even a month. They even had plantains in the pantry. She still had no idea how those had made their way to Alaska.

A second woman stepped forward from behind the pastry case, wearing a blue apron, wiping her hands on a bright yellow towel as her thick black braid swung behind her.

"And I'm Cheva," she explained. "Can I get you anything?"

Sola flushed slightly, murmuring, "Oh, no, thank you."

Before she could say anything else, Hyder's booming voice filled the café.

"She's already had three cups of coffee."

Sola shot him a look of disbelief and her cheeks flushed.

"From Lucia," he added cheerfully. "And it's so good I might never come back here again."

"Oh really?" Cheva raised an eyebrow. "How are you planning to get your chive and buttermilk scones then?"

Hyder paused, while his brow furrowed with exaggerated seriousness. Then he nodded.

"Alright fine," he conceded. "I'll still come for those."

Cheva laughed, a deep, free sound that seemed to indicate she was used to Hyder and his ridiculousness. Hyder even came forward, giving her a side hug and a big kiss on her cheek. She seemed used to that as well.

Sola was not sure why a twinge of irritation rose at the idea, but she quickly let it go as they continued through the café, stopping several more times as people introduced themselves, others just walking past, tipping their hats.

A thin, elderly man with deeply lined skin and thoughtful dark eyes approached them slowly.

"Koy," he said, placing a hand lightly over his chest, holding it there for a long moment, like the gesture mattered. "From Kisa'adi. You are most welcome here."

His accent was unusual, his words landing in places that felt guided more by rhythm than punctuation.

Sola shook his hand warmly, noticing arthritic twisting on his fingers and making a mental note to order some anti-inflammatory medication and have him come in for some hand therapy.

Then a woman with a gentle smile and soft graying red hair approached.

"I'm Clare," she said, her voice carrying the faintest hint of a Scottish lilt as she wrung her hands. "My daughter Bella has a bit of a cough. Would it be alright if we came by the clinic tomorrow, once you get settled?"

"Of course," Sola replied immediately. "You can come today if you'd like. Just give me an hour to figure out where the clinic is."

Clare blinked in surprise, then nodded quickly as her smile widened.

They stepped outside again through the opposite door and Sola stopped walking. The town square opened before them like something from a winter postcard. Or a Hallmark movie.

Yes, the cove side had been beautiful in its own way, but the water still held that quiet tension for her, clouding everything she saw.

The square felt different. It was safe and warm, despite the cold.

The buildings surrounding it were painted in bright colors that glowed against the snow.

To the east stretched a long white building trimmed in dark blue with a wide set of double doors and a large bell mounted proudly above them.

"The school," Willow explained quietly, noticing the direction of her gaze.

Along the southern edge of the square stood a tiny, weathered cabin beside a practical red building marked Alpenglow Volunteer Brigade.

Next to it rose a bright green barn with a hand-painted sign that read $0 Store.

Hyder chuckled when he noticed her curious frown.

"That's the junk barn," he told her. "When people replace something, they drop the old one there for whoever needs it."

Sola nodded as she turned to the west and saw a small peach-colored building that said Suds and Duds, and next to that stood a low blue building labeled Library.

Beside them was another structure that made Sola blink in surprise.

The building looked unmistakably Japanese. It had unpainted cedar walls. A gently sloping tiled roof with upturned edges. A small red gate, covered in snow, marked the entrance path, and an old-fashioned gas pump stood out in front.

"I've never seen anything like that," she murmured.

"That's Nobuhiro's shop," Willow shrugged nonchalantly. "He fixes everything."

Hyder added, "And sings karaoke like nobody's business."

In the center of the square stood a wide wooden covered pavilion beside a single towering spruce tree wrapped in thousands of tiny white lights. In fact, every building had lights wrapped around their eaves and windows, making them all sparkle, even with the falling snow.

It felt magical.

Sola was already imagining bringing August there later that evening when the sky darkened.

Maybe with some hot cocoa, she thought absently.

Then she saw it. Past the school, directly across the south-east corner of the square. A brand-new building painted a cheerful shade of yellow with bright white trim and shutters.

The sign above the door read: ALPENGLOW CLINIC

She did not realize she had started walking until she was halfway across the square. One of the narrow-shoveled paths angled straight to the door. Behind her she could feel Willow and Hyder watching and following, but neither said a word.

Sola paused at the door, noticing a small hand-carved wooden sign next to it.

Doctor Rivera-Kelly. She lifted her hand, letting her fingers trace over each letter, wondering who had bothered to do this, and felt something in her chest tighten.

Blinking her eyes, she focused on the door again, pushing it open. A small bell chimed softly overhead.

She walked into a waiting room that smelled faintly of eucalyptus and clean linen. It was welcoming, with two comfortable chairs and a small couch arranged around a low table stacked neatly with books and magazines. A wide woven rug blanketed the floor, and a small reception desk sat against one wall without feeling like a barrier between doctor and patient.

Behind it stood a doorway leading into an office. Her office. Inside sat a desk with a computer already set up and a set of lockable filing cabinets neatly arranged along the wall.

To the left was a small hallway with four doors. Behind one was a tidy bathroom. She kept going, opening the other doors.

The first held an exam room that looked exactly like she had imagined. A standard exam table sat in the center beside cabinets stocked with diagnostic tools. An otoscope, ophthalmoscope, blood pressure monitors, stethoscopes, and a small portable ultrasound unit she had requested were all neatly arranged inside.

The second room made her breath catch. The manipulative treatment room. A specialized osteopathic treatment table stood beneath a large window that looked out into the forest behind the building. Soft lighting filled the room, and a cabinet along the wall held therapy bands, anatomical charts, and supplies she would need for musculoskeletal treatment and manual manipulation.

It felt almost like a small wellness studio. Intentionally calm and quiet. Completely unlike the overcrowded clinic she had left behind in New York.

Sola stepped slowly into the room and placed her hand gently on the treatment table.

It was solid and real, and it was hers.

NINE

Hyder

If Hyder had thought Sola was beautiful when she was serious, seeing her face soften in awe was something else entirely.

Her lips parted slightly as she looked around the clinic, the tension he'd noticed in her shoulders earlier completely melting away. The sharp focus in her dark eyes gave way to wonder, and the faint color rising on her cheeks made her look suddenly younger, almost girlish in her excitement.

For the moment she seemed completely unaware of anyone else in the room. Hyder leaned one shoulder against the doorframe and watched her, unable to stop himself. She was magnificent and utterly captivating.

He imagined that it was what she would look like after being thoroughly kissed. After her breath had been stolen away and her worries pushed aside. Her body loose, her mouth soft, her eyes shining.

Pliant. The thought landed so suddenly in his mind that he jerked upright.

He dragged a hand down his face, knowing it was not the normal way he thought about women, and absolutely not what he should be thinking about right now. Not unless he wanted to be embarrassed by having to awkwardly adjust himself in front of not only the new town doctor but also his own sister.

Willow. Yes. Think about Willow. He knew that would absolutely kill the mood.

He forced himself to turn his head and look around the room.

The clinic was interesting, not at all what he had expected. Certainly nothing like the doctor's offices he'd been in during his time in the Coast Guard. Those had always felt cold and sterile, smelling strongly of antiseptic and something heavier beneath it. With a sadness that seemed to cling to the corners of the rooms where injured sailors usually went quiet, staring at the floor, bracing for words that could change everything.

This place felt nothing like that.

The air smelled clean and comfortable. The lighting was soft instead of harsh, and the furniture felt intentionally cozy instead of utilitarian.

He had not been inside since he'd helped Sutton finish the paint and trim a few weeks earlier. At the time it was little more than empty rooms and bare floors.

Now it looks...alive.

Willow had clearly done what Willow always did and turned a practical space into something welcoming and thoughtful. But even so, Hyder could tell that some of the choices here had not been hers.

The layout of the exam rooms, especially the one they were standing in, the arrangement of equipment, even the calming way the treatment room looked out toward the forest through the wide window. Those things felt different.

More peaceful and personal.

It gave him an interesting glimpse into the kind of doctor Sola might be. Someone who wanted people to feel calm instead of afraid. Someone who understood that healing sometimes meant more than prescriptions.

Behind him Willow cleared her throat lightly.

"Well," she said, hugging herself in satisfaction as though she too could tell how pleased Sola was. "I should probably tell you one more thing."

Sola turned toward her. "What's that?"

"I went ahead and hired someone to help you out up front so you wouldn't have to bother," Willow explained. "A receptionist. Her name is Galena."

She hesitated for a moment, waiting for Sola's reaction before continuing.

"She's from the village. But if you'd rather hire someone else, we can absolutely—"

"Oh, no," Sola interrupted quickly, shaking her head. "That's perfectly fine. I'm sure whoever you chose will be wonderful."

Hyder chuckled under his breath.

Sola glanced at him. "What?"

He lifted both hands innocently.

"Nothing."

Willow narrowed her eyes, and practically growled at him, "Hyder."

"What?" he echoed innocently, grinning. "I'm just imagining Galena's first day."

Sola looked between them curiously. "Should I be concerned?"

"No," Willow sighed.

"Yes," Hyder laughed out at the same time.

Sola raised an eyebrow.

"She's extremely organized," Willow clarified quickly. "She's helped at the Lodge a few times and she's wonderful with schedules."

Hyder nodded. "That part's true."

"And," Willow continued pointedly, "she's very friendly."

Hyder snorted. "That's one way of putting it."

"And what's the other way?" Sola crossed her arms.

Hyder leaned closer, whispering conspiratorially, "Galena's never met an opinion she didn't feel absolutely compelled to share. With absolutely everyone."

Sola blinked and Willow pinched the bridge of her nose.

"She also knows everything that happens in town or the village," Hyder added helpfully. "So, if you ever want the full story behind any patient who walks through that door, Galena will definitely provide it. Actually, she'll give it to you even if you don't ask."

Willow shot him another glare, gritting her teeth. "Hyder…"

"What?" he grinned again, completely unrepentant. "It's true."

Sola laughed softly, shrugging.

"It's okay. I think I can handle a little personality in the office."

Hyder's grin widened, watching as the determined glint came back to Sola's eyes.

Oh boy, he thought. *This is going to be fun.*

Willow clapped her hands again, redirecting the conversation.

"Well, it sounds like your first appointment might already be lined up."

Sola nodded. "Yes."

"Can we get you anything before we head out?" Willow added. "Coffee? Lunch? A tour of the rest of town?"

Sola shook her head, glancing around the clinic again with something close to disbelief in her eyes.

"No. I think I'd actually like a little time to go through everything before they get here." Her gaze drifted around the exam room again. "As long as the list I gave you all wasn't…too much."

Her voice faltered slightly on the last words and Hyder saw the flicker of worry there. Like she was afraid she *had* asked for too much.

"Oh, please." Willow waved a hand dismissively. "We got everything you asked for. Some of the stuff we weren't totally sure where to put yet, so it's in the storage room down the hall." She pointed. "But everything else is already set up in the drawers and cabinets."

Sola's whole face brightened again. Not with a polite smile. A real one. Her eyes deepened and sparkled at the same time, and for a moment Hyder felt like someone had reached into his chest and squeezed his lungs.

He froze. Again. Like his body hadn't quite checked with his brain.

This woman is going to be a problem.

Before he could stare any longer, Willow grabbed his sleeve and tugged him toward the door.

"Alright," she said briskly. "We'll let you get settled."

They were halfway out the door when Willow paused and turned back.

"Oh! I almost forgot. Would you and your family like to come to the Lodge for dinner tonight?"

Sola hesitated, almost like she was trying to decide if Willow actually wanted them to come, or if she was just being kind. She must have seen something in Willow's face, because she nodded slowly, smiling again.

"Yes," she said. "That would be great."

Willow beamed.

"Perfect."

They stepped outside again and crossed the square in companionable silence. Hyder kept his gaze firmly ahead. Absolutely not thinking about the way Sola's smile had looked just now.

Not at all.

They reached the other side of the square before Willow suddenly stopped.

"Alright."

Hyder glanced down. She had turned toward him with her arms crossed.

"Spill it, bro."

"What?" He managed to keep a straight face.

"What is going on with you?" she asked, her foot tapping impatiently in the snow.

"Nothing."

"Hyder...," the warning was clear in her voice.

"What?" This time the straight face was harder to keep. Willow was nothing if not persistent.

"Every time I look at you," she muttered, "you're staring at her like you won the whole pot at the elders' bingo night. You don't usually look at people...women...like that."

He forced his usual easy grin into place and casualness into his tone. "I have no idea what you're talking about, Wills."

She squinted at him.

"You still have a moony expression on your face."

"I do *not* have a moony expression. You're imagining things."

Willow studied him for another long moment, clearly not believing him. Finally, she sighed and started walking again.

"Well. Just be careful, Hyder."

"Careful of what?" he asked, even though he knew exactly what she meant.

"You know Sutton would freak out if you started messing with the new doctor."

Hyder rolled his eyes.

"Relax, Wills. I have *no* interest in messing with anyone."

"I mean, Sterling?" Willow continued like he hadn't said anything. "Well, we're all expecting that."

Sterling.

Their younger brother was due back from the North Slope any day now for his two-week break. And Willow was right. Sterling would absolutely notice the new doctor. She was exactly his type. Which essentially meant she was an attractive woman and not currently spoken for. He would charm her without even trying. Flash a smile, casually say something meant to melt her heart, and act like the whole world was a joke meant just for him. He'd done it a hundred times before.

The thought made something twist unpleasantly in Hyder's stomach. It could not possibly be jealousy. That would be ridiculous.

Besides, she was older than Sterling anyway. A few years younger than him, maybe, which would easily make her several years older than Sterling. And she had a kid. That was a level of responsibility even Sterling wouldn't mess with.

He hoped.

Hyder shoved his hands into his pockets against the cold, still thinking. Despite everything he had just told Willow, despite the way he kept insisting none of this meant anything, he realized something as they opened the door to the Raven and walked inside.

He was looking forward to dinner tonight. Not the food, and certainly not the usual family chaos.

But the simple fact that Sola would be there.

TEN

Sola

Her first day as Alpenglow's official doctor turned out to be surprisingly full.

Sola had expected Clare and her daughter, Bella, of course. The little girl arrived bundled in a thick pink coat and knitted hat that made her look more like a puffball than a patient, coughing once as if to prove her case. After listening carefully to her lungs, looking at her throat, and asking a few questions, Sola determined it was nothing more than a bronchial cough.

"Hot tea with honey," she advised gently. "And rest. If she develops a fever or starts wheezing, bring her back."

Clare thanked her three times before leaving, hovering like she wasn't quite ready to go even after being reassured.

After that came Amos.

He was a quiet young man who stepped through the door holding up his hand in a sheepish sort of apology.

"Sorry to bother you, Doc." He didn't meet her eyes when he said it.

His palm had a deep, clean slice across it, the kind that bled impressively but thankfully had missed anything critical.

"Woodworking accident?" Sola guessed.

He nodded, surprise flashing across his face as he looked up, as if he was just now seeing her.

Sola cleaned the wound thoroughly, irrigating it with saline while Amos sat stoically on the exam table.

"You know," she told him while preparing the suture kit and lidocaine, "sharp tools are not supposed to win the fight."

"Yes, ma'am," Amos replied seriously.

She stitched the cut closed with neat, careful sutures, telling him to keep it dry for at least a week, then gave him a tetanus booster just in case.

By the time he left, flexing his bandaged hand experimentally, the clock was creeping toward noon. Sola had just sat down at her desk to start some sort of organizational system for her patient notes when the bell above the door chimed again.

This time a large man filled the doorway.

He was big in the way men who had spent their whole lives lifting things tended to be, his suspenders stretched over a substantial belly, his beard thick and silvered with age, his head nearly bald when he pulled off his hat. In one hand he carried a heavy wicker basket that looked like it had wandered out of a Little House on the Prairie episode.

"Hiya, Doc," he gruffed.

Sola blinked.

"Hello."

"Name's Healy," he said. "I run the Raven across the square."

He tipped his head vaguely toward the building she could not see from where she sat.

"Brought you some lunch."

Before she could respond, he came over with a slight limp and set the basket down by the reception desk, flipped open a gingham cloth to cover it, then began unpacking.

First came a thick loaf of crusty sourdough bread wrapped in parchment, then a small crock of smoked salmon spread, flecked with fresh dill and lemon, a jar of pickled vegetables, a salad of roasted root vegetables and greens dressed lightly with vinaigrette, and finally, a slice of pie wrapped carefully in wax paper. Blueberry and still warm, the steam condensing on the paper.

When he was done, he gave the desk a quick, approving tap, while Sola stared, her eyes trying to take it all in but not quite understanding what was happening.

"This is…too much," she tried to protest.

He shrugged one shoulder and grunted.

"Town rule," he said matter-of-factly.

"What rule?"

"Feed the doctor." Then he gave a small nod and limped back toward the door. The bell chimed again as he left.

Sola stood there for a long moment, still staring at the spread. Until her stomach growled loudly.

"Well," she muttered. "It would be a terrible thing to waste good food."

She sat down and ate as much as she could. When she was finished, pleasantly full and feeling far more human than she had all morning, she began carefully repacking the basket so she could return it later.

Just then the bell chimed again.

This time it was Charlie. Her golden curls bounced around her shoulders and her smile looked a little nervous.

"Hiya," she said shyly, ducking her head, her lips trembling. "I know y'all just got here, and if you're too busy…"

Sola immediately straightened, slipping into doctor mode again.

"No," she said calmly. "I'm not busy. What can I help you with?"

Charlie hesitated, nearly whispering, "It's probably nothing."

"Well," Sola said gently, "why don't you tell me what it is, and we can decide together whether it's something or nothing."

Charlie nodded slowly.

"This morning, when I woke up, I felt…something."

"What kind of something?"

"A kind of ache," Charlie said, resting a hand lightly under her rounded belly. "Low down. Deep."

She shifted nervously.

"It went away once I got up and started moving around. But a little while ago I went to the bathroom and I saw some blood."

She lifted her hand quickly.

"Not much," she clarified. "Just a little."

Sola listened carefully, nodding slowly. It had been a while since her obstetrics rotation, but certain knowledge never left you.

"Is this your first pregnancy?" she asked.

Charlie nodded, her eyes getting shiny, blinking like she was trying desperately not to cry.

"What kind of prenatal care have you had so far?"

Charlie told her about seeing an OB in Anchorage at all the usual times, how she thought he was perfectly fine, but that they had not done an ultrasound yet.

"He scheduled one in two weeks," she explained. "Sutton is supposed to fly me over."

"Oh?" Sola said with mild surprise, glancing down at Charlie's belly again. She would have guessed she was further along. "How far along are you?"

"About eighteen weeks," Charlie said with a nervous laugh. "Give or take. I'm not all that regular and we were on our honeymoon. I had just stopped taking birth control right before the wedding."

Sola nodded thoughtfully, smiling reassuringly.

"Alright. It's not unusual to do the first anatomy scan around now. Would you like to do one today? Just to check that everything looks alright?"

Relief washed over Charlie's face immediately.

"Yes," she said quickly. "I think I would."

Then she hesitated.

"But would you mind if I called Sutton first? He'd want to be here."

"Of course," Sola agreed.

One of the strange things about Alpenglow that Sola was quickly learning was that if you did not use a landline, you were going to be FaceTiming or messaging people. There was no cell signal in the entire town. Yet the Wi-Fi worked beautifully.

Another interesting discovery was that, because the town was so small, it did not take Sutton long to arrive. The clinic door burst open only a few minutes later.

"Charlie!" He crossed the room in three long strides, his face tight with concern as he pulled her into his arms, then leaned back to search her face. "Are you okay? Why didn't you tell me this morning?"

Charlie shrugged, her brave smile starting to crumble now that she had him there. "I thought maybe I was just imagining it."

Sutton frowned. But before he could continue, Sola stepped in.

"Well," she said calmly, "why don't we head back and see what this baby wants to tell us."

She walked toward the exam room. At the door she paused and glanced back at them. "One question before we start," she said, "Do you want me to tell you the sex if we can see it?"

Charlie and Sutton's eyes met, and a small smile crept in to replace Sutton's serious look. Charlie nodded and was the one to speak. "Yeah, I think we do."

Charlie climbed onto the exam table and lay back while Sola opened a few drawers.

"I'm still learning where everything is," she admitted. Then she found the bottle she needed. "Ah, here it is."

She held up the ultrasound gel.

"I did order a warmer for this," she explained apologetically, "but I'm afraid I don't know where it is yet, so this is going to be a little cold."

Charlie laughed as Sola squeezed a generous amount onto her abdomen and wheeled the ultrasound machine closer. She placed the transducer gently against the gel and began moving it slowly across the surface of Charlie's belly.

The screen flickered to life.

At eighteen weeks the fetus was already clearly visible on the ultrasound. The head appeared first, round and bright against the dark fluid background, followed by the curve of the spine. The tiny vertebrae were aligned like a string of pearls. She adjusted the angle slightly, capturing the flicker of a steady heartbeat and the outline of small limbs shifting gently in the amniotic fluid.

Then Sola froze.

She adjusted the probe slightly.

Then again, her breath catching.

Two heartbeats. Two skulls. Two distinct spinal columns curving in opposite directions.

Both babies were clearly visible now, floating side by side within the uterus, each with their own fluttering heart, tiny rib cages expanding and contracting, arms occasionally twitching as if stretching in their watery world, reaching for one another.

She had never personally scanned twins before, but there was no mistaking it. Still, she took a moment to scan over both babies again, just to make sure everything was okay. Luckily, like most new parents, Charlie and Sutton were watching the screen with awe, seemingly unaware of what they were actually seeing.

She looked up slowly. First at Charlie. Then at Sutton. Her own heart was beating a little faster now too.

"Well," she said carefully, "Mom. Dad. I hope you're excited to hear that there is nothing wrong..."

She paused slightly. "...with your son..."

Her eyes flicked back to the screen. "...or your daughter."

Silence filled the room as she gave them a moment to absorb it.

She had heard that people sometimes reacted with panic upon hearing this news. Sometimes with laughter. Sometimes both.

"Wow...," Charlie breathed, watching the screen, her eyes squinting like she was still trying to see what Sola was seeing.

Sutton looked completely paralyzed. Like someone had unplugged his brain for a second. Then suddenly he turned toward Charlie.

"We need to move to Anchorage. Soon. Before they're born."

Charlie's head snapped up.

"What? Why?"

"Because it's not safe here," Sutton replied quickly. "My mother..."

Charlie placed her hand gently over his. Not saying a word. Giving him a moment.

Across the room, Sola sat quietly, deliberately still so she would not interrupt them.

She could admit she felt a little nervous herself. She had delivered babies before. Not many, but enough to feel comfortable.

Twins, however, carried more risk. There were simply more variables.

Still, moving entirely to Anchorage, months ahead of time, felt a bit extreme.

"Perhaps," Sola spoke carefully after a minute, "we could consider a compromise."

Charlie smiled. Sutton scowled.

"What if we keep a very close eye on Charlie here?" she suggested. "Let's say...weekly appointments for now. With twins we'll monitor growth carefully and keep an eye out for any complications. As we get closer to the due date, since twins usually arrive a little earlier, we can plan for you both to go to Anchorage a week or two before delivery. It can be a little babymoon for you guys."

Charlie's smile spread immediately.

Sutton, however...well, he was not convinced so easily. He studied Charlie's face. Then Sola's. Something he saw must have changed his mind. His expression softened slightly, but his eyes were still serious.

"Weekly appointments?" he confirmed.

"Yes," Sola nodded, meeting his gaze steadily. "And later we might increase the frequency."

But still, he just watched her as if he was still waiting for something else.

"I promise you," she vowed, "I will take care of her as if she were family."

That seemed to break through something in him. His shoulders finally loosened and he let his eyes drift back to Charlie who was still holding his hand.

"Alright," he said quietly.

They left a few minutes later, still hand in hand, both looking a little stunned.

Sola stood by the window as they walked toward the truck Charlie had driven over. Sutton opened the driver's door for her and leaned down to kiss her. It was not soft. It was solid. Like he was reassuring himself she was real and safe. Charlie wrapped her arms around his shoulders and kissed him back.

Sola quickly turned away, feeling slightly embarrassed for witnessing their moment. But also, something else. There was a quiet ache she had not expected. Somewhere deep, a hollow resonance.

What must it be like, she wondered, *to have someone love you that much?*

ELEVEN

Hyder

She's not coming.

Hyder had been watching the boardwalk door of the Raven for nearly twenty minutes, and every time it swung open without Sola walking through it, his grin loosened just a little more.

The usual family dinner that Sola had agreed to come to had been moved. He didn't know why. He had been working all day in the shop behind the Lodge, mending fishing gear and replacing the worn brass impeller housing he had pulled off the auxiliary pump on his trawler earlier that morning. It was the kind of job that required patience more than skill, but Hyder had always liked tinkering with engines and fittings, and it gave his hands something to do while his mind wandered.

His radio was up high, blasting some classics by Nirvana and Pearl Jam, so he did not hear the chat announcement. It was not the one with just his siblings, where actual problems like storm warnings, busted pipes, and guests arriving early were shouted out.

This chat included cousins. And neighbors. And most of the town. Apparently, Charlie and Sutton had some news, and they wanted to tell everyone at once.

Hyder had already guessed what that meant. A gender reveal sort of thing. The town was already buzzing about Charlie going to see the new doc today. Which, whatever. To each their own. But since it was going to be his niece or nephew, he decided not to mock it.

Too much.

However, in Alpenglow, that sort of announcement meant only one thing.

A party.

Or rather, a potlatch.

Normally Hyder would not have minded. He liked a good party. But Thanksgiving was less than a week away, and it seemed a little excessive considering they would be doing it all over again in a few days. And he found himself worrying that Sola and her family might not show. They had only been there for a little over a day after all.

Platters of smoked salmon, boules of sourdough, bowls of roasted vegetables, and a giant pot of spaghetti sauce and moose balls that Healy had been proudly stirring in the kitchen all afternoon were already beginning to fill the long trestle tables.

Someone turned on the music. Others helped to bring in two more casks of beer. The noise level of the Raven was steadily climbing.

The bell over the door jingled again. Hyder straightened, then grimaced.

Micah walked in carrying a massive glass bowl filled with something that looked like it had been assembled during a dare.

"Tell me that is not what I think it is," Hyder sighed.

Micah grinned, holding the bowl up higher, like it was a trophy.

"My famous twenty-layer dip."

"Micah, you know that looks like it could legally qualify as a biohazard."

Micah set the bowl on the table.

"Whatever, you know it's awesome. You're just mad you didn't think of it."

"Last time you made that," Hyder said dryly, "Kael thought the jukebox was flirting with him."

Kael called from across the room, "It was!"

The bell jingled again. Hyder looked. Still not her. The Raven continued filling.

Amos arrived, nodding once like that was more than enough greeting for everyone. Then Koy, holding on to Nan's arm, matching his steps to hers.

The Gordons walked in. Dan and Clare, holding hands like teenagers, and their son Finn trailing behind, raising his arms like he was holding up the roof. That kid was probably one of the coolest cats Hyder had ever met. He was gay, which luckily their town didn't care one way or the other, but beyond that, he was kind and happened to be his little sister Hope's best friend. For that, he would always think of him as family. The youngest Gordon was absent, but it was going around that she had a cold, so she was probably home with a sitter.

Willow, Hope, and Gemma burst through the door laughing loudly about something, hurrying over to the tables before the desserts were all gone.

"Gemma, lovey, slow down or you'll trip and lose your chance at the good ones," Willow said, catching her niece gently by the shoulder even as she continued laughing.

"But I want the pink one with the sprinkles!" Gemma squealed, bouncing on her toes while Hope grinned and handed her a plate.

"I don't know, Gems, I might get that one first," Hope teased her.

Gemma rushed over, grabbing not only the pink cupcake with the sprinkles but two others as well. Hyder halfway wondered if he ought to say something. He knew Charlie and Sutton would never let her have that much sugar. Then he shrugged. It was a celebration after all, and he wasn't the one who'd have to deal with her later.

Even Nobu came in, dusted with snow and already humming a tune to himself.

Within minutes it felt like the entire town had crammed into the Raven. The only ones missing, besides Charlie and Sutton and Sterling of course, were Dutchy, who never joined in a party if he could help it, and Ambler, who rarely even came to town unless he knew he was needed. Hyder glanced around at all the people he loved, trying not to feel disappointment that Sola wasn't there and to not look back at the door again when the bell chimed.

But he did.

And this time...she was there.

Sola stepped inside holding Gus's hand. The boy wore heavy noise-canceling headphones and carried a leather notebook under one arm. Behind them, Lucia swept in wearing a bright scarf wrapped dramatically around her shoulders and a smile that could have lit the entire room without electricity.

Hyder's grin returned instantly.

Clearly someone else likes a good party.

The town descended on them immediately. Hands were shaken. Introductions happened faster than Sola could possibly keep track of them.

Within seconds Lucia was swept into a group of older women who began talking animatedly with her, waving their hands and laughing as if they had known each other for years.

Hyder caught snippets.

"...Wednesday knitting circle..."

"...Friday bingo..."

"...Saturday soup exchange..."

Lucia looked delighted.

Sola, meanwhile, gently extricated herself and guided Gus toward a quiet table in the corner. She helped him settle into a chair, opened his notebook, and placed his pencils beside it while he kept the headphones firmly over his ears.

Hyder wandered over, his curiosity winning. He stopped beside the table and looked down at the page. His eyebrows lifted.

Spread across the paper was a meticulous drawing of the cove. Every curve of shoreline, every dock, every cluster of cottages captured with careful lines.

"Wow," Hyder said honestly. "That's incredible."

He was not even trying to hide his awe. Because it was.

Sola smiled. Another real one.

"Yeah," she said softly, her pride in her son clear. "Mapping is Gus's thing."

Hyder leaned a little closer. For a brief moment Gus looked up at him, his gaze flicking past Hyder's shoulder. Then back down again.

Suddenly he blurted out, "Hammer Time!"

Hyder blinked as it clicked. It was the type of trawler he captained. His aluminum boat that he'd special ordered after months of back and forth with Sutton about what would be best for fishing charters. He realized Gus must have seen the lettering on the hull.

"Yeah," Hyder said slowly, grinning. "My boat."

His gaze flicked to Sola, hoping he was not being too forward.

"When you and your mom get settled, after the weather gets warmer, you will have to come out with me on her. Would you like that?"

Gus did not say anything, but he gave a short nod.

Sola, however, looked a little upset, but she quickly smoothed over her features, the serious look coming back.

"Would you like something to eat?" Hyder asked, needing something else to say.

This time, it was surprise that flickered in her eyes as she glanced toward the food tables. Then anxiety.

"I think I'll wait until my mother comes back."

They both looked over. Lucia was listening to a story that had her laughing so hard she had tears in her eyes, gripping her sides.

Hyder chuckled. "She might be a while."

He didn't want to push, but he also hated the idea of her sitting there by herself, hungry. She was tiny enough that she definitely shouldn't be skipping meals.

"If you want, I can sit with Gus while you make a plate."

Sola's expression flickered with uncertainty at his offer. Clearly, she had spent years with her and her mother being the only ones responsible for her son.

And just as clear, trust did not come easily to her.

"I mean," Hyder added quickly, "I could go make you two plates, but you might not like what I put on there."

He gestured toward the tables again.

"The spaghetti and moose balls are pretty awesome, though."

Sola wrinkled her nose slightly, but after a moment she let her shoulders fall and nodded.

"Okay."

She drifted off toward the potlatch line, balancing two plates while glancing back every few steps, making sure her son was still alive.

Hyder noticed as he pulled up a chair and sat down beside Gus.

"Your mom's kind of overprotective, huh?" He said it casually, not expecting an answer.

"Yeah," came a quiet voice beside him. "She's mom."

Hyder grinned. Gus was still not looking at him but that was okay. It was enough that he knew Hyder was there.

Hyder pulled the chair closer and tapped the notebook gently.

"Can you show me your favorite one?"

Gus hesitated, then flipped several pages. The drawing that appeared made Hyder lean forward in awe.

It was a coastline, with deep fjords cut into steep mountains ending in calving glaciers. Wide coastal plains. Curving bays and coves.

Recognition came to him suddenly.

"Prince William Sound," he breathed.

Gus nodded slightly.

Hyder looked closer. He had spent his whole life on boats, reading navigational maps, charts with tides. Even satellite images.

But this...this was something else. It was art. Even he, who knew nothing of such things, could see that.

"And you did this from memory?" Hyder asked softly. "After flying over it yesterday?"

Gus did not answer, but he did not deny it either.

Hyder leaned back slowly.

"I have to tell you, Gus, this is incredible," he said seriously. "I would love one of these someday. To go on my wall. Do you think you could do that?"

Gus pressed his lips together. Then nodded.

"Hyde."

Hyder inhaled deeply, feeling something tighten in his chest at the quiet little boy saying his name.

Without another word, Gus flipped back to the page he had been working on and picked up his pencil again.

Sola returned just then and Hyder stood up.

"Your son is a genius."

She met his eyes.

"I'm glad you think so," she said quietly, staring. "Most people don't bother to notice."

That feeling hit him again. Like she was looking past his grin and into the real parts of him. Seeing things he did not always show. It made him feel oddly exposed.

And when she did not look away...

When she stepped a little closer...

Hyder had the strangest, nearly overwhelming compulsion to lean down and kiss her.

Luckily, for them both, the door burst open, and Charlie and Sutton walked in.

The Raven erupted, cheers filling the bar to the rafters. Someone banged a spoon against a mug. Gemma shrieked. Hope started whistling with her fingers.

Sutton raised his hands for quiet as Charlie grinned, her hand held absently and protectively over her lower belly.

"We have some news!"

"A girl!" someone yelled immediately.

Charlie laughed.

"A boy!" Amos shouted.

The room exploded again, discussing the merits of both. How Sutton did so well with girls. How he should have a boy to show him how to use a chainsaw.

"And just why couldn't he teach a girl to use a chainsaw?" came Tala from the other side of the room.

More cheers.

"Well," Sutton said seriously, "If you don't wanna know…" He grabbed Charlie's hand and made like he was leaving.

"No! No!" came more shouts. "Go ahead, tell us!"

Sutton broke out in a grin, then he looked over to see if Charlie was ready. She nodded.

"Well…it's a boy!"

More cheers.

"And," his deep voice boomed over the crowd, "it's a girl!"

For a moment, the crowd went quiet.

Then Micah yelled, "Called it! I win the pool!"

Hope practically bounced up and down.

Gemma rushed over, grabbed Charlie's legs in a hug, talking a mile a minute about how there would be two babies sharing her room.

Hyder came over and wrapped Sutton in a huge bear hug. For a moment their eyes met and Hyder saw it. The fear Sutton was not saying out loud. He understood it completely. Watching their mother die was something they would always carry together.

Hyder clapped his brother's back. Hard.

"It's gonna be all right," he said quietly.

Then he grinned and pulled away. Because this was a party. And Kings did *not* ruin parties.

Later, karaoke started. Nobu was halfway through a surprisingly enthusiastic rendition of "Sweet Caroline" when Hyder spotted Sola gathering Gus's notebook and pencils.

The boy's head was lolling sleepily, no longer wearing his headphones.

Hyder walked over, whispering, "Need some help?"

Sola flushed slightly. Whether it was from the offer or the two glasses of wine he'd watched her drink, he couldn't tell.

"Oh no, I've got it."

She glanced toward Lucia, who was still sipping her own wine and telling stories in a healthy mix of Spanish and English, to a very attentive audience.

It was obvious that Sola did not want to interrupt, but she also did not want to ask for his help.

Hyder smirked, then leaned down.

"Hey, Captain Gus," he murmured. "Want a piggyback ride?"

Gus looked up sleepily, thought about it, then said, "Hyde."

Hyder chuckled softly.

"Good enough."

He crouched more and lifted the boy easily onto his back. Gus held on so tightly he nearly choked him, but Hyder did not complain. Especially after he saw the astonishment on Sola's face.

The walk to Aurora Cottage was far too short. Hyder wished he had some excuse to stretch it longer, but he was drawing a blank.

He followed Sola inside and did not comment when she stopped to lock the door. Someone would eventually explain to her that nobody locked their doors in Alpenglow. But maybe that was something she needed to learn on her own.

She led him down the hall into Gus's room. Hyder waited quietly in the doorway while she helped her son change and tucked him into bed.

They backed out quietly and Sola walked him to the front door. He stepped outside.

She followed him out, stopping on her porch, her arms folded around herself almost protectively while she looked up at him with her knowing gaze again.

Hyder searched desperately for something, anything at all, to say that was not just "hi" once more.

His brain flashed back to over a year ago, when Charlie had first arrived in Alpenglow. Hyder had accidentally come across Sutton and Charlie kissing on her front porch.

If you wanted to say that all they were doing was kissing…

He flushed slightly. It would be incredibly cliché to do the same thing, especially after he'd mocked his brother over it. Plus, Sola had only just arrived, and she'd shown absolutely no interest in him whatsoever.

With a quiet sigh, he decided to say good night instead. He turned away, walking barely two steps.

"Hey, Hyder…"

He looked back. Somehow, she was right next to him, even though he hadn't heard her approach. He turned completely, his brow raised.

And she kissed him.

Twelve

Sola

Carajo!

It had to be the wine. That was the only explanation that made any damn sense.

Sola hadn't let herself be this reckless in years. Not since she'd learned, painfully and repeatedly, that giving in to raw impulse usually left her picking up pieces she didn't have the bandwidth to reassemble anymore. She liked simple and easy. Something she could walk away from and never see if she didn't want to. But the moment Hyder turned to leave, and the sharp bite of the night air began curling around her bare neck, something primal snapped awake inside her chest.

"Hey, Hyder..."

He pivoted back, and she didn't give her better judgment even a heartbeat to protest. If she had, she would've lost her nerve.

She closed the distance in one decisive stride, fingers curling into the thick wool of his jacket, yanking him toward her with more force than grace. Thank God for the high-heeled boots she'd chosen tonight. Even so, she had to rise onto her toes, slide one arm around the broad column of his shoulders, and drag that impossibly tall frame down to her level.

The first collision of their mouths was anything but tentative.

It was fierce. Greedy. A hungry, open-mouthed claim that swallowed the cold air between them. For one fractured second Hyder went rigid as though he was caught off guard, or maybe second-guessing the wisdom better than she was, but then his restraint shattered.

His hands found her like they'd been waiting years to do it.

One massive palm clamped around her waist, fingers splaying possessively over the curve of her hip. The other slid low, bracing at the small of her back, hauling her flush against the hard wall of his body. The kiss deepened in a single, devastating stroke, his tongue sliding against hers, slow and deliberate, tasting every gasp she couldn't hold back.

For one dizzying moment, the world collapsed to heat and him.

She could feel every inch of where they pressed together. The hard planes of his chest flattening her breasts, the ridge of his belt buckle digging into her belly, the unmistakable, thickening length of his arousal already straining against her through denim and layers of fabric. Her dreams had teased her with fragments of this last night. Soft, hazy fantasies, filled with sighs and muted colors. But reality was so much...more. So much more solid and hot. His body radiated like a furnace. His heartbeat thudded against her ribs. Heavy and fast. He was exactly enough to make her want more instead of less.

Up close, stripped of bar noise and winter wind, she finally caught his scent properly. Dark-roast coffee, a clean lemony bite of soap, and underneath it all the raw, musky undertone of aroused male skin. The kind of scent that would live in her sheets afterwards, making her want to bury her face in them and lose entire hours.

Hyder angled his head, deepening the kiss, the scrape of his day-old stubble rasping deliciously along her cheek and jaw. He kissed like he knew exactly how strong he was and was doing his best to keep that strength in check. She moaned softly into his mouth at the sensation, low and involuntary, and felt the answering vibration rumble through his chest.

Her fingers speared into his hair without conscious permission, tugging at the thick, surprisingly silky strands. The small, helpless hitch in his breathing sent a lightning bolt of heat straight between her thighs.

A rough, half-laugh, half-groan tore from his throat, then without warning, he simply lifted her. Effortlessly, the ease of it going straight to her head.

One thick forearm hooked under her thighs, scooping her up as though she were weightless. Sola gasped sharply against his lips as her boots left the boards. Her legs wrapped around his hips on pure instinct, locking tight.

The new position crushed them together even harder. Her core settled right over the rigid swell of him, the seam of her jeans pressing insistently with every tiny shift. Dizzying pressure sparked behind her eyes. Her dream, the one she'd spent all day trying to shove out of her mind, slammed back in vivid, X-rated detail. His hands, his mouth, the way he'd spread her wide and taken his time. Only now the fantasy was flesh and blood and devastatingly real. Real enough that if he took one step, two steps, turned and pinned her to the wall, she was not entirely certain she would bother to say no. She might even say yes.

She tasted the faint sweetness of pie on his tongue. Sugar and apples and cinnamon. But beneath it was something saltier, hungrier. Something that made her want to grind down and chase more.

She kissed him deeper, her teeth grazing his lower lip, tongue stroking in slow, deliberate drags that had him growling into her mouth. It wasn't theatrical. Just male and real. It made her want to pull another one from him.

Hyder matched her instantly.

His free hand roamed higher, the broad palm spreading across her shoulder blades, fingers digging in just enough to let her feel the restrained strength there. Like he was fighting the urge to rip fabric and touch skin. His breathing turned ragged, each exhale hot against her swollen lips. The kiss turned molten then. Long, languid pulls and teasing flicks of tongue that somehow felt hotter than the frantic beginning. He was kissing her like he was paying attention.

For long, drugged moments Sola completely forgot where they were.

The cottage porch. The icy night pressing at their backs. The distant, cheerful hum still leaking from the Raven's windows. It all thinned to static. Even her own name felt forgotten.

There was only sensation, and the dangerous, glorious relief of not thinking for once. The slick heat of his mouth, the iron grip of his arm cradling her ass, the relentless throb of his erection notched against her center, and the slow, torturous glide of his thumb tracing lazy circles along the knobs of her spine beneath her sweater.

That small, absent caress was what finally dragged a faint thought forward. An understanding of the real beginning of all of this.

This kiss.

It was not at the dock when she first saw him and felt an instant, extreme attraction. And it wasn't this morning at the clinic when she'd felt his warmth. Not even the dream last night.

It was earlier. Tonight. Watching Hyder bend down beside Gus at the Raven, his voice low and patient, treating her son like a person instead of a problem. That quiet decency had cracked something open inside her. Yes, she wanted him physically. But that was easily dismissed. Somehow the want went deeper now. It was suddenly dangerous and undeniable.

Not that physical was going to be a problem. The thick, insistent ridge currently pressing against her through too many layers of clothing promised more than enough to wreck her in the best possible ways. The thought nearly made her dizzy, and her mind tried to claw back some clarity.

And failed, still lost completely in him.

In the end, it was Hyder that pulled away, just far enough that their mouths parted with a soft, wet sound.

His chest heaved beneath her palm, his eyes wide and aroused, his lips slick from hers.

Neither of them spoke for a long beat. Then a short, stunned laugh huffed out of him.

"Well," he rasped, "that was…"

He shook his head once, his hands still flexing on her hips and ass like he couldn't quite believe she was real.

"…easily the best kiss I've ever had."

Pride flared in her chest. She let a slow, wicked grin curve her mouth as a pulse of savage feminine satisfaction ran through her.

His expression gentled, though the hunger in his eyes didn't fade.

"But," he added softly, regret threading through the word, "it's probably best if I head out for now."

She blinked. Not offended or hurt. Just…surprised. Her body was still needy. Her legs were still wrapped around him.

He lowered her with aching care, his big hands sliding to bracket her waist and lingering there as she steadied herself, his thumbs brushing the sensitive skin just above her jeans before finally letting go.

For half a second, she wondered if she'd miscalculated. Then her gaze dropped, deliberate and unapologetic, to the thick, unmistakable outline straining against the fly of his jeans, the denim pulled so taut she could trace the shape of him.

Understanding clicked. Pulling away was not an easy thing he was doing. He was stopping because he had to, not because he wanted to.

Sola eased back a single step, leaning one shoulder against the doorframe of her cottage, letting her posture relax into something lazy and inviting while she studied him.

"That's fine," she said, her voice low and far steadier than the liquid heat still pooling low in her belly.

Hyder searched her face, cautious.

"You're sure?"

She lifted one shoulder in a careless shrug, though the smile tugging at her lips betrayed her.

"I don't mind waiting."

Her eyes dragged over him again. Slow and shameless. Lingering on his mouth, his throat, the impressive evidence of his arousal still tenting his jeans.

"But not too long. *Entiendes*?"

The words pulled another laugh from him, this one deeper and edged with pure want.

His head tipped back for a second, and he breathed deeply through his nose, like he was trying to gather himself. Then he took a single step backward, down the porch stair, running his hands through his hair, still watching her like it physically hurt to turn away.

"Goodnight, Sola."

"Goodnight, Hyder."

He turned and walked away, not looking back.

Sola stayed where she was long after he had gone, one hand rising slowly to touch her swollen mouth. Her lips still tingled. Her body still hummed. And she knew she was going to be with him, sooner rather than later. But beneath all the leftover heat and need was a quieter truth she did not like nearly as much.

Nothing about Hyder felt simple.

THIRTEEN

Hyder

In the last few weeks, autumn, what little there was left, had officially surrendered, and winter had settled into Alpenglow with the quiet certainty of something inevitable. It would stay for the next five and a half months, perhaps six, if the storms kept it up. Long, dark, and cold. With a thick blanket of snow. The sort of winter that demanded patience from the people who lived here, who had long ago learned that fighting the season was pointless. You endured it and you adapted. You banded together and you waited. Usually with lots of celebration and flair to tell winter that it was not going to win.

These things were not new, but Hyder was starting to think the weather was mocking them. It had sent near-constant storms from the Arctic, delaying Sterling's return home. And it showed no signs of improving. In Alpenglow, the clouds had thickened since morning, heavy and swollen with more snow that had not yet begun to fall, though everyone in town knew it was coming. The air had gone strangely still, the wind dropping away until the cove lay dark and flat as slate. Even the gulls had disappeared and so had Lenny and Squiggy.

Hyder stood outside of the workshop, staring up at the sky as though it might personally apologize.

It did not.

He exhaled slowly, rubbing the back of his neck as he walked over to his truck. He had to admit to a growing sense of frustration beyond the weather. It was as if the whole world was against him. Or at least the town.

Persecuted. That's the word.

Well. Maybe that was a little dramatic. It was not as though half the town had intentionally come down with the flu, just after Thanksgiving, simply to prevent him from seeing Sola alone. Still, the result was the same. For nearly two and a half weeks now, the illness had swept through Alpenglow and the neighboring villages like a slow-moving tide, catching one household after another. Children, elders, fishermen who thought they were too tough to stay in bed, all of them eventually showing up at the clinic with fever and aching bones.

Which meant Sola had been working from dawn until well past nightfall. She was also making house calls, driving out to Kisa'adi and the smaller fishing camps. Dragging crates of medication and thermometers with her wherever she went.

He had seen her around, but usually it was only out of the corner of his eye. A glimpse of her orange Subaru rolling past the crossroads. A flash of dark hair as she hurried across the square in those damned heeled boots she still insisted on wearing. Boots that had absolutely no business being worn in an Alaskan winter, even if she did manage them with ridiculous grace.

And even though he happened to know someone had left her a perfectly good pair of Kamiks on her doorstep.

He knew. Because he was that someone.

He had left them in the dead of night, tiptoeing down the boardwalk like some sort of burglar, praying that no one in town saw him creeping around with a box under his arm. In Alpenglow that kind of stealth was almost impossible. Someone was always looking out a window, always walking a dog, always heading somewhere. But somehow, he had managed it.

Yet he still had not managed to get a single moment alone with her. He let out a heavy sigh as he pulled out on the dirt road to town.

He felt like a lovesick teenager who got kissed once and was ready for more. A lot more. To make matters worse, he already knew that Sola was not interested in anything serious. Because the one thing this town did better than banding together was gossip. Apparently, someone had asked her why she was not married. She had laughed and explained she did not need a husband...ever.

He had been thinking about that all week long. And Tala absolutely knew what was going on.

She had known from the moment he started avoiding certain topics, from the way his eyes followed Sola's car whenever it drove by the square. From the way he refused to mention her name.

"You look miserable," Tala had said last night as they were finishing up a swim in the natatorium, pushing her wet hair back from her face while she leaned against the edge of the pool.

"I am not miserable."

"Please," she snorted. "I know. I've seen you after three days of storms and broken lines. Not able to make it to shore 'cuz it's too risky. That's miserable. This?" She waved a hand at him. "This is pathetic."

Hyder glared at her, practically growling, "Careful."

"Oh, relax, puddle jumper."

He groaned.

"Do not call me that."

Her eyes went owl-wide in as close an approximation of innocence as she could muster.

"You flew in helicopters for the Coast Guard. That makes you a puddle jumper."

"That is not what that means." He pushed up from the edge of the pool, grabbing a towel. "You're insufferable."

"And you," Tala said sweetly, "are pining."

"I am not pining."

She raised a brow.

"You left her boots."

"That was practical," he insisted, not even asking how she knew. Because of course she did.

"You snuck down the boardwalk in the middle of the night."

"That was strategic."

"Hyder," she said patiently, "you have been watching her walking around town like a sad golden retriever who got told he can't have his favorite toy. Because that toy 'don't need no man.'"

He'd opened his mouth to argue. Then closed it. Because annoyingly enough, she wasn't entirely wrong.

Just then, Ellie walked in, wrapped in a towel and a cheerful smile.

"Hey, Hyder. Tala."

His comments last month still seemed to have merit. He quickly dried off as she dropped her towel and dove in cleanly.

He could admit that she had a nice body in her suit. Thin and average height, small-chested with long limbs. Hell, she was pretty. Any other time he would not have minded noticing. He still would not have been inclined to do anything about it, but he could be objective.

Now, it just frustrated him. Not because of her. She couldn't help it. But the moment he saw her he immediately thought of Sola.

Of their differences.

Sola's dark, intense beauty. Her voice that had him hearing music even when she was simply asking a mundane question. Her lips. Her breasts as they pressed against him. A perfect handful.

He'd never wanted anyone so much whom he was not supposed to have.

Now, as Hyder pulled up in the gravel lot near the town square, he looked down at the cove, seeing the extra lights that had been strung along the boardwalk last month, right before Sola and her family came to town. They glowed warmly against the dark water, reflecting softly on the surface of the harbor.

Has it really been that long?

Yes. It damned well had been. And he was determined to do something about it.

Hyder walked down past the Salty Netter, waving to Dan as he sat behind the counter fiddling with a box of lures. Lures that he honestly knew nothing about, but did his best to stock whatever anyone convinced him was the finest. Dan jumped down from his stool and stuck his head out of the door.

"Evening, Hyder," he called.

"Hey, Dan."

"I got in some new heavy halibut gear. Ya know, those super-stout rods with five hundred-pound mono and giant twenty-ounce cannonballs for dropping way down in the deep Gulf." He grinned and pulled back his flannel so Hyder could see his shirt underneath. "Perfect for hauling up the big one!"

Dan was incredibly proud of his shirts. They were long-sleeved with a huge fish and the words "Ask me About the BIG One" emboldened across the top, and "the Salty Netter, Alpenglow, AK" in smaller letters at the bottom. He wore a different colored one every day and, in the summer, they were the best-selling items from his shop. Tourists loved them.

His wife, Clare, had them made a couple of years ago, based on the town's gentle teasing over Dan's penchant for bold tall tales about the big fish that once got away from him. Even Dan was aware of the joke and that he really knew nothing about fishing or gear. But he still tried, and he was happy. Really, you couldn't beat that.

He had once come to the King Wilderness Lodge on a business retreat, from a corporate job that was killing him, and he fell in love with Alpenglow. By the next summer, he had quit his job, and his whole family had moved with him. Hyder sometimes wondered what it must be like to have someone like Clare, someone who trusted and loved you so much that they were willing to come to a new place, sight unseen, just because you needed it.

Fortunately, their whole family fit right in and they stayed, becoming part of the fabric that wove Alpenglow into something special. Unfortunately, everything he was saying about the fishing gear was wrong, but Hyder liked him far too much to correct him, and he was already trying to edge away.

"Sounds great, Dan. I'll pop in tomorrow and take a look."

"Okie doke. See ya then." Dan grinned and backed into his shop, his gaze shifting from Hyder to the boardwalk behind him.

Hyder knew everyone would know within half an hour where he was going.

The Aurora cottage looked much the same as it always had, the same small porch overlooking the cove, the same wide windows glowing softly with lamplight. But there were small changes now. A colorful tile with a tiny coquí frog hung beside the doorframe, and someone had strung a bright woven ribbon along the railing, its reds and yellows a cheerful splash of color against the snow. A new doormat that read: Welcome to Our Casa.

He knocked, waiting while he heard footsteps inside.

"Coming!"

Lucia.

He hoped Sola was home too.

Lucia opened the door, a small look of surprise crossing her face before her smile broadened warmly.

"*Señor* Hyder." She waved him inside and said, as though the two things were synonymous, "You're hungry, I have some arroz con pollo."

Hyder chuckled, rubbing his stomach.

"I wish, *Señora* Rivera. But my brother made some steaks for us tonight. I'm stuffed."

She frowned, genuinely disappointed, as though feeding him had been the natural order of things and he had somehow disrupted it. Her expression brightened again instantly.

"Well, there is always tomorrow. You will come. I'm making *asopao*." Her tone brooked no argument and Hyder could only nod.

"Yes, ma'am."

"You are here for Sola, *no*?" she asked casually, her wise eyes twinkling.

He felt his face warm. At thirty-two years old.

Blushing.

"Yes, ma'am," he repeated. "Is she home?"

"Ah," Lucia said, glancing toward the window. "No. There is someone in the village. Sick. She is down there."

Hyder glanced out the window too. The sky had darkened even further. The snow looked close now, the clouds swollen with it. Any minute it would begin falling and probably not stop until morning. He didn't like the idea of her driving home in that.

"She drove?"

"*Sí,* yes. In the car your brother got her."

"Yeah, okay." Hyder nodded slowly, still gauging the sky. "Well...tell her I dropped by."

"*Sí,* I will tell her. But you will be here for dinner tomorrow. Don't forget." She wagged her finger.

Hyder raised his hands in surrender.

"I won't. I promise."

Satisfied, Lucia walked him to the door. Her small frame, wrapped in a bright shawl, her dark eyes making him think again of her daughter.

Out there. Alone.

On his way back to his truck, Hyder saw Cheryl peeking out of the Mercantile.

"Yoo-hoo, Hyder!" She waved him over energetically.

Hyder forced his grin to stay where it was and walked toward her, going inside.

"Hey, Cheryl. What can I do for you?"

"Well," she said conspiratorially, lowering her voice even though there was no one else around, "I was wondering if you were the one picking things up from the barge next week."

Hyder shrugged.

"Probably. Haven't looked at the schedule yet, but that sounds about right."

"Well, whoever it is," she said, leaning forward over the counter, "you need to bring more than one truck."

Hyder blinked.

"Oh?"

Usually, one truck was more than enough unless they were hauling construction supplies or someone had ordered something special. Like before Sola came, when it had taken three trucks just to get all the equipment and furniture for the clinic.

"Yeah," Cheryl lowered her voice even further. "The new doctor ordered something. Something real big."

Hyder felt a faint prickle of curiosity.

"What?" He tried for nonchalant and failed. Miserably.

"A new bed," Cheryl whispered dramatically. "I guess the one she had in there wasn't big enough. Can you imagine? As tiny a thing as she is."

Hyder wondered at that too, but he also felt a flicker of irritation. Sometimes it frustrated him how little privacy anyone had in their town. But he only nodded. After all, he'd asked.

"All right. We'll make sure it gets here."

Finally, back in his truck, he backed out of the small lot and headed toward the crossroads. And then, as if his hands had a mind of their own, he turned right instead of left. Toward Kisa'adi.

By the time he reached the village, the road had turned into a swirling tunnel of white, the headlights reflecting off flakes so thick and close it felt like driving through fog. The village had always been a second home to Hyder. He had spent just as much time there as he had in Alpenglow when his mother was alive. When she died, he spent even more time there. They all had. The twins were practically raised there by Nan and Koy.

Of course that had been at the old village.

Years ago, a flood basically wiped old Kisa'adi off the map. A village that had stood for as long as anyone could remember, for as long as the stories themselves could remember.

But Alpenglow did what they could. What they always did. They rebuilt. Only on higher ground and a little closer to town.

The new Kisa'adi was its own little miracle. A little more modern, yes, but still with a central plankhouse and the yearly totems surrounding the clearing, blessing the people who lived there and reminding them of the past that still shaped them.

By the time he arrived, the road was nearly a whiteout, and Kisa'adi had apparently lost power. Hyder found the turn by muscle memory rather than sight.

Snow gave way beneath his boots as he stepped out of the truck, the heavy wet flakes already piling up past his ankles as he hurried toward the plankhouse through the darkness.

Sola could be in any one of two dozen houses. But most likely, in weather like this, people would gather in the plankhouse, keeping the fire going just in case. Hopefully someone there would know where she was if she wasn't inside already.

He pushed open the heavy carved wooden door, his fingers involuntarily tracing the Chiltak symbols, and stepped inside, closing it quickly behind him as his eyes adjusted to the dim light.

Most of the village was already there. They sat on old logs laid out at angles around the central fireplace, their faces lit by the glow of the flames. The old plankhouse had only a simple pit with a smoke hole in the ceiling, but even Koy had finally admitted the new hearth was better. Thick stone, carefully laid, holding the heat and radiating it slowly through the room. And there was less smoke in the air.

He nodded to a few cousins, aunts, and uncles, old friends, as he stepped farther inside, stomping snow from his boots. Unlike Alpenglow, Kisa'adi did not ask questions. You were there because you belonged, or because you needed to be. That was enough.

Then he saw her. Across the space, on the raised platform toward the back, she was sitting beside a narrow cot, reading a book out loud by candlelight, the aria of her voice already calling to him, his legs already moving.

Nan lay on the cot beside her, wrapped in blankets and shivering.

Nan was the village healer. Normally the village would never have called for a doctor, preferring to take care of their own unless something was truly serious. The problem was it was always Nan who did the caring.

"Hey," Hyder said quietly as he reached them. "How is she?"

Nan had been the one who sang healing songs over him when he was a boy, making him drink potent herbal concoctions that made his nose wrinkle, but always seemed to do the trick. Seeing her like this tore at him.

"She has the flu too," Sola said softly. "I gave her some Tamiflu, but it might be too late."

Hyder blanched.

"Oh," she added quickly, realizing how that sounded. "I'm sorry, I didn't mean it like that. I just mean she's probably going to have to fight this one on her own."

Hyder relaxed slightly.

"Well," he replied gently, glancing down at Nan again, "not completely on her own. You're here."

Sola gave a weak smile.

"Yes. I only hope it doesn't get too cold tonight. We lost power half an hour ago."

Hyder frowned, looking around.

"Has anyone done anything with the generators?"

She glanced up at him, surprised.

"No. I didn't know that was an option."

"Well," he said, looking around the room, "the elders like to forget that we put them in several years ago, when the village was rebuilt. I'm not sure they've ever used them. Probably because this is how it always was and they hate change."

He pulled his gloves back on.

"But they were tested this summer and worked fine then."

He turned back toward the door.

"Give me five minutes," he called over his shoulder. "I'll get 'em running."

FOURTEEN

Sola

A mechanical cough began, then a steadier, low rumble, the sound carrying through the walls of the plankhouse. Sola heard it from where she sat beside Nan's cot, the vibration traveling up through the floorboards and into her bones. She sighed, focusing on the sound for several minutes until it began to comfort her, realizing one of her fears was now gone.

Nan was finally sleeping, her feverish breathing smoothed out by the medicine and the warmth that was even now returning to the room from ticking metal heaters that lined the outside of the large room. Sola closed the book she had been reading, setting it carefully on the low stool beside the cot, thinking.

I wonder why he's here.

She had seen him in the last couple of weeks. He was impossible to miss, the very definition of tall, dark, and handsome, often out on one of the boats in the cove, helping to haul in nets and crab traps, or winterizing engines. It was Willow who had caught her staring once, and casually explained that in Alaska, boats were not just tied up and forgotten. They were prepared like living things being put to sleep, carefully tended so they would survive the winter and wake again in the spring. Like flowers.

Then there were the times he drove by in his truck, and she had to do everything in her power not to turn her head. But she'd been so damned busy, she barely had time to sit and breathe or hang out with August and Lucia, let alone chase after a guy she found attractive. Not that she minded being busy. If anything, it made her transition to Alpenglow feel natural.

Yet it did mean that Hyder remained an itch she had not yet scratched. Though none of this had stopped her from thinking about him or dreaming about him. Of his hands on her. The way his lips felt. His body. She definitely still wanted him.

And he's here.

Unfortunately, they were not alone.

The plankhouse smelled of woodsmoke, time, and people. The central hearth threw long shadows across the logs where more than three dozen people sat or lay bundled in wool blankets and furs. Conversations had quieted to murmurs, as though the storm outside made words feel heavy. Someone had brought out a pot of bear stew earlier, and the scent still lingered, comforting in its greasiness. A few children slept in a pile near the fire, their small bodies rising and falling in rhythm. Several elders dozed upright on benches against the wall, their heads nodding. The storm howled beyond the thick cedar planks, but inside, it was safe. And now, warm. Held together by firelight and people, and now, a generator.

Hyder came back inside several minutes later, snow still clinging to the shoulders of his parka. He stomped his boots again near the door, then shrugged out of the heavy coat and hung it on a peg. His hair was damp, dark and spiky from the wind and the wet flakes, his cheeks flushed from the cold. He caught her eye across the room and gave a small nod, the kind that said everything was all right now.

Sola felt something. Not gratitude exactly, though that was there too. He was just so capable. Something she was not used to. And he did not crow about it or smile in some slimy, mannish way.

He just...was.

Hyder made his way over, stepping around sleeping bodies and low conversations. He lowered himself to sit on the edge of the narrow platform where the hosts had made space for her earlier, the most private corner they could offer in a building that had never been built for privacy. A heavy wool blanket had been draped over the low partition, and another lay folded at the foot of the sleeping area, with piles of furs and quilts. They had insisted she take it, the doctor from Outside who had come, despite the storm, to check on their Nan.

He sat close. Not touching. Angled just enough that their knees almost touched. The cold still clung to him, but beneath it she could feel the warmth of his body, solid and alive, even across the distance. She shifted slightly, coming closer without really meaning to. He was just there, his citrus and dark coffee scent comforting.

"They're running good," he said quietly, voice pitched low so it would not carry. "Should hold through the night. Maybe longer if the fuel lasts."

She nodded. "Good. *Gracias.*" Sola rubbed her hands together, the chill from earlier still lingering in her fingers despite the returning heat, looking over at Nan again. "I just wish I'd gotten here sooner."

"You got here. That's what matters."

His voice was not placating or dismissive. Just laced with honesty.

"The road is gone by now," he added. "Nothing's moving until they plow, and that won't be till early morning."

She looked toward the door, though she could see nothing but darkness and the faint swirl of white against the small window. "Figures. I told *Mamí* I'd be back before midnight."

"She'll know you're safe. We can't text because Koy keeps stonewalling the idea of putting in Wi-Fi. But someone will get word to Alpenglow by SAT phone."

Sola gave a small laugh, more breath than sound. "She's probably already planning how to yell at me in two languages when I get home."

Hyder smiled at that, a charming lopsided grin that started in his eyes and made the corners crinkle. It made her belly flutter.

"Yeah, well, no one can yell at us as good as family. Right?"

They sat in silence for a while, the fire crackling and the low hum of voices around them. The pile of blankets between them felt like an invitation and a barrier at the same time. She was aware of every inch where their bodies nearly touched, the way his thigh finally brushed lightly against hers when he shifted to ease his back. The cold had forced them close, but the closeness was doing something else now.

Heat. It was low and steady. But there was no denying it. At least not for Sola.

She turned her head slightly, studying his profile in the firelight. A strong jaw, straight nose, dark clear blue eyes. He was watching the flames, but she knew he was aware of her too. The way his breathing had changed, and how he refused to look directly at her, like he already knew what might happen if he did.

She decided on something the way she made most decisions. Quick, with no second-guessing.

She leaned in and kissed him. Again. Pressing her mouth to his, one hand coming up to curl around the back of his neck, fingers threading into the damp hair at his nape. He froze for half a heartbeat, surprise flickering through his eyes, and then he kissed her back. His lips were warm, tasting faintly of coffee and mint, and he made a low sound in his throat, barely audible, and his hand found her waist.

One minute they were sitting, the next lying on the pile of fur and quilts, side by side with a light blanket pulled over them. The kiss deepened. She parted her lips and he followed, tongues sliding together in a slow, deliberate rhythm. Heat rushed through her and she shifted closer, pressing her chest to his, feeling the hard plane of his body against her softer one. Her free hand slid under his thermal shirt, palm flat against the warm skin of his stomach. He was solid muscle, heated from the inside out, and she felt him tense under her cool touch.

He pulled back just enough to breathe, forehead resting against hers. "Sola," he growled. "They're right there."

"I know." She kept her voice just as low, lips brushing his as she spoke. "But I'm not stopping unless you tell me to."

His breath hitched. His hand tightened on her waist, fingers digging in slightly. "I don't want to stop."

"Then don't."

She kissed him again, hungrier this time. Her hand moved higher under his shirt, tracing the ridges of his ribs, then sliding around to his back. She felt the play of rippling muscles there as he shifted to pull her closer. The blanket slipped lower, but neither of them cared. She hooked her leg over his, pressing herself against the growing hardness between his legs. He groaned softly into her mouth, the sound swallowed by the kiss.

Her fingers found the waistband of his jeans. She slipped them under, her palm curving over him through the fabric of his boxer briefs. He was thick, heavy, and hot, straining against her hand. She stroked him slowly, feeling him pulse under her touch. His hips jerked once, involuntarily, and he broke the kiss to press his face into the side of her neck.

"Sola," he breathed against her skin. "God."

She smiled into his hair, nipping lightly at his earlobe. "Shh. Quiet."

He nodded, but his hand was moving now too. It slid under her sweater, his callused palm skimming up her side until he cupped her breast through her bra. His thumb brushed over her nipple, and she arched into the touch, biting her lip to keep from making noise. Pleasure sparked, sharp and insistent. She rocked subtly, seeking friction, and he answered by grabbing her thigh, hiking it higher, and pressing even closer. She ground against him once, twice, the pressure nearly perfect, but not nearly enough, especially through all their layers of clothing.

They moved like that for long minutes, hands exploring, mouths finding each other again and again. Like young teenagers discovering things for the first time. She pushed his shirt higher, wanting more skin, and he helped her, tugging it up so she could press her palm to his chest. His heart hammered under her fingers. She kissed down his jaw, his throat, feeling the vibration of his swallowed sounds.

His hand slid lower, cupping her ass through her jeans. She was aching, her body trembling, and she knew he could feel her need. She didn't care.

She reached for his zipper, fingers fumbling only slightly in the near-dark. He caught her wrist gently but firmly, pulling it up while rolling her over onto her back, deliberately shifting to the side so he was no longer in the juncture of her thighs.

"Wait," he gritted out through his teeth. "We can't. Not here."

She froze, looking up at him. His eyes were dark now, pupils blown wide in the low firelight. "Why not?"

"Listen." He tilted his head slightly. Somewhere across the room, an elder coughed. A child shifted, muttering something in their sleep. The planks creaked under someone's weight as they put another log on the fire and sparks lifted before settling again. "They're right there. The aunties. The kids. Nan. If we keep going, someone's going to hear."

She knew he was right. She had known it the whole time. But the want was so strong it drowned out caution. "Then be quiet."

He exhaled shakily, resting his forehead against hers again. "I want you, Sola. More than I've wanted anything in a long time. But not like this. Not hiding under blankets with half the village breathing ten feet away. I want you alone. I want to take my time to savor you. And I want to hear you. Really hear you when you call out my name."

The words landed heavy, settling somewhere deep, stirring things Sola usually kept locked away. She wanted to argue, to tell him she did not need romance or privacy or any of that. She just needed release. Bodies. Heat. Him, between her thighs, giving her his thick length until she came.

But the way he looked down at her, earnest and open and a little wrecked, made the argument die on her tongue.

She swallowed. "You're serious."

"Dead serious." His thumb brushed over her wrist where he still held it. "I want more than a quick fumble in the dark because the storm trapped us."

She stared at him for a long moment. Her body was still humming, frustrated and unsatisfied, but something else was there too. A reluctant warmth. Affection, maybe. Or at least the beginnings of it.

She let out a slow breath. "You're killing me, Hyder."

His answering grin was pained, but real. "Feeling's mutual, Doc."

She lifted up and kissed him once more, softer this time. Slower. An acceptance instead of a demand. When she finished, he rolled to his back and she followed, resting her head against his shoulder, listening to his heartbeat slowing gradually.

They stayed like that, tangled under the blanket, bodies pressed close for warmth and something more. The fire popped. Someone stirred nearby and the storm raged on.

Sola did not sleep right away. Her mind turned over what he had said, what her body still wanted, what her life back in the Bronx and even here in Alpenglow had taught her about needing people. She thought about her son asleep in the cottage, safe with her mother. She thought about how she had come to this place, telling herself it was only to get her foot into a practice and find a place for August. Certainly not to find a relationship. Yet here was this man. Steady and cheerful and impossible to ignore. And he wanted to take his time with her.

It was irrational, really. When she stopped to think, she realized they barely knew one another. She looked down, staring at her boots warming by the fire. Heavy, ugly, winter things that someone had left like a shoe elf one night, a couple weeks ago. She knew it had to be him. In fact, she had deliberately not worn them before today, because she did not like whatever they might represent. That someone cared enough to get them for her. But today, with the cold and snow making her wince, she finally relented.

Why did he come tonight? She did not have an answer, and she certainly was not about to ask him.

Eventually her eyes grew heavy. His arm came around her, careful and protective. She let herself relax into it, the ache between her legs fading to a dull throb, and he kissed the top of her head, whispering something she could barely hear.

"...*Sha'aéil.*"

She almost asked him what he meant, but for some reason, it felt like knowing would be too much.

Tomorrow the road would open, and she could decide what came next. For now, she closed her eyes, his heartbeat steady under her ear, and let herself go. Back into her dreams, where Hyder's hands wouldn't stop her.

FIFTEEN

Hyder

Morning light came through the small windows of the plankhouse in weak lines, telling Hyder the storm had passed but the cold had settled in deep. He was still half asleep, wrapped in the thick wool blanket with the faint scent of woodsmoke clinging to everything, when a familiar voice cut through the quiet.

"Heya, Hyder."

The words barely registered before a swift kick landed squarely on his backside. Hyder sat up fast, one arm already swinging out in an old reflex, until his eyes focused on the man standing over him. Koyuk grinned down at him, missing more teeth than he still had left, his wrinkled and creased face carrying more life than most men half his age ever managed, his eyes sparkling with the kind of mischief that came from eighty-five winters and no plans to slow down any time soon.

"Hey, Koy," Hyder grumbled, rubbing the spot where the boot had connected. "You still got it."

Koyuk nodded once, as if he had never doubted it for a second. He leaned on the carved walking stick he had carried since Hyder was a boy and waited while Hyder pushed the blanket aside and swung his long legs over the edge of the sleeping platform.

Memory came back all at once. The storm. The generators. Sola. The way she had kissed him first, again, her bold hands sliding under his clothes while the village slept only feet away. He turned his head quickly toward the rumpled area beside him, but the space was empty, the blankets pushed back and already cold. Like she'd never been there at all.

Koyuk watched him with knowing eyes. "Yeah, the doc is already gone. The plow came through about an hour ago. She took her Subie and headed back to town before the sun was barely thinking about showing itself."

Hyder nodded, trying to keep his face neutral even though the news landed harder than he expected. She left without saying goodbye. Not a word. Not even a shake to his shoulder. He stood up, stretching the stiffness out of his back. The plankhouse was already stirring. A few people moved around the central hearth, feeding the fire and heating water for tea and coffee.

Koyuk jerked his chin toward the door.

"Come on outside with me, boy. We can talk while you help clear some snow."

Hyder pulled on his boots and parka, and they stepped out into the cold morning. The sky had cleared to an intense, bright blue that promised no more snow. But it could still change its mind. The snow lay thick on every roof, every totem, every path. The plow had carved a narrow channel through the main road, but the rest of the village looked like it had been buried.

They walked toward the shed where a couple of younger men were already pulling out the snowblowers. The machines roared to life in short bursts, throwing white plumes into the air. Hyder grabbed a spare shovel from the rack by the door and fell in beside Koyuk. The old man did not do much heavy lifting anymore, but he directed with the confidence of someone who had seen every kind of winter this island could throw at them.

They talked while Hyder worked, voices raised against the sound of the blowers. Koyuk asked about what supplies had made it on the barge schedule. He mentioned a few families in the village that could use extra fuel and food if the next storm hit hard. Hyder listened and made mental notes. Even though Kisa'adi was not officially part of Alpenglow, blood and history made them family as far as the Kings were concerned. Koyuk was actually his great-uncle, his grandmother's brother, and was the oldest elder in the village. Which meant his words carried the most weight.

After a while, Koyuk leaned on his stick and looked out over the clearing they had made, his eyes suddenly serious.

"You be careful this winter, Hyder. The skies will be cold and beautiful. The northern spirits will dance across the heavens like they have something to prove to us. But the snow is going to take its toll. More than usual, I think."

Hyder nodded solemnly. He would trust Koyuk about Chiltak Island weather more than any forecast or satellite image. The old man had a way of reading the wind and the ice that came from a lifetime of listening when most people only looked.

"I hear you," Hyder said. "We'll make sure the village has what it needs before the next big blow."

Koyuk clapped him on the shoulder with surprising strength. "Good. Now go finish clearing that path by the smokehouse. I will check on Nan."

Hyder worked for the next hour, moving snow with steady, practiced swings of the shovel, relishing the hard work. His mind kept drifting back to the night before, no matter how hard he tried to focus on the task. He could still feel the press of Sola's mouth on his, the way she had taken control and kissed him like she had been waiting weeks to do it. Her hand slid under his shirt, then lower, stroking him until he had to bite back a groan and almost came in her hand like some inexperienced kid.

He had to stop them.

Again.

He had meant every word. He wanted her, but he wanted her right. Not rushed and hidden and quiet. And not when she could slip away at first light without even saying goodbye.

One of the younger men gave him a knowing look as he passed with the snowblower. Hyder kept his expression even. They knew he had not gotten to finish what Sola started. They knew she had left early. In a village this size, nothing stayed private for long, even if everyone pretended not to notice when things were happening.

He tried not to give too much meaning to her leaving. She was a doctor. She had patients waiting. A son and a mother back in Alpenglow. And she had never promised him anything more than the heat of the moment. Still, the space beside him this morning...was empty of more than just her body.

He shook his head, knowing he was being ridiculous, but it still didn't change how he felt.

When the main paths were finally clear enough and sanded for safe walking, Hyder carried the shovel back to the rack and brushed the snow from his gloves. He went inside the plankhouse to say goodbye before heading out. Koyuk was sitting beside Nan's cot now, the old woman propped up against a pile of blankets. She looked much better this morning, her color returned and her eyes clearer. She sipped from a blue enamelware cup, the steam carrying a sharp, eye-watering herbal smell that Hyder remembered well. The same tea she used to make when anyone in the family got sick. Whatever was in it, Sola probably would not approve of the lack of measured doses, but Nan would not care either way. This was the medicine her grandmother's grandmother had made, and that was enough.

Hyder crossed the room and crouched down near the cot. "Good to see you sitting up, Auntie."

Nan gave him a slow smile that reached all the way to her eyes. "Ah, you know it would take more than a little cold to take these old bones."

She took another sip of the tea, then set the cup aside. Her wise gaze caught his with a serious look that made him straighten a little.

"Your mother would like her," Nan told him quietly. "You picked well."

Hyder felt heat rush into his face. Once again, he was blushing like an idiot. "I don't know what you mean, Auntie."

Nan just kept staring at him, patient and unblinking, until he was the one who had to break away. He cleared his throat and looked down at his hands. "I need to get back. See if my boat needs a little help after all this snow."

He stood up, gave Koyuk a nod of thanks, and touched Nan's shoulder gently. She patted his hand once before he turned to leave.

Outside, the cold air felt good against his warm face. He climbed into his truck, started the engine, and let it warm up while he scraped the snow from the windshield. The road back toward Alpenglow had been plowed wide enough for one vehicle, the banks piled high on either side like white walls. He drove slowly, careful of hidden ice, and let his thoughts turn fully to Sola again.

This was twice now that he could have had sex with her. No, that word felt wrong for what he felt. Made love. That sounded ridiculous too, like something out of an old movie. Anyway, it was twice, and both times he had been the one to stop them. What was wrong with him?

Perhaps the third time could be the charm. But he realized he wanted to take the good doc out on a date first. Maybe she didn't do marriage or relationships, but she never said she didn't like to date. To have a good time. But he wasn't sure what she might like to do. It was not like he could take her to TAO for sushi, drinks, and dancing.

Listen to me, he thought as he navigated a curve in the road. *I might as well write to Dear Abby or something.*

One thing was for sure. He was not going to ask Tala for advice. She would get way too much amusement out of the whole situation and never let him live it down.

He pulled into the plowed lot near the town square and sat there for a minute with the engine running. In the distance he could see people shoveling sidewalks and snow blowing, the steady rhythm of a small town digging itself out after a heavy storm.

It was not long before the Yøl celebrations started, a twelve-day-long festival that always began on the shortest day of the year with a bonfire and went on until New Year's Day. Hyder hoped the weather was going to be kind. Nothing like trying to carol or decorate the town tree in a blizzard. But they had done it before. They could do it again.

Maybe Sola and Gus would like to go out to Lake Sletta'a and go ice skating, he thought suddenly. It was not Rockefeller Center, but the lake had its own kind of pretty when the lights were strung along the edge and the ice was smooth and clear. Once winter took hold and the lake froze, the town began grooming the trails out there and keeping the shed stocked with cocoa and hot cider for the kids. And gløgg for the adults.

But is that a good first date...? He wasn't sure. They certainly wouldn't be alone out there.

He looked up and saw Tala walking toward his truck, breaking him from his thoughts. The cheesy, sly grin on her face told him she had already heard about last night. And next to her, with his own huge smile, was his little brother, Sterling. Clearly, he had finally managed to fly in this morning, probably hitching a ride with Marshall. It crossed his mind that he could just drive off before they got there. But the thing with Tala was she would chase him down until she had her say. Also, it would be rude not to welcome his brother home after months of being away.

Instead, he just waited for the inevitable, his engine still idling, one hand resting on the wheel.

As he did, he heard Nan's voice again in his head, *"Your mother would like her. You picked well."*

Hyder could not help but smile. Because she was right. His mother would have liked Sola.

A lot.

SIXTEEN

Sola

Morning brought too much clarity.

The kind that arrived unwelcome after sleeplessness and too many second thoughts.

Sola had left plenty of men sleeping in beds that weren't hers, slipping out before dawn so she could be home before August woke up and started asking questions she didn't want to answer. But this was the first time guilt had twisted in her chest like a dull hook, catching somewhere deeper than she cared to examine. The first time the phrase *walk of shame* actually landed, even though she and Hyder hadn't finished what they started.

She kept her head down as she hurried down toward the boardwalk, past the early morning crowd gathered outside the café. But it didn't help. Cheerful, knowing smiles followed her anyway. A couple of older women nodded with open approval. One of the fishermen raised his coffee cup in a mock toast. Another winked.

Alpenglow, apparently, did not believe in subtlety.

When she got home, even her mother didn't chide her for staying out all night. Instead, she casually mentioned, too casually, that

Hyder was coming for dinner. Sola would have grouched about the meddling if August had not perked up at the news, his small voice bright with recognition.

"Hyde?"

She wondered at her son's sudden excitement, but he was already rushing off to get dressed for school, leaving her no room to stay frustrated. It was hard to resent a town that had welcomed her boy so thoroughly he actually looked forward to going to school now.

She walked him there on her way to the clinic, the cleared path already sanded under their boots. The air was cold enough to sting her lungs, and their breaths came out in heavy white puffs.

"How was school yesterday?" she asked, keeping her tone light. She always asked this question, and the usual response, if there was one, was a shrug.

"Sledding," August answered this time, his eyes on the ground ahead of them. "The big hill."

She smiled, letting the simplicity of his words settle in her chest like something fragile and precious.

As they approached, a little boy named Noble called out, "Gus!"

August lifted his gaze, let go of her hand without a backward glance, and ran toward him. Sola didn't mind the lack of goodbye. Her heart swelled at the sight of her son with a real, live, actual friend.

Charlie was standing by the front door and lifted a hand in greeting. Sola waved back, grateful for the woman who seemed to already understand August on a level that had taken her years of careful work. It was comforting to know she could leave her son without worry. Not once had there been a call about Gus having a meltdown or someone teasing him. Instead, he was bringing home homework that asked him to draw maps of things and places they were studying or calculate distances for math. All things he looked forward to.

And if anything ever did happen, she was only across the road.

The clinic waited, its cheery yellow paint making her smile even more. She paused for a moment, taking in the cleared walkway, the careful shoveling that meant someone had come by before dawn to make sure she and her patients could get in safely. It still caught her off guard how much the community worked together. Not just one or two people. Everyone. And not because they had to, but because they wanted to.

She had several appointments lined up. Mostly flu cases, the tail end of the wave that had kept her running since she arrived. She yawned as she opened the door, the exhaustion from the night before settling deeper into her bones now that she had stopped moving and no longer had Gus with her.

Galena was already walking up the path behind her, her heavy boots squeaking. The woman had turned out to be one of Willow's best decisions. She was a great receptionist, organized in an effortless small-town way, and she really did know everyone in Alpenglow, Kisa'adi, and even Williwaw.

"Morning, Galena," Sola tried to keep her voice professional as they stepped inside and hung up their coats. "Any messages from yesterday?"

Galena's grin was immediate and wicked.

"Oh, I've got messages all right. Mostly from people who saw a certain Subie parked outside the plankhouse all night." She leaned against her desk, arms crossed, clearly enjoying herself. "So. Second hottest King brother, huh? How was it? Did he live up to the hype, or do we need to lower expectations for the whole family?"

Sola froze for half a second, her professionalism cracking under the direct hit. She busied herself with the stack of magazines, trying to sound composed. "Galena, that is...not appropriate clinic conversation."

Galena snorted, completely unrepentant.

"Doc, we're in Alpenglow. Appropriate swam away with the last barge. Spill. Was it worth sneaking out at the crack of dawn looking like you got hit by the snowplow and a guilty conscience at the same time?"

Heat crept up Sola's neck. She turned, hands on her hips, fighting a smile she didn't want to give in to just yet. This was the first time Galena had pushed the boundary this hard, but there was something disarming in the teasing that made it hard to shut down completely.

"Second hottest?" Sola asked finally, raising an eyebrow. "Who's the first?"

Galena's grin widened with pure mischief.

"Sterling, obviously. You haven't had the pleasure yet, since he's been stuck on the Slope. But he's a hound. Wouldn't surprise me one bit if he comes back with fleas. Still pretty to look at, though."

Sola couldn't help the laugh that escaped.

It felt good. It had been years since she had a real friend, too. Most of hers had drifted away when she got pregnant with August. They all said they would keep in touch, but her life became about things none of them could understand. She never blamed them, not really, though it still stung.

She shook her head, the tension in her shoulders easing just a fraction. "You're terrible."

"Yeah, but you like me," Galena shot back, already sorting the day's files with practiced efficiency. "And you're blushing, Doc. It's cute."

Sola sighed and turned to head into her office. Then she stopped and turned back.

"Hey, Galena…"

Galena looked up. "Yeah?"

"What does…" Sola looked up at the ceiling, trying hard to remember something. "What does sha-a-eel mean?"

Galena's brows rose. Then another grin came to her lips.

"*Sha'aéil*, you mean?"

Sola nodded.

"Well, Doc, someone called you their sun and sea in Chiltak. I wonder who that could be?"

Sola blushed more, then rushed into her office, closing her door behind her to cut off Galena's laughter.

The day moved on in a steady rhythm. The flu cases were lighter than they had been, mostly people with the last dregs of it, hoping for Tamiflu even though it was too late. Sola explained patiently, again and again, how the antiviral worked best in the first forty-eight hours. Most took the news with good-natured shrugs, the way she was learning Alpenglow did.

Then Elim arrived, a man she had only briefly met last night at the village when she heard him coughing. She had told him to make sure he came in soon for a checkup, and he'd given her a non-committal shrug. She'd halfway assumed he wouldn't come, so she was glad he was there.

She listened to his chest and frowned at the crackling rales in the upper lobes. Wet, persistent sounds that had no business being there in a man who insisted it was just a stubborn cold.

"How long has this cough been bothering you, Elim?" she asked gently, stepping back to meet his eyes as he sat on the exam table, his shoulders still shaking from his last cough.

He shrugged, wiping his mouth with the back of his hand. "Few weeks, maybe a month or two or three. It comes and goes. Can't seem to shake it, but you know how it is with the fishing season winding down and everything. No big deal."

Sola's frown deepened as she noted the subtle sheen of sweat on his forehead despite the cool room, the way his cheeks hollowed, and the quiet weariness in his dark eyes. "Any fevers? Night sweats? Chest pain when you breathe deep?"

Elim hesitated, then nodded slowly. "Yeah...I wake up drenched sometimes. And my appetite's been off. Nothing tastes right lately."

Her pulse ticked up.

Chronic cough. Night sweats. Appetite loss. Fatigue. The chest sounds. Tuberculosis climbed to the top of her differential fast.

Without a word, Sola reached for a surgical mask and slipped it on, then handed one to him.

"Elim, I need you to wear this," she said calmly. "This could be tuberculosis. TB. It spreads through the air, so we must be careful. We need to collect some samples for testing, and I'll ask Sutton if he can fly you over to Seward for a chest X-ray as soon as possible." She watched him as he wearily pulled the mask on, reaching for his hand when he was done. "If it is TB, it's treatable, but we need to act fast. Okay?"

Elim's eyes met hers and she saw the caution and uncertainty there. Then his hand tightened on hers and he nodded.

"Okay, Doc."

She arranged for isolation in an empty cottage, the best that could be managed in a place like Alpenglow, and made a note to begin contact tracing in the morning.

But in the back of her mind, worry gnawed.

The plankhouse.

The whole village of Kisa'adi had been in and out of there during the storm. Including Elim. And most of them moved through Alpenglow on a regular basis. Not to mention the kids who went to the school. Realistically, she would need to test a lot of people, and it would mean a lot of cooperation. She was still new, barely a month in. Everyone had been kind, but she heard the good-natured *cheechako* comments. The quiet bets on how long she would last. Would they listen when she told them this was important? If she couldn't handle it, the state would probably step in with a full public health team. She wasn't sure how that would land or how it would make her look.

She and Galena wiped down the clinic thoroughly after Elim left, every surface, every instrument, the quiet heavier now than it had been that morning.

When they finally closed near dinner time, Sola waved to Galena with a new sense of camaraderie.

"See you tomorrow. And...*gracias*. Thanks for everything."

Galena winked. "Anytime, Doc. Try not to sneak out before breakfast next time, though. I gotta know if the Kings are everything we've always thought they were!"

Sola laughed again, then stepped out into the cold, the sun already setting. She walked home through the cleared paths, noticing the twinkling lights were even more prominent than when she'd first arrived, and Christmas music was drifting softly over the square from speakers in the pergola. It hardly seemed possible that

Christmas was so soon. She had not even had a chance to do any shopping for Gus or decorate their cottage.

By the time she got home, she had completely forgotten Hyder was supposed to come for dinner until she pushed open the door and the warm smell of her mother's cooking hit her.

He wasn't alone.

A slightly younger version of him and Sutton stood in the living room. Same dark hair and blue eyes, perhaps not quite as tall, and a little leaner, but with an effervescent energy that seemed to vibrate off of him. Where Hyder was all easy cheer and confidence, and Sutton was serious and certain, this man felt like he was still working out where he fit in the world and enjoying the search.

Sterling, she guessed. Though if Galena were here, she would have to argue on the hottest King brother rankings. Her eyes flicked over to Hyder involuntarily.

Her mother introduced Sterling smoothly. His grin was immediate as he stepped forward, taking her hand with a little too much charm. Almost like he knew it was expected of him.

"Doc! You're even prettier than the gossip said."

Sola managed a polite smile, noting the way the flirtation rolled off him like breathing. He did the same with her mother a moment later, complimenting the meal before it was even served. It didn't feel targeted, more like a reflex.

August watched him with open curiosity, but still drifted toward Hyder, carrying a rolled-up sheet of paper.

Hyder took it with careful hands, unrolled it, and scanned it.

"This is amazing, Gus." His expression turned solemn. "I'm honored."

Sola wasn't sure what it was. She figured it was some kind of map, but the weight Hyder gave the moment made her chest tighten.

Sterling leaned in. "Can I see?"

Hyder showed him. Sterling's eyes scanned the drawing, and he let out a low whistle. "That's some amazing art, kid. I like to visit museums all over the world, and this is better than some of the stuff I've seen."

Sola blinked. For a moment, Sterling's charming façade had parted and honesty had come through. She knew August was good, talented in that quiet, focused way of his, but the praise felt like a lot. She wasn't sure how to respond, so she didn't, letting the words sit. For his part, her son just nodded. He always struggled with social nuance, but he understood truth when it was that obvious.

Later, after dinner, she walked the King men to the door. Sterling moved first, reaching down to pull her into a quick, easy hug like his sister Willow would have done. Sola felt a small spike of panic at the unexpected contact, but her eyes found Hyder's over his brother's shoulder.

His gaze was stormy. Possessive, almost. The realization was ridiculous and fascinating all at once.

Sterling released her, oblivious to his brother's mood, and turned to her mother, kissing her cheek with theatrical flair.

"*Señora* Rivera, that meal was one of the best I've had in months. Glad you're here."

Her mother, still in her element, giggled like a girl.

Hyder came closer. Sola wondered if he would touch her. Hug her the way his brother had. But he didn't. Instead, he leaned down, his hands in his pockets as if he did not trust himself, his voice low and rough around the edges.

"Can I take you out on Friday?"

SEVENTEEN

Hyder

How did one plan a date meant to impress someone when there was exactly one place to eat dinner in town, and that place was already so familiar it felt more like another living room than a destination?

The thought had kept Hyder up most of the night, staring at the exposed wood beams over his head as they creaked softly with the shifting cold outside. The Lodge was too warm, the kind of dry, insulated heat that stretched his skin tight after a day out in the wind, and sometime after midnight he had kicked off his covers entirely, dragging a hand over his face and exhaling into the dark as if that might somehow shake loose a better idea.

He had gone through every option he could think of. The Raven, obviously, but that felt...lazy and predictable. Like he had not even tried. Williwaw crossed his mind next, but the logistics of driving her over the mountain pass for dinner, only to haul her back again in the cold and dark, did not feel like the kind of evening he wanted to give her. It could be kind of tetchy in the winter, especially after this much snow. Not to mention that the few places to eat there made the Raven look like a Michelin star.

And he wanted something that felt special. Something that might surprise her. That might make her look at him the way she had in the doorway the other night.

Think, idiot.

Before dawn arrived, Hyder had given up on sleep entirely.

He threw on an old T-shirt and a pair of worn athletic shorts and made his way downstairs, running a hand through his hair as he went, the smell of coffee already drifting up the stairwell like a promise. When he stepped into the kitchen, he let out a quiet breath of relief.

Willow.

She stood alone at the counter with her back to him, pouring hot water into a mug for her tea, her long dark hair braided loosely down her back, a soft sweater hanging off one shoulder like she had not quite decided whether she was awake yet. She had likely just come in from her tiny greenhouse studio, trading the humid warmth of her plants for the crisp morning air of the Lodge.

Hyder leaned his shoulder against the wall.

"Thank God it's you," he grumbled.

Willow did not turn right away, but he saw a small smile lift the corner of her mouth as she stirred milk into her tea.

"That bad?" she asked lightly.

"You have no idea."

She glanced over her shoulder at him then, taking in his bare legs and rumpled hair, and lifted one brow.

"You look like you got in a fight with your own thoughts and lost."

"That is...uncomfortably accurate," Hyder muttered, pushing off and walking toward the counter. He grabbed a mug and poured himself black coffee, not bothering with anything else, then leaned his hip against the opposite side of the island.

Willow turned fully now, cradling her tea in both hands.

"Alright," she said, studying him. "What did you break?"

"My dignity, mostly."

She snorted softly. "That's been hanging by a thread for years."

"Helpful," he deadpanned. Then he took a breath, running his fingers through his hair again. "I asked her out. For Friday."

Willow stared, then slowly smiled.

"The doctor."

"Yeah."

"And she said yes."

"Yeah."

"Well...," Willow said, drawing the word out as she blew over the top of her tea and took a small sip, "I suppose miracles do happen."

Hyder shot her a look. "You're supposed to be the supportive one."

"I am being supportive," she said mildly. "I haven't said anything terrible."

"Yet."

She tilted her head, considering him, and he could practically see the thoughts lining up behind her eyes, the warnings she was choosing not to say. For once, she held them back, letting the unspoken words sit between them.

"So," she said instead, setting her mug down. "What's the problem?"

Hyder let out a breath.

"I have no idea what to do with her."

Willow's lips twitched.

"That's a new problem for you."

"Not like that," he said quickly, scowling. "I mean...I want it to be...good. The date, I mean. I don't want to just take her to the Raven." He gestured vaguely. "And let Nobu belt out some ballad as the grand finale."

Willow hummed softly, turning slightly, her gaze drifting toward the window as she thought.

"I'm not sure," she admitted after a couple of minutes.

Hyder opened his mouth to say something, but before he could, the mudroom door swung open.

"Morning!" Tala's voice cut in.

Hyder closed his eyes briefly.

Of course.

Tala stomped into the mudroom, bringing a gust of cold air with her, snow still clinging to her boots. Ellie was right behind her, brushing flakes off her coat as she stepped inside. They both pulled off their gear and came into the kitchen. Tala took one look at Hyder's face and grinned like she had just been handed a gift.

"Oh, this looks good," she said, rubbing her hands together. "What did I miss?"

"Nothing," Hyder blurted out quickly.

"Hyder asked out the doc for Friday night, but he doesn't know where to take her," Willow said at the same time, entirely too cheerfully.

Hyder turned to her in betrayal. "Wills."

"What?" she said innocently. "You needed help."

Tala's grin widened into something wicked.

"Oh, this is *rich*," she said, dropping into a chair and lifting her feet onto another. "Captain Coastie over here can jump out of helicopters but can't plan a date."

"Rescue swimmer," Hyder reminded her yet again, knowing it wouldn't change anything.

"Puddle jumper," Tala shot back without missing a beat.

Ellie moved quietly to get some coffee, but Hyder felt her presence like a weight he could not shake. He avoided looking at her entirely.

"Well," Tala continued, leaning forward with interest, "have you considered taking her somewhere truly romantic? Like the fuel dock? Nothing says love like the smell of aviation fuel."

"Or the net shed," Willow added. "Very atmospheric. Especially when it's been cold and they freeze in those weird shapes."

Hyder glared at them. "You're both hilarious."

"We know," Tala retorted.

Ellie's voice came then, " think you should take her up to the igloo."

The room quieted and Hyder looked at her despite himself.

"The igloo?" Willow repeated.

Ellie nodded, smiling shyly. "Yeah. The reports say the aurora is gonna be pretty strong this weekend, so you should have quite a show. It's private, but different." She glanced briefly at Hyder. "Seems like the kind of thing she might like."

Hyder felt something shift, like a weight had suddenly lifted. He had completely forgotten about the geodesic dome up on a high ridge on the mountain to the north of town. It was built two summers ago as something half practical, half whimsical, a place to watch the sky from above the low clouds if you were willing to make the trek. Getting there would take effort. Almost as much effort as going to Williwaw.

But...it would be just us.

"Yeah," he nodded slowly. "That could work. Thanks El."

Ellie's smile deepened just slightly, then she took one last swallow of coffee and rinsed out her cup.

"Well," she added lightly, "I've got to get an order to Cheryl before those guests come in next week. See you all later."

She slipped on her coat, and headed out the door, letting in another whisp of cold air.

The second it shut, Tala burst out laughing.

"Oh, that is *perfection*," she pointed at Hyder. "Your girlfriend just planned your date for you."

Hyder groaned. "She is not my—"

"Girlfriend," Tala finished for him, still laughing. "Yeah, I know, I know. You're just accidentally dating her without realizing it."

Willow looked between them, her brows lifting. "Wait. What are you two talking about?"

Tala leaned back in her chair. "He's convinced Ellie's got it bad for him."

"Tala," Hyder warned.

"Apparently she follows him around like a puppy, shows up everywhere, probably writes his name in the margins of her notebooks with little hearts," Tala went on, ignoring him entirely. "It's tragic, really."

"Oh, Hyder," Willow chuckled softly, shaking her head. "So now you're going to lose us a doctor and our manager?"

"I am not," he grumbled, and he really hoped it was true.

But Willow's expression shifted, turning thoughtful, clearly not listening to him.

"I really don't think Ellie's into you," she said after a moment.

"Thank you," Hyder muttered.

"Told him she's probably just lonely," Tala added with a shrug.

Willow nodded slowly, her gaze drifting again.

"Maybe we need to do more for her. Cheryl and the elders have their bingo nights and stuff, but Ellie doesn't really fit into that."

Tala made a face. "Yeah, I'm not playing bingo."

"Me neither." Willow laughed. "I'd say movie night, but it kinda defeats the purpose of gettng some humans to be around for conversation."

Tala snapped her fingers. "Book and wine night."

"Ooh, that I like." Willow's eyes lit up.

"A few books," Tala suggested. "More wine."

"Definitely more wine," Willow agreed, already reaching for her phone to make notes. "I'll set something up."

Hyder looked between them, feeling oddly like he had been removed from his own conversation, grinning despite himself.

Maybe it would help. Maybe giving Ellie something else to focus on would ease whatever this strange tension was that had settled over everything. It certainly couldn't hurt.

And as for Friday...

He straightened slightly, the idea of a date up at the igloo settling into place now.

It could work.

It was not as easy as he had first assumed.

In fact, it had turned into something far bigger than he had intended, something that had grown legs and taken on a life of its own the moment he had to ask one person for help and then another and then another, until suddenly the entire town seemed to have a hand in what was supposed to be a single, simple first date.

The problem was, he couldn't do it all himself. He needed food, and not just food, but food that would actually impress her. Which meant not something he had burned or microwaved. So, he had to bring in Healy. Involving Healy meant opinions. Loud ones. About seasoning, portions, and what constituted "romantic" food in a place where most romance involved either whiskey or smoked salmon.

Then there was the matter of getting it up there, still hot, which meant asking one of the Johnson kids to head there ahead of them with the food in an insulated bag, swearing up and down they would set it up neatly and not just in a messy pile. Hyder had his doubts, but at that point, he was committed.

And then, because apparently, he had completely lost his mind, he decided the igloo should look a certain way.

Which meant decorating. Which meant Willow. And once Willow was involved, it took exactly three minutes for Hope to know, and exactly three seconds after that for Tala to give her opinions, and from there it might as well have been announced over a loudspeaker at the Mercantile.

All week, people had been stopping him on the boardwalk, leaning out of doorways, calling his name from across the square with suggestions, advice, and entirely unsolicited commentary.

"Make sure you bring extra blankets!"

"You better not burn the food!"

"You bring her back smiling, boy, or don't come back at all!"

By the time Friday evening rolled around, the whole thing had been built into something that felt dangerous.

Not physically. But socially. If this went well, everyone would know.

And if it didn't...well, everyone would *definitely* know.

Hyder stood in his room for a long moment before he left, staring down at himself like he was assessing a stranger. He had on a pair of chinos he had not worn in years, or ever if he was being honest, and a button-down shirt that Charlie had quite literally stolen from Sutton's closet, holding it up against Hyder with a critical eye before declaring it "perfect." He had politely refused the tie she tried to force on him, drawing a line somewhere between effort and complete humiliation.

He flexed his shoulders once, then twice.

You've jumped out of helicopters, he reminded himself. *You can survive a date.*

Still, his stomach twisted as he grabbed the extra gear he had gathered that day for Sola. Heavy gloves, a snowsuit, everything but the boots he knew she did not need, and he ran down the stairs. Most of his family was in the kitchen. Absolutely waiting for him, everyone but Sutton grinning. Sutton, well, he stopped just short of scowling, but probably only because Charlie had threatened him.

"You look *fine*," Hope whistled. In the past, she would have just stood back, sullen and quiet. For her to be so open now brought weight to her words.

"Yeah, Uncle Hyder," Gemma agreed, hopping up and down in her excitement, her dark braids swinging.

Hyder smiled nervously. "Thanks, guys." Then he turned to Willow. "And thanks again for going up there and getting it all ready."

Willow shrugged. "Well, I couldn't have you heading up there with a picnic blanket and chicken wings."

Hyder didn't bother to argue about the merits of chicken wings and said goodbye before running out the door. The ride to town was mercifully quick and he rushed down the ramp to the boardwalk.

As he walked, voices carried from the front of the Raven.

"Hey! Don't screw it up, Hyder!" Kael chuckled.

"Yeah, don't trip on your way up the mountain!" This time, it was Micah.

He lifted a hand in acknowledgment without turning, forcing a grin he did not entirely feel, and kept walking.

By the time he reached Sola's cottage, his pulse had picked up in a way that had nothing to do with the cold. He knocked and the door opened almost immediately.

Sola stood there, framed in the warm light behind her, her dark hair falling over her shoulders. She was dressed in fitted black pants and a soft camel sweater that clung just enough to make his brain stall for half a second.

She waved him inside and he stopped. So fast he almost *did* trip. Sterling was there.

Hyder's jaw tightened just slightly, his gaze flicking from his brother to Sola and back again, something intense and unwelcome twisting low in his gut.

"What are you doing here?" he asked, keeping his tone light, even if it did not quite reach his eyes.

Sterling did not look remotely bothered. He was sitting casually at the table, leaning on his elbows like he had always belonged there.

"Relax, bro," he said easily. "I came to see Gus."

Sola's eyes moved between them, quick and assessing, as if she could feel something under the surface.

"He brought him art supplies," she added, her tone neutral but curious.

Hyder glanced past Sterling toward the table.

Gus sat there, completely absorbed, a brand-new art pad spread in front of him, thick charcoal sticks scattered nearby instead of his usual yellow pencils. His small hand moved in careful, deliberate strokes, his tongue poking out slightly as he tested the medium, learning it, adjusting pressure and angle like it was a language he was already beginning to understand.

Hyder's irritation dissolved immediately.

"That's great," he said quietly.

Then, because he could not stand there any longer feeling like a third wheel in a space he had been thinking about all day, he turned back to Sola.

"You ready to go?"

Her eyes dropped to the pile of gear in his hands, then down to what she was wearing, then back up to him, suspicion flickering across her face.

"...What is all that?"

"You'll need it," he said, stepping closer and handing it to her. "And your heavy boots. Just until we get where we're going. Then you can take it off."

She took it slowly, still looking at him like she was trying to decide if this was a good idea or a terrible one, then nodded once and began pulling it on.

Behind them, Sterling straightened.

"You're taking her to the igloo?" he asked casually.

Hyder did not look at him, still watching Sola.

"Yeah."

Sola's head snapped up.

"The igloo?"

Hyder kept his face carefully neutral, even as his heart kicked harder against his ribs.

"It's not...exactly an igloo," he said, deliberately vague so he did not ruin the surprise.

She studied him for a moment longer, clearly trying to read what he was not saying, then went back to adjusting the oversized gear.

Hope's snowsuit swallowed her slightly, the sleeves a little too long, the bulk of it making her look smaller somehow, not bigger. Hyder made a mental note to get her one of her own.

She finished, still looking dubious, but she turned back toward the living room.

"Bye, *Mamí*. Bye, GusGus. I'll be home late."

Lucia waved a hand from the couch, busy with her knitting, entirely unbothered by any tension in the room.

"No worries, *mija*. We will be fine." Then she looked up, meeting Hyder's eyes. "Go, have a good time you two."

Hyder found himself blushing yet again, and nodded back to her, not trusting his voice. He did manage a quick goodbye to Gus, who didn't look up but lifted his chin slightly in acknowledgment. He ignored Sterling entirely and followed Sola out the door.

They walked past the Salty Netter, the cold settling deeper now that the sun had fully dipped. Hyder led her to where he had parked.

The snowmachine was a long-track touring model, built for two, wide and stable with a high windshield and a cushioned, stepped seat that allowed a passenger to sit slightly elevated behind the driver. The rear cargo rack was packed tight, bags of extra gear secured beneath bungee cords, and the whole machine looked less like something built for speed and more like something designed to glide over the land in quiet, steady comfort.

The Cadillac of snowmachines.

Hyder looked over at Sola as he handed her a helmet, watching as it dawned on her that they were going to be riding on it.

"You just need to climb on behind me," he explained. "I'll do all the work."

She hesitated, and for a moment Hyder thought she might refuse. Then she shrugged, raised her gloved hand and made the sign of the cross as she gave a chuckle, then pulled on the helmet and slid on. Hyder grinned and pulled his own helmet down and sat in front of her.

The engine roared to life beneath them, deep and powerful, the vibration running up through his legs as he eased them forward, then out over the snowbank and toward the trail that wound its way up Mount Raven.

Sha'a Yéil. His mind reminded him with near reverence, hearing his mother's voice instead of his own.

The ride took nearly forty-five minutes. He could have made it in thirty, but he didn't want to scare her.

At first, she sat stiff behind him, unsure of where to put her hands, but as the terrain shifted, she settled, her arms wrapping around his middle, her body aligning with his as the machine cut through the snow.

At some point, she rested her head against his back and Hyder's chest tightened.

Don't screw this up.

The closer they got, the louder his thoughts became.

What if she hated it? What if it was not what he thought it would be? What if the sky stayed dark and empty, with no aurora, no magic, just cold, gray disappointment? He had seen it happen before. People came looking for the ribboned lights and found nothing, while on nights no one expected anything, the sky would explode with color.

He crested the final rise and slowed. Behind him, he felt Sola lift her head. He did not say anything. He didn't need to. Because the igloo was there. Looking exactly as he had hoped.

The geodome glowed against the snow, soft golden light spilling through its glass panels, fairy lights strung around its frame like something out of a dream. It looked both completely at home on the ridge and entirely unreal, like it had been placed there by something other than human hands.

Hyder felt the tension he'd been holding for the last few days drain out of him. Then he gunned the engine one last time, closing the final distance, pulling up right to the entrance before cutting it off.

Silence rushed in around them as he pulled off his helmet, turning slightly.

"Well," he said, his voice rougher than he intended, "we're here."

EIGHTEEN

Sola

Sola had not expected to feel nervous. That, more than anything else, unsettled her.

She had been on dates before. Probably too many of them if she was being honest. Enough that she'd long ago lost count. Men in suits, men in scrubs, men who knew exactly how to order the right wine and exactly how to flatter her in ways that felt practiced and smooth. Men who did none of that and had somehow felt easier to manage. There had been dinners, drinks, nights that blurred into mornings, all of it uncomplicated. Simple. Where she was always in control and never had to question where it was all going.

This did not feel like that. This felt...anticipatory. Like something important was about to happen.

The anticipation started earlier that evening, when Sterling King had shown up at her door, all charm and careless confidence as usual. But something had been different this time. It was subtle and took her a minute to realize what it was.

He hadn't flirted with her. Not once.

Instead, he'd stepped inside with a polite nod, his attention shifting almost immediately past her to where her son sat at the table, drawing with his pencil.

"Hey there, Gus, my man. I brought you something," Sterling said, crouching down beside August, pulling a slim case from under his arm and opening it with a quiet snap.

Charcoal sticks, smooth and neatly arranged, dark to light, sat inside.

"I like to draw too," he added easily. "But I use these. Ever tried them?"

August hadn't answered, his gaze instead fixed on the unfamiliar tools, his fingers hovering just above them like he could already feel what they might do.

She'd watched them, holding her breath, not quite understanding what was going on.

When August finally reached out, taking one of the sticks in his hand, Sterling had simply sat with him. There was no pressure or expectation. Just...a steady presence and a gaze that understood.

It surprised her. Men usually did not know how to exist around her son. But ever since she came to Alpenglow, all the King men seemed to instinctively know what August needed from them. And it was something different from each.

Then, just as she was about to cry, to thank Sterling for his thoughtfulness...the knock came.

Hyder.

Her brain snapped to attention, and she opened the door with...*excitement*. Yeah, she was actually excited.

He walked in, and the shift in the air was immediate and palpable. For one fleeting second, Sola had again thought Hyder might be jealous of his own brother. But it'd slipped away just as quickly, vanishing the moment Hyder's attention moved past everything else and landed on August. His face changed then, to recognition and approval.

Something inside her had relaxed after that. Like all the ridiculous anticipation was unnecessary. This was going to be an easy night, just like all the others.

Until she saw the gear. She'd stared at it like Hyder had just handed her armor for war.

"You'll need it," he said simply.

It had not been until she saw the snowmachine waiting outside that it clicked. Even then, she hesitated. But she'd ridden motorcycles before. Fast ones with reckless drivers. Rides she would absolutely never admit to her mother. She figured snow had to be softer than asphalt.

So she climbed on, and the moment the engine roared to life beneath them, something inside her shifted again.

The ride was...exhilarating.

Cold air sliced past them, the world blurring into streaks of white and dark green as spruce trees rushed by on either side. The engine thrummed beneath her, powerful and steady, and instinctively, she wrapped her arms around Hyder's middle.

His body was solid, a shield against the wild wind, and at some point, she stopped thinking about the cold entirely and leaned into him, letting the rhythm of the machine and the steady certainty of him carry her forward. She felt safe. And that realization was far more dangerous than anything else. Even more than the anticipation.

When he slowed, she lifted her head and saw the igloo, and she almost laughed. Whatever her brain had conjured up when she heard the word *igloo* had been wildly, hilariously wrong.

This was something else entirely. It glowed in isolation. Soft gilded light spilling through curved glass, fairy lights twinkling like stars caught just beneath the surface of the clouds, the whole structure sitting lightly upon the snow, on top of a mountain ridge like something magical.

"Okay..." she murmured as she pulled off the helmet, unable to stop her smile as she gestured. "That is not what I was picturing."

Hyder laughed quietly beside her as he took hold of her hand, and they walked toward the door.

"Yeah. We get that a lot."

Inside, it was warm and inviting. The space curved gently around them, maybe fifteen feet across, the back wall insulated and solid while the entire front opened in a wide arc of glass facing northwest. Clouds hung low tonight, but she could imagine what it would look like under a clear sky, with stars spilling endlessly above them.

A tiny wood stove burned near the back, casting a flickering glow that danced along the walls. Fairy lights were strung overhead, their light delightful, and in the center of the space stood a small table.

With two chairs. Two covered plates. Two wine glasses. And a single white daisy in a narrow bud vase.

Sola blinked. Somehow the impossibility of it all, especially the fresh flower, stunned her.

"Hyder…"

He shrugged, suddenly looking almost shy.

"Figured I'd try."

Her chest tightened, the anticipation pushing back in again.

He helped her out of the heavy gear, brushing her arms, her shoulders, the small of her back, just long enough to make her aware of every place he touched. But he left it at that.

Then he pulled out her chair and, once she settled, lifted the metal cloche. Soft steam rose immediately, carrying the rich scent of a savory, buttery sauce and herbs.

Perfectly cooked halibut with a panko crust sat on the plate, draped over a bed of creamed potatoes and sautéed spinach. A delicate beurre blanc pooled beneath it all, flecked with thyme and lemon oil. Beside it was a small roll of buttered sourdough, still somehow warm.

Sola inhaled, her eyes closing for a moment.

"That smells incredible."

Relief flickered across Hyder's face as he sat across from her.

"Good."

He poured them both a glass of chilled white wine, and they began eating.

Dinner was...awkward at first. In the way most first dates were. They talked about small things. The town. The weather. The food. The way people here seemed to know everything about everyone. She asked about the igloo and he explained.

"This mountain we are on is pretty important to the Chiltak People. To the village."

"How so?"

"I know it will sound silly," he grinned, "but for as long as anyone can remember, we have hiked up here, to *Sha'a Yéil*, or Mount Raven, every year on the night of the light spirits. The *Yéik*. And we thank them for bringing us out of the darkness."

For a moment Sola watched him, to see if he was serious, until she realized he was. Very serious.

"This is a religious thing?" she asked.

He looked out toward the gray night, then explained, "No, not religious exactly. Just thankful. In our stories, there is a time when everything was dark. Raven, the trickster, a completely white bird, flew up to the home of the god who held the light in a box."

"A box?"

"Yeah, a bentwood box." He chuckled, then went on, "Somehow, Raven managed to trick him into letting him play with the light, but Raven stole it, escaping up the chimney. That is why he is black now."

Sola laughed, then turned thoughtful.

"If Raven stole the light, and I presume gave it to your people, how come there is still darkness?"

"Ah, *that* is a good question," his grin tugged even harder on one side, "and one that Koy would explain has to do with a big battle against the darkness. It went on for generations, too many to count. In fact, to this day, it is still being waged, and explains why sometimes it is darker than other times. And it is why we hike up here, every year, when it is usually so cold it hurts to breathe, and we watch the light spirits in the sky and give them our thanks for still waging that battle."

He looked around the igloo.

"We built this place because a few years ago, Koy almost didn't make it all the way up. It was simply too cold, and he is getting a little old." He paused and looked a little sheepish. "But don't *ever* tell him I said that."

Sola grinned back, understanding.

"Anyway," he went on, "now we come up here, warm up for a little while, then finish the hike up to the peak."

"Hike?" She looked out of the glass again as well. "Up?"

"Yeah, we're pretty high now, about as high as we can snowmachine up. We go on snowshoe from here." He laughed again, then became serious, catching her eyes and holding them. "I know it seems nuts, but when you see the aurora, dancing across the sky, you really understand that there is something else up there."

Sola swallowed and nodded, knowing what he meant. She was not really a religious person. Her mother was, and Sola had been brought up in the church, even taking her first communion. Until one day she declared she was not going anymore, and her mother, though disappointed, did not try to change her mind.

Now, she believed more in helping people. That actions meant more than words. She could tell that she was not alone in this sentiment. This igloo was just more evidence of how the Kings did whatever they could to take care of their people. *That* she could understand.

Then, almost as if he realized the conversation had gone too heavy, Hyder tried to lighten it. He told her about the fishing charters. Funny stories of guys from the "Lower 48" who came to Alpenglow thinking they wanted a great big Alaskan experience, then got queasy at the smell and sight of a gutted 200-lb halibut. Then he talked of his boat and how he'd named her after his mother. About sleeping on the water when his family got too noisy.

He barely touched on his time in the Coast Guard. But Sola heard something there and made a mental note to learn more, when the moment felt more right.

Instead, she told him about New York. About her college days and medical school. A little about the clinic, and her patients who slipped through the cracks because the system was not built for them. She realized she was glossing over the rough stuff too and wondered if he knew.

Slowly, the edges softened, and they started to talk about real things. Things you just did not tell someone who didn't mean something to you.

"Gus," Hyder said at one point, quieter now. "He's...something else."

Her fork paused as a familiar tension coiled in her chest.

"Yes," she said carefully.

He leaned forward slightly, resting his forearms on the table.

"I mean that in a good way, Sola."

She studied him. Then, because she believed him, she relaxed and told him more.

"I had him with my college boyfriend," she explained. "He told me to get an abortion."

Hyder went very still.

"I didn't, obviously," she continued. "But he decided he didn't want any part of it. We spent the next two years on the same campus, him pretending I didn't exist. That *we* didn't exist. I never saw him after we graduated."

The silence that followed was electric. Sola could feel tension rolling off Hyder.

"That's not a man," Hyder finally ground out, a muscle in his jaw twitching.

The anger in his voice startled her. It was not loud or explosive, but it felt deep and real. For a moment Sola was grateful August's father was not anywhere around because she was not sure what Hyder would do to him. Not that she would care for his sake, but it definitely would've ruined their date.

Sola looked out of the glass again, realizing she should not be feeling the warmth that kept spreading through her chest. Because it was not something she could control, and control was still important.

They finished dinner slowly after that, and when Hyder stood and walked over to a bag briefly, she leaned back in her chair, letting out a quiet breath. When he returned, he carried a small dessert. A dark chocolate lava cake. Still somehow warm with ganache falling over the sides.

She took a small bite. A soft, involuntary groan escaped her as the rich taste hit her tongue and her eyes fluttered closed for just a second.

When she opened them, Hyder was staring at her mouth.

Not in a subtle way. He was hungry.

Sola's pulse kicked, and instead of looking away, she leaned forward.

"Are you ready," she whispered, "to finish what we started?"

He blinked, surprise flickering across his face. Then came that slow, dangerous half-smile. The one she felt in her lower belly.

"Well," he murmured, leaning closer, "I did say I wanted to be alone. So I could take my time."

He leaned closer still, and his voice dropped.

"And I wanted to hear you. Especially when you say my name."

That was all it took. They stood at the same time, the table wobbling as it was pushed aside, forgotten entirely, and his mouth found hers. Hard, almost like an inevitable crash.

Her hands fisted in his shirt, pulling him down closer, as his arms wrapped around her, lifting her just enough to press her fully against him. Heat flared, intense and undeniable, her body responding before her mind could catch up.

This. This was what she understood. This she could control. She could. *Really.*

She kissed him deeper, chasing his taste, his warmth, his solid presence.

He walked her backward, step by step, until her spine met the cool curve of glass. Then he turned her, lifting her hands until her palms pressed against it.

"Stay there," he told her, his tone rough.

He stepped away, leaving her alone, shaking, her breath fogging the glass.

The lights clicked off, one by one. Darkness settled around her, broken only by the faint glow of the cloud-filtered sky and the flickering from the low fire. She could not see him. But she could feel him.

Coming closer.

And closer.

Until his lips brushed her ear again.

"Tonight," he growled, "I'm going to remind you of something, Sola."

Her fingers curled against the glass, desperate to touch him, but somehow managing to restrain herself.

"That you exist," he continued, softer now, "and up here...you're the only thing that matters."

Her breath caught, and when his hands finally found her, she believed him.

And she let herself lose control.

NINETEEN

Hyder

I need to slow down.

That was Hyder's first coherent thought, somewhere between the moment her back met the glass and the moment she chose to listen to him and stayed exactly where she was.

There was no hesitation or smart remarks masked as confidence. Just a deep inhale and stillness, her palms splayed against the cold curve of the glass as though she had always been meant to stand there, waiting for him.

That was what undid him.

Hyder had known desire before. Plenty of it. It was almost as if each of his past romances was him trying to find something that could be his. To fill some void. But this...this was something else entirely. This felt like stepping onto uncertain ice and realizing too late that the surface might not hold him. But it would be worth whatever cold splash he might feel later.

He came back to her after he turned out all of the lights. She had been turned into shadows and shapes, into breath and heat and the faint outline of a woman who had somehow taken up far more space in his head than she had any right to. He moved slowly, deliberately, not because he lacked urgency, but because he had too much of it, because if he rushed, he was not sure he would be able to be slow or careful.

When he reached her, he did not touch her right away. Just reminded her how important she was. To him.

He stood just behind her, close enough to see the slight tremor in her shoulders as she exhaled, fog blooming briefly against the glass before disappearing again. Moments passed. Still, he just breathed her in.

Then his hand came up and settled at her waist, his thumb pressing lightly into the curve of her side as though he needed to anchor himself before he did something reckless.

"You're sure?" he asked, though he already knew the answer.

She turned her head just enough that he could see the edge of her profile, the line of her cheek, the dark sweep of her lashes.

"I don't do unsure."

That did something immediate to his chest, though he was not sure if her confidence unsettled him or was the best thing he had ever heard.

He laughed quietly, more breath than sound.

"Yeah," he murmured. "I'm starting to get that."

Then he finally moved again.

His other hand slid up her arm, his fingers brushing along the length of it until he reached her shoulder, and from there he eased the fabric of her sweater aside, baring the smooth line of her collarbone.

He took his time, watching her as he exposed each inch, watching the way her body responded even when she tried to keep it still. The slight lift of her chest. The way her breath caught and then steadied. The way she leaned back, almost imperceptibly, into him.

He bent his head and pressed his mouth to each place he revealed.

Warm, soft skin met his lips, and he inhaled, letting himself linger there for a second longer than necessary, just to smell the crisp mint and faint green sugar on her neck. She was cool and refreshing, like a chilled mojito, with the barest creamy whisper of coconut that spoke of sun-warmed islands far from the Alaskan snow.

"Hyder…"

There it was.

He closed his eyes for a moment, savoring the harmony in her voice, then pulled back just enough to continue.

Her sweater came off slowly, drawn up and over her head, his hands brushing her ribs, her back, and the slight tension in her muscles as she lifted her arms to help him. When it was gone, he let it fall somewhere behind them without looking.

His gaze dropped to her back. She was wearing a tiny lace red bra. For a moment, he forgot to breathe.

She was exactly as he had imagined and somehow entirely different. Small, yes. Delicate in frame. But there was strength there too, subtle but undeniable, in the lines of her shoulders, in the way she held herself.

"Jesus," he muttered under his breath.

She shifted slightly, as if the weight of his gaze alone was enough to make her aware of every inch of herself. Even though she still couldn't see him.

"Is that good or bad?" she asked with a hint of challenge, and he knew she had to understand just how sexy she was.

He grabbed her hips and turned her closer again, one hand coming up to her nape and threading through her hair.

"Very good," he said simply, knowing it was nowhere near enough.

He kissed her again.

Not like before. Not like the impact of mouths and heat and urgency that had brought them here. This was slower, more intentional, his hand tightening slightly at the back of her neck as he angled her exactly where he wanted her, as he took his time exploring the taste of her, the feel of her responding beneath his hands.

She met him, matching him perfectly, but there was a difference now.

He was leading, and she was letting him.

That realization sent a fresh wave of heat through him, more acute than before, more dangerous.

He broke the kiss only long enough to draw her backward, guiding her away from the glass and toward the center of the small space, to the rug that had been laid out in front of the window.

"Here," he murmured, his hands firm at her waist as he turned her.

She followed without question, her breath uneven now, her composure beginning to crack in small, telling ways. He smiled against her skin as he bent his head again, pressing his mouth to her shoulder, then lower.

Her answering sound was soft and involuntary, and it went straight through him.

Piece by piece, he continued to kiss her.

He still did not rush, did not grab or take without thought. Every movement was deliberate, and he watched her as he touched her, watched the way her reactions deepened, the way her hands began to move of their own accord, finding him, gripping his shirt, his shoulders, whatever she could reach.

At one point, she pulled back, laughing softly, breathless and a little disbelieving.

"You knew this would happen tonight," she accused gently.

He leaned back just enough to meet her eyes.

"Well," he said, then added, "but I hoped."

Her gaze softened for a fraction of a second, something deeper flickering there before it was swallowed again by heat.

"Dangerous man."

He did not disagree. Normally he would. He was never the risky brother, not when it came to women. But there was still that realness between them, a visceral wanting that felt dangerous. Not wanting to think about it, he let the world outside fade.

The clouds seemed to press closer, blurring the edges of everything beyond the dome. Inside, the shadows of the stove wrapped around them, the air heavy with heat and breath and something that felt perilously close to inevitability.

He guided her down with a certainty that left no room for hesitation. She went with him, her fingers gripping his arms as she adjusted, meeting him where he wanted her.

"Sola," he rasped.

She looked up at him, her eyes dark, her expression open and slightly confused.

"Yes."

He kissed her again, letting himself get lost in it for just a moment longer than he should have.

Because he knew. He knew this was already more than it should be. Knew that somewhere between the dock and now, they had already crossed a line they might not be able to come back from.

Still, he didn't stop. And neither did she.

Her hands moved against him, and he felt a shift in her, the way she leaned into the moment, letting herself feel it instead of analyzing it or attempting to control it.

"That's it, *Sha'aéil*," he murmured, half encouragement, half something else.

She made a soft, frustrated sound, her head tipping back slightly.

"Don't—" she started, then stopped, her breath catching.

He stilled.

"Don't what?"

Her eyes opened, locking onto his.

"Don't talk. Don't make me think. I don't want to think."

He nearly laughed but realized she was serious.

He nodded, just as sincere. "I can do that."

Hyder pulled back just enough to strip off his own shirt in one smooth motion, revealing the hard lines of his chest and shoulders. Her dark eyes tracked every movement, hungry and unguarded. He let her look, watched her gaze drift over his tattoos. Then he reached for the rest of her clothes with deliberate hands.

He eased her bra straps down her shoulders, kissing each newly bared inch of skin before unclasping it and tossing it aside. Her breasts spilled free, small, upright, and perfect, her nipples already tight, begging for him. He groaned low in his throat at the sight, then lowered his head, lavishing them with slow, open-mouthed kisses. He sucked one peaked nipple into his mouth, his tongue circling, teeth grazing just enough to make her arch and gasp. His hand cupped the other breast, his thumb brushing over the sensitive tip in lazy strokes while he worshipped the first with his lips and tongue. He took his time, switching between them until her chest was flushed and her breathing had turned ragged.

Only then did he move lower, trailing kisses down her stomach, over the curve of her hip. He unbuttoned her jeans, hooking his fingers into the waistband, and tugged them down. He left the thin fabric of her matching red panties on, a final, teasing barrier, as he settled between her thighs.

His mouth returned to her breasts, sucking and licking while his hand finally slipped beneath the edge of her panties. His fingers found her slick and hot, already drenched with need. A low, satisfied sound rumbled in his chest.

"Fuck..." he breathed against her skin, even though she had told him not to talk. He couldn't help it. The proof of her desire made something primal go through him. This wasn't just want anymore.

He circled her with two fingers, then slid one finger inside her, then the other, taking his time. She writhed beneath him, her hips rolling, a soft moan escaping her lips as he pumped steadily, slowly. He kept his mouth on her breasts, alternating between them, sucking harder as his fingers moved faster, deeper, coaxing her higher.

He wanted to see her fall apart. Needed it. Needed to watch this controlled, confident woman lose every ounce of composure until the only word left on her tongue was his name. Maybe then this wouldn't feel so temporary. Maybe then he would be burned into her the way she already felt burned into him.

Her back arched sharply, her thighs trembling around his hand. Her fingers dug into his shoulders, nails biting into his skin as her hips bucked against his touch.

"Hyder…" Her voice cracked, breathless and desperate.

"That's it," he murmured, not stopping. "Let go for me, Sola."

The world narrowed to the space between them, and time ceased to exist. All he knew was Sola.

And then…

A sound. Faint at first. Distant. Almost lost in the mountains.

Hyder froze. It took a handful of seconds for his brain to catch up, for recognition to cut through the haze of desire.

A snowmachine.

Coming in fast.

He pulled back abruptly, his chest heaving, his mind snapping back into place with sharp, unwelcome clarity.

"Sola—"

She blinked up at him, disoriented for a second before she heard it too. The engine grew louder. Closer. Almost there.

"*Mierda!*" she breathed.

They moved at the same time, scrambling for their clothes, for anything that would restore some semblance of order and reality.

Hyder dragged on his shirt, his body still thrumming with everything that had just been interrupted.

Sola reached for her sweater, her fingers still trembling as she yanked it on without looking, the fabric landing inside out against her flushed skin. She didn't notice. In the same frantic motion, she hopped into her jeans, fastening them as the roar of the snowmachine thundered up just outside.

Hyder shoved his boots on, barely tying them, his gaze flicking once more to her, to the way she looked, taking in her wild hair and swollen lips, the faint sheen of sweat still glowing on her collarbone, the unmistakable flush of need still coloring her cheeks. The moment still clung to her even as it dissolved around them.

A knock came, sharp and urgent. Hyder strode to the door and pulled it open.

Amos stood there, his breath fogging in the cold, his helmet hanging in his hand.

"Doc!" he exclaimed with urgency. "Someone's hurt."

TWENTY

Sola

Hijo de la gran puta!

Sola couldn't believe it.

It was like the universe itself had decided to intervene at the exact worst possible moment, like some cosmic joke designed specifically to test her patience, restraint, and sanity. Never had she been so sexually frustrated, not even in college when everything had been messy and confusing and tangled up in emotions she had long since sworn off.

And the worst part?

She did not even have the time to sit in it. To process it. To *do* anything about it.

They were flying down the mountain.

Not riding. Flying.

The snowmachine roared beneath them as Hyder pushed it much harder than he had on the way up, the engine snarling as it cut through powder and carved down the narrow trail. Amos's taillight flickered ahead of them, weaving through the dark like a guide they could not afford to lose.

The trees blurred into streaks, indistinguishable from one another in the darkness, and Sola's earlier exhilaration was gone, replaced by a tight, instinctive fear that had her gripping Hyder hard around the waist, her gloved fingers locked into the fabric of his jacket.

She pressed into his back, her helmet against him, not for closeness now, but for stability. For something to ground her.

Her mind, however, refused to stay grounded. Because even as adrenaline surged, even as the cold bit into every exposed inch of her, even as the roar of the engine filled her ears...

I can still feel him.

Her body hadn't caught up. It was still back up at the top of the ridge. She could still feel the ghost of his hands. The heat of his mouth. The way she had responded, the way her body had wanted him. How close she had been before they had to stop.

"Focus," she muttered to herself, the word swallowed by the wind and roaring engine.

Because she knew what waited at the bottom of the mountain.

Nobuhiro.

The shift happened then. She shut it down. All of it. Her thoughts were suddenly clean and clinical as she slipped into full doctor mode. By the time they burst out of the tree line and onto the groomed path beside the plowed road, Sola's mind had locked into place, pushing everything else aside.

Nobuhiro had been fine when he visited just days ago, shyly explaining his problem. He'd been stiff, yes. With chronic lower back pain, particularly through the lumbar region, and reduced mobility through his hips. She had already started him on a combination of osteopathic manipulative treatment, focusing on soft tissue release and gentle articulation, with plans to work toward more structured corrective treatment once his inflammation settled.

And she had explicitly told him to avoid heavy lifting, which he had apparently not listened to.

Now he was in her clinic, unable to feel his lower legs.

Her jaw tightened.

Neurological involvement.

Possibly an acute disc herniation. Lumbar, likely L4-L5 or L5-S1, given the distribution. And if there was compression of the nerve roots, or worse, involvement of the cauda equina…

Her stomach dropped at the thought. Because she didn't have imaging. Or anyone to consult just down the hall. It was just her.

No. She shook her head. It was too early to assume anything.

But numbness. Loss of sensation. That wasn't something she could ignore.

When Hyder swung the snowmachine up in front of the clinic, the place was lit up and overflowing, a cluster of people spilling out into the cold, their breath heavy in the air, their voices low and anxious.

He barely had the machine stopped before she was off, pulling off her helmet and pushing through them.

"What happened?" she demanded, her voice in more control than she actually felt.

"Doc!" Cheryl grabbed her arm, her eyes wide. "He was at the shop, said his back went, and he just dropped. He tried to stand, but he said he couldn't feel his legs right."

Healy stood just behind her, his beefy arms crossed, his usual gruffness replaced by something more serious. "He's inside. Says it's more numb than pain. Numb."

Sola nodded once.

"Okay. I need space."

They didn't move. They just stood there, worried. Because this was not just a patient to them. Not just someone who lived in their town.

This was Nobuhiro. *Their* Nobu.

She softened her tone just a fraction.

"I need to examine him properly. I promise I will tell you everything once I know more, but right now I need everyone out of here."

There was a pause, a collective hesitation. Then Healy huffed.

"You heard the doc. Move."

Grumbling and reluctant, the crowd began to thin, filtering out into the cold, though Sola knew they would not go far.

Inside, Nobuhiro lay on the exam table, one hand gripping the edge, his face tight with pain, though he still managed to give her a small, apologetic smile.

"Ah...Doc," he winced. "I believe I did not listen to your wise words."

She sighed, stepping closer.

"No," she said gently. "You didn't."

She placed her hands carefully along his lower back, fingers pressing along the lumbar spine, testing for tenderness, for muscle guarding, for the exact point of failure.

He hissed when she reached the left side.

"There!" he cried.

She nodded, continuing, still methodical, her mind creating a picture of the anatomy.

"Can you feel this?" she asked, running her fingers lightly down his leg.

"...less," he admitted.

She tested reflexes. Movement and sensation. On both sides. Each response painting a clearer picture.

Disc involvement. Likely a herniation pressing on the nerve root. Possibly severe.

She exhaled slowly.

"Okay," she said, keeping her voice calm. "I think you've aggravated a disc in your lower back. It's pressing on the nerves that run down your legs, which is why you're feeling numbness."

He listened quietly.

"We're going to start with reducing inflammation and stabilizing you," she continued. "No movement unless absolutely necessary. I mean it! I want you flat and supported. I'll give you anti-inflammatories and something for the pain."

She paused.

"If the numbness gets worse or if you lose control of your bladder or bowels, we need to get you to Anchorage immediately. That would mean surgical evaluation."

His eyes tightened at that while she held his gaze.

"We're not there yet," she explained. "But we are not ignoring this."

He nodded once.

"Understood, Doc."

She softened then.

"And next time," she added, pressing lightly along his spine again, earning another hiss, "you listen to your doctor."

Nobu gave her a faint smile at that.

"Yes, Doc."

It took time.

Time to stabilize Nobuhiro, to explain to his friends what the plan was, to reassure everyone that he was not dying, though he would be out of commission for a while.

Hyder and Amos were still in the waiting room when she came out. Which she was grateful for, because she trusted them both to carefully do as she asked.

"He can't be alone or get up by himself," she explained. "Not for a few days at least."

They nodded and moved past her.

"I'll go ahead and stay with him tonight," Hyder offered as they lifted Nobu, supporting him between them. Nobu winced and made a deep groan, but they were slow and steady, and they eventually made it out the door and began crossing the square to his home.

Sola stood in the doorway of the clinic, her arms wrapped around herself, watching them.

Hyder looked back. Just once, over Nobu's shoulder. And the look in his eyes...it hit her like a physical thing. The want and frustration, and something deeper and unfinished.

It mirrored exactly what she felt.

Her breath caught. Then he was gone, and so was everyone else, leaving her in a silence that was nearly overwhelming.

She exhaled slowly, forcing herself to move, to reset the space, wiping down the exam table, organizing instruments, until everything looked exactly as it should.

Only then did she pause, her hands resting against the counter for just a moment longer than necessary, her shoulders dropping, the exhaustion and disappointment finally catching up to her.

Then she turned off the lights and stepped outside. The cold hit her immediately. Sharper than before. Colder, if that was possible. For the first time since they had left the mountain, she looked up and stopped.

The sky had changed, the clouds finally parting.

And above her...

Color.

Not just color.

Movement.

Ribbons of greenish-blue unfurled across the sky, twisting and folding over one another like something alive, like silk streams caught in an invisible current. Threads of violet flickered at the edges, faint but unmistakable, while streaks of pale white light shimmered through the center, bright enough to cast a soft glow across the snow below.

Sola stood there, frozen, her mouth open.

She had seen pictures, heard it talked about, and thought she had understood.

She hadn't.

It was vast. Endless. Alive in a way that made her chest ache, made her feel awestruck and completely, utterly infinitesimal. Yet somehow more aware of herself than she ever had been.

"*Ay Dios...*" she whispered.

The lights shifted again, stretching, dancing, painting the sky in colors she had no words for, and for a moment she remembered what Hyder had said to her earlier. About how, when you saw the aurora dancing across the sky, you really understood that there was something else up there.

Standing there, her body still tight, still thrumming with everything that had been interrupted, everything that had almost happened, she felt that same strange contradiction.

The sky moved freely. Boundless and untamed.

And I... Her mind drifted. She wasn't sure what she was.

She felt wound tight. Paused in the middle of something that refused to finish.

Without warning, tears stung her eyes. Not from fear or relief. From something she didn't have a name for yet. He'd called her *Sha'aéil* again. And she'd stopped him. Not because of the sun and sea part. That was her name after all. Marisol meant the same thing. But because she knew it meant *his* sun and sea.

Why did I stop him? she wondered as she kept watching. But she still had no answers.

Reluctantly, she turned toward home, each step feeling heavier than it should.

She paused once more at the edge of the boardwalk, glancing back toward the mountain, then higher to the lights still dancing above.

Her lips pressed together.

"We're not finished," she murmured, knowing that whatever was going on between her and Hyder, it was not done. He knew it. Now, so did she.

She walked on. She couldn't stay out and watch the lights anymore, even if she wanted to. It was too cold.

TWENTY-ONE

Hyder

For the last two weeks, time had begun moving in a way that did not make sense.

It was both too fast and too slow. Hyder couldn't decide which one bothered him more.

On one hand, every day felt like it dragged, stretched thin with work and weather and the constant hum of winter setting in even deeper. The snow had not let up, the days had shortened to little more than a suggestion of light, and the cold had sharpened into something that bit straight through every layer if you were not careful.

On the other hand, entire stretches of time had vanished in a blur. Just like Sola, who seemed to always be everywhere and nowhere.

Between the TB testing kits finally arriving, the town lining up one after another to get cleared, Nobu's recovery, which had thankfully turned in the right direction but still required careful monitoring, and her now twice-weekly appointments with Charlie, whose belly seemed to grow a little more every time Hyder caught sight of her, the woman barely stopped moving.

He had seen her. He was just never *with* her. At least never alone.

Just more flashes of her driving past in her Subaru, her hair pulled back, those damned heeled boots still somehow on her feet like she had something to prove to the entire state of Alaska. Though he had also seen her wearing the Kamiks when the snow was fresh, which he supposed was a small improvement.

He also saw glimpses of her in the clinic window, bent over paperwork, her brow furrowed in concentration. And once, just once, across the square, when she had looked up at the exact same moment he had, and the air between them had gone charged and incomplete.

Then someone called her name, and she turned away.

Still persecuted.

He snorted under his breath now, walking through the quiet, early morning dark, as he made his way along the boardwalk toward Aurora Cottage. It was still ridiculous, but it felt true nonetheless, because on top of all the busyness, the town had decided it was time to celebrate.

Yøl.

The festival had started four days ago, and it would run for another eight days. Twelve days when the town refused to be quiet or still. A fight against the darkness, letting it know it didn't get to win.

Which meant there had been no avoiding anyone. No slipping off unnoticed. No finding a quiet moment that had not already been claimed by some tradition, some gathering, some event that had half the island involved and the other half showing up anyway.

Not that he minded. Not really. It was Alpenglow at its best.

Still...

He exhaled slowly, his breath curling white in the dark as his mind slipped back over the last several days, one moment folding into the next like a series of snapshots strung together.

The Yule log was always the first sign.

Like clockwork, at sunset on the twenty-first of December, though sunset felt like a generous term for the dimming of an already dim sky. The entire town always gathered as they carried the massive log through the square.

"Careful, you *oosik*, you're gonna drop it on your own foot. Or mine!" Healy had barked at Micah, who nearly lost his grip.

"I got it!" Micah shot back, though the log dipped dangerously anyway.

Hyder had laughed, adjusting his own hold, glancing over. And there she was.

Sola...

Bundled in layers this time, thank God, though he could still see the shape of her, the line of her jaw tucked into a scarf, her dark eyes reflecting the glow of the torches as they all walked. Lucia walked ahead of her, chatting easily with Cheryl and two of the elders, already fully folded into the rhythm of the town like she had always belonged there. Gus had stood just off to the side, his headphones on, his notebook tucked under one arm, watching everything with that same intense focus Hyder had come to recognize.

When the log had finally been set and lit, the flames climbing high into the dark, sparks snapping upward into the sky, Sola had looked up, her face caught in the firelight, and Hyder felt that same pull low in his gut, that same awareness that hadn't eased since their night on the mountain.

Hell, since I first heard her voice.

He had not gone to her, held her hand, kissed her how he wanted. There were too many people. Too many eyes that would have loved nothing more than to make such a moment part of the celebration.

But he had watched her.

The tree decorating had been worse. Or better. Depending on how you looked at it. Because at least they'd managed to talk. A little.

"Absolutely not," Sola had said, standing with her hands on her hips as Tala tied a long red ribbon to a branch. "That is not how you tie a bow."

Tala pursed her lips. "It's a ribbon, Doc. Not stitches."

"It is an *ugly* ribbon," Sola had shot back, already taking it and retying it into a proper bow with quick, efficient movements. "If we are doing this, freezing our asses off, we are doing it correctly."

Hyder had leaned back against a wooden pillar of the pavilion, his arms crossed, watching as she fixed not just one ribbon, but three, then stepped back, assessing the tree like it was a surgical procedure she intended to perfect.

"You gonna charge us for that, Doc?" he'd called out.

She'd turned, her eyes narrowing, but there had been a spark there, that same pull. "Only if you keep talking, *Señor* King."

"It would be worth it," he called back as she walked around to the other side of the tree, looking for more ribbons that needed help.

God, he wanted to cross that space between them. Not for any other reason than to be closer to her.

Okay, maybe one other reason. Or two.

Tala had snorted beside him. "Ooh! You are *so* far gone."

He had straightened. "I am not—"

"You are," she'd cut him off, grinning. "You're looking at her like she's the last piece of pie at the Raven. Or worse, the last beer."

"I do not—"

"You do," Willow had chimed in from his other side, not even looking at him as she grabbed another box of ornaments.

Hyder had rolled his eyes. "I hate all of you."

"Liar," Tala said cheerfully, then had walked away before he could say anything else.

Then there were the gingerbread houses. They had been chaos. Absolute, glorious, tasty chaos.

Candy everywhere. Icing in places icing should never be. Children running around, their own houses half-done and forgotten. Adults pretending they were not more competitive than the kids.

And Sola...

Sola, who could handle a medical emergency without blinking, had been utterly defeated by frosting and cookies.

"It won't stay," she'd muttered, trying to attach a wall that promptly slid sideways.

"Because you're using too much," Hyder had explained, crouched beside her, his own structure already perfect.

She'd shot him a look. "I am following the instructions."

"The instructions are wrong." He'd taken the piping bag from her and demonstrated, slower this time. "You need less, and you need to let it set."

Her eyes had tracked his hands, like there would be a test afterwards.

"You're enjoying this," she accused him.

"Immensely."

She scoffed, but when she tried again, it held.

"See?" he'd said.

She had glanced up at him then, and for just a second, something softened in her expression.

"Don't get used to it," she declared.

He grinned. Because it was too late. He never wanted to experience *Yøl* without her again.

Then there was Christmas Eve.

It was always loud and wonderfully overwhelming in the best possible way, the kind of joyful chaos that wrapped Alpenglow in warmth and laughter, despite the cold. The day always began with the mushing race, an event that drew teams from across the island and even a few from the mainland. Mushers and their dogs arrived in a flurry of excited barking and colorful gear, chasing nothing more than bragging rights and the simple pleasure of letting the dogs stretch their powerful legs after weeks of shorter training runs.

After that came ice skating up at Lake Sletta'a, up in the foothills of the eastern mountains. Sola was surprisingly good at it. She wore a borrowed pair of Willow's skates and laughed brightly as she spun across the fresh ice. Hyder had pulled on his old hockey skates and took a few slow laps to reacquaint his feet with them after eight months away. As he watched Sola steady Gus, her hands gentle on the boy's shoulders while his legs wobbled beneath him, Hyder remembered how he had once wondered whether the two of them would enjoy any of this. A quiet wave of gratitude washed over him now that it was clear they did.

As the light began to fade, everyone gathered their gear and made the trek back to town for the Christmas Eve feast.

Lucia had been seated between two older women who had taken it upon themselves to explain everything about ribbe and crackling and why one version was better than the other, while she listened with bright interest, occasionally chiming in with her own opinions that had them all laughing.

Gus had sat quietly, focused on his food, occasionally glancing up when something caught his attention, his notebook never far from reach.

And Sola...

She relaxed. Not completely and not enough for anyone else to notice. But enough that he did. It was the way her smile came easier, the way she leaned into conversations instead of standing just outside of them. It could have been the gløgg, but Hyder suspected it was more than that.

He had wanted to sit next to her. He hadn't.

There were still too many people. Too much of everything except what he actually wanted. He knew everyone thought he was being a chicken, but he still didn't feel like *she* was ready. Not yet.

Hyder huffed out a breath now, shaking his head slightly as he finally reached Aurora Cottage. The whole boardwalk felt soft in the early hour, just before Christmas morning. Snow layered thick along the roofs, illuminated by the faint glow from the lights, which cheered him up despite his frustrations.

He slowed, holding the bundle in his hands carefully.

Though he'd volunteered for this mission, it had turned into a whole family operation.

"You cannot just give him something normal," Willow had insisted. "It has to be something he'll *love*."

"Something useful," Sutton added, taking a sip of his coffee.

"Something fun," Hope chimed in.

"Something artsy," Sterling suggested, leaning back in his chair.

"Something not loud," Charlie advised firmly.

"Something for his maps," Hyder finally muttered, half to himself.

That had been it. When he knew exactly what to get Gus for Christmas.

Now, tucked inside the wrapped paper, was a leather-bound atlas-style sketchbook, custom ordered through Cheryl, its pages thick and unlined, paired with a full set of charcoal pencils, graphite sticks, fine liners, and a small field compass engraved with a simple marking on the back.

For Gus.

From the Nisser Elves.

That was how they had decided to leave it. Because in their neck of the woods, Santa had his helpers, and they were the ones who left the gifts.

Hyder crouched, setting the package carefully beside the boots lined up outside the door, loving that they had decided to participate in the town tradition. He adjusted it just enough that it would not tip over into the snow. Then he took one of the cookies they had left on the doorstep and took a big bite. He had watched his brother do the same thing over the years for Gemma and Hope, and it gave him warm satisfaction to be doing it for Gus.

For a moment, he just stayed there, listening to the pre-dawn calm, the only noise the soft lapping of the cove against the boardwalk, the faint creak of the wood as the cold settled into everything, and his crunching on the half-frozen cookie.

He imagined Gus waking up tomorrow, coming outside, and finding the gift and the missing cookies. The way his eyes would light up, the way his hands would move immediately to the pages, to the tools, already thinking, already mapping.

He imagined Sola watching him. That soft look she always got when she forgot to guard it. Especially when she was happy for Gus.

His chest tightened. He wanted to be there, to be a part of it.

Damn it.

He straightened slowly, brushing his hands together, then shoved them into his pockets, rocking back slightly on his heels as he looked at the door.

He could knock. It would be easy. It was still early, but he knew Sola often got up before dawn anyway.

Instead, he exhaled and stepped back.

Because this felt like something more than a gift from the elves for someone else's child.

He turned, his boots crunching softly as he made his way back down the boardwalk, the lights of the town tree twinkling in the distance, the sky still dark, still holding onto the last of the longest nights.

Hyder figured he'd been patient for a lot of things in his life. He could wait for her. For them.

TWENTY-TWO

Sola

Christmas morning began with thunder.

Not the kind that rolled across the sky, but the kind that pounded down a narrow hallway with small, frantic feet and the unmistakable sound of a front door being thrown wide and banging against the wall.

Sola's eyes snapped open.

For one disoriented second, she did not know where she was. The unfamiliar ceiling above her, the lack of sirens and cars, the stillness. Then everything rushed back at once. The cottage, the town, the water outside. And her heart slammed hard against her ribs.

"Gus!"

She was out of bed before the panic could fully take hold, grabbing for her robe as she burst into the hallway, bare feet cold against the floor, her mind already spiraling through every worst-case scenario she had ever carried as a mother before she even reached the living room.

Through the mudroom, the front door was still wide open, with cold air pouring inside. Her son was outside, standing on the front porch in nothing but his favorite PJs and winter boots.

Lucia stood beside him, one hand braced on the door, the other resting lightly on August's shoulder, calm as ever, as if none of this were alarming in the slightest.

"Relax, Marisolita," her mother said without even turning around. "He is fine."

Sola forced herself to breathe.

In...

Out...

In...

Out...

Her pulse slowed, though it took effort, the instinct to panic still clinging stubbornly to her chest. She stepped forward, wrapping her robe tighter around herself as she moved to the doorway, her eyes scanning Gus.

He was fine. Better than fine. He was smiling.

Not just a small, subtle lift of his lips she had learned to treasure. This was different. He pointed down at the porch with excitement.

"Cookies are gone."

Sola blinked, her gaze dropping to the small plate they had set out the night before, now empty except for a few crumbs.

For a moment, she just stared at it. Then she laughed softly, the sound catching somewhere between relief and something deeper.

"Looks like the nisse came," she said.

"Of course they did," Lucia added, entirely satisfied. "We left the good cookies."

Sola shook her head, still smiling despite herself. When Willow had explained to her about their Nordic tradition of leaving their boots and cookies out for the nisse, she had snorted.

Yet here they were, and the cookies were gone, despite the fact that she had fallen asleep and forgotten all about them. She thought about who might have come by, but she figured she already knew, and it was a little unsettling. She shrugged, deciding it was not the time to worry about such things, and looked out across the cove instead.

She wondered briefly if she would ever truly relax living this close to the water, with no fences or barriers, nothing between her son and the unknown except her own vigilance.

Probably not.

But the thought slid away as quickly as it came, because Gus was still smiling.

"Come on," she said gently. "Let's go inside. It's freezing."

"Present." He pointed again. There, leaning by the boots they had lined up the night before, was a beautifully wrapped package. Someone had clearly put in effort, tying a large bow with a flourish.

"Yeah, GusGus," she said softly, a bit in awe, "it sure is. Bring it in, okay."

Inside, Gus barely paused, already moving toward the tree, his attention held with the same intensity he brought to everything. He dropped to his knees on the rug, already peeling back paper with careful hands.

Sola sank onto the couch, pulling her feet up as she watched him, Lucia settling beside her with a soft sigh.

"He is happy," her mother said quietly, not taking her eyes off him.

Sola nodded.

"He is."

It was not a small thing to say that. The change had been gradual and subtle, and almost hard to track in the nearly two months that they had been in Alpenglow. But moments like this made it undeniable.

He was more at ease in Alpenglow. More present and less overwhelmed. Talking more, and not just to her and Lucia. And he had friends. A community. Which was all she ever wanted for him.

Lucia glanced at her then, her dark eyes serious despite the softness of the morning.

"You did a good thing, Marisolita."

Sola let out a slow breath, leaning back against the couch, not even pretending not to know what her mother meant.

"I hoped I did," she admitted. "But I would be lying if I said I was always sure."

"And now?"

Sola watched August's hands still. Then they moved quickly as he pulled out a large leather-bound book, more like a tome or a huge dictionary than anything else. He flipped it open, one page and then another, touching the textured paper reverently. He then pulled out a case and opened it. Inside was a collection of charcoals, much more extensive than the ones Sterl ng had shared with him. And lastly, an antique-looking compass.

"Maps," he whispered.

Sola felt something in her chest tighten.

Lucia leaned closer. "From the nisse," she whispered, like a secret she was sharing just w th him.

Gus nodded, already reaching for the charcoals, testing the weight of them, the feel of each one. He did not look up again.

Sola swallowed, blinking a little harder than necessary.

"Now I think..." she hesitated, searching for the right words. "...I think we got lucky. I just can't believe they knew exactly what to get him."

Her mother hummed knowingly. "This town sees people, *mija*. That is what makes it different."

Sola let that sit for a moment. Because it was true.

In the months since they had arrived, she had been busier than she had ever been in her life, pulled in a dozen directions, needed in ways that left her exhausted and fulfilled all at once.

And yet, she had never felt more supported and seen.

"What about you?" her mother broke into her thoughts. "Are you happy, Marisolita?"

Sola hesitated.

Then, slowly, with a soft sigh, "Yeah, *Mamí*, I am too."

It was the truth.

So why...

She frowned slightly, her gaze drifting toward the window.

Why did she feel...off. Not unhappy and not even unsettled. Just...aware.

Something is missing.

Her jaw tightened at the thing she did not want to admit out loud.

Hyder.

She missed him. Missed the way he filled a space, the way his presence seemed to shift the air around her, the way he looked at her like she was something he had already decided to claim but did not want to force her into anything. Missed that he wasn't there with them.

Sola's frown deepened.

That was not how this worked. It never had been. She did not need anyone around her but her family. Her mother and August and her work. That was what made her complete.

"Everything okay, *mija*?" Lucia asked, watching her too closely.

Sola blinked, forcing a smile.

"*Perfecto*," she said lightly, turning to watch her son as he made the world come alive on the paper in front of him. That was much safer.

In Alpenglow, the days after Christmas blurred in a way that felt entirely different from the weeks before.

Less frantic, but more alive.

Yøl did not slow down after the twenty-fifth of December. If anything, it only grew louder. The morning after Christmas, she found herself pulled into the cross-country ski tradition whether she liked it or not.

"I do not know how to do this," she told Willow flatly, staring down at the narrow sticks strapped to her feet.

"You will," Willow said cheerfully, already gliding forward with unnatural ease, then adding over her shoulder, "or you will fall. Either way, it's fun."

"It does not look fun," Sola muttered.

Hyder snorted from somewhere behind her. "Give it five minutes, Doc."

She turned just in time to see him push off smoothly, his body moving with practiced confidence, as if he belonged to the motion itself.

It irritated her.

"How hard can it be?" she muttered.

Three seconds later, she was on the ground, flat on her back, staring up at the pale winter sky, her ski boots popped out from the tension.

"Well," Hyder said, skiing backward now, coming to a stop beside her and offering a hand. "That answers that."

The ice fishing huts were worse.

"You want me to sit in a box on frozen water," she said slowly, looking at Micah as if he'd just suggested they take a vacation on the moon, "and wait for something to maybe bite a hook?"

"That is exactly what I am asking," he said proudly.

"...why?"

"Because when it works, t's great."

"And when it doesn't?"

"We drink."

Sola considered that.

"...fine, but I like my gløgg hot."

Micah laughed outright, and when Sola looked up, she saw Hyder watching.

The snow maze had been anarchy.

Children running in every direction, adults pretending they knew where they were going, Tala shouting directions that were definitely wrong.

"I swear you just sent us n a circle," Sola accused, breathless as they turned another corner.

"Trust the process," Tala shot back.

"What process?"

Charlie, who was walking slower and holding Sutton's hand, turned when she got close and admitted, "There is no process. Or an exit."

Sola laughed then, surprised at herself. Hyder was several paces behind them, and when Sola turned, she saw he was watching her again. It might have unnerved her, but eventually she realized she was more upset that he was not closer.

At some point, in between all the cookies, activities, and cheerful madness, Sola stopped feeling like a total outsider.

People continued to greet her, but now some even stopped her in the square, asking after her patients, her family, her day. They gossiped with her instead of about her. She began to hear *cheechako* whispered less and less. And once, she thought she heard *sourdough* murmured instead.

Before Sola realized it, it was New Year's Eve. Like most things, New Year's meant a party at the Raven, complete with fireworks over the cove as the first strains of "Auld Lang Syne" poured out of a speaker. The entire town gathered along the boardwalk, bundled in layers, faces turned toward the sky as the first burst of color lit the darkness. It was no ball dropping, but Sola did not mind one bit.

"Beautiful, isn't it?" Lucia said beside her. She was holding Gus close as he covered his ears while watching the explosions at the same time.

"It is," Sola whispered.

Suddenly, she felt a hand at the back of her neck and fingers threading into her hair. She turned, knowing exactly who it was.

Hyder.

There was no hesitation this time. No worry over who might see them. He pulled her in, his mouth finding hers as the sky exploded behind them, color and sound and light crashing together in a way that felt almost too much, too alive.

Sola leaned into him, her hands coming up to his chest, gripping his coat as if she needed him to keep standing right there and never move.

Whether it was for the fireworks or for them, Sola wasn't sure, and she didn't care. Right now, it was just them, and she had missed this.

When he pulled back, his forehead rested briefly against hers.

"Happy New Year, Doc," he murmured.

She grinned. "Happy New Year."

Then, remembering where she was and who was around, she gasped, turning toward her mother. And Gus.

They were both watching. August with a brief, curious glance before returning his gaze to the fireworks, and her mother, not bothering to hide her wide, knowing grin. Sola blushed, but she realized she was just too happy to feel embarrassed, so she shrugged instead, and turned back to the fireworks, and let Hyder stand close to her, as she'd been hoping for all week long.

The next morning, New Year's Day, came with cold. And insanity.

Sola again stood firmly on the boardwalk, her arms crossed, watching as what appeared to be half the town prepared to throw themselves into freezing water. Apparently thinking that calling it a Polar Plunge made it okay.

"You cannot be serious," she said flatly.

"Oh, they are." Charlie stood beside her, bundled up and very much not participating. "I did it once."

Sola turned. "Once?"

"Once," Charlie confirmed. "Last year. Before the water got this cold."

"And?"

Charlie smiled sweetly. "Never again."

"Smart woman." Sola nodded as her mind, unhelpfully, began listing potential complications.

Cold shock response. Rapid heart rate. Arrhythmias. Hypothermia.

"This is medically irresponsible," she muttered.

Charlie laughed softly. "You'll get used to it."

"I sincerely hope not."

A cheer went up, and Sola's attention snapped back just in time to see Hyder surface, water streaming down his body as he hauled himself back up onto the dock.

Her breath caught.

He was...barely dressed in just boxer briefs. Water slicked over muscle, over his inked shoulders, over skin that looked carved from stone and alive all at once.

"Careful," Charlie nudged her lightly. "You're drooling a little."

Sola blinked, dragging her gaze away, only to have it snap right back.

"I am not..."

"Mmhmm."

Sola flushed but didn't deny it again.

Charlie leaned closer, her voice dropping slightly. "You know he's one of the best."

Sola frowned faintly.

"I am biased," Charlie continued, smiling, "and I think Sutton is better, of course. But Hyder...he's special."

Sola's jaw tightened just slightly. She knew Charlie meant well. But she didn't need that. She didn't need someone special. She just wanted him. A physical thing, that was all this was.

Her mind whispered back.

Liar!

She ignored it. Instead, she watched as Hyder wrapped himself in a towel, roughly drying his hair with another as he made his way up the ramp toward them.

"You sure you don't want to try?" he asked, giving her the half-grin she liked so much. "It's exhilarating."

Sola lifted a brow. "I think you're *loco*. I like my extremities exactly as they are."

His gaze dropped, slowly taking her in from her toes back up to her eyes.

"Yeah," he said easily. "Me too."

Her breath hitched, just slightly. Then he was gone, turning toward the Raven, whistling as he disappeared inside with the rest of them.

Just like that, the new year had begun.

Sola stood there for a mcment longer, watching the empty place where he'd been, the cold biting at her cheeks, the world alive around her.

She tried to think of where she had been this time last year. She was sure she had either been working or hanging out with August and her mother. She tried to picture it. To feel it. But she couldn't. Not clearly.

Yet somehow, she did not think she ever would forget this New Year. Because it hadn't just sl pped past her. It had pulled her in, and she let it.

TWENTY-THREE

Hyder

The ropes creaked softly as Hyder pulled them tight, securing *The Ahnah* to the town dock, his breath coming out in a slow puff as he leaned his weight back against the line, testing it, then gave a satisfied nod when the trawler barely shifted against the pilings. The weather had settled in the last week since the new year began, and for once it was not blistering cold. Which did not mean it wasn't cold, just more tolerable.

It was also early. Too early for most of the town, the sky still barely going purple to the east. But not for him. He liked this quiet time, when the world seemed to belong to him alone.

The red fuel pump stood just up the dock, its metal sides dulled by years of salt and weather, the hose coiled neatly where someone, probably Dan, had taken the time to do it right. Hyder grabbed it, dragging it back across the boards with a low scrape, then climbed down onto the deck and popped open the fuel hatch, the sharp smell of marine diesel rising up to meet him.

"Let's get you well fed," he muttered under his breath, more out of habit than thought.

They'd had some good short runs for the last couple of days, mostly ferrying guests back and forth along the cove, from the Lodge to town. Not that they couldn't drive there faster, but the winter bookings had changed things. These guests thought a quick ride on the boat was a novelty and if it kept them busy during the day, he didn't mind. Much.

Luckily the aurora had cooperated too. Hell, it had more than cooperated, with ribbons of green and blue tearing across the sky like something alive, shifting and curling above the mountains while the guests soaked in the hot springs below. Even Hyder, who had grown up with it, had found himself standing still, his hands in his pockets, just watching.

He twisted the nozzle, listening to the steady glug of fuel filling the tank, then glanced out across the cove. The sky was clear and the water was still, in that early morning way that promised stability instead of trouble.

The weather will hold today. He was sure of it. Which was good, because today was not going to be a short run inside the cove.

The guests had decided they wanted more, but not fishing. They wanted open water and wildlife. Some otters and eagles. Possibly some sea lions or a pod of orcas. Maybe even a glimpse of the glacier calving if they were lucky enough to catch it.

It was ambitious for early January. He did not usually start with charters until mid-February at the earliest. Sometimes even March, when the wind was less of a twitchy bitch. But it was still doable, if they did not go too far from Alpenglow and stayed near the coast. Just in case.

Hyder capped the tank, coiled the hose back into place, then moved on, checking lines, securing extra gear, making sure everything that could shift would not. Out there, it did not take much for something small to become a problem.

The Sound did not forgive mistakes. It never had.

Hyder paused for a moment, his hand resting on the worn edge of the rail, his gaze drifting out over the cove. It looked calm now.

Almost harmless. A mirror of dull steel stretching toward the mouth where it opened into something far bigger.

He knew better. He had seen what it could do.

Men twice his size, stronger than him, tougher than him, were swallowed whole because they thought they knew better than the tide, the wind, or worse, the cold. Because they thought they had time and thought they were invincible.

And Dad...

His jaw tightened slightly. His father had known better too, but somewhere along the line, he'd forgotten about one very important thing.

Respect.

That was the word he always remembered. Not fear. Hyder didn't fear the water. He couldn't, not with the life he'd chosen. But he respected it. Every line he tied, every piece of gear he checked, every life vest he made someone wear, it all came back to that.

Respect the water. Or it would take what it wanted.

He was crouched near the stern, tightening a strap over a crate of emergency supplies, when he heard it.

A soft scuff of boots on wood.

He looked up.

Gus stood on the dock, just past the red pump, small and still against the wide stretch of gray water and the still dark sky.

He was all alone.

"Hi, Hyde," Gus said quietly, watching the air just above Hyder's shoulder.

Hyder straightened slowly, his brows pulling together as he glanced instinctively toward Aurora Cottage.

There was no movement. No frantic mother running down the boardwalk.

Not yet.

But he suspected it was only a matter of time.

"Hey there, Captain Gus," he said, keeping his voice easy, like him being there was the most normal thing in the world. "Whatcha doin' out here, bud?"

Gus shifted his weight slightly, his gaze drifting away from Hyder for a second, then coming back.

"Boat," he explained.

Hyder huffed out a soft breath through his nose, a smile tugging at his mouth despite himself.

"Yeah," he said. "This here's my boat. And I bet you were thinking about when I said you could take a ride. Right?"

Gus waited, thinking, then he nodded.

Hyder moved closer to the rail, resting his forearms against it, bringing himself down just a little to be more at Gus's level.

"Where's your mom?" he asked gently. "Or your grandma?"

Gus did not answer right away. Then, after a beat, "Sleeping."

Hyder's jaw tightened as he glanced again toward the cottage, then back to Gus.

"Alright," he said, his tone shifting just enough to broach something serious. "Listen to me, okay?"

Gus's eyes snapped back to Hyder's shoulder, the way that Hyder had learned meant that he was paying close attention. In his own way.

"You don't ever come out on the dock by yourself," Hyder said, calm but firm. "Not without me or your mom or grandma. And you definitely don't get on a boat, any boat, unless someone's with you. Understand?"

Gus nodded once more.

"Say it," Hyder added, wanting to make sure he got it.

Gus blinked, his mouth working like he was trying to get his words out.

"No boat," he finally agreed.

Hyder grinned. "No boat without asking. And if you are on a boat, what do you wear?"

Gus looked down, his confusion obvious.

Hyder reached behind him, grabbing a small life vest from where it hung near the cabin door, holding it up.

"This," he said. "Every time."

Gus nodded again, more certain now.

Hyder studied him for a second, then exhaled. He should take him back. He knew he should.

But he was already running late to head back over and pick up the guests, and he could not help but feel like it would hurt Gus's feelings if he did.

"Alright," he said finally, pushing off the rail. "Come here."

He reached down, lifting Gus carefully over the side and onto the boat deck. Gus let him.

"Arms up," he said.

Gus complied, and Hyder slipped the vest on, tightening the straps and tugging each one to make sure it was snug.

"There," he said, giving it one last check. "Now you're good."

Gus looked down at himself, then back up at Hyder.

"Now, I can't take you out today, but you can sit right there and watch, okay?" Hyder added, pointing to a spot near the cabin. "No moving around."

Gus sat immediately, his fingers curling around the bench seat.

Hyder snorted softly.

"Good man."

He went back to work, but now he talked.

"This here's the emergency ditch bag," he said, tightening the bag down with a strap. "We keep it where we can get to it quick. That's the thing about boats. You don't get a lot of time to think when something goes wrong."

Gus watched him.

"That line there keeps us from drifting," Hyder went on. "And this..." he tapped the side of the engine housing, "...this is what gets us home. I can go out today, because the weather is good, but if the weather is bad, I wouldn't go. And I always have a backup plan, just in case."

Gus listened, watching carefully while Hyder finished going through his checklist. He was nearly through when a door slammed.

Hard.

"Gus!" Sola's voice tore across the cove.

Hyder winced.

"Uh oh," he said under his breath, glancing at Gus. "Captain Gus, I think your mom's mad."

Gus looked at him seriously.

"She's mom."

Hyder huffed a quiet laugh. "Yeah," he agreed. "She is."

Sola came into view a second later, running down the boardwalk, with no coat or gloves. Just sheer panic carrying her down the ramp, her hair loose, her breath coming hard and fast in the cold air.

Hyder moved immediately, stepping toward Gus, one hand steady on the boy's shoulder as Sola reached the dock.

"Gus!" she cried again, her voice breaking now as she closed the distance.

"*Estoy aquí*," Gus said quietly, like that explained everything.

Sola reached them, her hands already reaching, grabbing for him as Hyder lifted him down, pulling him in tight.

"What are you thinking, *mijo*?" she demanded, her voice a mix of anger and fear, words tumbling over each other. "*No puedes hacer eso! No puedes salir así!*"

"He's okay," Hyder murmured.

Sola did not look convinced, and she did not even look at him.

"Come on," she said, breath shaking as she pulled back, her hands moving to the straps of the vest. "We're going home. Right now."

Her fingers fumbled in the cold, unable to take it off.

"*Mierda!*" she cried out, her head bowing, the emotion in her voice real.

"Hey," Hyder said gently, already swinging himself onto the dock in one smooth motion, landing lightly beside them. "It's okay," he added, reaching out, his hands steady as he guided hers. "Here. Like this."

He unclipped the first buckle, then the second, quick and practiced.

"He had the vest on," he said, keeping his voice calm. "He didn't go near the edge. He did exactly what I told him."

Sola's eyes snapped up to his, still wild and brimming with angry tears.

"He came out without telling me," she shot back.

"I know," Hyder said. "And that's something we fixed."

She hesitated. Just for a second.

"Gus promised," Hyder added quietly, glancing down at the boy. "Right?"

Gus nodded.

"No boat alone," he repeated.

Sola's shoulders dropped just a fraction and Hyder decided to take a chance she might be willing to listen.

"I can teach him," he explained, the words coming out before he could overthink them. "How to be around boats and water. How to swim. So he can be safe."

Sola stilled, her gaze flicking between him and Gus.

"He listens to me," Hyder went on. "And I won't let him ever do anything he's not ready for."

The morning was no longer as quiet as it had been. Hyder became aware of it all at once, and he looked up.

The Forget Me Not's door was open, and a few people were standing just outside. Further down the boardwalk, several others were standing on their porches.

All watching them.

Sola noticed too, and her jaw tightened, and for a moment, Hyder thought she might refuse. But when she looked back at Gus, something softened again.

"...Fine," she finally said, her voice quieter now. "But not alone. Never alone."

"Never alone," Hyder agreed. Gus even gave a small nod.

Sola let out a deep breath, then took Gus's hand, her grip firm as she pulled him back toward the boardwalk.

"*Vamos*," she murmured, the edge still in her voice, but it was softer now.

Hyder watched them go, and it suddenly hit him, how much he wanted to go after her. To pull her in and convince her it was okay.

But this was not the moment.

Tala passed them on the ramp as she headed down toward the dock. She watched Sola and Gus for a second, waiting until they were out of earshot, then let out a low whistle.

"Damn," she said. "She's a spicy one, isn't she?"

Hyder's mouth curved slowly into a grin.

"Yeah," he agreed, watching until Sola and Gus disappeared into the cottage. "But I like that."

TWENTY-FOUR

Sola

It was hard to let go. To let someone help her. Correction: it was hard to let a whole town help her.

Because that was what was happening, whether Sola was ready for it or not. Not in grand gestures, not in anything she could easily refuse or politely sidestep, but in small, persistent ways that seemed to weave themselves into her life without asking permission.

It had started simply enough. With the clinic walkway always cleared of snow. With her favorite foods and coffee showing up in the market. Someone stacking firewood outside their cottage. Thick, home-knitted scarves and hats in a box on their porch. And perhaps most important, arranged rides for patients to come in so she could get all the TB testing done before the State decided she was taking too long.

Or at least all these things had felt simple at the time. Now there was something that felt deeper. It began that cold morning, a couple of weeks ago now.

The sheer terror of it still lived sharp in her chest if she let herself think about it too long. Waking to silence, to a room that should not have been so quiet. To August's bed, haphazardly made, the covers pushed aside in a way that told her he had gotten up on his own instead of being woken by her or Lucia. Then the slow, creeping realization that he was nowhere in the cottage. Not in the bathroom. Not in the kitchen. Or tucked into one of his quiet corners with his notebook.

And then the front door. It was unlocked and cracked just enough that the cold was seeping inside.

She did not remember grabbing her boots. Or even the way her heart had pounded so hard it made her vision blur as she ran. Only the thought. Over and over again.

Too close to the water. Too close to the water. Too close...

Hyder had tried to calm her then. But his presence was somehow both grounding and infuriating all at once. But if she was honest with herself, it had not been him who stopped her spiral. Not really.

It was August. The look on his face. Not of fear of the water or confusion. But with fear of her.

That was what had cut through everything else, making her swallow the anger that had been rising up like a tide she could not stop. Forcing her to take a breath and step back. To remember that her son had not done something wrong out of defiance. He had simply...gone.

The way he sometimes did.

The idea that Hyder would teach him to swim, when she had first agreed to it, had felt like a concession more than anything else. A temporary solution. Something to make herself feel like she was doing something instead of nothing.

She had not expected it to work.

Now Gus was going up to the Lodge almost every day, after school. For lessons. And not once had he come back upset. Not once had he resisted going again. Which, in and of itself, should have told her everything she needed to know.

Her mother, of course, had gone with him each time. It was usually during Sola's clinic hours, while she was still getting to the last stubborn holdouts for the testing, which meant she had no choice but to trust what she was told when they came home.

Lucia, frustratingly, had taken to offering only the bare minimum.

"He is doing well," she would say, with that knowing little smile that made Sola want to shake a better answer out of her.

"Okay...how well?" Sola had pressed more than once.

Lucia would only shrug, practically singing as she told her, "You will see, Marisolita."

It was enough to make her want to scream. But she would see. *Tonight*.

Because tonight was the first official meeting of what Willow had very enthusiastically christened *Wine About It Book Club*.

Sola had tried to beg off. Truly, she had.

"I am too busy," she'd told Willow truthfully, one hand still on a patient chart, the other already reaching for the next file. "And I have not read anything that qualifies as a book in months. Maybe even years if you don't count medical texts."

Willow had just smiled at her, completely unmoved.

"That's okay," she returned cheerfully. "You can come and *not* talk about the book."

"That seems counterproductive," Sola had muttered.

"It's mostly about the wine anyway," Willow added.

Which, unfortunately, had not helped Sola's argument.

Now she was closing up the clinic, stacking the last of the day's charts neatly on her desk while Galena leaned against the counter, already shrugging into her coat with far more enthusiasm than the situation warranted.

"You sure you don't mind giving me a ride?" Galena asked, glancing over her shoulder.

"Of course not," Sola said, slipping her own coat on, reaching for her keys.

"Good," Galena grinned. "Because I plan on getting absolutely sloshed."

Sola paused, one brow lifting as she turned toward her.

"You know excessive alcohol consumption has well-documented negative effects on the liver, cognitive function, and—"

"Oh my God," Galena cut in, laughing as she shoved her toward the door. "You are not allowed to be a doctor right now."

"I am always a doctor," Sola replied dryly.

"Not tonight," Galena shot back. "Tonight you are a woman who is going to drink wine and pretend she has hobbies. And friends."

Sola laughed despite herself, locking the clinic behind them. She had been told no one locked doors in Alpenglow, but her New York mind was still resistant. Plus, as she'd argued with Galena more than once, there were still HIPAA laws and privacy concerns.

"I have hobbies," she insisted as they stepped out into the cold.

"Name one."

Sola opened her mouth. Then closed it. She normally would have said yoga, but her mat was somewhere under her bed, gathering dust ever since their move.

Galena cackled with far too much pleasure. "That's what I thought."

The drive north was short, but the sky had already deepened into that soft indigo that came before full dark, the snow catching what little light remained and reflecting it back in a way that made everything feel further than it really was.

Sola had been to the Lodge a handful of times now. Usually for dinners and a few quick checkups on Charlie during the worst of flu season. But it had been a while, and as she pulled up, she felt that same strange mix of anticipation and hesitation settle low in her chest. The one she always noticed whenever she knew she was about to see Hyder.

Inside, she found Charlie cooking in the kitchen.

Or rather, Charlie standing in the kitchen while Sutton was doing most of the work and telling her to sit down and rest.

Sola paused just inside the mudroom, taking in the scene with a faint smile.

"You know," she said lightly, shrugging off her coat, "it is generally acceptable for pregnant women to cook."

Sutton snorted without even looking up from the cutting board.

"You don't understand, Doc," he said, shaking his head. "It was never acceptable for Charlie to be near a kitchen."

Charlie gasped. "That is slander."

"It is fact," he replied calmly.

Sola's smile widened.

"Duly noted," she murmured. Then, glancing around, she asked, "Where's Gus?"

Charlie turned, lifting a wooden spoon and pointing it toward the back windows.

"He's in the pool house."

Sola nodded, leaving the way she'd come in, and made her way to the wood-and-glass structure that sat just behind the main Lodge. It was modern in contrast to the rustic logs of the Lodge, and the light from inside reflected outward into the dark like a blue lantern.

She paused for a moment, just taking it in, then reached for the door.

The moment she stepped inside, humidity kissed her skin, and the sharp, clean scent of chlorine, mixed with something softer, eucalyptus maybe, wafted around her, creating a space that felt both alive and calm at the same time.

Then she heard it. A sound that stopped her completely, shorting out her mind while she tried to recognize it.

Laughter.

Her breath caught.

Gus.

She had heard him laugh before, of course. When he was very little. When the world had been simpler, before everything became something to navigate and manage.

But this was different.

Her son sounded unrestrained and vibrant with pure happiness.

Sola took a step forward, then stopped herself, instinctively pulling back into the shadow of an Areca palm near the door, not wanting to interrupt whatever this was. Not wanting to risk breaking it before she got to see it for herself.

Hyder was in the water, moving easily, like it was an extension of him, splashing lightly toward Gus with a grin that was equal parts challenge and encouragement.

"Come on, my man," he called, his voice echoing softly off the walls. "You can't swim from way out there."

August stood at the edge, nodding, his small body stiff with focus.

Then...he jumped.

Sola's heart dropped so fast it made her dizzy. Her body reacted before her mind could catch up, coiling, every instinct screamed at her to move, to run, to grab him.

Then August's head broke the surface. And his arms moved.

It was not perfect or smooth, or even coordinated in any traditional sense. But it was working. His arms were pushing. His legs kicking. Carrying him forward across the water toward Hyder, who was moving backward just enough to give him space, his hands out, ready just in case.

But August didn't need him. He made it all the way across.

And the pride on his face...

Sola felt the tears before she even realized they had started. She did not wipe them away. Did not even dare to breathe. She just stood there, watching.

Clapping broke the moment, and Sola leaned forward slightly, shifting her angle, and saw her mother sitting in a teak chair halfway down the length of the pool.

"Good job, *mijo*," Lucia told him.

She was not alone.

Hope sat beside her, Gemma too, both girls in swimsuits, quiet until now, as if they understood that Gus needed that stillness to find his footing. Or perhaps they'd been told, and instead of making fun of him, they had given him that respect. Either way, more tears came.

Something broke wide open inside her in a way that felt...right. Like a grip she had been holding for too long was finally, slowly, beginning to release. It had its own sort of pain that was easing toward relief if she would only let it.

Awareness prickled, like a current moving over her, and Sola lifted her gaze.

Hyder was looking at her, and for a moment everything else fell away.

The water. The voices. Everyone else.

It was just him. And her.

"Thank you," she mouthed silently, not caring if he saw the tears streaming down her face.

He didn't answer her, just nodded once, briefly.

When she turned, stepping back toward the door, needing a moment to gather herself, to feel what she was feeling without the weight of anyone else seeing it...he understood enough to let her go.

It started with wine. That Sola would later decide was both the problem and the solution, deliberately ignoring the fact that she'd used this excuse before. When she'd first kissed Hyder.

Because the moment she left the pool house, stepping out into the evening cold with one hand pressed over her mouth, breathing in air so frigid it burned all the way down, it was all leading her to something inevitable. She went for a walk, down a path in the snow that someone had cleared. She stood at a cliff, overlooking the vast expanse of the Sound, still crying, realizing she was not just feeling gratitude. It was an understanding that Hyder was doing this *for* her son. Not because he was trying to impress her, but because he was a good man. Eventually, as the idea settled, she wiped her tears and went back, just as her mother was coming out with August, already bundled up, his hair still slightly damp at the ends, curling.

"Sola!" Her mother exclaimed, "when did you come?"

"I just got here," Sola fibbed a little, knowing that if she talked about what she saw, she would lose what little composure she'd managed.

"Well, he is ready to go home," Lucia said gently, as if she did not notice Sola wiping her nose.

Sola nodded, grateful for the dimness hiding her blotchy face and red-rimmed eyes.

"I'll come with you in a minute."

"No, no," Lucia said at once. "You stay. Your son is happy and tired. I will take him home, and I will put him to bed. You need to be with other adults before you forget how."

That almost made Sola laugh. Almost, but the truth of it stung. She gave August a quick kiss instead.

"Goodnight, *mijo*." Then she met her mother's eyes. "Thank you, *Mamí*."

Lucia sniffed. "Of course." Then they walked away.

Sola watched them get in the car and drive off, until the cold was finally too much on her damp cheeks and she went back inside the Lodge.

Hope's voice drifted down to the kitchen from the steps leading upstairs. They must have just come out of the pool house and she realized she was lucky they hadn't seen her.

"Gems, we gotta go! Finn's dad is gonna be here any minute."

"But I can't find Grizzlette!" came Gemma's shout.

"Your bear is down here." This was from Charlie, who was busy pulling out a pitcher of milk and pouring herself a glass.

A honk came from the parking area out back, and Sutton straightened.

"Girls, your ride is here."

Hope and Gemma came rushing down the stairs, their hair also still wet, apparently with plans of their own for the night.

"Hiya, Doc." Hope brightened when she noticed Sola standing just inside the mudroom.

"Hi, Hope, where are you off to?"

Hope shrugged. "Nothing too fancy. Gemma is going to have a sleepover with Bella, and I'm gonna hang with my friends, Finn and Kake."

"That sounds like fun." Sola smiled, trying hard to bring herself into the moment, rather than mulling over what she had seen at the pool.

"I guess..." Hope rolled her eyes. "But I think it would be more fun to hear what *you* guys are gonna talk about all night."

"All right," Sutton lifted his gaze from the platter of warmed brie and bread he was arranging, trying his best to look stern. "You still have some growing up first, young lady."

"Yeah, yeah." Hope rolled her eyes, then gave him a quick hug, then another to Charlie.

"Bye, bug," Sutton swooped Gemma up into his arms and rubbed his stubble into her neck, making her giggle.

"Bye-bye Daddy. Bye Mommy," she added, waving to Charlie.

"Have a good time, sweet pea. You, too, Hope."

Another honk sounded and Sola watched as the girls rushed out. It was almost like the Lodge immediately shifted, and noise that was decidedly more adult began to drift from the other side of the kitchen, where the guest area usually was.

"Come on!" Charlie grabbed her arm and pulled. "We can't hide out in here all night."

"Wait," Sutton called after them, coming over with the brie. "Can you take this in for me? I'm afraid to go in there."

Sola nearly laughed, until she realized he was at least partially serious.

"Sure," she said as she took it, then followed Charlie.

"Doc!" Galena called out once they made it through the swinging kitchen door. She was already halfway through her first glass, if the flush in her cheeks was anything to go by. "You made it. I was starting to think you were going to escape into the woods or fake a medical emergency."

"I considered it," Sola replied dryly, her eyes glancing up toward the double height ceiling. "But unfortunately, the biggest emergency seems to be in here."

"True story." Galena shook her head solemnly before immediately ruining it by grinning and taking another sip.

The Lodge itself was something Sola had yet to get used to. Rustic and solid, with thick exposed log beams, and an enormous double-sided stone fireplace. It was designed to hold large groups of wilderness seekers, but when none were around, the King family used the space to spread out. Tonight, the long table, usually kept clear, was laden with an arrangement of mismatched wine glasses, several open bottles already breathing, and a spread of food that looked far too thoughtful to be casual but far too chaotic to be formal.

Willow was at the center of it, of course.

She turned the moment Galena shouted, her face lighting up in that way that always made Sola feel both welcomed and mildly ambushed.

"You're here!" Willow crossed the room in a few quick steps, pulling her into a hug before Sola could even decide if she wanted one.

"I was told attendance was mandatory," Sola grumbled into her shoulder, awkwardly holding the platter of cheese out to her side.

"It is," Willow replied cheerfully, pulling back. She then took the serving dish and walked back to the table, calling over her shoulder, "But also, I wanted you here."

Something in the simplicity of that landed. Sola nodded once, then glanced around.

Tala was sprawled in one of the chairs, lounging like she owned the place, her dark eyes amused as she watched everything unfold. Ellie sat nearby, a glass in her hand but not drinking much, her posture composed in a way that felt almost deliberate, like she too was not sure whether she belonged or not.

Melodie and Sofiya were near the table, deep in conversation about something that involved hand gestures and wild laughter. Esther Kinew sat with Cheva, the two of them quietly observing with indulgent, fond expressions that suggested they had outgrown such lively nonsense.

Then there was Charlie. Openly pouting. With her glass of milk.

"I would like to state, for the record," Charlie announced, "that this is deeply unfair."

Sola glanced at the glass in her hand. Then back at the wine on the table.

"Yes," she agreed. "That does seem like a design flaw. Though, as your doctor, I would say that a *small* sip or two of wine is okay now that you're nearly in your third trimester."

Charlie sighed dramatically. "I know. But everything makes me nauseous. Wine. Beer. Even cider. Do you know how tragic that is during something called a wine book club?"

"You could rename it," Sola offered mildly. "Milk, metaphors, and mild resentment."

That earned a surprised laugh.

"I like her," Cheva said from across the table.

"Careful," Tala added lazily. "She's still pretending she doesn't like us."

"I never said that," Sola replied, straightening her shoulders.

"No," Tala said, lifting her glass. "You just think it real loud."

There was laughter at that, easy and unforced, and before Sola could overthink it, Galena pressed a glass of red wine into her hand.

"Drink," she instructed.

Sola looked down at it. Hesitated. Then, because apparently it was a night for poor decisions or because she wanted to ease the tension she still felt, she took a sip.

It did not take long. That was the thing.

The first glass warmed her. The second softened her edges. By the third, she found herself laughing and actually enjoying herself.

At Tala, who had somehow taken over the conversation with a story about Hyder that was clearly exaggerated and only getting worse with each retelling.

"And then," Tala was saying, gesturing wildly, "the poor Lil' Frogger swore he could fix it with duct tape."

"Absolutely not," Willow chuckled, wiping tears from her eyes.

"I'm telling you," Tala insisted, "men have entirely too much confidence when it comes to duct tape."

"That is not a male-exclusive trait," Sola said before she could stop herself.

Nine heads turned toward her. Waiting impatiently.

"Well," she added, lifting her glass slightly, "in medical school, there was this guy that came in with a...broken appendage from his girlfriend being a little too...enthusiastic. I needed a creative approach to securing certain equipment."

There was a beat.

Then Esther leaned forward. "No...!"

"Oh yes," Sola nodded, the wine loosening something that had been too tightly wound for years. "It was temporary. And highly discouraged. But also...effective. At least until it was time to take it off. But that was his fault for not letting me shave him first."

"Doc," Tala said, eyes gleaming, "I knew I liked you."

Ellie smiled faintly at that, but it did not quite reach her eyes.

Sola noticed. Not because she was looking for it. But because she was starting to notice everything. It was as if everything was moving around her at once and it all wanted her attention.

"Clare's not here?" Melodie asked suddenly, glancing around.

Willow shook her head. "I invited her. But she said she was too old."

There was a chorus of no ways and snorts.

"Ha," Tala said. "She just likes her husband too much."

Charlie grinned, one hand absently resting over her stomach. "Well, I can't fault her for that. If I wasn't so preggo, I might've stayed upstairs with mine too."

There was a soft ripple of laughter at that, a shared understanding that passed between the women without needing explanation.

Then Galena leaned back in her chair and swirled her wine. "So...Doc."

Sola narrowed her eyes slightly. "That tone suggests I should be concerned."

"You should be delighted," Galena corrected. "We were just wondering something..."

"Were you?" Sola said flatly.

"Mmhmm," Tala added. "Specifically, we were wondering about your...integration into the community."

Sola took a slow sip of her wine. "I am the town doctor. I am already integrated."

"Not like that," Melodie chimed in, grinning.

"I don't understand," Sola looked around.

And then, like a coordinated attack...

"Hyder!"

It came from three directions at once.

Sola managed not to choke. Which, frankly, was a small miracle.

"I fail to see how that is relevant to my integrating—"

"Oh, please," Tala cut in, waving a hand.

"It is entirely relevant," Galena added.

"Hyder is part of the town infrastructure," Sofiya explained with a straight face.

Sola set her glass down carefully.

"Is this an official interrogation?" she asked. "Or are you all just incredibly nosy?"

"Yes," Willow said brightly.

There was laughter again, louder this time, and Sola felt heat rise up her neck. She knew it was definitely the wine that had not just told them to mind their own business.

"Nothing has happened," she said, perhaps a little too quickly.

Silence, and shared, doubtful looks.

"Nothing?" Tala repeated.

"Nothing," Sola confirmed.

Galena leaned forward. "Not even a little something?"

"Nope."

"Not even—"

"No."

There was a pause. And then, from the side, softly, "That's a shame. You guys would be good together."

Ellie.

Sola's eyes flicked to her, and she saw Tala shift almost immediately, her posture changing as she moved her chair slightly closer to Ellie, her expression unreadable now.

The conversation moved on, but not quietly or neatly, and certainly not in a straight line. It sprawled, branching and looping back on itself, growing louder and warmer with every sip of wine that disappeared from their glasses. Voices overlapped, laughter came quicker, and whatever small hesitations Sola might have clung to earlier in the evening were steadily worn down by the sheer momentum of it all.

One thing that did not happen was anything even resembling a discussion about books, and by the time the night began to wind down, if it could even be called winding down, Sola knew two things with absolute certainty.

One: she was drunk. Not disastrously so or enough to lose control of herself entirely, but enough that the tight guard she usually kept on her thoughts had loosened, enough that everything felt just a little softer, a little slower, a little more...honest.

And two: she did not want to leave.

Which was...new.

Sutton appeared at some point, as though summoned by the rising volume of the room itself, drawn in by instinct or long practice. Now he stood near the door, moving with that same quiet efficiency Sola had already come to recognize, collecting coats, shepherding people out into the cold without ever seeming hurried.

"I've got you," he said to Galena, who lifted her glass in a sloppy salute, her grin wide and entirely unrepentant.

"Hero," she declared.

"Menace," he tossed back without missing a beat.

Charlie was already slipping on her coat, still pouting slightly, though it had changed into something almost playful, leaning into Sutton as he guided her toward the door, one hand steady at her back as if he could not quite stop himself from checking that she was fine.

"Text me when you get home," Willow called after them.

"I live here," Charlie shot back, her voice drifting back through the open door.

"Still text me," Willow replied, entirely serious.

More laughter followed that, the sound echoing through the Lodge as the chaos unraveled in a series of small departures, each one taking a little more noise, a little more warmth, until, suddenly, it was quiet.

Sola found herself standing near the fireplace, the heat warming one side of her body while the other cooled, her glass still in her hand, though she could not remember the last time she had taken a sip.

She was alone.

Sutton must have done a head count before driving off, because a moment later he poked his head back through the kitchen door, one hand braced against the frame.

"You good?" he asked.

Sola blinked up at him, the question taking a second to process.

"I was supposed to drive home," she admitted, the words coming out slower than she intended, as though they had to travel a little farther than usual.

His gaze dropped briefly to the glass in her hand, then lifted back to her face.

"No," he said simply.

Something about the certainty of it made her laugh.

"Fair."

"I can take you," he offered. "There's just enough space left, if you don't mind sitting on Galena's lap."

Sola turned her head slightly, her eyes drifting toward the French doors, where the cove stretched out and the faint glow of the town lights flickered below. Somewhere down there was Aurora Cottage. Her mother. Her son. Her safe, contained world.

She looked at it for a long moment, then back at the Lodge. At the quiet. At the feeling still humming low beneath her skin.

"No," she told him, the word forming with more intention than she expected. "I'll...wait..."

Sutton studied her for a moment, something thoughtful passing through his expression, but he did not question her.

"Don't burn the place down," he told her finally, already stepping back.

"I make no promises."

"Good," he replied, then he was gone.

The kitchen door was still swinging, slower, then it too was still.

Sola stood there for a while longer, with the last few months, everything that had led her to this moment, swirling in her mind.

Then, without entirely deciding to, she moved. Through the swinging door and into the k tchen. It was the same place she had first come into that night. But different too. More intimate now that it was empty.

Beneath it all, that familiar, insistent pull rose again.

Her eyes lifted. Toward the stairs. She knew where they led, even if she had never had reason to go up them before.

Her mouth twisted slightly, the expression caught somewhere between disbelief and reluctant amusement.

"Well," she murmured under her breath, straightening her shoulders as though bracing herself for something she had already chosen, "this is a terrible idea."

She set her glass down and started climbing, each step surprisingly steady despite the high heels of her boots, her hand brushing lightly along the railing as she went. At the top, the hallway stretched out before her, longer than she expected, lined with doors. A lot of doors.

Of course, she thought wryly.

A family as large as the Kings needed space. Needed rooms to hold all their lives and their noise.

But tonight, there was none of that. For the first time since she had arrived in Alpenglow, the Lodge was empty.

Except for her.

And him.

Her pulse picked up with a quiet drumbeat beneath her skin.

Hyder is somewhere behind one of those doors.

Sola swallowed hard and went looking.

TWENTY-FIVE

Hyder

He hadn't planned to fall asleep.

Hyder had meant to wait it out, to let the noise burn itself off, to give the women downstairs time to drink their wine and tell their stories and eventually scatter back to their own homes, leaving the Lodge quiet again. He had even tried to drown it out, pulling on a playlist he only ever used when he needed peace, something low and rhythmic, a slow pulse of sound that gave his thoughts somewhere to settle instead of spiraling.

Willow had stood in his doorway earlier, her eyes clear and threatening.

"Do *not* come downstairs," she warned.

"I wasn't planning on it," he'd replied.

"Good," she said, not believing him for a second. "Because if you do, I will make your life very unpleasant."

He'd believed that. Willow had the uncanny ability that most little sisters had at torture.

So he stayed, stretched out on his bed, one arm thrown over his eyes, listening to the muffled rise and fall of laughter through the floorboards, trying not to picture who was at the center of it, trying not to imagine Sola, her mouth softened by wine, her guard slipping just enough that something warmer might show through.

That had been his first mistake. Because once the image formed, it didn't leave.

At some point, between one song and the next, between one thought and another, his body gave in where his mind would not, pulling him under before he could stop it, and he began to dream of her.

Nothing specific. Just her, smiling over her shoulder, beckoning him closer, calling his name.

"Hyder..."

He heard it. Not the way anyone else said his name. Soft, but musical.

His eyes opened slowly, his body still heavy, his mind lagging just a fraction behind as he turned his head toward the sound.

"Hyder."

It came again, and he blinked, still groggy, still thinking of the Sola in his dream.

There she is.

Framed in the doorway, backlit just enough that he could see her outline, her hand already reaching back to close the door behind her as though she decided that whatever this was did not belong anywhere else, and it did not need anyone else.

"Sola?" His voice came out ragged, still caught in sleep.

She didn't answer. Instead, she came closer...and she started removing her clothes.

Not slowly. With a kind of quiet urgency that made something in his chest tighten as he pushed himself up on his elbows, his breath catching as he tried to reconcile what he had just been dreaming about with what he was seeing, what he knew had to be real.

Her boots were unzipped and kicked off first. Then her sweater was dragged up and over her head and thrown somewhere behind her without a second thought. Her bra quickly followed. Her pants were next, pushed down, stepped out of, discarded just as carelessly. As though her clothes were something she no longer had the patience to deal with.

His first instinct was disbelief. His second was awareness.

"You're..." he started, but the words went nowhere, dissolving the moment she moved closer.

Because now he could smell her. That faint, clean mint and coconut that he'd thought of every moment since their night up in the igloo.

Dreams did not have scent. They did not have weight. And they certainly did not make his pulse hit this hard.

She climbed onto his bed without asking, her hands bracing on either side as she moved over him, and the moment her skin brushed his, other parts of him rose to awareness, his dick punching up, almost painfully, already harder than he could ever remember being before.

Everything in him locked, and for one suspended beat, he stopped breathing entirely.

Because she *was* real. Warm and completely bare. Solid against him in a way that made every nerve in his body come alive all at once.

His hands came up slowly, hovering for the smallest fraction of a second, giving himself one last chance to question this, to stop before it started.

He didn't take it. He slid his hands to her, up her arms, over her shoulders, down her back, pulling her in.

Her skin was softer than he expected, but there was nothing fragile about the way she held herself or hesitant in the way she responded to him, leaning into his touch immediately, meeting him with a kind of certainty that erased whatever doubt he might have left.

"You're real," he muttered.

Her answer came in the form of her mouth. She kissed him like she had already decided, her tongue twisting with his. Her hand slid into his hair, tightening just enough to pull him where she wanted him, and something in him answered that without thinking, his hands flexing, shifting her closer, pulling her fully against him until there was no space left.

She made a sound, low and unguarded, and it went straight through him.

"Sola," he said against her mouth, the name rough now, edged with something that felt dangerously close to control slipping.

She still did not answer him and she did not slow.

If anything, she pressed closer, tilting her hips, grinding, her body fitting against his in a way that made his grip tighten more, his instincts take over before his thoughts could catch up.

He rolled them, settling himself between her thighs, one hand braced beside her head, the other sliding along her side, mapping her in a way that was both instinct and intention.

She didn't resist. Instead, her hands came up to his shoulders, nails digging in just enough to make him know he was going to feel it in the morning. He moved over her, his mouth leaving hers to find the line of her jaw, the curve of her throat, the places where her breath hitched without her meaning it to.

There. That reaction. He felt it and made a mental note. *And there.*

He felt the way her body responded to him. He took his time, slowing just enough to learn. To figure out where and what she liked best.

"Sola," he said again, quieter now, his mouth brushing the skin below her collarbone as he spoke. "Tell me to stop."

Her answer was immediate.

"Don't."

That single word snapped the last thread of restraint he had left.

Hyder leaned up to kiss her harder, deeper, tasting the wine on her tongue and the quiet hunger underneath it. His hand slid down her body, cupping her breast, thumb brushing over her nipple until it tightened under his touch. She arched into him with a soft gasp, and the sound went straight to his cock.

He had never felt this kind of pull before, the kind that made him want to slow down just to see what she would do next but made him too weak to do it.

He broke the kiss and moved lower, mouth trailing over her collarbone, between her breasts, then further down. When he settled between her thighs, he pushed them wide with his shoulders, opening her completely to him. Sola's breathing had already turned ragged.

He looked up the length of her body once, just long enough to meet her eyes. They were dark, a little wide, but burning with the same need he felt. Then he lowered his head and licked into her, slow and deliberate.

Fuck.

She tasted spicy and sweet and something else that was unmistakably her. He groaned against her folds, the vibration pulling a sharp cry from her throat. He did it again, firmer this time, tongue circling her clit before sucking it gently between his lips. Her hips jerked. One of her hands flew to his hair, gripping tight, forcing him closer, and he loved the sting of it.

He took his time, learning every reaction. How she shivered when he flattened his tongue and dragged it through her slick heat, how her thighs trembled when he slid two fingers inside her and curled them just right. She was tight, so fucking tight, and the thought of finally being inside her made his cock throb painfully against the mattress.

"Hyder..." Her voice cracked on his name, half plea, half warning.

He didn't stop. He worked her with his mouth and fingers until her legs started to shake and her grip in his hair turned desperate. Only when her back bowed and she came with a broken moan did he ease off, kissing the inside of her thigh as she came down.

When he crawled back up her body, he was shaking with how badly he wanted her.

He kissed her again, letting her taste herself on his tongue. She kissed him back just as fiercely, legs wrapping around his waist, pulling him closer. The head of his cock nudged against her entrance, hot and slick, and for one dizzy second he almost pushed inside.

Then reality slammed into him.

"Shit," he rasped, pulling back just enough to look at her. "Condoms."

Sola blinked up at him, dazed. "What?"

"I bought a box before the igloo. I think they're in the bathroom. Don't move."

He hated every second it took to roll off the bed and cross the room. The cold air hit his skin like punishment. He yanked open the bathroom drawer, found the unopened box he'd casually tossed in weeks ago, and tore it open with more force than necessary, small foil-wrapped squares exploding across the floor. He didn't care. His hands were sure as he rolled one on, heart hammering the whole time.

When he turned back, Sola was sitting up on her elbows, watching him with dark, glossy eyes. Her hair was messy, lips swollen, skin flushed. She looked like every fantasy he'd tried not to have for months.

He climbed back onto the bed and pulled her on top of him before she could overthink it. "Like this," he said, voice low and rough. "I want to watch you take me."

Her breath hitched. She straddled his hips, one small hand bracing on his chest as she reached down between them. He gripped her waist, steadying her, but didn't pull her down. This had to be her pace.

Sola bit her lip hard as she positioned him at her entrance. She was still slick from his mouth and her own release, but he was big and she was petite. The first press of her body against the head of his cock made his jaw clench so tight it hurt.

She sank down, slowly, inch by inch, gasping.

Hyder's hands tightened on her waist, every muscle in his body locked as he fought the overwhelming urge to thrust up into her. She felt impossibly tight and hot and perfect. The stretch made her breath come in shallow pants. Her teeth dug deeper into her lower lip as she worked herself down, trying to settle fully around him.

He stayed perfectly still, even though it was killing him and sweat was breaking out across his chest. "That's it," he murmured, voice strained. "Take your time, *Sha'aéil*. I've got you."

When she finally sank all the way down, seating him to the hilt, a low groan tore from his throat. She was so full of him he could feel himself pressing against the end of her. Her eyes fluttered, then glossed over with pleasure as she adjusted to the feeling.

Then she leaned back, bracing her hands on his thighs, her hair caressing him like silk.

The new angle thrust her breasts high, her nipples tight and begging for his touch, silhouetted in the light coming from the bathroom. Hyder's gaze dropped between them, mesmerized by the sight of where they were joined. He could see himself disappearing into her, her slickness coating every inch of him as she slowly dragged herself almost all the way off, until just the head remained inside her, then sank back down again.

The wet glide of her body over his was obscene and beautiful. Every time she lifted, he saw her stretched around him, his length shining with how wet she was. Every time she came back down, she moaned as he felt her take him deeper, her inner walls fluttering around his length.

"Fuck...Sola," he breathed, the words raw.

She started moving faster, finding her rhythm. Her head tipped back, lips parted, small sounds spilling out with every drag of her hips. He kept his hands on her waist, guiding but never forcing, letting her ride him exactly how she needed.

When her pace grew uneven and her breathing turned soft with desperate whimpers, he knew she was close.

Hyder sat up suddenly, wrapping one arm around her back, the other at the back of her neck. In one smooth motion he flipped them, putting her beneath him again without ever leaving her body. He settled between her thighs, his hips pressing her into the mattress.

"Come, baby. I need to feel you come around me," he growled against her ear.

He started grinding into her. Deep, slow, rolling thrusts that kept constant pressure on her clit. Her nails dug into his shoulders. Her legs locked around his waist. He could feel her pulsing, the tension coiling tighter and tighter around him.

"Come on, Sola," he whispered, voice rough with restraint. "Let go for me."

"Hyder..."

She shattered with a cry, his name breaking on her lips like a song, as her body clenched hard around him, rhythmic waves pulling him deeper.

The feeling of her coming undone beneath him snapped the last of his control.

He thrust once, twice, then buried himself as deep as he could go. Pleasure slammed through him, white-hot and blinding. He came hard, groaning her name into the curve of her neck while the low music from his playlist still pulsed softly in the background, mixing with the sound of her gasping and the frantic beat of his own heart.

For a long moment afterward, the only sounds in the room were their ragged breaths and the quiet music.

Hyder stayed inside her, holding her close and pressing soft kisses to her damp skin as the reality of what had just happened settled in.

She was here. In his bed. In his arms.

For the first time, he let himself think about what it would mean if she stayed with him. Not just for the night.

Forever.

TWENTY-SIX

Sola

Sola woke wrapped in warmth, the kind that made it very difficult to remember why she ever bothered getting out of bed at all. Her body was loose in a way that felt earned, her mind drifting just beneath the surface of sleep as sunlight pressed faintly against her closed eyelids. For a long moment she simply stayed there, suspended between dreaming and waking, content to exist in the quiet, steady rhythm of breath that was not entirely her own.

Then she realized there was weight at her middle, a heavy arm draped across her, anchoring her in place, pulling her back against something solid and very, very warm, the heat of it curling along the length of her spine. Behind her, she could feel the broad plane of a chest, the slow rise and fall of it against her back, the subtle shift of muscle under skin that was very much alive, and very much not something she was used to waking up to.

There was the sound too. It was soft and steady. Not the quiet hum of a New York morning filtered through walls and distant traffic, but something else entirely. A low, almost contented snore, just enough to register, just enough to remind her again that she was not alone.

That she had not been alone all night.

Her lashes fluttered, her body shifting just slightly as awareness continued its slow climb upward, and she let her eyes open at last.

The first thing she saw was thick, dark beams stretching overhead, speaking of something built to last through winters that she was only just beginning to understand. A wide dresser stood against the far wall, heavy and practical, a big leather chair draped with clothing that was decidedly not hers.

It clicked. This was not her room. She was not in her bed. This was not her life.

She went still, refusing to breathe. Because she knew exactly where she was. And more importantly…who she was with.

"*Mierda*," she finally breathed as her eyes flicked toward the clock on the bedside table.

9:30.

Her entire body jerked before she could stop it.

Normally, by now, she would already be dressed, already halfway through her morning, already moving through patients and charts and the constant urgency of her work, her mind running three steps ahead of everything else. Instinct kicked in immediately, her thoughts scrambling, pulling up her schedule, mentally flipping through appointments.

She stopped just as suddenly.

Saturday.

The clinic was closed. The realization eased some of her panic, though not entirely. Because even if she was not late for work, there were still other things to consider.

August.

Her son was absolutely awake by now. There was no version of the morning where he was still asleep at this hour, not unless something was wrong, and the thought alone had her heart stuttering for a fraction of a second before logic returned and told her that no, he was fine, he was home, he was with Lucia.

Lucita.

Ah. That was a different problem entirely. There was also no universe in which Sola would be able to walk through that front door unnoticed. No careful slipping inside, no quiet retreat to her room, no avoiding the knowing gaze of her mother and the inevitable clucking tongue and admonishment that would follow.

With exaggerated care, Sola began to shift, inching forward, testing the weight of the arm draped over her waist, trying to slide out without waking the man attached to it.

It was not easy. Hyder did not so much sleep as he occupied space, his body relaxed in a way that still managed to feel substantial, his limbs loose but heavy, his presence undeniable even in stillness.

It took longer than she liked, but eventually, she managed. Free, she paused, turning just slightly to look back at him.

Hyder lay sprawled across the bed, one arm now stretched out where she had been, his chest and arms bare, his breathing deep and even, his lips parted just enough to let out that same soft, almost boyish snore. There was something disarmingly unguarded and innocent about him, like this.

She scoffed at herself, folding her arms loosely across her chest. Because there was nothing innocent about Hyder King. Not even a little.

Her mind, entirely unhelpful, supplied her with images of the night before. Vivid and erotic, her body remembering before she could stop it, heat curling low in her belly as sensation followed thought.

Once had not been enough. Not for either of them.

They had found each other again, and then again after that, as though the weeks of tension that had built between them had finally snapped, leaving nothing but instinct and want in its wake. She had never experienced anything quite like it, not in all her years, not in all her carefully compartmentalized encounters that had always been clear and exactly what she said they were.

Last night had not been that.

It was...

She cut the thought off before it could finish forming, knowing it was not helpful.

Still.

She could admit, at least to herself, that it had not been just about release. Though, to be fair, the release had been...impressive.

Her mouth twitched. Last night had proved to her that it was not just about the motion of the ocean. The size of the boat definitely had something to recommend it.

And the stamina.

Dios mío.

There had been a moment, somewhere in the middle of the night, or perhaps early this morning, when she had pushed at his shoulders, breathless and overwhelmed, insisting that she could not possibly come again.

Then she had. He made sure of it.

Now, standing there, her body pleasantly sore in places she had not even realized could ache quite like this, she found herself wondering something that unsettled her far more than she wanted to admit.

Could she ever go back? To anything less than *that*?

With another man?

The unwelcome idea hit her like a sudden jolt, her brows drawing together as she took a step back.

It was ridiculous, utterly ridiculous. She and Hyder had not made any promises to one another. They were not in a relationship. They had not even had a conversation about what this was.

They had one night.

One very...thorough night.

That was it.

So why did the thought of being with another man suddenly feel...wrong? Like losing something she hadn't agreed to want.

Sola shook her head once, sharply, and frowned, forcing herself to turn away. She scanned the room for her clothes, gathering them quickly and quietly, dressing with efficient movements that spoke to years of practice.

She knew, logically, that leaving without saying goodbye was not her best move. It was, in fact, the move of a coward. But she also knew herself well enough to understand that if she stayed, if she looked at him, if she saw those eyes open and that mouth curve into that easy, lopsided grin...she might not leave at all. She might just crawl back into the bed and ask for more.

Fully dressed, she slipped toward the door, easing it open, holding her breath as she closed it behind her, and then, barefoot and silent, she made her way down the stairs.

The Lodge, of course, was no longer empty.

Sterling was at the kitchen island, leaning back with a mug of coffee in hand, Charlie perched on a stool beside him with a bowl of something that looked suspiciously like oatmeal and a deeply unimpressed expression on her face, while Willow stood at the stove, stirring something that smelled far too good for Sola's current state of mind.

Three heads turned at once. Followed by a shocked silence.

"Oh...," Sterling said finally, his mouth twitching as his gaze flicked from her face to her disheveled hair and back again. "Well, good morning, Doc."

Charlie's eyes lit up, her grin entirely too delighted. "Look who decided to join us for breakfast. We have glue in a bowl."

Willow didn't say anything at first. She just looked at Sola. Really looked. Then one brow arched slowly.

Sola straightened her shoulders, lifting her chin with as much dignity as she could muster, which, considering the circumstances, was not nearly enough.

"I...have to go," she said, already edging toward the mudroom, reaching for her coat.

Sterling snorted. "Do you, though? Because I feel like we've missed a good story here."

"Sterling," Charlie said mildly.

He held up both hands. "What? I'm just saying. It wasn't my room she was sneaking out of."

"Do you need a ride?" Charlie cut in brightly, enjoying herself far too much. "Because I'm pretty sure Sutton is heading into town anyway, and I would hate for you to…what's the phrase…walk of shame?"

Sola shot her a look, because her words hit too close to home.

"There is no walk of shame."

"Oh, honey," Charlie said sweetly, "there absolutely is. I know, because I've been there!"

Sola shoved her arms into her coat. "I'm leaving."

"Smart," Willow finally chimed in, nodding once. "Before he wakes up."

That made Sola pause, just for a fraction of a second. Then she grabbed her keys and fled.

The cold hit her like a slap, clearing her head just enough to let her breathe again as she hurried toward her Subaru, her thoughts still tangled somewhere between satisfaction and something dangerously close to panic.

She could still feel him. That was the problem.

Not just in memory, not just in thought, but physically, as though her body had not quite caught up to the fact that she had left him behind, that she was no longer in his bed, no longer wrapped in his warmth. No longer had his hands holding her.

It clung to her. Pulling at her like a riptide.

And it did not fully release until she was halfway down the road, the Lodge shrinking behind her, the familiar shape of the town coming into view, giving her something safer to recognize.

By the time she parked and stepped out onto the boardwalk, she had her expression mostly under control, her shoulders squared, her breathing even.

"Morning, Doc."

Sola froze.

Galena stood just outside the café, bundled up and grinning like she had just been handed the best gossip of her entire life, Melodie beside her with a far more subtle, but no less knowing, smile.

Sola exhaled slowly. "Good morning."

Galena's eyes swept over her once, sharp and assessing. "You look...well rested."

"I am," Sola replied evenly.

"Mmhmm," Galena hummed. "I'm sure you are."

Melodie spoke softly, in that cadence that was uniquely hers, "We were just heading in for coffee, if you'd like to join us."

"No, thank you." Sola shook her head. "I have to...go home."

"Of course you do," Galena practically sang. "Wouldn't want to be late."

Sola narrowed her eyes. "Late for what?"

"Breakfast." Galena's grin widened. "With your mother."

Ah, yes. That.

"Have a good day." Sola forced a smile as she walked away before they could say anything else.

Behind her, she could hear Galena's laughter. This time Melodie joined her.

The cottage door opened easily, left unlocked, something she was still getting used to. Inside, the familiar scents of coffee and eggs and something faintly sweet that spoke of home and family.

August sat at the table, already halfway through his breakfast, his notebook open beside him, his pencil moving in precise strokes as he ate.

Lucia stood at the counter, rinsing a pan.

She turned, saw Sola, and smiled. Her expression was not one of surprise or concern, merely knowing.

Sola stopped short.

"...*Mamí.*"

"*Buenos días*, Marisolita," Lucia said lightly, as though her daughter had simply stepped out for a morning walk and not spent the night elsewhere entirely.

Sola narrowed her eyes. "You are not going to say anything?"

"What is there to say?" Lucia lifted one shoulder.

"You know exactly what there is to say."

Lucia turned back to the sink, rinsing the last of the soap away. "Sola, you are an adult. You made a choice. I trust you."

That was somehow worse than the scolding she was expecting.

Lucia dried her hands and turned back around, picking up a plate and sliding it toward her. "Sit. Eat."

Sola glared at her, but she sat.

"Thank you, *Mamí,*" she muttered.

"There is more if you are still hungry," Lucia added sweetly. "I am sure you worked up an appetite."

Sola choked slightly on her coffee.

Across the table, August did not look up, but she could see the faintest hint of a smile tugging at the corner of his mouth. Sola decided to ignore it. And to ignore her mother's obvious approval.

She ate instead. But somewhere, in the back of her mind, uninvited but persistent, she wondered what Hyder's face had looked like when he woke up. And whether he had reached for her and found...nothing.

TWENTY-SEVEN

Hyder

She did it again.

"Son of a bitch!"

The words cracked through the quiet of his room as Hyder stared at the empty space beside him like it might somehow fix itself if he looked hard enough.

It didn't.

The sheets were already cold, rumpled in a way that told the truth of what had happened there, and the faint scent of her lingered everywhere, in the cotton, in the air, in his own skin, like she had soaked into him sometime in the night and refused to leave.

But she had left. Left him with nothing but the aftermath and his own memories.

He swung his legs over to the side of the bed, dragging in a breath and letting it out slow, dropping his head forward, his elbows braced on his knees as the truth settled into him.

There was no chance, none, that he was ever going to want another woman again.

Not after that. Not after her.

Every time before, every woman he had been with, he had gone into it thinking he cared, thinking maybe this one would stick, that maybe it was something more than just convenience or timing or proximity, that maybe it was something real enough to build on.

Now he knew he'd been wrong. Because whatever he had thought those things were, whatever he had told himself they meant, none of it even came close to what last night was.

Being with Sola hadn't just been good. It had not just been intense, the kind of physical connection that left his body aching and satisfied in equal measure.

It was...complete.

That was the word that kept coming back to him, settling into his chest like it belonged there.

Complete.

Like something had finally clicked into place. And yeah, physically, she had more than held her own.

He let out a short, breathless laugh, scrubbing a hand down his face.

The woman could definitely move. His body was still paying for it, his muscles sore in places that had nothing to do with work or cold or hauling lines, and everything to do with the way she had met him, matched him, pushed back against him like she had been waiting just as long as he had.

Like it mattered. Like *he* mattered.

That was what had him sitting there, staring at the empty side of the bed, feeling something dangerously close to unease crawl under his skin. Because if he did matter to her, why was she gone again without even a word?

Groaning, Hyder pushed himself upright, his knees giving their usual protest as he shifted his weight, though not from cold, but from the kind of use they had seen the night before. He rolled his shoulders once, before glancing back over his shoulder in the mirror.

The sight of his own skin made him let out another quiet chuckle.

Long, red streaks ran down his back, thin and sharp where her nails had caught and dragged, marking him in a way that felt both ridiculous and deeply satisfying.

"Yeah," he muttered under his breath, reaching back and tracing one lightly with his fingers, wincing. "Totally worth it."

He would carry them proudly, and if he had anything to say about it, they would not be the last.

He crossed to his dresser, reaching into his drawers to pull out a pair of sweats and his oldest, most comfortable T-shirt, the faded Coast Guard one with the hole near the hem that Willow had been threatening to throw out for years.

"Not today," he muttered, dragging it over his head.

If she had survived this long, she was staying.

Dressed, barefoot, and still half caught between satisfaction and something a little more complicated, Hyder made his way toward the door, pausing for just a second with his hand on the frame, looking one last time at his bed. His empty bed.

"Great," he muttered. "Good start, King."

He blew out another breath and headed downstairs. The moment his foot hit the second-to-last step, he knew something was off, and he froze.

The Lodge had a particular kind of energy when something was about to happen, a hum just under the surface, voices layered over each other, movement that was just a little too coordinated to be accidental.

And right now? That hum was loud.

Hyder stayed where he was, bent forward, and glanced into the kitchen, so he'd hopefully have at least a few seconds to think before he had to react.

Sutton stood at the counter, his arms folded with the kind of focused precision he usually reserved for work, while Charlie sat perched on a stool nearby, a glass of milk in one hand and an expression on her face that said she was enjoying whatever was happening far more than she should.

Sterling leaned back against the far counter, already grinning like he had been waiting for this exact moment.

And Willow?

Willow stood by the stove, stirring something with entirely too much calm, her back to him.

"Well, well, well," Sterling drawled, straightening just enough to take him in properly. "Look who finally decided to come up for air."

Hyder finished stepping into the kitchen, doing his best to keep his face neutral, wondering, without asking, just when his little brother was going back up to the Slope.

"Morning," he said evenly, reaching past Sutton to grab a mug.

"Is it?" Charlie asked sweetly, tilting her head as she looked him over. "Because you look like a man who has had a very long night."

Sutton snorted under his breath.

Willow still didn't turn around to look at him. She kept stirring as if whatever was in the pot had personally offended her. Which, if he'd learned nothing else over the years, meant that she was worried about something.

"Coffee's fresh," she said softly.

Hyder poured it, took a long sip, and leaned back against the counter like he had all the time in the world.

"Appreciate it."

Sterling let out a low whistle.

"Wow," he said, glancing around at the others. "He's not even trying to deny that he bumped uglies with the doc."

"There is nothing to deny," Hyder replied, then grimaced. "And don't call it that."

That earned him a full laugh from Sterling.

"God, I love this," he said, pushing off the counter. "I've lost count of the number of times you guys have called me on the carpet for this exact thing."

Sutton grunted, then turned to Sterling, the implied shut-up almost louder than if he'd actually said it.

Sterling raised his hands in surrender, and stepped back, but his look suggested he was nowhere near done giving Hyder shit.

"Where is she?" Hyder finally asked, looking around just in case.

"Home." Charlie's smile softened just slightly. "She left about fifteen minutes ago."

Sterling winced theatrically. "Ouch, that's gotta hurt."

"Sterling," came another warning from Sutton.

"What?" Sterling lifted both hands again. "Listen, you could all do with some of my extensive knowledge about women. And I'm just saying, historically speaking, when a woman leaves before you wake up—"

"It's not!" Hyder interrupted him. He exhaled and shook his head again. "It's not like that."

"Hmmm," Willow still did not turn around. "Isn't it?"

Hyder narrowed his eyes at the back of her head.

Et tu, my sister?

"Wills."

Now she turned, one brow lifting as she studied him. "What?"

He held her gaze for a second, then sighed.

"It wasn't just a casual thing. Not like the *encounters* of others in this family. It meant something."

Sterling coughed, not the least bit ashamed to know Hyder meant him and that everyone else knew too.

The rest of the room quieted. Sutton watched him for a moment longer, then nodded once.

"All right. But just so we're clear," Sutton went on, his voice edged in a way that meant he was choosing his words carefully, "she's not just anyone."

Hyder's jaw tightened.

"I know that."

"She's the only doctor we've got, and she's a damn good one," he added, glancing briefly toward Charlie as if to prove his point. "People are already counting on her. Not just for scrapes and coughs either."

"I know," Hyder repeated as he leaned back against the counter. "You think I don't know that?"

Charlie tilted her head, suddenly less amused, watching him with a soft, patient look that somehow managed to be tougher to take than one of Sutton's scowls. He could only imagine how it must work for her students.

"She's got a whole life tied up in her," she reminded him gently, one hand resting over her belly without thinking about it. "You can't mess with that unless you're sure."

"I'm not," he said immediately, pushing off the counter now, his shoulders squaring as he looked between them. "That's what I'm trying to say. I'm not. I want that life too."

Sterling's face suddenly lost its amusement.

"Man," he muttered, glancing toward Willow. "He's serious."

"Obviously," Willow shot back, though her eyes never left Hyder's face, searching him, weighing something only she could see.

"Listen, guys. I don't know what she's thinking yet," he admitted, and there was no defensiveness in it now, just honesty. "Hell, I don't even know if she's thinking about it at all. She might have woken up this morning and decided last night was a mistake, or that it was just something that happened. She certainly left in a hurry."

Willow was still looking at him, but her shoulders had softened just a fraction.

"But?" she prompted gently, knowing he wasn't done.

Hyder laughed quietly, shaking his head like he couldn't quite believe himself.

"But I know what it was for me," he said, lifting his gaze again. "And it wasn't just the one night. I want all the nights."

Sterling leaned forward slightly, his interest sharpening.

"Man, you got it bad…"

Hyder held his brother's gaze for a moment, then looked at all of them in turn, making sure they were all listening before he said what he needed to say.

"I want to marry her."

Willow's lips parted slightly and Charlie went very still. Sterling blinked, once, like he hadn't quite processed it yet.

And Sutton? Sutton didn't move at all for a moment, then suddenly, a huge grin broke out across his face.

"Well," he finally said, glancing at Charlie, then back at Hyder. "It took you long enough."

Hyder's own grin was less convincing, because he knew it was not just up to him. Now he needed to figure out a way to explain to Sola that she should get over all her old notions about getting married *and* stop running away from him in the morning. He still needed to have patience.

"Okay," Willow's voice brightened suddenly, her entire posture changing like someone had flipped a switch. She set the spoon down and wiped her hands on a towel, turning fully toward him now with a look that Hyder knew very, very well.

It was the look she got when she had already decided something and was about to drag the rest of them along with her. Hyder narrowed his eyes, concerned. He wasn't sure if he wanted his family to be a part of asking Sola or if he wanted to figure it out himself. Not that he wouldn't appreciate their efforts, but he was worried that all their...*Kingness* might make things worse.

"If that's where we're at," she continued before he could stop her, "what can we do to help?"

TWENTY-EIGHT

Sola

She was annoyed and had been for more than two weeks. Which made absolutely no sense, and she knew it.

Sola sat at her desk in the clinic, flipping through a chart she had already read twice, her pen tapping lightly against the paper in a rhythm that matched the irritation sitting just beneath her skin. A feeling she couldn't quite justify but also couldn't seem to shake, no matter how many times she told herself she was being ridiculous.

Because it was ridiculous. Hyder had not done anything wrong. Absolutely nothing. And that was the problem.

He hadn't pushed, hadn't asked for more, hadn't cornered her with questions or expectations or any of the things she'd been so sure she would have to deal with after that night. Which meant she had *nothing* to push back against.

He had simply...continued to show up. In the way he always did. With his big, genuine, lopsided grin and those deep blue eyes always lighting up when he saw her, bringing his bright, relentless sunshine energy that somehow managed to make even the most chaotic day feel a little easier.

And for some reason, that was what was bothering her.

She pressed her lips together, setting the chart aside and leaning back in her chair, staring up at the ceiling as if it might offer some kind of explanation for the mess her brain seemed determined to make out of something that, logically speaking, should have been simple.

They had slept together again since that night.

More than once, now.

The first was a few nights later, when she had been alone at the clinic, long after she should have gone home, doing inventory she did not actually need to do, just so she could avoid thinking too much.

He had shown up. With coffee and snacks.

"Don't tell me." She did not even stop what she was doing at first, her voice dry even as something in her chest tightened at the sight of him in the doorway. "You just happened to be passing by."

He'd shrugged, leaning one shoulder against the frame, holding out the cup like it was the most normal thing in the world.

"It's Alpenglow," he said simply.

For some reason, that had been enough of an explanation, and enough of an incentive for them to end up on her desk, ripping clothes off.

Then there was the truck, about a week ago.

Her tire had gone down halfway between the clinic and the village. She stood there glaring at it like that alone might fix it, debating her options before finally pulling out her phone and sending a message to Willow, asking for a ride.

Which had apparently been a mistake. Because Hyder was the one who showed up.

She could still see the way he'd climbed out of his truck, his expression shifting from concern to something else the moment he saw her face.

"You okay, Sola?" he'd asked.

"It's just the tire," she'd explained, crossing her arms like that might somehow make the situation less irritating. "I had it checked last week when it seemed a little low."

"Mmhmm." He'd crouched down, running his hand along the edge of it. "Well, it's flat."

She could not refrain from rolling her eyes.

"Thank you for that very helpful observation."

He'd glanced up, that one corner of his mouth lifting.

"You're welcome." Then he stood, motioning to his truck. "Let's go. I'll come back later with a new tire."

Then, somehow, they'd ended up on the side of the road, proving that one was never too old for sex in a car. If you put in the effort, watched your head, and didn't stop to think about why you shouldn't.

She pressed her fingers to her temple now, dragging in a breath.

That was the problem. None of it had required thought. It had all just happened. And now here she was, sitting in her clinic, annoyed because he had not asked her for anything more. Not even a date or a heavy, awkward conversation.

He just showed the fuck up. He accepted every dinner invitation her mother extended, seemingly infatuated with Lucia's arroz con pollo. Which perhaps was the most annoying part of all of this. Night after night, he would sit at *her* table, laugh with Gus, let Lucia pile food onto his plate like he was starving and couldn't possibly get food anywhere else.

Then he left. With no expectations. No pressure. No...anything. Not even a kiss goodnight.

"Unbelievable," she muttered under her breath, pushing back from the desk and pacing across her small office before turning back again, her mind churning.

What exactly did she want him to do? Corner her? Demand something? Ask her where this was all going?

If she was being honest, she didn't even know the answer to that herself. Yet something about the fact that he was not asking bothered her more than it would have if he had.

"Okay, that's enough," she grumbled out loud, shaking her head as she grabbed her coat and shut her office door behind her. She would just go home, have a hot bubble bath, go to sleep early, and maybe by tomorrow she would be over it.

"Absolutely not."

Sola stopped in her tracks, her coat barely half on.

"What?"

Galena did not even look up from the papers she was sorting, her expression one of complete certainty as she continued writing something down, her voice carrying that matter-of-fact tone that meant she had already decided this was not a discussion, merely an actuality.

"You're going," she said, like it was obvious.

"Where?"

Galena finally looked up, giving her a look that suggested Sola had just asked the most ridiculous question imaginable.

"To *Yéik*," she said slowly. "Obviously."

Sola stared at her. For the last week she had heard everyone talking about making the run up Mount Raven to see the aurora tonight. For Yéik Fest. She even remembered when Hyder told her, on their first date, how important this night was to the villagers. But never once had she considered going with them. For one reason, it was too cold up there. And for another, she didn't need to be reminded of Hyder any more than she already was.

"I don't think so."

Galena's brows lifted.

"Oh, I do."

Sola laughed, crossing her arms.

"You're very confident for someone who has absolutely no authority over me."

Galena shrugged.

"Maybe." She set her pen down and leaned back slightly. "But I do have the advantage of knowing how this place works, and right now, it works like this: you don't go, people notice."

Sola rolled her eyes. "I'm pretty sure they'll survive."

"Mmhmm," Galena tilted her head. "The town? Probably. Your reputation? Not so much."

"My reputation?" Sola repeated, incredulous.

"Yes." Galena nodded once. "Because this is one of those things. One of those...Alpenglow rites of passage, I guess you could call it. You're young enough, strong enough, and new enough. Everyone is watching to see if you'll do it."

Sola scoffed. "That's ridiculous."

"Is it?" Galena asked mildly, her mouth twitching before she conceded. "Maybe you're right. But if you don't go, the elders will absolutely judge you."

Sola snorted. "I think I can live with that."

"Can you?" Galena asked, now leaning forward slightly. "Because Koyuk will definitely have opinions, and I'm just saying, you really don't want to be on the receiving end of those."

Sola paused.

Damn it.

Her mind immediately went to the older man, to the careful way he spoke, the quiet authority he carried, the trust he had slowly placed in her as she worked on his hands.

The thing was, she *didn't* want him to think less of her.

"Plus," Galena added casually, like she had not just landed a solid hit, "the rest of us will think you're just chicken."

Sola narrowed her eyes. "Do you really think calling me a chicken is going to work?"

Galena shrugged, entirely unbothered.

"Maybe not," she conceded. "But if that doesn't, I can always start clucking at you every time you walk into a room. Maybe flap my arms a little."

Sola tried not to laugh and failed. "You wouldn't."

"Oh, I would." Galena grinned. "I'm nothing if not consistent."

Sola shook her head, already losing the battle. "You're absurd."

"And you're going," Galena shot back.

Sola exhaled slowly, trying to come up with another reason, besides the truth, that would get her out of this. In the end, she decided Marisol Rivera-Kelly was no chicken.

"Fine," she muttered. "I'll go."

Galena beamed.

"I knew you would. I believe a new snowsuit was already delivered to your cottage earlier today."

The ride up to the igloo was not the same as last time. For one thing, it was far colder than anything she had willingly subjected herself to in the past, the air cutting through even the extra base layers she had piled on. And she was holding on to Micah, her arms wrapped around his middle as they followed the others along the trail in a single long line.

Not Hyder.

Not because she'd chosen it, but Hyder had simply not been there when they left, so he wasn't an option.

Which, fine. Bien.

It was not like she cared.

Micah shouted something over his shoulder, his voice barely audible over the engine, and she leaned closer instinctively, catching only part of it before nodding anyway, her cheek brushing briefly against his back as the machine dipped and climbed over the uneven terrain.

The trees blurred past, dark shapes against the snow, the trail winding as the air grew thinner, the world opening up as they climbed higher.

It was beautiful in a stark, unforgiving kind of way.

They pulled up near the igloo, the machines slowing one by one as people began to dismount, laughter and voices carrying through the cold air as everyone gathered, stamping their feet, adjusting gloves, shaking out stiffness and cold.

Sola slid off behind Micah, her legs protesting slightly as she steadied herself, pulling her gloves off as she followed him into the igloo and looked around.

Then, there he was.

Hyder.

Standing just off to the side, his gear already half off like he'd been there for a while, his hair pushed back, his grin easy as he spoke to Tala, something comfortable in the way he stood there, completely at home in this place. Unlike Sola, who couldn't stop picturing him the way he was the last time they were there.

His gaze shifted and found her, and he paused. Then, nothing. Just the same steady, calm look as he nodded once and went back to his conversation.

Sola's jaw tightened.

"*Bien,*" she muttered under her breath.

Totally fine.

The space inside the igloo quickly became crowded with people shrugging off top layers, laughter bouncing off the curved walls as everyone jostled for space by the tiny wood stove, the easy camaraderie settling around her whether she wanted it to or not.

Someone bumped into her with a muttered, "Move your giant boots, Micah! You're taking up half the dome," while another voice shot back, "That's because he *has* giant boots, Cheryl had to order them special."

Micah laughed and shouted, "You know what they say about big boots!"

Sola didn't even pause.

"Yes," she began dryly, "that there's no statistically significant correlation, and anyone who believes otherwise probably has a small penis."

There was a beat of silence, then Tala barked out a laugh.

"Oh my God," she said, pointing at Micah. "Doc just mad burned you, bro."

Micah shook his head, grinning despite himself.

"Wow. That felt targeted."

Sola finally looked up, one brow lifting slightly.

"You opened the door, *mi amigo*," she smiled.

"Yeah," Tala added, still full-belly laughing, "and she closed it on your ass. Hard."

Willow came over then and handed her snowshoes.

"Here," she said. "You'll need these."

Sola took them, staring like they might bite.

"Great."

Willow grinned.

"You'll be fine," she said. "Just don't step on yourself."

"Helpful," she grumbled as she crouched, trying to make sense of the straps, her fingers already clumsy because they were still cold.

"You're doing it backwards," Tala said, not even looking at her.

"I am not," Sola shot back, immediately defensive.

Tala finally glanced down, took one look, and grinned.

"Doc...you're absolutely doing it backwards. The wide end is at the front."

Micah leaned down, helping without making a big deal of it. "Don't worry. First time I wore these I walked straight into a tree drift and disappeared."

"That makes me feel significantly worse, not better," Sola muttered.

Tala clapped her hands once, drawing everyone's attention.

"All right, peeps," she called. "Time to move. Remember, don't leave the line, and if you need to turn back...well then, you're a great big puss—er, loser."

Groans and laughter echoed off the dome. Clearly this was something they'd all heard before.

"But for reals," Tala's voice got serious, "if you do need to come back, no one goes alone."

Everyone shifted, zipping their snowsuits back up, tugging on gloves and hats and face covers again, filing toward the door in a loose line.

Sola followed, adjusting the straps on her feet now that they were facing the right way, her movements slow, the weight of the snowshoes unfamiliar as she stepped out into the cold again.

The climb was challenging. There was no other word for it. Sola took deliberate, awkward steps, the snow resisting her, the incline just enough to make her legs burn and tremble as they moved upward in a steady line, the only sound the crunch of snow and the occasional voice breaking through the quiet wind.

Her breath came faster, loud in the cold, her heart pounding.

Somewhere in the back of her mind, she was already questioning every decision that had led her here.

"This is insane," she eventually muttered.

Someone ahead of her laughed.

"You're doing great, Doc!" Kael called out.

She wasn't, and she was beginning to regret all the days of cardio she'd skipped. But she kept going. One foot in front of the other. Until the whole group stopped. And when she lifted her head…

The sky. Madre mía!

She forgot how to breathe. It was even more spectacular than when she'd first seen it from the town square.

Light that was not light, but something alive that looked close enough to touch from this high. Shifting and flowing, almost among them, in ribbons and waves, green and violet and pink and a color she did not have a name for, stretching endlessly above them, dancing in a way that felt almost intentional, almost aware. Dancing for them, dancing around them.

Sola had no words. No way to explain the way it made her chest ache, the way it made everything else fall away for a moment. The exhaustion, the irritation, the confusion. All of it dissolving into something quiet. Until suddenly, the world was peaceful.

She stood there, unmoving, her gloved hands hanging uselessly at her sides, the pain in her legs and her labored breath forgotten as she stared, letting the light wash over her.

Then a hand slid into hers. She startled slightly, her gaze turning just enough to see Hyder standing beside her, his fingers curling around hers like it was the most natural thing in the world.

"Hi." His voice was softer, almost reverent in the face of everything around them.

She swallowed.

"Hello."

He gave her hand a small squeeze, his eyes lifting back to the sky.

"I'm glad you could make it."

TWENTY-NINE

Hyder

If anything, Sola was even more attractive when she was pissed off. Her eyes would darken in a way that made them look almost ebony, her accent would curl and deepen, and her expressive mouth would settle into a small, stubborn pout that made him want to drag her in close and kiss her until she forgot what she was mad about in the first place.

It was not a delicate kind of wanting, either. It was the kind of wanting that sat low in his gut and pulled at him until his hands itched and his jaw tightened, until he had to remind himself, sometimes more than once, that there was a difference between taking and earning.

Sola had been looking at him like that for weeks now.

At first, he had been worried it was regret. That maybe she had woken up that morning, after she had come apart in his hands and under his mouth, and decided that it had all been a mistake. A mistake brought on by attraction and maybe too much wine. He wouldn't have blamed her, not really. Her life was not simple, and neither was he, no matter how easy he tried to make things look on the surface. There was a child involved, and a mother, and a town that relied on her.

So he had done the only thing that had made sense to him. He'd been there for her.

Not with expectations or pressure, not with that unspoken demand that men sometimes carried after a night like that, as though what had been given freely was now owed again. He had no interest in being *that* man. Instead, he had shown up whenever he could make the time. Ready to eat when Lucia insisted on feeding him, with support when Gus needed it, and the simple willingness to sit and be part of their space without trying to take it over.

He wanted her to see that he could be relied on. That he was not just someone who could take her apart in the dark and leave her to put herself back together in the morning, but someone who would still be there when the lights were on and the day was long and the work was hard.

Someone who could stay and always acknowledge her existence. More than acknowledge it...celebrate it and remind her that she mattered to him more than anyone else.

It had taken him longer than he cared to admit to realize that she was not upset because she regretted him or their night together. She was mad because he was not taking her back to bed. Twice now, she had not even bothered pretending.

The first time had been at the clinic, late enough that the lights in the square had already dimmed and the rest of the town had settled in, but word had gone out that the doc was still working. He had brought her coffee, and she had barely said two words to him before her hands were on him, dragging him close, her mouth hot and impatient like she had simply decided she was done waiting.

He had not said no. He was not *that* strong of a man.

The second time had been on the side of the road, with the engine of his truck still running, the world wide open around them and not a single thought in his head that resembled restraint. She had looked at him, just looked at him, and something had snapped. She was straddling him before he could blink.

He had not said no then, either.

But both times, afterward, he had stepped back again.

Not because he didn't want more, because God knew he did, but because he wanted more than that. He wanted all of it. The mornings and the evenings and the quiet in-between moments, the weight of her beside him when they woke up, when there was nothing happening at all, with the sound of Gus in the next room and Lucia humming in the kitchen. He wanted the life that came with her, not just the heat of her body.

So he waited. And it was driving her absolutely insane.

Tonight, though, he could admit that he had been a little irritated himself.

He had hoped, maybe more than he should have, that he would be the one bringing her up to the mountain. That she would climb on his sled behind him, her arms sliding around his waist, her body pressed close to his as they cut through the trees, and that the ride itself would be enough to bring back the memory of their first night up there. The way she had looked at him through the glow of the fire and the lights, the way her breath had fogged the glass, the way she had said his name like it meant something.

Instead, he'd been sent ahead to get the igloo prepared. Not even asked, really. It had just been assumed. Sutton had done it the last two winters, but this year he had shaken his head, one hand resting on Charlie's shoulder in that absent, protective way of his, and said he was not leaving her alone all night. Hyder hadn't argued. There was nothing to argue about. Of course, Sutton would stay, and someone else would go ahead. And of course, that someone would be him.

He'd come up early, started the fire, checked the stove twice for good measure, adjusted the lights and made sure everything was ready and warm, and then stood there like an idiot, staring out through the glass as the minutes stretched longer than they should have.

More than half an hour by his count.

Long enough that he started pacing, then forced himself to stop pacing, then went back to the door just in case he had somehow missed them. Which would be impossible because twenty snowmachines coming at him made a lot of noise.

When he finally heard the growling sound bouncing off the trees and the long line of machine headlights came into view, his chest tightened, catching him off guard before he even had time to think about it.

She was on the back of Micah's machine. A wide-track touring sled, one of those long, stable ones that rode smooth and steady even when the trail got uneven. It made sense. It was exactly the kind of machine someone would put a newcomer on.

That didn't stop the way his gut twisted when he saw her arms wrapped around Micah's waist, her helmet turned slightly as she leaned into him for balance.

It was fast, his reaction. Instant and ugly, though he shook it off almost as fast, because it was absurd. She had to come up with someone, and he had not been there, and Micah was safe and not a threat to anything except maybe the last piece of Cheryl's apple pie if it was left unattended for too long.

Still, the image stuck with him longer than he liked, while he waited inside for her.

Then their eyes met, and everything else disappeared. Except her frustration, which nearly made him laugh out loud and he seriously considered rushing over, sweeping her into his arms, and kissing her.

Instead, he'd walked behind her the whole way up, there in case she needed help, or if she decided she couldn't make it and wanted to go back. He should have known she was too stubborn not to get to the top. And when she got there, her face changed again, filled with something he could only describe as astonishment and wonder. It softened her in a way nothing else did, stripped away the sharp edges she normally carried, leaving her wide open.

He got it. He'd been coming up for *Yéik* since he was seven and had watched the lights his whole life. Seen them every winter, in every kind of weather, had watched them stretch across the sky like they belonged there, like they had always been there. They had never felt new to him.

Until now.

Until he saw them reflected in her dark eyes.

Until he slipped his hand into hers and felt her fingers curl around his like she had made a choice without saying it out loud, like she was standing there in the cold and the dark and deciding, maybe without even realizing it, that she was alright with him being there.

He squeezed her hand, just a little, and when she squeezed back without hesitation, something relaxed inside him that had been restless for weeks.

Maybe it was the magic of the lights. Maybe it was just her. Either way, he was not going to waste it.

Because he had a plan.

If he tried to explain that plan to anyone outside of his family, they would have thought he had lost his mind completely. Even some of his family had looked at him like he might have finally tipped over into something unfixable when he first laid it out, though to their credit, they had not said no. They had laughed, of course, because that was what they did, because there was no version of this where Tala did not make at least three inappropriate comments and Willow did not immediately start rearranging things in her head to make his plan better.

But they were helping.

Every spare moment he had, every hour that was not already claimed by the Lodge or the boats or the endless list of things that needed doing in a place like Alpenglow, or when he was not spending time with Sola and her family, he had been working on it. Hauling and clearing, asking for favors he would be paying back for the next six months.

Somehow, it was all coming together.

Tonight, though, was not about that. Tonight was about this. About standing at the edge of something bigger than himself and feeling, for once, like he was not just passing through it, but sharing it. And about the sound of the others around them, the quiet laughter and the steady crunch of movement in cold snow that meant no one was alone, not really, not ever. Not in Alpenglow.

244

it. And about the sound of the others around them, the quiet laughter and the steady crunch of movement in cold snow that meant no one was alone, not really, not ever. Not in Alpenglow.

THIRTY

Sola

For years, Sola had tried many things to find some semblance of inner peace.

There had been a stretch in her mid-twenties where she paid an alarming amount of money to sit in a dimly lit studio in SoHo while a guy with a man bun and quest onable hygiene told her to "release her attachments to the material world." Which would have been more convincing if he had not been wearing sneakers that cost more than her rent and food budget at the time. There had been a meditation app, which she abandoned after three days because the calm British voice kept reminding her to breathe as though she might forget. Then there had been a brief flirtation with sound baths in Brooklyn, where she had spent an hour lying on a mat while someone struck a gong and she tried very hard not to think about her mounting student loans. And failed.

Yoga had been the only thing that had ever really stuck.

Or at least, the only thing she had found a way to keep doing, though even she could admit that her dedication had less to do with enlightenment and more to do with stubbornness. She did not like quitting things, especially when she had paid for them, and especially when she was not immediately good at them. Over time, though, it had become something more. A place where her mind could, if not quiet down completely, at least stop shouting at her for a little while.

Unfortunately, since arriving in Alpenglow, yoga had slipped out of her routine.

There was always something else to do. A patient who needed her. A medical supply order that had gone wrong. Storms that required preparation. A child with a cough. An elder with pain. The flu and TB testing. Work and life had filled every available space, and she had let it, because that was what she did.

But ever since that night on the ridge, standing beneath the aurora with her hand in Hyder's, she had missed that feeling. That strange, steady calm that had settled over her, not because she had forced it, but because it had simply...happened.

"I was thinking," she casually mentioned to Willow as they walked around the co-op, smelling all the new soaps and lotions, "maybe I could start a yoga class. Up at the church. Nothing fancy. Just once a week."

Willow had looked at her wide-eyed, and then, like a spark catching dry kindling, the idea had taken off so quickly Sola barely had time to process it.

"Oh, we're *so* doing that!" Willow exclaimed, already reaching for her phone to make notes. "We are absolutely doing that. I'll make a sign-up sheet. No, I'll make two. One for participants and one for people who will pretend they're not interested but will show up anyway."

"I didn't say—"

"You said enough," Willow cut in brightly. "This is perfect. We need something like this. Oh, Tala is going to hate it."

"She's going to what?" Tala's voice called from across the store.

"Love it!" Willow answered without missing a beat.

Tala appeared around the corner. "I will only hate it if I have to wear stretchy pants."

"You already wear stretchy pants," Willow pointed out.

"These are functional stretchy pants," Tala argued. "Not bendy feelings pants."

Sola laughed despite herself, and just like that, her simple idea took on a life of its own. By the time she walked into the church a week later, she was not entirely sure what she had expected.

It was not...this.

There were more than twenty people already inside, from both the town and village, scattered across the wide plank floor, some standing awkwardly with rolled mats tucked under their arms, others already attempting stretches that looked less like yoga and more like they hadn't found their toes in quite some time. Another fifteen lingered along the edges, leaning against the walls or perched on the benches, clearly only there for the entertainment value.

Sola stopped just inside the door, her brows lifting slightly as she took it all in.

"This is a lot of people," she murmured under her breath.

"Welcome to Alpenglow," Galena said cheerfully beside her, already kicking off her boots. "Word travels fast. Especially when it involves the possibility of watching someone fall over in slow motion."

"I am not going to fall over," Sola returned automatically.

Galena gave her a look. "Oh, honey. I wasn't talking about you."

Sola followed her gaze.

Healy stood near the front, his beefy arms crossed over his broad chest, looking deeply suspicious of everything happening around him, including his own presence there.

"You signed up?" Sola asked, unable to keep the amusement out of her voice as she approached him.

Healy grunted. "I was told there would be stretching."

"There will be stretching."

"And that it might help my back and stiff leg."

"It might."

He considered that. "All right then."

"And," Willow added from behind him, "he said if he can balance a tray of chowders in sourdough bowls across a busy dining room, he can handle standing on one foot."

Healy snorted. "That tray's heavier than any of you, missy."

"Not me," Tala said, dropping her mat with a thud. "I've been bulking."

"You've been eating," Willow corrected.

"Same difference. Don't be jelly over my winter weight."

Sola pressed her lips together, trying, and failing, not to smile as she moved toward the front of the room.

"Okay," she called to get everyone's attention, her voice carrying far more confidence than she felt. "So. Full disclosure. I've never taught a yoga class before."

A ripple of laughter moved through the room.

"Good," Melodie called. "We've never taken one."

Sola took a breath, letting it out slowly, grounding herself the way she had been taught.

"Okay. Let's start simple. Everyone find a space, unroll your mats, and try not to hit your neighbor. That is step one."

"Already failed that," Micah said, elbowing Dan in the ribs.

"You're too close," Dan muttered.

"You moved," Micah argued.

"Gentlemen," Sola said dryly, "if you could save the territorial disputes for later, that would be great."

They quieted, though not without a few lingering mutters, and slowly, somewhat chaotically, the room began to settle. What followed could only loosely be described as yoga.

There were moments, brief and shining, where everything aligned, where people stood steady, breathing in unison, and where Sola could almost pretend she knew what she was doing.

And then there were the other moments.

"Why is my leg doing that?" Tala demanded, wobbling aggressively.

"Because you're trying to balance," Sola replied.

"I don't like it."

"Then stop trying to fall," Willow quipped.

"You're not helping." Tala grimaced, windmilled her arms, then fell.

Across the room, Healy stood in what was, to Sola's surprise, a nearly perfect tree pose, one foot pressed firmly against his calf, his arms steady as his hands came down to prayer, his face solemn as his eyes closed.

"Well, I'll be damned," Willow murmured, staring at him. "Healy, you're actually good at this."

Healy opened one eye. "Told you. Years of balancing trays."

Then there was Hyder.

Sola did her best not to stare at him. And failed. Spectacularly.

He moved through the poses with an ease that was not fair, his balance steady, his body controlled. There was no stiffness in him or hesitation, just a quiet concentration that made something low in her belly tighten. Unfortunately, now was not a time for her to jump him.

"Focus," she muttered under her breath.

"I am focused," Galena whispered back beside her.

"Not you."

"Oh..." Galena did not bother to whisper again, but was in fact very, very loud. "Him."

Sola shot her a look.

Galena shrugged, completely unrepentant.

Sola turned away, heat creeping up her neck as she moved them into the next position, deliberately placing herself where she could not see him.

It didn't help. Because she could still feel him.

When the class finally came to an end, there was a collective exhale, a mix of relief and satisfaction that filled the room as people stretched, laughed, and compared notes on who had fallen over the most.

"That was...not terrible," Tala finally admitted.

"I'm exhausted," Micah added.

"You only did two poses," Dan pointed out. "Over and over. The down dog thing and the mountain."

Sola laughed, the sound coming easier now, her body loose in a way she had not felt in weeks. Maybe it was not the calm she had been chasing. But it was something.

As she rolled up her mat, she became aware of him again.

Hyder.

He was watching her, that familiar grin tugging at his mouth, and when their eyes met, it hit her fast, that same pull she had been trying hard to ignore.

"Good class," he said, stepping closer.

"Thanks," she replied, hoping her voice sounded steadier than she felt. "You have pretty good balance and flexibility. Have you done yoga before?"

He shook his head. "Nah. But if you don't have balance on deck, you're pretty much gonna be taking a dunk into the Sound."

"Ah," she said, a smile slipping through. "That makes sense, I guess."

They fell into step together as they headed out, the chatter of the others surrounding them as people called goodbyes and made plans for the next class.

"Well..." he let the word drift off, shoved his hands into his pockets as they reached the path through the town square that split, one way to parking, the other to the clinic. "I gotta go. But I was wondering...you wanna come by this evening? Gus has another lesson. Figured you might want to see how he's doing. You could even put on your suit and join us."

She hesitated, just for a second. Not because she didn't want to, but because she did, and after having him witness her emotional breakdown the last time she'd seen him teaching her son, she was not sure if she was ready.

He didn't push. He just waited while her mind sifted through everything.

"Yeah," she agreed finally. "I think I'd like that."

His grin deepened, just slightly, then he nodded.

"All right. I'll see you later, Doc."

"Later," she echoed, watching him walk away, hearing a little whistle coming from him.

The clinic hours moved quickly.

Nobu was first, shuffling in with far more ease than he had a few weeks ago, though he still carried himself carefully, as though he did not entirely trust his own body yet.

"You're improving," Sola told him, her hands firm but gentle as she worked through the familiar sequence of adjustments, guiding his spine into alignment, feeling the subtle shifts beneath her fingers.

"Because I listen," Nobu replied.

"Now you listen."

He grinned.

"I listened before. Just...selectively."

She smiled back, despite herself.

"That is not the same thing."

Koyuk followed, his hands weathered and still stiff, though the exercises she had given him were helping.

"You're cheating, Koy," she told him mildly, watching the way he favored one side.

"I'm adapting," he countered. "Adaptation is what has kept me on this earth so long."

Sola didn't have an answer for that, so she just let it go.

Cheryl came in with Kenai next, her grandson squirming under Sola's examination with the kind of energy that suggested he had been up since dawn and had way too much sugar.

"He's fine," Sola assured her, finishing up. "Healthy and strong. But he is ready for his first dose of the HPV vaccine."

Cheryl blinked, surprised. "HPV vaccine? At his age? What on earth for?"

Sola smiled gently as she peeled off her gloves. "It protects against the HPV virus, which is very common and can cause several types of cancer later in life, including in men. We start the series around ages 9 to 11 because it works best before any possible exposure. It's safe, quick, and part of the routine schedule now for both boys and girls."

Cheryl still looked uncertain. "I've never heard of giving it to boys..."

"It's been recommended for years," Sola replied calmly. "One less thing to worry about down the road. We can do it today if you're comfortable, or schedule it for later."

In the end, she had Galena print off some information, and Cheryl had begrudgingly taken it. Though Sola was sure she was going to hear about it later. Something about how the new doctor was trying to treat little boys for STDs.

She had a few more patients come in to have their TB tests read, though thankfully the situation had not spiraled into the kind of outbreak Sola had quietly feared in the first days after Elim's diagnosis. So far, only two additional cases tested positive, both caught early enough that neither patient had developed symptoms.

Elim remained the most serious case by far, but even he was responding well to the antibiotics, his fevers finally breaking and the angry rattle in his lungs easing enough that he could move for longer stretches without exhausting himself.

For a town as small and isolated as Alpenglow, it could have been devastating. The thought had sat heavy in Sola's mind ever since Elim first came to her. Too many people living in close quarters through the long winter. Too many families sharing meals, rides, childcare, and air.

But luck, and a community that had actually listened and come in for testing, had managed to stop things before they became catastrophic. For once, she allowed herself a small breath of relief as she reviewed the next patient chart waiting on her desk, her last one of the day.

She glanced down, frowning slightly. She had been in Alpenglow for a little more than four months now and thought she'd met everyone from the town and village. Even Ambler, probably most notorious for his self-imposed isolation, had made it into the clinic once to take care of an infection in his leg.

"Galena," she called, stepping out, tapping the chart. "Who is this?"

Galena glanced up, her eyes lighting with recognition. "Oh. Whittier Harlan. Goes by Whitt."

Sola blinked. "I don't know him."

"He's from Williwaw. Runs a fishing operation. Has for...thirty, maybe forty years."

"Why is he coming here? They have a pretty good PA over there."

Galena shrugged. "Heard you're good with backs. Figured he'd see what the fuss is about."

"Huh," Sola murmured, knowing enough about the area now that she understood coming over the pass from Williwaw in winter was slow going.

Whitt Harlan looked older than his fifty-eight years. He was broad-shouldered despite a stoop in his posture, his clothes worn in a way that suggested they saw more use than care. There was a faint odor of stale whiskey rolling off him, lingering just enough to make Sola's nose wrinkle before she smoothed her expression.

"Doc," he nodded once.

"Mr. Harlan," she replied evenly. "What seems to be the problem?"

"My back," he bit out. "It's been acting up somethin' fierce lately."

"Alright. Let's take a look."

The exam was a little challenging. Whitt followed her instructions, but with a reluctance that suggested he was not used to taking directions. Especially from a woman. His responses were clipped and grumbled.

"You lift a lot?" she asked, pressing gently along his lumbar spine.

"Comes with the job," he grunted.

"And you don't ask for help."

He snorted. "Don't need it."

"You do," she explained calmly.

He eyed her for a minute. Like he was studying her, and then, unexpectedly, he barked out a short laugh.

"Maybe," he conceded. "I got me two boys, but they aren't so keen on workin' on the boats no more."

Sola gave a nod of understanding. She was coming to learn that in rural Alaska, one needed people, and when you didn't have that, life could be very hard.

By the time Whitt left, Sola had a plan in place for him to do PT at home, and a follow-up scheduled in two weeks. Whether he did either remained to be seen.

"Interesting," Galena commented after he walked out and they began cleaning up and setting up the'clinic for the next day.

"That's one word for it," Sola agreed.

Galena glanced at her, a smile spreading across her face. "So. You going up to the Lodge tonight?"

Sola sighed. "Do you ever *not* know everything?"

Galena grinned. "Nah. But to quote my favorite philosopher: 'Those who simply wait for information to find them spend a lot of time sitting by the phone. Those who go out and find it themselves have something to say when it rings.'"

Sola blinked. "And who said that exactly?"

"Dawson," Galena shrugged. "Or maybe Gilmore Girls."

Sola laughed, shaking her head. "Of course, how could I not know *that*?"

"So...," Galena pressed. "You going?"

Sola hesitated. Then nodded.

"Yeah. I'm going. But just to see Gus's progress."

"Uh huh." Galena was entirely unconvinced. "Well, make sure you make some of your own progress. Us girls are losing our patience."

Sola rolled her eyes, but she didn't argue, and when Galena left for the night, Sola realized she did not really mind the teasing or the butting in.

Well, not as much as she once had.

THIRTY-ONE

Hyder

The water lapped quietly around them, softly, echoing against the wood and glass of the natatorium. Steam curled up from the surface in thin, ghostlike ribbons, blurring the edges of everything just enough to make the world safe and contained.

Hyder kept himself afloat easily, treading water without thinking about it, his body moving on instinct as his eyes tracked Gus across the shallow end.

Back and forth. Again and again.

The kid was getting better. Not just better. Confident. Hyder could see it in the way Gus pushed off the side with more certainty, how his arms moved with purpose, how his legs had a rhythm to their kicks.

"He's getting pretty good." Hyder's voice was filled with quiet pride.

Beside him, Sola let out a soft breath, the sound almost disbelieving.

"Yeah," she said, and there was no mistaking the awe in it. "He is. I never thought he would learn."

Hyder glanced at her then, taking in the way her eyes followed Gus.

"*Mamí* and I tried," she went on, shaking her head slightly, water droplets catching in her dark lashes. "We tried everything. Classes, taking him to the Y, those little inflatable arm things that he hated and tore off before we even made it to the water. He just...wouldn't."

"Yeah," he nodded slowly. "Lucia told me."

She turned her head at that, just slightly.

"She did?"

He shrugged one shoulder. "We were talking when she first started bringing him in. She said you both gave it a hell of a shot."

Sola laughed, though it came out humorless.

"Hell of a shot," she repeated. "That's one way to put it."

Hyder watched Gus reach the edge again, slap the side of the pool with one small hand, then turn himself around for another pass.

"I think," Hyder said after a moment, "we just need to keep at it until he can do it with some noise and distractions. People moving around, ya know? Not just quiet like this."

Sola looked up at him, really looked at him this time, her brows pulling together slightly.

"What?"

"That," she gestured vaguely toward Gus, toward the whole situation. "That idea. The noise. I'm just surprised you thought about it. Most people don't."

Hyder shrugged again, though there was more behind it this time.

He had spent hours coming to that conclusion. Weeks, really. Sitting with his phone in one hand and a notebook in the other like he was cramming for a test he didn't even know how to take. Reading everything he could find, watching videos, trying to understand something that, the more he learned, the less it seemed to follow any kind of rule.

Autism.

It was like trying to map the ocean with a stick in the sand, while the waves kept coming to wipe away all you'd done.

The only thing that had stuck, the only thing that had made any kind of sense, was that line he had read over and over again.

If you meet one kid with autism, you've met one kid with autism.

There didn't seem to be a consistent pattern. No guarantees or shortcuts or manual.

There was just...Gus.

At one point he'd stopped trying to understand it like a problem to solve and started paying attention instead. Watching what worked and what didn't. When to push. When to back off. When to talk. When to shut up and just be there.

He had learned more from Gus in a week than any article had given him.

"Well," Hyder said, keeping it simple, "Gus is a good kid, Sola. I'm sure it hasn't always been easy, but he's loved. That much is clear."

Sola's expression softened at that, something in her shoulders relaxing, just slightly.

"Yeah, he is."

Hyder watched her for another beat, noticing the way that quietness didn't quite reach all the way through. There was still something there. A tension. Like she was holding herself together out of habit more than necessity.

"Sola," he murmured.

She turned toward him again, her mouth parted just slightly, and he had to remind himself that this was not the time for kissing.

"Yeah?"

He hesitated for half a second, choosing his words carefully.

"I was wondering. Any time we talk about Gus, you seem like you're worried."

He saw a shift happening in her emotions. It moved across her face in quick, flickering layers. First irritation, bitter and defensive, then something deeper, sadder, before finally settling into something that looked a lot like acceptance.

She drew in a deep breath and let it out again.

"You might be right," she admitted, and he could hear the honesty.

"I think," she went on, her gaze drifting back to Gus for a moment, "after all this time, I've lived in this constant state of worry. It's just always there. I only ever really breathe when he's home. With me. With *Mamí*. When I know he's safe."

Hyder didn't interrupt. He just listened.

"Even then," she added, her mouth tightening slightly, "there are times when something happens, and Gus will just…" She trailed off, her hand making a small, helpless motion in the water before falling still again.

Hyder swallowed. He'd seen it once, watching helplessly as Gus had folded in on himself, overwhelmed by something no one else could hear or feel. Then he saw Lucia step in without hesitation, wrapping him tight in a towel, holding him close, and murmuring soft Spanish words until the storm passed.

That had been the moment Hyder understood. It was the noise and stimulation. There was too much of it. He thought back to how he liked to be on his boat, alone, because the world was sometimes too much. For Gus, it had to be even more.

He shifted closer to her without thinking too hard about it, closing the space between them until their shoulders brushed beneath the surface. Then, slowly, he reached for her, wrapped his arms around her, and pulled her in. Her back pressed to his front. He held his breath the whole time, bracing for the possibility that she might pull away.

She didn't. Instead, she softened, almost imperceptibly at first, then fully, her body melting into his like she had been holding herself upright for too long and had finally decided to stop.

He let his chin rest lightly against the top of her head, pressing a quiet kiss there, breathing in the faint, minty scent of her hair.

"Maybe," he murmured, his voice barely more than a whisper, "there can be more safe places for Gus."

He paused, just long enough for the words to land and for her to take them in.

"And more safe people."

She leaned back then, just enough to look up at him, and their eyes met. She didn't answer him, but something passed between them anyway.

"Mom! Look!"

Sola turned immediately, instinct snapping her attention back to the pool, though she didn't push out of Hyder's arms.

Gus stood at the edge, further down, by the deep end, water dripping off him, his small chest rising and falling quickly with excitement. He pinched his nose, and jumped.

Sola tensed instantly, her body going rigid against Hyder's while she watched Gus pop back up and swim to the other side again.

Hyder leaned down slightly, his lips brushing close to her ear.

"Relax, Sola," he whispered. "He knows how to swim now."

By the time they all climbed out of the pool, Hyder was beginning to feel like maybe all the time he'd given Sola to realize he was here was beginning to work.

But he still had to do his best not to look at her. Because Sola, standing a few feet away in that bikini, the water still tracing slow paths down her skin, was a problem he did not have a solution for. Not with Gus there.

He cleared his throat, focusing instead on Gus as the kid wrapped himself in a towel.

"So," Hyder swallowed, forcing his voice back into something resembling normal, "we can't do lessons for a few days, Gus, my man. I'm sorry."

Sola's head turned toward him immediately, the question clear in her eyes.

"We've got an early season charter that flew in tonight," he explained. "I'm taking them out about fifty miles to find deeper water, first thing in the morning. Try to snag some halibut."

"It's still winter, though, no?" she asked, her tone thoughtful but edged with concern.

"Yeah," he said. "The good fishing doesn't really start until next month, but these guys are here for backcountry snowboarding and wanted to get some fishing in too."

She hesitated. "Is it safe?"

There it was again. That worry and tension in her shoulders. But this time, it wasn't for Gus. It was for him. He couldn't help the way that made him feel.

"It's safe enough," he told her. "If the weather holds, I'll take them out past the strait to Black Rock Channel. But if it starts looking dicey, I'll keep us closer and go to Eaglet Deep. We might not catch much there this time of year, but it's safer. Nearer to land."

She studied him for a moment, then nodded.

"Oh. Okay."

Hyder hesitated, then decided maybe it was time. Maybe Sola had reached a point where she was ready to start something.

"But," he added, softer now, "when I get back, and the guests head out... maybe we can go out."

She blinked. "Go out?"

He gave her a half-smile. "Nothing fancy. This is still Alpenglow after all. Maybe just drinks at the Raven. I hear Healy's got a new tequila in."

She made a face.

"Tequila is not my friend."

Hyder laughed. "No?"

"No," she said firmly. "But make it rum, and you have a deal."

His grin widened.

"Rum it is."

They walked out together, the cold air hitting them immediately and freezing their wet hair.

At her Subaru, Hyder paused, realizing he should probably just say goodnight, open her door like a gentleman, and watch her drive away.

Instead, he stepped closer, and he kissed her goodbye.

She kissed him back.

THIRTY-TWO

Sola

Ay, coño, qué feliz me siento!

Sola could not stop smiling.

It was ridiculous, really. From the moment she'd woken up that morning, when that weak but unclouded rising sun had slipped through the edge of her curtains, she had been happy. It sat under her skin, vibrated in her chest, making her want to stretch and laugh and move, as if her whole body had finally remembered what it felt like to be light.

"Ay, Marisolita!" her mother was the first to notice, as always, appearing from the kitchen as Sola stepped out of her room, tying her robe loosely at her waist. "I have the coffee in just one moment. But I think maybe you do not need it today."

Sola would normally have tried to smother her smile with a shrug, pretending she had no idea what her mother meant. But she was just too damned happy.

"Thank you, *Mamí*," she said, leaning in to press a quick kiss to her mother's cheek before giving her a side hug as she passed. "I would love some coffee."

Lucia lifted one brow, the corner of her mouth curving knowingly, but she did not ask. She didn't need to. Her mother had already woven herself neatly into the fabric of Alpenglow, especially with the older women, and those women thrived on shared stories and observations the way hummingbirds thrived on nectar.

The idea that the entire town might already know that Sola was going on another date with Hyder should have made her bristle.

It didn't.

She was just...too happy.

She took the small cup her mother handed her, the coffee dark but softened with a splash of evaporated milk and just enough sugar to take the edge off the bitterness, the way she had always liked it, and carried it back to her room.

She hit her favorite playlist, and Bad Bunny's *Estamos Bien* began to pulse through her speaker, instantly turning her room into a sun-drenched sanctuary with pure, defiant positivity. She sang along as she pulled her clothes from the closet, then she let go and spun, dancing like nobody was watching because, for once, she was exactly where she wanted to be.

When the song ended, moving to something a little softer, she finished getting dressed, pulling on thick leggings and a sweater, her thoughts drifting again and again to the night before, to the way Hyder had looked at her, to the way his mouth had felt...

She stopped herself. The joy still there, but now she was trying to contain it. At least a little.

Coffee, maybe a scone. A normal morning.

Except nothing felt normal, and maybe she didn't want it to. The singing began again.

Once she was dressed, she moved down the short hall and tapped lightly on August's door before pushing it open.

"Hey, GusGus."

He was already awake, sitting cross-legged on the bed, his hair sticking out in every direction as if he had argued with his pillow and lost. His charcoal moved steadily across the page of the large sketchbook Hyder, nisse elf extraordinaire, had given him, his attention so focused that the rest of the world barely seemed to exist.

Sola paused in the doorway, just watching him.

Even though she had watched him draw for years, she had to admit there was something different now. His lines were more confident and more deliberate. It was as if his hands were finally catching up to the complexity of his thoughts, translating what he saw in his mind with a new clarity.

"I'm heading out in a few minutes," she told him gently. "To get something sweet from the café for breakfast. Wanna come?"

He stilled. Then, after a longer pause, he nodded once and set the charcoal down carefully beside the page.

Sola's grin widened.

"Okay," she said softly, pulling the door mostly closed behind her to give him space. "Get dressed."

Her soft singing continued as she walked back into the main room.

Lucia had obviously heard them and was already shrugging into her down coat.

"You normally don't do the carbs for breakfast," her mother said lightly, adjusting her scarf. "What has changed, hmm?"

Sola just smiled again, unable to help herself, and wrapped her arms around her mother in a quick, tight hug. Even Willow would have been proud.

"Nothing," she said, entirely unconvincing.

August came rushing out moments later, passing them both without a word, shoving his feet into his boots before yanking his own coat on, his excitement unmistakable. Since discovering Healy's cinnamon rolls, he treated any mention of the café like another kid did with Disneyland.

They stepped out together, Lucia taking one of his hands, Sola the other.

The sunlight was brighter now, reflecting off the snow and water in a way that almost hurt to look at, and for a moment, everything felt perfect.

When they reached the café door, they all paused. Not because of anything they saw. Because of what they didn't. The Forget Me Not was completely empty.

"Are they closed?" Lucia asked, though the open sign hung plainly in the window.

Sola reached for the handle and turned it. It was unlocked and the door opened with a soft chime that sounded far too loud in the silence.

"Hello?"

Nothing.

The café was never empty. Not in the mornings. A thin thread of unease began to wind its way up Sola's spine, but she forced a lightness into her voice that didn't quite belong there anymore.

"Come on, GusGus," she said, taking his hand again, a little tighter this time. "Let's go over to the Raven. Maybe Healy's still working on the cinnamon rolls."

Everyone was in the Raven.

Not sitting or scattered in their usual easy clusters, eating or laughing, but gathered together in a way that immediately felt wrong. When she stepped inside, the door swinging shut behind her with a dull, echoing thud, they all turned, as if the room had been waiting for her.

Voices cut off mid-sentence, collapsing into a heavy, suffocating silence, and for a brief, suspended second, no one moved at all.

The unease shifted, clawing and curling around her ribs and squeezing tight.

"What's going on?" she asked, realizing her voice had lost all the joy it had earlier.

Sutton moved first, weaving through the gathered people, his expression set in a way she had not seen before. Not even when he was worried about Charlie and the babies.

"Sola," he stopped just in front of her. "Can you...?" His eyes flicked down briefly to where Gus stood pressed close against her side, before returning to her face, something measured settling into his features. It was obvious he needed to talk to her, but he didn't want to say anything in front of August.

She resisted immediately, especially when Gus's hand tightened on hers. Like he also realized what was happening.

"No," she said, shaking her head once, ignoring the pulse that had begun to pound in her ears. "Just tell us."

Sutton exhaled through pursed lips, running a hand through his hair, and for the first time she noticed that his fingers were not entirely steady.

"About ten minutes ago," he said, choosing each word with care, "Hyder tried to radio in."

Her stomach dropped, as if the floor beneath her had shifted without warning, and for a split second, her mind simply refused to accept that this strange moment had anything at all to do with him.

"It was garbled and quick," Sutton continued, his voice steady in a way that felt practiced, "but he said he was taking on water."

No.

Her mind rejected it instantly. She had just seen him. She had just felt him. He kissed her goodnight, and when she drove off, she saw him standing in her rearview until she made the turn toward the bridge.

"No one's been able to raise him again. Not on the radio or the SAT phone," Sutton added. "And there's fog rolling in. Fast."

Sola turned toward the windows without thinking, her gaze snapping to the bright stretch of sky beyond the glass and the sunlight turning the cove into a blinding prism.

"It looks fine," she said, her voice nearly unrecognizable now, like she was the one underwater.

"Yeah," Dutchy's voice cut in from somewhere to her right, rough and impatient, "up here it does. But it's coming in from the southwest, and it's moving quick. We've got maybe an hour before it's pea soup out there."

Movement rippled through the room then. As if Dutchy's words had reminded everyone of the urgency. Sutton spun on his heel, going back to where he was when they'd first entered. Sola saw that there was a rolled-out chart on the table and Dutchy was busy pushing one of his fingers down, tracing a path. The words Black Rock drifted over to them, and Sola vaguely remembered Hyder telling her that was where he was going today.

Gus tugged on her arm.

"Wrong."

Sola blinked down at him, her chaotic thoughts still struggling to catch up with whatever Sutton and the others were doing.

"What, *mijo*?" she murmured, still half focused on Sutton.

"Wrong," he said again, louder this time, nearly shouting.

Heads turned, the attention shifting to them again. But something in the way Gus looked up at her made her remember something else.

"They're looking in the wrong place," she said back to him, suddenly understanding what he was trying to tell her.

Dutchy overheard her and let out a short, incredulous sound, already shaking his head.

"Nah." He waved his hand back at her in dismissal. "He was headed for Black Rock. That's where he—"

"Eaglet."

The word cut cleanly through the noise as August pulled hard on her arm.

"Yes, *mijo*, I remember."

Then she turned and shouted too, not caring if anyone thought she was crazy or not, "Sutton! He didn't go there. He went to Eaglet Deep."

Sutton froze, lifting his eyes, locking his gaze onto her.

"Eaglet Deep?" he asked.

Sola nodded quickly, her heart now slamming hard enough that she could feel it in her throat.

"He said if the weather turned, that's where he would go," she said, the memory snapping into place. "You just said the fog is coming, right? He would have changed course."

Dutchy shook his head again, more forcefully this time.

"He left more'n two hours ago, girlie," he argued. "Before the sun even came up. He wouldn't have known about any fog. We only just heard about it."

"Hyder would know," Sola insisted, and Dutchy waved a dismissive hand.

"If my daughter and grandson say so, then it is so!" Lucia stepped closer to Dutchy with a deep frown, daring him to argue with her.

"Boy," Dutchy scoffed to Sutton, "Ya can't seriously be listening to all this."

But Sutton wasn't looking at Dutchy anymore. He wasn't even looking at her. He was looking at Gus.

Slowly, he came over again, lowering himself down to his haunches, bringing himself level with him, his expression shifting into something careful.

"Are you sure?" he asked.

Gus met his eyes. Not for long. Just a brief, steady connection. Then he moved over to the chart, studied it for only a few seconds and pointed at something.

Sutton straightened, following him, watching. As soon as Gus placed his finger, Sutton was already moving before anyone else knew where he was going.

"Dutchy," he called over his shoulder, "you head out toward Eaglet Deep with your boat. Now, just in case. I'm taking the Kodiak. It's close enough that I should be able to make it there and back, before that fog rolls in."

Dutchy opened his mouth, ready to argue, but whatever he saw in Sutton's face stopped him. He snapped his mouth shut, grabbed the charts and turned on his heel.

"Fine," he muttered, already moving. "But if we're wrong—"

"We're not," Sutton cut him off cleanly, already heading toward the town square door.

Both doors slammed open at once, cold air rushing in as Dutchy disappeared out toward the cove, and Sutton to where his truck was parked. With them gone, the room fractured into motion, people grabbing gear, calling out instructions, getting ready for whatever came next.

Sola didn't move. She couldn't. Her body felt rooted to the spot, her fingers locked around Gus's hand as if letting go would somehow make everything real. Right now, it was only words.

Through the windows, she saw Dutchy's trawler pull away from the dock, cutting through the water, and five minutes later, the rising whine of the yellow plane that brought her there filled the air, lifting off from the far end of the cove and banking toward open water.

Everything was happening so fast. Less than fifteen minutes ago, she'd been happy. They were going to eat baked goods and ignore the calories. Hyder was going to take her out. They had a future they had not yet talked about. Because she'd been so worried about control that she'd nearly missed what she could have, if only she reached out for it.

"Don't worry, *mijo*," she whispered, the words automatic, pulled from somewhere deep inside her where comfort for her son lived even when she did not feel it for herself. "They'll find him."

Gus stepped closer, pressing into her side.

"I know, Mom."

THIRTY-THREE

Hyder

Leaving before the light was even a hint was never easy. Hyder didn't mind, but Tala always grumbled, and the clients usually had the same glassy-eyed look, that particular expression people wore when they were questioning the choices that had brought them to a frozen dock in the dark, dressed in expensive tech gear and clutching travel mugs like coffee might save them.

At least the group he was taking out today was a little more used to roughing it than most. They were dot-commers from California, men in their late thirties who had made fortunes in things Hyder did not entirely understand, and then spent chunks of that money chasing places no one else had touched yet. Backcountry skiing and snowboarding, heli drops on glaciers, ice climbing. Apparently, the greater the inconvenience, the more they liked to brag about it afterward.

Hyder didn't exactly get it. Then again, he *liked* the water in winter, liked the silence before an icy dawn, the feeling of being one of the only people awake in the world. So perhaps everybody had their own particular brand of crazy.

The dock boards were black with cold and slick with frost crystals when he first stepped onto *The Ahnah*, his breath rising in slow white clouds. The deck lights cast shallow gold across the aluminum and gear. Enough to work by, but not enough to feel warm. Behind him, the Lodge shone on the rise, while farther down the cove, the town was mostly dark, save for the marine lights still glowing on the boardwalk. He did his usual safety checks first, making sure all the gear was where it was supposed to be. Immersion suits. Life vests. Locator beacon. SAT phone. Life raft. Throw bag. Flares.

When he was satisfied, he resecured it all, just in time for Tala to show up with the clients, yawning while she began untying the stern line, muttering under her breath.

"I swear to God," she grunted, hauling the rope in and flaking it neatly over her arm, "if I ever say yes to a charter before sunrise again, just knock me unconscious and put me back in bed."

Hyder snorted as he stepped into the wheelhouse and started his other checks, his fingers moving from habit more than thought. Battery switch. Panel. Gauges waking one by one. Bilge light silent. Fuel where it should be. Oil pressure not yet relevant. He turned the key and the diesel caught after half a breath, coughing once before settling into a low, familiar rumble that vibrated up through the hull and into his bones.

"You say that every time," he called out.

"And every time, I mean it more."

The clients were clustered awkwardly near the cabin bulkhead, trying to stay out of the way while still looking like the kind of men who did not need to be told where to stand. Hyder had seen that look before too. Men who thought competence was transferable, who assumed because they could negotiate venture capital or drop down a mountain in six feet of powder, they also understood boats.

They usually didn't.

One of them, a guy in a neon jacket named Brent or Brett or maybe Bryce, stamped his boots and leaned toward the wheelhouse door.

"How long till we hit the fishing grounds?" he asked.

"Depends which grounds," Hyder answered with a grin.

The man laughed like he thought that was a joke. Hyder let him.

He stepped back out onto the deck just as Tala came up from the bow, the last line loose. She pushed them off with one boot and hopped aboard in the same movement, easy as breathing. The hull drifted away from the dock, the gap widening with a slow pull, and Hyder glanced up instinctively as a low breeze slid across his face.

He stilled. Lifted his chin. Closed his eyes. Breathing the wind.

It was nothing he could point to. Not really. No obvious shift in pressure, no hard gust, no mineral smell of a storm riding in from the Sound. The sky above them was clear enough to break your heart, stars bright and endless, the darkness beginning to thin only at its farthest eastern edge. The water inside the cove was steady, the tide moving out and not fighting them. Everything, by all outward signs, looked fine.

And yet...

A low wariness moved through him all the same. Nothing he could point to with certainty. Just that quiet little hook in his gut, the one he had learned a long time ago, after thousands of days on the water, in all kinds of conditions, never to ignore.

Tala handed out life vests to the clients, quipping about how they were the latest in Paris fashions, and completely non-negotiable. That was something rough-and-tumblers usually didn't like to be told about either. They figured if they could swim, there was no point. But he'd pulled enough lifeless bodies from the cold water of Alaska to know it had a way of making even the best swimmers forget to move their limbs.

Finished, Tala came up beside him, shoving her gloves tighter on her hands as he took the helm and eased *The Ahnah* ahead at a crawl. The boat answered him, her stern settling slightly as they moved free of the dock, her wake barely more than a soft curl in the black water.

Behind them, Alpenglow began to fall away. First the Lodge. Then the boardwalk and cottages, and lastly the church up on the bluff, lit up as the town's version of a lighthouse. Ahead of them, the sheltering island at the mouth of the cove loomed as a deeper shadow against the western horizon, its long shoulder blocking the worst of what Prince William Sound could throw at the town on a bad day. Hyder steered them toward the narrow passage he'd threaded a thousand times, the engine barely above idle, prop wash whispering behind them.

For a few minutes, neither of them said anything. The clients had gone quiet too, their excitement not yet fully awake enough to overcome the cold. Only the engine, the hush of water along the hull, and the occasional rattle of gear broke the silence.

Then Tala tipped her head back, looking at the sky.

"You're in one of your moods," she muttered.

Hyder kept his eyes ahead. "Am I?"

"Yep."

"How can you tell?"

"You get this little line right here." She tapped her own forehead. "Like you're trying to outthink something. Usually, the weather or the water."

He grunted noncommittally.

She followed his gaze out past the narrows, where the open Sound waited in dark, flat bands beneath the stars.

"There isn't a cloud in the sky," she said. "The barometer hasn't dropped. Wind's barely doing anything. Your sensor might be off."

"My sensor?"

"Yeah." She flicked him a glance. "Must be all the mooning."

He finally looked at her, then he turned back to the water.

"Shut up, Tala."

She grinned, her chipped tooth flashing in the deck light. "Touchy Lil' Frogger."

They passed the shelter of the island and the water changed almost immediately. Not badly. Not yet. Just enough to remind everyone aboard that they were no longer inside the cove. The swell out in the Sound was long and low, lifting the bow in patient, rolling motions as they met it. The dot-commers had to widen their stances so they didn't have to discover whether the life vests worked or not.

Black Rock Channel lay starboard, farther out and deeper, the best bet this early in the season if you wanted to put clients on halibut and had the four hours to make the run. Eaglet Deep lay the other way, more protected and much closer in, with a decent structure beneath but not much payoff this early unless luck was on your side.

Hyder kept one hand light on the wheel and let the choice sit for a second longer. Then he turned them to port.

Tala's head snapped toward him.

"Oh, come on," she groaned. "Seriously?"

He didn't answer immediately, just adjusted their heading and watched the compass settle.

"Eaglet?" she said. "This early? We'll be lucky if we catch a cold over there."

He gave the throttles a little more, enough to bring them up onto a reasonable cruise without throwing the guests overboard. The hull responded cleanly, slicing across the dark surface with the steady, confident push of a boat built to work.

"I know," he answered.

Tala leaned one shoulder against the frame of the wheelhouse door, studying him now, less teasing, more curious.

"Then why are we going there?"

He exhaled through his nose.

"My gut."

She was quiet for a beat. Then another.

"That's annoying."

"I know."

She looked out over the water again, then back at him. Whatever she saw in his face must have been enough, because the grin disappeared and something more serious settled in its place.

"Alright," she shrugged. "Eaglet Deep it is."

He nodded once. It wouldn't matter to the clients, because they didn't know Black Rock from Fraggle Rock. He only hoped they would catch something. Maybe some lingcod or a very confused salmon. They didn't seem like the type who just wanted a long boat ride.

The water was smoother than it usually was that time of year, and Hyder pushed the throttles just a touch more as the horizon slowly changed shape around them while night gave way by degrees rather than all at once. The black softened to charcoal, then to steel. The stars thinned overhead. The outlines of far-off islands sharpened and separated from the dark.

At their speed, with the water cooperating, Eaglet Deep lay a little over an hour out. He took a swig of his own coffee and began thinking through drift, bottom structure, what he might tell the clients when the fishing turned out to be thinner than promised.

The sun rose fully and g.inted over the Sound, and Sola's face rose before Hyder. Something happened last night. It was subtle, but he was sure of it, and he couldn't wait to get back tonight and spend more time with her and maybe figure out exactly what it was.

As an hour passed and the weather was still looking clear and perfect, Tala began shooting him irritated glances. He started to wonder if maybe she was right. Maybe his sensor was off.

Not that I'm mooning, of course.

But perhaps he had subconsciously made a choice that would have them all home before dinner, instead of what was best for the client. His lips pursed as the idea settled, and he was halfway considering if it would be best to turn around, when he felt it first through the soles of his boots.

A change. Nothing big, but definitely wrong.

It wasn't the swell or the usual vibration of the diesel under load. It was a shudder almost too brief to name.

He frowned and glanced down at the gauges. The oil pressure was steady. Temp just fine. RPMs where they should be. Tala was looking ahead and the clients were joking with one another. No one else had felt anything, and he started to relax.

Then the engine coughed. Once. Just enough to make Tala straighten.

"You feel that?" she asked, turning.

"Yeah."

He pulled the throttle back a touch, listening. For ten long seconds, everything smoothed out, and he almost decided it must be a bad batch of fuel or time for a filter change, even though he'd just replaced it last month.

Then the engine stumbled again, harder this time, and somewhere beneath them he heard a sound no captain ever wanted to hear. A heavy, irregular slap from inside the hull. A terrifying thud of the engine's spinning flywheel slamming into deep, rising water.

His head turned sharply toward the bilge alarm panel. He waited for a breath, still hoping he was wrong. Instead, the red high-water light flashed, and the alarm shrilled to life.

"Fucker!" Tala swore.

Hyder was already moving, his mind outrunning adrenaline by a hair.

"Check the bilge," he snapped.

She didn't hesitate, just spun and disappeared aft.

The clients had heard the alarm now and their curious eyes were staring at him, the questions beginning.

"What's that?"

"Is that normal?"

"You guys got an issue?"

Hyder ignored them all, his eyes scanning ahead, looking for something he knew had to be there. Off their port bow, not far enough to be comforting but close enough to matter, a black hump of rock broke the waterline. It was the kind of little nothing island nobody bothered naming and most captains hated and called a boat killer. It was barely more than a slab at high tide, slick with bird crap and sea lion stink most of the year.

But it was there.

Tala reappeared at the wheelhouse door so fast she nearly hit the frame.

"We're taking water," she said, her voice low and tight for his ears only. "Not spray. Real water, rising fast."

"How fast?"

"Fast enough."

Hyder had already decided, but this made him sure.

"Get the safety gear ready."

Her face changed. Serious all the way through now.

"We're going down?" she asked quietly, careful not to carry that question to the clients.

"Maybe," he said, already swinging the wheel toward the rock. "But if our luck holds, I'm gonna run us aground first."

Her eyes flicked ahead, saw what he was aiming for, and she nodded once.

"Got it."

Then she was gone again, barking instructions before fear could catch up with anyone.

"Everybody listen up," she called, her voice even like calm was a weapon. "I'm gonna give you some immersion suits, just like the one we showed you last night. I want you to put them on. No arguing, no questions, just move."

That got their attention better than the alarm had. The men stared at her for half a beat too long, then scrambled. They watched as Tala ran through unrolling them from their bags and shaking them out. Then they tried to hop into the boots before awkwardly kneeling and almost falling over. It was a little like watching three grown men wrestling with giant rubber dolls.

Hyder did his best to ignore them as he pushed the throttles just enough to keep steerage without making what was happening under them worse. The engine still didn't like it. It coughed again, a wet, ugly stutter that sent a pulse of anger through him.

The stern was settling lower now. He could feel it in the trim of the boat, in the way the bow rode up a touch more than it should, in the sluggishness just beginning to creep into her response.

He grabbed the radio mic and keyed it.

"King Air, King Air, this is The Ahnah, copy."

Static.

"King Air, King Air, this is The Ahnah, copy."

More static. Then a burst of garble. If it was a response, it certainly wasn't a clear one.

He keyed again, jaw tight.

"Ahnah taking on water. Repeat, taking on water. Making for a rock east of Eaglet Deep. Need immediate—"

The signal shredded in his ear, squealing, swallowed by interference or terrain or pure bad luck. Either way, he was almost out of time for it to matter.

"Damn it."

He tried again, this time switching frequency, then again on the local working channel, but either he was being stepped on, or the signal was bouncing wrong because all he got back was more broken squealing. All he could do was hope somebody might have heard him, but he wasn't holding his breath.

Frustrated, Hyder grabbed for the emergency locator beacon instead, tearing it from its bracket and flipping the manual activation switch instead of waiting for it to go off if they went down. For a moment he watched for the reassuring strobe light. Nothing happened. He smashed his finger onto the test switch, over and over, eventually growling as he tossed the useless plastic box to the deck.

What the fuck!

He knew he had to keep it together, and his mind refocused on the little island growing larger ahead, ugly and bare and perfect. He didn't need comfort at this point. He needed ground.

Behind him, one of the clients was breathing too fast, as if he were only now catching on to the seriousness of their situation. Or perhaps putting on the immersion suit, which was still hanging low on his waist, was too much of a workout.

"What do you mean we're taking on water?" he demanded. "How much water?"

"Enough that I need you to shut up and put that suit on properly," Tala answered for him, then went back over the safety protocols once more. The ones the clients usually only half-listened to. Now she had their full attention.

Hyder would have laughed if he'd had any room for it.

The bow lifted over a swell, then dropped. The engine sputtered hard enough this time that he thought it might die right there. If it did, they'd lose the last of their approach speed and drift broadside before they ever made the rock, and things would get significantly more complicated in a hurry. They would still make it to the rock, but they would have to swim there instead.

"Come on," he muttered to the boat, one hand firm on the wheel, the other feathering the throttle. "Come on, girl."

She answered with one more shaky surge. It was enough.

Maybe.

Tala came up beside him again, already half-wearing her suit and holding his in one hand and a large bag in the other. She put both on the seat next to him.

"Clients are geared up. More or less. Ditch bag's ready."

He nodded.

"Once we hit, get 'em off on the lee side if there is one. If not, keep 'em together on deck till I tell you different."

"You think she'll hold?"

"I think she'd better."

The island was close now, the water breaking white around its shoulders where submerged rock pushed the swell up into chop. Hyder adjusted a few degrees, aiming not for the highest point but for the shallow shelf he knew was just under the surface along the eastern side. Enough to ground them without stoving the bow in entirely.

It was a gamble. But they were out of any other options.

The bilge alarm screamed and the engine shuddered hard. The steering went heavy for half a second, then light again.

"Brace for impact!" Tala yelled, and the clients grabbed the side rails.

Hyder set his jaw, fixed his eyes on the strip of rock ahead, and drove her in.

The collision was not the violent, bone-jarring crash most people might think of when a boat runs aground.

It was worse in its own way.

A grinding, dragging shudder ran the full length of the hull, metal scraping over submerged rock with a sound that made Hyder's teeth clench as he imagined whole strips of *The Ahnah's* aluminum plating being shaved away like the skin of a potato. The bow lifted higher than it should have, climbing the shelf beneath them, then stuck fast, held there while the stern sagged lower into the water, heavy with everything they had already taken on.

The engine choked once more, coughing like it was trying to clear its throat, then died.

Just like that, silence dropped over them, broken only by the slap of water against the hull and the relentless scream of the bilge alarm, which now seemed impossibly loud without the diesel rumble to compete with it.

Hyder didn't waste a second.

"Engines off," he said out of habit, even though they already were, his hand moving automatically to kill what systems he could, cutting power before anything electrical had a chance to complicate things further. "Tala, status."

She was already moving past him, checking aft again, her voice carrying back over her shoulder.

"Still coming in," she called. "But it's slower now."

Hyder stepped out onto the deck, already calculating, running through the next ten decisions in his head. The radio was acting wonky and the locator beacon was suddenly busted. He needed to send out a distress call.

SAT phone!

Tala had just checked it yesterday and he'd made sure it was in the ditch bag before he left. He grabbed the bag and unzipped it, pulling out the black handset, stabbing the power button with a trembling thumb. The screen flared to life, and he almost kissed it. But his relief quickly vanished as the words "SEARCHING FOR SIGNAL…" blinked across the display and stayed there.

"Motherfucker!" he growled under his breath after another minute.

Behind him, the clients had gone very still, and he knew he still needed to keep it together for them.

They were standing at the edge of the tilted deck, staring down at the rock and water below, their earlier bravado gone entirely, replaced with expressions that ranged from tight, controlled concern to outright, unfiltered fear.

"Is this normal?" came the first question.

Hyder turned, forcing calm into his expression, because right now he was no longer running a boat, he was running them.

"It's not ideal, guys," he said, his tone easy. "But we're fine. We've got a solid bottom under us, and we're not taking on water like we were a minute ago."

Another one of them, the neon jacket, looked over the side.

"That's water…"

"Good eye," Tala said cheerfully from behind him, already hauling a coil of line and tossing it down toward the rock. "Lucky for you, it's shallow right here. You might get your boots wet, but you're just gonna have to bill me later. Or better yet, bill the Kings. They can afford it."

A weak laugh flickered through the group.

Good, Tala.

Keep them moving. Don't let them be afraid. Hyder nodded once toward the stern.

"Tala's gonna help you take off your gear, since we *won't* be going in the water today."

They grumbled, but truthfully none of them had managed to get their suits all the way on anyway.

"I know, it's a pain in the ass, but you don't want to be climbing over the rail with those suits on. Once you're done, you're going to go down one at a time," he instructed. "Grab the rail, watch your footing, and step where Tala tells you."

"What about rescue?" one of them asked quickly.

"It's coming," Hyder told them without hesitation, without allowing even a fraction of doubt into his voice. "They'll be coming soon."

That part is...optimistic.

He didn't bother explaining that he'd told everyone before they'd left that he was headed toward Black Rock, not Eaglet Deep. He didn't explain that this stretch of water was not exactly a highway for passing traffic, that most captains avoided it unless they knew every rock and shelf by memory the way he did. And he certainly was not about to tell them that every option they had to let anyone know where they were seemed to be mysteriously out of commission.

That was not information they needed. Not yet. Instead, he started gathering the ditch bag and a few other items they might need right away while Tala showed them how to take off their suits. It took them another ten minutes of pulling and complaining.

"Alright, let's move," Tala said, clapping her hands once, bringing their attention back to her. "Big guy first. Yeah, you. If you fall, try not to land too hard on me."

"I'll do my best," the man muttered.

One by one, they climbed down, splashing through the cold shallows as they made the short step onto the rocks, slipping a little, catching themselves, then up onto drier rock.

Hyder stayed on deck until the last of them was off, his eyes still tracking the waterline, the angle of the hull, the shift of the tide. It was just starting to come in, and he was worried it might just take *The Ahnah* completely when it did. But that was not his main concern at the moment. It was the clients. They were his responsibility. He needed to make sure they made it through this.

When the last client got down safely, Hyder grabbed the ditch bag, slung it over his shoulder, and followed.

The rock was worse up close. It was uneven, narrow, with barely enough room to hold all of them without someone standing too near the edge.

"Up," Tala grunted, already moving. "Let's find the highest point. We're making camp, boys."

"Camp?" one of them echoed, seemingly mystified.

Hyder knew it was probably shock. These guys might be used to jumping onto lonely mountains to make their way back down. But he was pretty sure they usually ended those days in sheets with a high thread count in thousand-dollar-a-night hotel rooms.

"It's a temporary inconvenience," Tala corrected brightly. "A great story you can tell your buddies about back home."

She had already pulled a small stove from the ditch bag. A compact, stainless-steel burner, which she was setting up on the flattest section of rock she could find. Within minutes, a small blue flame flickered to life, and she set a pot over it to make some coffee, more for morale than necessity.

The clients drifted closer, drawn to it instinctively, their shoulders hunched, hands rubbing together. Their earlier confidence had been replaced with the uneasy stillness of people who just realized they were very far from in control. And that they didn't know anything about boats.

Tala straightened and walked back toward Hyder, her grin still in place, but her eyes sharper now.

"You got a plan?" she asked lightly.

"Always," he said.

She snorted. "Love that answer."

"Come on."

They stepped away from the group together, back to the boat, climbed back up over the rail.

"We grab what we can," he said quietly. "Anything useful. Extra thermal blankets, hand warmers, food, flares."

"And if she slides?" Tala asked.

"Then we move faster."

She nodded once, her usual smart remarks gone as they split without another word, moving through the boat quickly, grabbing what mattered, leaving what didn't.

Hyder found himself looking around the hull, looking for something to explain how they'd ended up where they were. He hadn't felt a collision. When he got to the stern, he almost missed it. But there was something. Something about the way the water moved.

He crouched, leaning over, bracing one hand on the rail as he peered down into the churn behind the prop. It was small, almost too small. A clean, round puncture just above the normal waterline, half hidden behind the prop wash, in a spot that made no sense. To punch through his hull like that, it would need speed. Or force. Neither of which would happen in the back like this.

His breath stilled as his mind tried to reach for something else. A rock strike. Or debris. Some kind of random damage. A fluke.

But it wasn't jagged or torn. It was precise, tiny, and in one of the few places where it would take just long enough for water to reach the bilge and sink them. So they wouldn't be close to shore when it did.

His stomach dropped as he added this to the malfunctioning equipment, and last year flashed through his mind.

Sutton's plane crash. The way the oil line had been halfway severed. So it would take a while for the plane's vibration to cut through it the rest of the way.

"Hey," he called quietly. "Tala."

She came up beside him, wiping her hands on her pants.

"What, Cap'n?"

He shifted just enough to give her the angle.

"Take a look," he said under his breath. "And don't say anything."

She leaned over. Paused for a second, then leaned closer.

Then, before she could stop herself, "Son of a bitch."

She straightened slowly, her eyes meeting his, and in that look, there was no question. She knew as well as he did that someone had done this.

"That's not all. There is something wrong with the radio. And the beacon and SAT phone."

Her brows lowered and it was clear she was making the same connections he had. Hyder held her gaze for half a second longer, then gave the smallest shake of his head.

Not now.

She nodded, then they filed it away without another word and let their training take over again.

Keep everyone warm and dry and wait it out until they were rescued. The hole would still be there when they got back to safety. The equipment would still be busted.

Hyder swung himself back over the rail, forcing a small grin to his face as he started back toward the group, knowing they were still watching him.

He made it halfway. Then stopped.

At first, it was nothing. Just a sound at the edge of hearing, a low hum threading through the wind. He tilted his head slightly, listening.

There!

It was faint but growing. An engine for sure, though not a boat.

A plane.

Hyder's head snapped up, one hand coming up to shield his eyes from the bright, hard glare of the low winter sun as he scanned the sky. Waiting and hoping it was not just some random flyby.

Tala was already moving, the flare gun in her hand.

"You see it yet?" she asked.

"Not yet," he said, still searching.

Then to the east, the smallest glint of metal catching light.

He locked onto it, his breath catching when he saw the way it was moving. It wasn't wandering or searching. It was coming straight for them, like it already knew where they were.

A real grin broke across his face before he could stop it, and as they waited, the yellow plane dipped its wings once in acknowledgment. A mechanical howdy.

Cheers broke out from the dot-commers, and they began waving their arms.

"That's for us, right?"

"Yeah," he almost laughed in his relief, "it's for us." And even before it came close enough to make out clearly, Hyder knew exactly who it was.

It was Sutton, in the Kodiak.

The floats skimmed the water as his brother came in, skipping once, twice, before settling cleanly into the swell, turning toward them with practiced ease. Tala was already scrambling for rope and as soon as the plane's engines died down, Sutton tossed open the hatch and she threw it to him, pulling the Kodiak closer.

Sutton's eyes met his, the enormity of everything passing between them.

"About damn time," Hyder called to him, his legs feeling shaky now that the adrenaline was draining out of him.

Sutton smiled and gave a shrug.

"Well, luckily you happened to tell a nine-year-old where you were going."

Hyder let that sink in, as he realized how his brother had found him so quickly. Then he turned back to their guests.

"Okay, guys. Time to go home."

THIRTY-FOUR

Sola

The Raven did not feel the same. Normally it was the beating heart of Alpenglow, near the crossroads and where every intangible road of gossip, celebration, and quiet comfort eventually led. It was as though time was playing tricks and the usual warmth and amusement had been stripped, warping into something unrecognizable, each second dragging just long enough that Sola became aware of it, aware of the space between one breath and the next, the space between one person and the next.

She had moved at some point, though she didn't remember doing it.

One moment she'd been near the cove door, the next she was deeper in the Raven, standing just off to the side of the main room, her back against the rough wood of one of the beams, her head angled toward the bar where the radio now sat like the center of gravity for the entire town.

Everyone was there. Moving, too, but only in that restless way people did when they had nothing to do but wait for news they couldn't control, speaking in low voices that never quite rose into full conversation, as if anything louder might break whatever fragile thread was still connecting them to those who had not yet come home.

Healy had stationed himself behind the bar, though for once he was not wiping anything down or reorganizing bottles or fussing over details that didn't matter. His hands rested flat against the wood, fingers splayed, his eyes also fixed on the radio as though he could will it to tell him something.

Cheryl stood nearby, shifting her weight in slow, deliberate motions, arms crossed and then uncrossed again, her gaze moving from the door to the windows to the radio and back again, as if she could not quite decide where she was needed most.

Willow was at her family's usual table, the booth Sola had seen the Kings gather at too many times to count. Her arm was looped loosely around Hope's shoulders, though it was not entirely clear who was comforting whom. Hope sat stiff beside her, her guarded composure more fragile than usual. Gemma sat at Willow's feet, under the table, unusually quiet and still, her small hand buried in Sitka's fur. Charlie was there too. Sitting with her hands draped over her belly, with her eyes staring at the sky outside, her face set in something that spoke of past trauma, and despite her own worries, Sola made a mental note to give her an extra checkup this week.

Amos had taken up position near the door overlooking the cove, one hand braced against the frame, ready to move the second he was needed, though he had to move each time the door opened.

It did swing open. Again, and again. Bringing more people, more movement, more waiting.

Not just from town. From Kisa'adi too. Filling in the edges of the spaces, standing shoulder to shoulder with the people of Alpenglow without distinction, without separation, because in moments like this, there was no difference between them.

Some of their own were still out there. And that was enough.

Sola looked around once more, noticing that Ellie was there too. She stood in one of the back rooms where the pool table was, almost in shadow, her arms wrapped tight around herself, her shoulders drawn in, her head slightly bowed as if she were trying to make herself smaller.

Her face was pale. Not the shy, pleasant expression Sola had grown used to seeing, but something stripped down, her mouth pressed tight, her eyes bright with tears she was not even attempting to hide.

She looked exactly how Sola felt. Except Sola was...locked. As if something inside her had frozen over. As if the panic had gone too deep, too fast, and now it sat there, heavy and unmoving, refusing to let anything else through.

And it was still morning. Though the brilliance of earlier had given way to something more muted, and when she turned her head toward the southern windows, Sola could see the fog Sutton had mentioned, just beginning to drift over the square, creeping forward in slow, pale, swirling tendrils that blurred the edges of the horizon. It reminded Sola of how cold cream looked when you poured it into hot coffee and it wasn't ready to mix quite yet.

Just then the radio beeped, the sound cutting through everything else. Every head turned at once and every murmur stopped.

Sola's breath caught somewhere halfway to her lungs, her heart fluttering. If she was talking to anyone else, she would have reminded them to breathe. Doctor's orders. But she couldn't.

The speaker crackled, and there was another beep.

Then, "Got 'em all, Alpenglow Town."

It was unmistakably Sutton's deep voice.

"If you read me Alpenglow, this is the Kodiak. All five from The Ahnah are accounted for. I repeat, we have all five from The Ahnah, safe and sound. We are in the air and will land in twenty minutes. Repeat. ETA twenty minutes."

For a split second, no one moved. As if the room needed to understand the words before it could react to them. Then it broke, and sound rushed from every direction at once. Cheers, laughter, sharp exhalations of breath that turned into something like joy, people clapping each other on the back, voices rising, overlapping, relief spilling out of them in waves.

Sola felt it too. A surge of emotion that should have been relief, that should have unlocked her chest and let her breathe again. It should have allowed her to smile.

But it didn't. Because something else had already broken open, deep inside her. And now that it had, it would not close again. Her knees felt weak and her hands trembled.

She glanced across the room again, drawn without meaning to.

Ellie.

This time, Ellie was not trying to hold it together. She was sobbing. Her shoulders were shaking as she let herself go, grasping the pool table as if that were the only thing keeping her upright.

It hit Sola hard. That recognition. That mirror. Because it was still exactly how she felt. Except her tears wouldn't come. They were there. She could feel them burning behind her eyes, pressing. Part of her wondered about that.

What is wrong with me?

Why couldn't she celebrate or let her relief show? She stood where she was, as the town continued to move around her. When it was nearly time for the plane to show up, they began spilling out of the Raven and onto the boardwalk, every eye lifted toward the sky.

Sola finally moved with them, even though she did not remember deciding to. She only knew that suddenly she was outside, the cold hitting her face, the fog now making everything soft but her.

Gus was beside her. Lucia was just behind, holding him by the shoulders. Everyone else was lined up at the railing of the boardwalk, still waiting but engaging in loud, teasing chatter. Mostly about the party they would have later, the celebration. Sola got it, but she still couldn't let go.

Above them, the sound came first. A mechanical hum that soon became a throaty growl, cutting through the fog, drawing every gaze.

"There," someone said, pointing.

The Kodiak was coming in low over the water, cutting through the increasing fog, the floats skimming the surface, then kissing the water with practiced ease before it turned toward the dock, cutting a clean line through the cove.

Amos was already moving, running forward with the lines as the plane eased in, tightening them like he'd done it a thousand times before, and Sola realized he probably had.

The hatch opened.

Three men came out first. Sola didn't recognize them, but she realized they must be the charter guests. They moved carefully, as though stiff from cold and shock, their faces still pale but, to their credit, they all tried to smile when they saw everyone watching them.

The town managed to contain themselves while they waited. Just barely.

Until Tala stepped out. Grinning.

She paused on the deck, took a small, exaggerated bow, then, for good measure, dropped into a curtsy that was far too practiced to be entirely a joke or to be her first time giving one.

The cheers broke again, and Sola almost laughed with them. Almost.

Then Sutton emerged, frowning as he turned back to hear someone still inside.

Hyder.

He stepped out behind his brother, their heads now bent slightly toward each other as they spoke, whispering with urgency, their expressions serious.

He was right there. Right there. Yet he had not looked up.

That icy sensation was still inside her, and she realized she needed his eyes. She needed to see him see her. To know he was actually okay.

As if the thought itself reached him, he paused mid-sentence, lifted his head, and his gaze found hers. Everything else fell away and she unfroze.

Without any other thought or hesitation, or even the faintest awareness of anything or anyone around her, Sola ran.

She ran down the boardwalk, past nearly the entire town, past the people who parted instinctively to let her through, past voices calling out, laughing, cheering, saying her name, past Ellie, who, despite her red eyes, was now grinning through fresh tears, past the three men who stared at her like they were watching something out of a rom-com.

Past Tala, who saw her face and said, "Oh, boy, here we go."

She barely registered Sutton stepping aside just in time, his brows lifting as she nearly collided with him, his hands coming up in reflex as if to steady her and then dropping again when she didn't slow.

Even when she reached Hyder, she didn't stop.

She launched into him with full force, her arms wrapping around him, her legs lifting without thought as she clung to him, as if letting go was no longer an option she possessed, as if the space between them had become something unbearable.

He caught her, his arms coming around her like it was the most natural thing in the world and he understood exactly what this was without needing any explanation.

When their mouths met, it was not slow or careful. It was not even, at its core, passion. It was relief. A desperate, undeniable need to confirm what her eyes had already told her, what her body had already begun to believe, what her heart had already claimed without her permission.

Hyder was alive.

Her fingers curled into him, into his neck, into his shoulders, into whatever part of him she could hold, grounding herself in the simple fact of him.

Behind her, the town erupted in applause and whistles. Cheers that rose and echoed across the water and were swallowed by the fog.

Tears streamed down Sola's face, and she didn't care that every single person in Alpenglow and half of Kisa'adi was watching her lose every ounce of composure she had ever prided herself upon.

For the first time in her life, she didn't want to hold it together. She just wanted to be held by Hyder.

THIRTY-FIVE

Hyder

Hyder pulled back first. Not far. Just enough that he could see her. His forehead rested against hers, their breath still tangled, her fingers still gripping the back of his jacket like she didn't trust the world. For a moment he couldn't speak, because seeing her like that, seeing tears spilling freely down her face, hit him even harder than the moment the engine had died beneath his hands.

"Hey," he murmured, "it's okay, *Sha'aéil*. I'm okay."

Her breath hitched.

"I know." The words came out watery and uneven, her voice catching halfway through them as a small, almost disbelieving laugh followed, like she did not quite trust the relief yet. "I know. I just...needed..."

Her voice trailed off and she didn't finish the sentence. She didn't have to. He knew. He'd known for months, but he was grateful that she had finally figured it out too.

Reluctantly he loosened his hold on her just enough to set her back on her feet, his hands lingering at her waist for a second longer than necessary, steadying her as she found her balance again on those ridiculous heeled boots she continued to wear half the time.

He glanced down at them briefly, a corner of his mouth lifting despite everything.

"Still wearing those things, huh?" he muttered.

She sniffed, swiping at her face with the back of her hand, her chin lifting just a fraction.

"They're cute," she said defensively, though her voice still wavered.

He chuckled, but the sound felt like it didn't quite belong after the morning he'd had.

He looked up. Sutton was still watching him with concern that spoke of the conversation they hadn't finished. Right before Sola had collided with him, he had been explaining to his brother what had happened. About the hole he and Tala had found. About the malfunctioning safety equipment.

He held Sutton's gaze for a second, giving a small shake of his head, explaining without words that he did not want to talk about it anymore. Not now. Not with Sola still pressed up against him.

Sutton frowned and Hyder could see the worry and frustration there. He still wanted to discuss what it all meant and what came next. But he nodded once in return, accepting it, shelving it, even if it was already burning in the back of his mind.

Hyder reached for Sola's hand, threading his fingers through hers without thinking about it, enjoying the fact that she was there and being so public about it.

"Come on," he said quietly.

They turned together, moving up the ramp toward the boardwalk, and the town closed in around them immediately. Hands clapped against his back. Then came the teasing.

"Nice job, genius," Micah called out. "Only you could sink a perfectly good boat on a clear day."

Hyder snorted.

"Wasn't me," he shot back easily. "Boat just decided it needed a nap."

"Expensive nap."

"Send the bill to Tala," he added without missing a beat. "She was driving."

"Liar!" Tala called from somewhere behind them. "I'd have hit the rock cleaner."

"Yeah," he said over his shoulder, grinning now despite himself. "That's exactly what I'm worried about."

The laughter came easier, rolling through the crowd, relief loosening something in everyone, letting the tension bleed out in jokes and noise and the kind of ribbing that only came when people knew things had turned out alright and it was how they showed their gratitude.

Hyder took it all in stride, but his hand never left Sola's.

As they neared the Raven, his gaze shifted, and he saw Gus standing just off to the side of the door, Lucia holding him close. Hyder dropped to his knees without hesitation, bringing himself level.

"Hi, Hyde," came his small voice.

"Hey there, Captain Gus," he answered him, his voice softer now. "I hear you're my hero today."

Gus looked at him. Really looked at him, for almost a full second, long enough to blink.

"I hear you knew exactly where to find us," Hyder continued.

Gus's gaze shifted, sliding away to Hyder's shoulder, but he nodded.

Hyder felt something in his chest tighten, and he stood slowly, holding out his other hand. He knew Gus might not take it, and he was okay if that was the case.

After a moment, Gus placed his small hand in his. Hyder's fingers closed around it, gently, like he was holding something fragile and important all at once.

"Come on," he repeated, and the three of them walked into the Raven together.

When Alpenglow wanted to party, nothing much could stop it. Right away, the Raven became exuberant and loose with the kind of energy that came when fear had nowhere left to go but out.

Hyder barely registered half of it because as they were walking in, he saw Ellie. Her face was still blotchy from crying, her hands twisting together in front of her like she didn't know what to do with them now that the worst had passed.

Guilt hit him right away. He'd let her infatuation for him go on too long. Probably, if he was honest with himself, because he was a coward, and because he'd been so swept up with Sola that he didn't want to take the time to do it the right way. But now, it was past time. He needed to deal with her.

Now, he told himself, understanding that life was short and there was no time like the present.

He opened his mouth to tell Sola he would be right back, already preparing to cross the room, to say something, to fix it.

But Tala beat him to it.

She slid into the booth beside Ellie, talking low, her body angled in a way that shut the rest of the room out without making a show of it.

Hyder couldn't hear what she said. But he saw a change in Ellie right away. Her shoulders loosened and her mouth turned into a small, shaky smile. Then Tala pulled her into a quick, tight hug. After she leaned back, she must have said something else, because Ellie's smile turned into a laugh. She tried to cover it, as though she almost couldn't believe it had slipped out. Then she just went with it, laughing loud enough for Hyder to hear her now.

Hyder exhaled slowly, grateful for the reprieve.

Tomorrow.

He would still need to do something about it. Because he was already stepping into whatever this was with Sola, and he didn't want to bring any unfinished business with him.

It took a long time before they were able to extricate themselves. Especially after the food appeared and drinks were poured and the music started.

The charter guests were pulled into the middle of it all, their shock turning into cheer as they were handed glasses they did not ask for and stories they did not quite understand but enjoyed anyway. Dan Brown even had them convinced to come back later in the season, explaining how he would set them up with all the latest gear, sure to land them the biggest fish they'd ever seen. Which was good, because Hyder could only imagine the Google review they had been about to get after today.

By the time the sun dipped, and the fog had completely engulfed the cove, they had become honorary townies, filled with the best beer on tap, and clapped on the back and teased like they had always belonged there. And they were all wearing T-shirts that Clare had given them, each proudly pointing to the fish and drunkenly saying, "Hey! Ask me about the big one!"

Eventually, the current of it all carried them back to the Lodge.

Lucia had already taken Gus home after his head began drooping, so Sola came too. Which was good because she had yet to let him go. Every time he shifted, she shifted with him, like she had not quite convinced herself that he was real. Hyder didn't mind. Having her at his family's home made the space feel more comfortable, the sensation of being lonely completely gone.

The guests were upstairs already, probably passed out, and the Kings were all in the kitchen, sitting around the table, starting to finally relax. Hyder stood to grab another drink when Sutton finally caught him without Sola, who was still listening to a story that Willow was telling about their childhood.

"Alright," Sutton grumbled under his breath. He was done waiting. "Talk to me."

Hyder didn't pretend not to understand.

Neither did Tala. She got up from the table quietly, and leaned back against the counter, her arms crossed, all humor gone.

Hyder exhaled slowly, running a hand through his hair.

"It wasn't a punch from debris," he began. "Definitely not anything natural."

Sutton's eyes narrowed.

"How small?"

"Small enough we didn't notice it right away," Hyder said. "Just a slow leak until it wasn't. But it was too clean."

Tala nodded once.

"Yeah, it was perfectly round," she added. "Like something had punched through quick. Maybe an ice pick with a hammer."

Sutton's jaw tightened.

"Where?"

"Behind the prop wash," Hyder said. "It was hidden. You'd have to know where to look to see it."

"And none of the equipment worked?"

"Well, I guess you guys got the radio, but it was only garbled on my end. The beacon was definitely messed with and so was the SAT phone. It had to be late last night, though. Because Tala checked them both."

"Yeah," she agreed. "They were fine before I went to bed, after I put the suits back from doing the safety demonstration."

Silence settled over the three of them for a beat.

"That's twice now," Sutton said finally, and it was clear he was pissed. "And once was already too much of a coincidence. We need to keep a better eye on everything. Dutchy sent word that he was gonna pump her out and patch her. Then tow her back in the morning. Maybe we can see something more after we pull her out."

Hyder would have liked to be the one to bring *The Ahnah* back, but he didn't argue. There was still too much to figure out here. Ever since Sutton's plane crash last year, they had been careful. But clearly someone knew enough about their equipment, and they were quick enough that they were able to do this without being caught.

"Maybe we can start having some kind of watch," Hyder suggested. "Both here and on the town dock. That's really all we can do that we aren't already doing."

Then he looked up, realizing the table had gone silent. Sola was staring at them, looking back and forth like she was trying to work out what she'd overheard. So were Charlie and Willow.

"What are you saying?" Sola finally asked, as if she'd found all the pieces but they didn't quite fit. "That someone did this?"

No one answered her right away, but their uncomfortable silence was all the confirmation she needed.

"No!" she exclaimed, jumping to her feet. "No, that doesn't make sense. Who would…why would…we need to call the police."

"Sola," Hyder started, keeping his tone calm, trying to ease her back before she went too far down the spiral he could already see forming in her mind.

But she was already there.

"No," she said again, louder now, her hands speaking just as much as her voice. She ran to the phone on the wall, already dialing.

"Hey," he said, taking the phone from her and hanging it up, running his hands along her arms, glancing toward the main part of the Lodge. "We've got guests upstairs."

"I don't care about the guests," she shot back immediately, her accent thickening. ""Why are *you* not more angry? Why are we not calling the cops?"

He recognized it. The inability to understand how things worked in the bush. Charlie had looked exactly like that after Sutton's crash. The same disbelief that the world could work this way. That there could be no immediate answer or clear authority. No one to fix it.

"We'll file a report," Sutton explained, stepping in. "We'll document everything. But out here—"

"*Eso no es suficiente*! That's not good enough." Sola cut him off, shaking her head harder now, her voice rising again. "No. You don't just *accept* that someone tried to hurt the people you care about!"

Charlie forced herself up now, one hand resting over her belly as she waddled over, her brows drawn together. Willow was right behind her.

"They're saying someone sabotaged his boat, nearly killing him." Sola gestured to Hyder, her frustration spilling over. "And last year someone, presumably the same someone, crashed his plane," now she pointed to Sutton, "and still, they're not going to do anything about it!"

Charlie's eyes snapped to Sutton.

"What? The boat?"

"We don't know that for sure," Sutton said carefully.

An argument ensued. Sola, Charlie, and Willow, standing shoulder to shoulder, facing Hyder and Sutton. While the King men did their best to placate them. And Tala, her arms still folded, now grinning as she watched. She should have had popcorn.

"Then we get one," Sola finally said.

Hyder lowered his brows, confused.

"Get one?" he repeated.

"*Sí*," she said, lifting her chin. "We go and get a detective. Someone who knows what they're doing."

"That's not how this works," a hint of disbelief creeping into his voice despite himself. "We can't just go kidnap a cop."

"Fine," she snapped. "Then we call. We call everyone until someone comes."

Charlie nodded immediately.

"She's right."

"Of course she is," Willow added.

Sutton closed his eyes briefly, then exhaled.

"Okay," he said finally, holding up both hands in surrender. "Okay. I'll make some calls. I'll do what I can. I promise."

Charlie seemed to settle at that, her shoulders easing slightly as she turned back toward the table. Willow took a little longer, but eventually she also agreed to let Sutton handle it.

Sola didn't. Hyder could see it in her. In the heat still burning behind her eyes. She was not done, not even close. She could argue about it all night.

Despite everything, despite all the unanswered questions, he grinned. Because God, she was something. All passion and fire. He was turned on, and if he didn't get out of the kitchen soon, it was going to get embarrassing. Real quick.

He leaned down, close enough that only she could hear him, and whispered.

"Hey, Sola. Wanna come upstairs and play doctor?"

He felt the shift immediately. The fire in her eyes didn't disappear. But it changed. She didn't smile, still not ready to let everything go, but she did nod and take his hand. And she pulled him up the stairs.

THIRTY-SIX

Sola

I'm not going to leave.

The thought came to Sola almost as soon as she woke, with a quiet certainty that surprised her, without the usual internal debate that accompanied nearly every decision she made.

She was staying.

Hyder was wrapped around her, his arm heavy across her middle, one leg slipped between hers in a way that would have irritated her once, would have made her pull away in search of air, of the quiet solitude she had always needed in order to rest.

His bed was warm. He was warm. She allowed herself to sink into that warmth without resistance, without the instinctive tightening that usually came when someone else occupied her space.

She simply stayed.

Well. As much as someone like her could stay. Her mind still worked. It always worked. Even now, it flickered through details, through timelines, through possibilities, through the problem that sat waiting for her the moment she stepped out of this room and back into the world where answers were expected and action was required.

Someone did this.

Even as her mind continued to circle back to the day before, to the hole in Hyder's boat and the sabotaged equipment, to the implications of what that meant, to the unsettling reality that someone had deliberately tried to harm him, she found that one truth remained steady beneath it all. It would no longer be ignored. The very idea that the Kings had simply let the other incident sit, to dangle unanswered, for more than a year, without finding a solution, frustrated her.

But even as those thoughts pressed in, she found her focus shifting, edging back to the night before, to what had happened after they left the kitchen. To the way Hyder looked at her, the way his voice had dropped when he had whispered in her ear, the way he let her lead him up the stairs like there had never been any question that he would follow.

She knew what he'd been doing. She wasn't a *boba*. An idiot. He was distracting her. Pulling her away from the problem.

She let him. She had let him because some part of her had recognized that she needed it. That if she did not allow herself to be with him, she would have burned herself out trying to fix something she could not immediately fix.

When they got inside his room, it was not so much making love as it was an affirmation of life.

Hyder kicked the door shut behind them with his heel, the sound barely registering before his mouth was on hers and Sola met him. The kiss was deep and messy from the first second, tongues sliding, teeth grazing, breaths already ragged. He tasted like salt air and the faint trace of the rum they'd shared earlier, and she drank him in.

His hands roamed her back, his broad palms pressing her closer until there was no space left between them. She could feel the hard line of his cock already straining against her stomach through their clothes. A low, needy sound escaped her throat, and he swallowed it, kissing her harder, walking her backward until her shoulders hit the wall beside his dresser.

"Sola," he growled against her mouth. "I need you naked. Now."

They tore at each other's clothes with zero patience. Her fingers yanked at the buttons of his flannel, and one popped off and pinged across the hardwood. He ripped her sweater up and over her head in one rough motion, nearly tearing the seam. She laughed breathlessly into the next kiss, then moaned when his hands cupped her breasts through her bra, thumbs brushing her nipples until they peaked tight and aching, before it too was torn off. Her leggings, panties, and socks went next.

Naked and impatient, she shoved his thermal up his chest, and he bent forward to help her pull it all the way off, exposing the lean, corded muscle of his torso and the intricate line tattoos that wrapped around his shoulders and upper arms. Her palms skimmed over them, tracing the bold black patterns she had only half-noticed before. Now that she had been in Alaska for months, she understood the stylized Native symbols of sea creatures. Salmon, seals, and there, curving along his left bicep, the powerful sweep of a killer whale.

"These..." she whispered as her fingertips followed the orca's tail. "They're beautiful."

Hyder's breath hitched. His hand fisted gently in her hair, tilting her head back so he could look at her. "Later," he promised, his voice dark. "Right now, I want you."

His confession sent liquid heat flooding between her thighs. She dropped to her knees without hesitation, hands already working his belt and zipper. When she tugged his jeans and boxer briefs down together, his cock sprang free, thick and heavy, and already glistening at the tip. Sola's mouth went dry at the sight. He was big, bigger than she'd fully registered in their frantic earlier encounters. The veined length curved slightly upward, the head flushed.

"*Dios mío*," she breathed. She glanced up at him through her lashes. "You're huge."

A wicked smirk tugged at his mouth. "I know you can take it."

She did. Wrapping one hand around the base, Sola leaned in and dragged her tongue slowly up the underside, savoring his salty taste. Hyder groaned, low and guttural, his hand tightening in her hair. The small bite of pain at her scalp only made her clench below. She swirled her tongue around the head, then took him deeper, lips stretching around his girth. He was velvet steel on her tongue, pulsing as she bobbed slowly, hollowing her cheeks.

"Yes, just like that," he rasped, his hips rocking gently.

She moaned around him and his other hand came down to cradle her jaw, his thumb stroking her cheek as she worked him, taking him as deep as she could until the head nudged the back of her throat. Tears pricked her eyes, but it felt perfect. Hyder's control was iron. He didn't thrust wildly, just guided her rhythm with that firm grip in her hair, the occasional shallow pump that had her desperate and needy.

After long, delicious minutes he bent down, grasped her shoulders, and pulled her off him, breathing hard.

"Up," he ordered, hauling her to her feet. He spun her and lifted her onto his wide oak dresser in one smooth motion. The wood was cool against her bare ass as he shoved her thighs wide, kneeling between them like a man on a mission.

"Look at you," he murmured, his eyes dark with hunger as he spread her with his thumbs. Feeling confident, she did look. She was slick with arousal for him.

"Hyder...please," she gasped, the words tumbling out.

He didn't make her beg twice. His mouth descended, hot and relentless. He licked a broad stripe up her center, then sealed his lips around her clit and sucked. Sola's head fell back against the mirror, a broken moan ripping from her throat as one hand grabbed the top of the mirror and the other threaded in his dark hair. He ate her like he was starving, with long, firm strokes of his tongue, his fingers sliding deep inside her.

The pleasure built fast and brutal. Her hips bucked against his face until he pinned her down with one strong forearm across her pelvis.

*"Ay, Dios...*Hyder, right there, *por favor."*

He groaned in approval, the sound vibrating straight through her core until she was right on the edge, her thighs trembling. Then he pulled back abruptly, his lips shiny with her. She whimpered at the loss, reaching for him.

"Not yet," he told her, his voice rough with restraint. He stood, towering over her, and in one fluid move he pulled her off the dresser, spun her around, and bent her forward so her palms braced against the wood. He kicked her feet wider, so she was open for him.

"Stay just like that," he commanded. She watched him in the mirror as he grabbed a condom and rolled it on. Then, with one hand gripping her hip, he guided himself to her entrance. He rubbed the blunt head through her folds, coating himself in her, teasing her clit until she was shaking. Then he pushed in with one smooth motion.

Sola moaned long and loud at the stretch, the burn, as she was almost too full. *"Mierda..."*

Hyder bottomed out with a guttural sound, waiting, his hips flush against her ass. "That's it. Take me." Then he started moving. Deep, powerful thrusts that rocked her against the dresser and had her lifting onto her toes, the angle hitting that perfect spot inside her. His free hand roamed up her spine, then fisted in her hair again, tugging just enough to arch her back and make her gaze meet his in the mirror.

The slap of skin on skin filled the room, almost indecent, mixed with her breathless cries and his low growls. "You're so fucking perfect," he praised, his pace quickening. "You were made for me."

She was close again, trembling on the brink, when he suddenly pulled out. Before she could protest he dropped to the floor with her and pulled her on top of him. She straddled him backwards, her back to his chest. Hyder sat up slightly, one arm banding around her waist to pull her tight against him while the other hand drew slow, teasing lines down her spine and arms.

"Ride me, Sola," he murmured hot against her ear, nipping the lobe.

She sank down onto him with a shared groan, the new angle letting him fill her even deeper, dragging against every sensitive nerve as she began to move. She rolled her hips, grinding back against him. His fingers continued their path along her side, then dipped lower, finding her clit and rubbing firm circles in time with her rhythm.

The pleasure coiled tighter, and she leaned back into his chest, her head on his shoulder, one hand reaching back to grip his neck. He kissed and bit along her shoulder, whispering filthy praise between thrusts up into her.

"That's my good girl...fuck me...you feel so goddamn good."

They moved together in a desperate rhythm, sweat-slick skin sliding, her moans turning into sharp cries as she chased release. Hyder's hand left her clit only to grip her hips again, helping her bounce harder. The coil snapped without warning, her orgasm crashing over her in waves, clamping around him as she came with a broken shout of his name.

Hyder didn't stop. He fucked her through it, drawing it out, then flipped their position in a fluid roll so she was now facing the carpet, her fingers grasping for purchase. His hands gripped her ass, guiding one leg up high as he entered her hard and fast. A second climax slammed through her almost immediately, leaving her weak and trembling.

Only then did he let himself go. With a deep, animalistic groan he buried himself to the hilt and came.

They stayed locked together, panting, hearts hammering. Hyder's arms wrapped around her, pulling her onto her side against him.

After long moments he pressed a softer kiss to her shoulder. "You okay, *Sha'aéil*?"

She managed a shaky laugh, still floating, loving that he'd called her that again.

"More than okay. I think you broke me."

"Hmmm." He smiled against her skin. "That's too bad. Because I'm not done with you yet."

But at that moment, he was gentle. He gathered her limp, sated body into his arms and stood, carrying her the few steps to the bed as if she weighed nothing. Sola felt utterly boneless, every muscle liquid and warm. He laid her down carefully, then slid in behind her, curving his bigger frame around hers.

She drifted off slowly, her body still humming, her mind quieter than it had been in weeks, her awareness settling into the steady rhythm of his breathing behind her, the solid presence of him curved along her back, his hand resting at her waist like it belonged there.

Somewhere in that small space between before sleep took her, she made another decision.

This is how I want it from now on. I never want to fall asleep alone again.

The thought should have startled her and sent her mind racing, listing reasons, building arguments, creating distance where there was none. But it didn't. Which, in itself, was a novelty.

She had always valued her space.

Even in their apartment in the Bronx, even in a place where space was a luxury that had to be negotiated, she had needed that quiet before bed, that sense of emptiness, of being alone with her thoughts before she allowed sleep to take her.

Luckily, her mother and Gus both slept like the dead, so the two of them sharing a bedroom made sense.

Sola had always been different. She woke at everything. At the distant bark of a dog down the street. At footsteps in the hallway, at voices through thin walls, or the creak of pipes and the shift of the building settling around them.

Not fully awake, but always aware. Having someone in her bed, that had always been the most noticeable thing of all.

Hyder in bed was extremely noticeable. He took up space. Not just physically, though he certainly did that, his body large and solid and entirely unconcerned with the idea of staying on his own side of the mattress. But also in a way that seemed to fill her mind, as if his presence extended beyond the boundaries of his body.

And yet...I like it.

If anything, instead of keeping her alert or making her hyper-aware, it had eased something in her so completely that she'd slept deeper than she could remember. No drifting just beneath the surface. She couldn't even remember dreaming.

She had read a study once, about the way early humans had adapted to fear, about how vulnerability in sleep had once meant real danger. It was not until they learned to control fire that they had found a way to feel safe in the dark, to create a barrier between themselves and whatever might come out of it.

Fire had meant protection and survival.

She shifted slightly in his arms, her fingers brushing over his wrist where it rested against her, feeling the warmth of him, the steady beat of his pulse beneath her touch.

Maybe Hyder is my fire. A smile came to her lips at the idea. She didn't even care if it was ridiculous.

Behind her, he moved. His arm tightened around her, pulling her closer, drawing her back into him as if even in sleep he was aware of her presence and unwilling to let go.

"You're still here," he murmured against her, his voice rough with sleep.

He leaned down, pressing his mouth to that spot just below her ear, the one he had found far too easily, that sent a shiver through her every single time.

She inhaled sharply despite herself, her body reacting before her mind could catch up, before she could even pretend that she had any control over that response.

She turned in his arms, shifting until she faced him, her hand coming up to rest against his chest, feeling his heartbeat and the solidity of him.

"*Sí,*" she said softly. "I stayed."

His eyes opened fully then. There was no mistaking how sleep fell away, replaced by something far more focused, his deep-blue gaze settling on her with an intensity that made her breath hitch.

"I'm glad," he said, then he leaned in and kissed her.

His mouth moved against hers with a kind of quiet confidence, as if there was nowhere else he needed to be, nothing else that demanded his attention more than her.

Her fingers slid into his hair without thinking, tangling there, pulling him closer even as she shifted against him, her body aligning with his, her awareness sharpening in a completely different way now, no longer dulled by sleep but heightened by proximity, by the lingering heat that had never fully faded from the night before.

His hand moved to her jaw, his thumb brushing along her cheek. She let herself lean into it. Let herself feel the way her body responded, the way her mind quieted again.

He broke the kiss just long enough to look at her again, his gaze searching her face in a way that made her heart beat faster.

"What?" she asked quietly.

A hint of his normal, lopsided grin lifted one side of his lips.

"Just making sure you're real," he explained.

She laughed softly at that, her hand lifting to smooth over his shoulder.

"I could say the same thing."

"I'm real." He kissed her again, just one soft brush this time. "I'm not going anywhere."

Sola felt something else. Another certainty.

Waking to him kissing her...she could get used to that too.

THIRTY-SEVEN

Hyder

Coming down to the Lodge kitchen, Hyder was in a good mood. That was putting it lightly.

He was in such a good mood that if anyone had been around to witness it, they might have been concerned, or at the very least suspicious, because while he was generally a happy person, he didn't typically descend stairs in the early morning with the extreme urge to whistle and a huge grin that refused to leave his face no matter how hard he tried to tamp it down.

Sola walked beside him, one hand in his, the other lightly trailing along the railing. She was also smiling, but he could tell she was wishing for her usual coffee and some clean clothes. And possibly her hairbrush. He'd definitely done some damage there.

He, on the other hand, was already wide awake. Almost embarrassingly so. Because his mind, which should have been on the day ahead, on the repairs that needed to be made, on the questions that still lingered about what had happened, had instead latched onto something else entirely.

Sola.

Their future. The very real, very sudden realization that at some point, soon, he was going to need to ask her to marry him. Not because she was expecting it, but because he wanted to.

He glanced down at her hand. It was bare. She never wore jewelry. Not even a watch.

That complicated things a little.

Does she like gold? Or platinum?

Something simple or something bold? Or did she hate jewelry altogether and he was about to embark on a mission that would end with her politely thanking him and then never wearing the thing again?

Or worse, saying no as he popped the question.

He frowned slightly now, his mind already turning it over, trying to problem-solve in the same way he would approach anything else. Logically and efficiently.

He could ask Willow. Willow would probably know. Willow always knew little things like that.

But the second the thought formed, he dismissed it just as quickly, because asking Willow about this would be even worse than his vague notion of wanting to marry Sola.

She would take the concrete idea of a ring, run with it, expand it. And to her credit, probably improve it. But it would involve at least six other people and, in the end, it would not mean as much.

No, he would figure it out for himself.

Sutton had. He remembered going with him on a quick trip to Anchorage, the way Sutton had dragged him through store after store, waiting until he saw something in one case and pointed, his voice certain as he said, "That one."

That had been it.

Hyder wanted that certainty. He wanted to look at Sola and know exactly what she wanted.

They reached the bottom step, and for a brief moment, he was surprised by the quiet. By the lack of Kings. Though he supposed it made sense. He and Sola slept late, and there were still guests, guests that were *not* out fishing. Sutton and Willow were probably busy entertaining them. Charlie would already be down at the school. She only had one more week until the agreed-upon date for her and Sutton to head to Anchorage to be closer to the hospital. The girls would be at school too.

He stepped into the kitchen fully, Sola just behind him, and stopped.

Because the kitchen wasn't empty like he'd thought. Sitting at the island, her legs crossed casually, a mug of coffee in her hand, was Tala. She had a wide grin that could only be described as shit-eating, and she was obviously waiting for him.

And next to her...was Ellie.

Hyder's good mood didn't disappear. Not completely. But the guilt he had deliberately pushed aside yesterday came back all at once, settling heavy in his gut.

It's time.

He opened his mouth, already running through what he was going to say, trying to find the right balance between honesty and kindness, between clarity and not making things worse than they needed to be.

Sola spoke before he could.

"Well," her tone shifted slightly as she took in the scene, though she did not linger on it. "I really need to get home."

Hyder blinked.

"What?"

"I'm sure *Mamí* already walked Gus to school," she continued, brushing a hand through her hair, already edging toward the mudroom. "But I have appointments that got skipped yesterday, and I need to see if I can drag them in before they disappear on me entirely."

That made sense. He knew she couldn't stay there with him forever. Not yet anyway.

"Hey," he said, catching her hand lightly before she could move past him completely.

She turned back. He leaned in, pressing a quick kiss to her mouth.

"Don't work too hard," he murmured.

She gave him a small laugh.

"No promises."

He walked her out through the mudroom, holding the door open for her as the cold air rushed in, though he felt her absence more than the cold.

She glanced back over her shoulder once, catching his eye, and something passed between them again.

She'll be back.

Then she was gone.

He shook himself slightly, straightened his shoulders, and stepped back inside the kitchen. It was time to deal with this.

"Hey, El," he said, keeping his tone easy as he crossed over to the other side of the island so he could face her.

Tala's smirk widened immediately, and Ellie looked up, curious.

"Listen," he started, rubbing the back of his neck, suddenly aware that he had not actually practiced this part as well as he thought he had. "I, uh...I wanted to talk to you about something."

"Okay..." Ellie said slowly, her brow raised.

Tala took a slow sip of her coffee, her eyes dancing with something that looked dangerously close to anticipation.

Hyder narrowed his eyes at her. She only smiled wider.

"Look," he continued, focusing back on Ellie. "I'm really sorry if I've...I don't know...if I ever gave you the wrong idea about anything. That wasn't my intention. I just..." He exhaled. "I feel bad. And I think this needs to stop."

Ellie blinked.

"What needs to stop?"

Hyder frowned slightly.

"I mean...you know," he said, gesturing vaguely between them, already feeling himself losing the thread. "The hanging around. The...you being around. I mean, I get it. And I appreciate it. I do. I'm even flattered, honestly. But I'm with Sola. Really with her. And I just...there's nothing that can happen between us. There never was."

Silence. A long beat of silence as Ellie stared at him with wide eyes, like she still wasn't sure what she was hearing.

Tala pressed her lips together so hard they disappeared entirely, her shoulders shaking.

Hyder glanced at her, realizing she looked like she was about to explode, and he scowled.

"Come on, El," he added, trying to recover. "I mean, you're always around. It's kind of obvious—"

"Hyder," Ellie interrupted him. "I was never hanging around to be around you."

Now it was his turn to feel confused.

"What?"

Ellie smiled, a wide one he did not often see from her. It brightened her whole face, and though she was always pretty, she now looked beautiful. Hyder shook himself, knowing that even if it was just an objective thing, it was not helpful. She then looked over at Tala, who nodded, then back at him.

"I was trying to spend time with Tala."

The words landed, and he had to sort through them for a moment before they connected. Heat flooded his face so fast it was almost impressive.

"Oh…" Then, because apparently his brain had abandoned him entirely, "Oh."

Tala lost it. Full, unrestrained laughter burst out of her, loud and delighted, as she pushed away from the counter and stepped closer to Ellie, slipping an arm easily around her waist.

"You sure?" she murmured, leaning in just enough that Hyder could hear the teasing edge in her voice.

Ellie rolled her eyes, but she was still smiling.

"Yeah," she said. "I'm sure."

They turned together, Tala still grinning like she had just been handed the best entertainment of her morning. Of her life.

"Well," Tala said, looking back at him, "Lil' Frogger, I guess you could still learn a thing or two about women."

Hyder let out a breath that was half chuckle, half relief.

"Yeah," he admitted. "Yeah, I'm starting to see that."

Tala tilted her head.

"But don't worry," she added sweetly. "I'm still willing to teach you."

He snorted.

"Somehow that doesn't make me feel better."

Ellie laughed again, and the tension, whatever had been there, whatever he had built up in his own head over the last five months, was gone.

"Speaking of," he said, glancing between them, realizing this might be a good opportunity. After all, Ellie was the one who came up with the idea for his first date with Sola. "You know my plan, right?"

Tala raised a brow.

"Oh yeah," she sighed. "We *all* know the plan, puddle jumper."

Hyder winced slightly at the nickname but let it pass.

"Well," he continued, leaning his elbow on the island, lowering his voice slightly. "I think I want to add one more thing to it."

"Oh yeah?" Tala said, clearly intrigued now. "You've already had half the town working overtime. I'm not sure what else we can do. At least not until spring. After breakup."

Hyder hesitated for just a second.

"When I show Sola, I also want to give her...a ring."

That seemed to surprise Tala. Enough that she didn't answer him right away and her expression shifted from amusement to something that looked almost like confusion, like he had just said something in a language she didn't speak.

"A ring?" she repeated.

Ellie, however, lit up.

"A ring," she echoed, excited. "Now *that* we can do."

THIRTY-EIGHT

Sola

She should've known this would happen.

Not the specifics or the exact conversations. Or the particular way each person would tilt their head or smile just a little too knowingly when she walked by. But the inevitability of it. The way a place like Alpenglow did not do anything halfway, especially not something as interesting as a new relationship.

Being certain about Hyder was one thing. That had come on her quietly, then all at once. Sola hadn't expected it, but she was no longer questioning it.

But the town's involvement was something else entirely. Because now it wasn't just her and Hyder. Now it was everyone else seeing them. Talking about them. Folding them together into something singular.

A couple.

That wasn't something she had practiced in a very long time. You could use August's age and add another nine months to get the exact date. Years of singlehood didn't simply dissolve because she had spent a night, or two, in a man's bed, no matter how compelling that man was, no matter how much her body and heart seemed to recognize him as something essential.

Independence was not a coat you shrugged off at the door. It was something you carried. Something that had kept her steady when everything else had been uncertain.

Now she was walking through her day and everyone seemed to find the need to bring up Hyder.

Galena was only the first. She accosted Sola as soon as she walked into the clinic, standing by the coffee machine, wearing a look on her face that could only be described as predatory interest.

"Well," Galena drawled, taking a slow sip before lowering her mug, her eyes sweeping over Sola from head to toe with exaggerated care. "You look...well rested."

Sola rolled her eyes, setting her tote down with more force than necessary.

"I'm always rested," she retorted, moving past her, already reaching for the first chart sitting on the desk.

"Mmhmm," Galena hummed, entirely unconvinced. "And I'm the Queen of England."

"That would be difficult," Sola said dryly, without looking up. "Considering she is dead."

Galena laughed, then moved closer.

"Come on, Sola. Details," she practically whined. Then, leaning forward slightly, lowering her voice just enough to make it worse, not better, "Did he go all night? 'Cause I always figured he'd be the one."

Sola nearly choked and she felt her face flush, and the smile that came to her lips was involuntary.

"Ooh, I'm totally taking that as a yes." The glee in her eyes was obvious. "So," she continued, "should I start planning the wedding now?"

Sola froze. Then she straightened slowly, turning to face Galena, her brows lifting in a way that was meant to communicate disbelief and annoyance but likely failed at both.

"Wedding?" she repeated. "You've jumped several steps there, no?"

Galena shrugged, completely unbothered.

"I'm efficient," she said. "Also, this is a small town. We don't do 'slow burn' very well. We go straight to casseroles and commitment."

Sola snorted despite herself, shaking her head as she turned back to her work.

"You're insane. You're all insane."

"Correct," Galena said cheerfully. "But you like us anyway."

Sola did not answer that. Because the problem was...she did.

Sighing, she grabbed her white coat and tried very hard to get back into professional mode. Her first patient of the day was Clare Brown.

Clare swept into the clinic with her normal cheer. Her graying red hair was escaping from the bun she'd had up at some point, her bright scarf half-hanging off her shoulders.

"Hey, Doc," she inclined her head slightly as she came into the exam room.

"Clare," Sola returned, gesturing toward the table for her to sit. "How are you feeling?"

Clare smiled.

"Oh, you know," she sighed. "A bit warm at night, a bit...unpredictable during the day. Nothing I can't handle."

Sola nodded, already reaching for her notes.

"When you made the appointment, you mentioned some hot flashes," she said. "Sleep disturbances. Mood changes. We can—"

"And how are you feeling?" Clare interrupted gently.

Sola paused.

"Excuse me?"

Clare's smile deepened.

"With Hyder," she clarified. "And what happened with the boat."

Sola pursed her lips.

"Clare," she said slowly, "I believe you came here to talk about perimenopause."

Clare tilted her head.

"Aren't we?" she asked.

Sola stared at her and Clare held her gaze. Then, after a beat, she relented with a soft laugh, lifting her hands slightly.

"Very well," she said. "But you must admit, it is a topic of interest. You and Hyder. The town is invested."

"I'm aware," Sola muttered.

Clare's eyes sparkled.

"And have you considered more children?" she asked, as if it were the most natural follow-up in the world.

Sola did choke this time.

"What?"

"Well," Clare continued calmly, as if she didn't notice Sola's shock, "Gus is such a delightful child, and Hyder...well, he has always been *very* good with children. He'd be a great dad. Almost as good as my Dan."

Sola stared at her. Then slowly, deliberately, she set the chart down.

"Clare." Her tone was now unmistakably professional. "We are going to discuss your hormone levels, your symptoms, and your treatment options. We are not going to plan my reproductive future."

Clare shrugged, then smiled again.

"Fair enough," she said. "Though I do think you two would make beautiful babies."

Sola pressed her lips together.

"Sit back and relax," she said. "I'm taking your blood pressure."

By the time Clare left, Sola was already tired. Which was ridiculous because it was barely mid-morning.

Her next patient did not help.

Nan arrived with the careful steps of someone who had lived a long life and intended to keep living it, her eyes clear despite the years.

"Ah," she murmured, staring at Sola with a kind of quiet approval. "You look different."

Sola narrowed her eyes slightly.

"That seems to be the consensus today."

Nan chuckled softly.

"Happy, my child," she clarified. "You look happy."

Sola hesitated, thinking that maybe Nan was just being kind.

"Maybe..." she admitted.

Nan nodded, as if that confirmed something she had already known.

"Hyder's mother was like that," she said.

Sola blinked.

"Ahnah?" she asked, curious now, despite her irritation.

Nan nodded, her gaze softening as she leaned back slightly, her hands folding in her lap.

"She had that same look," she said. "When she found something worth keeping. And she was strong like you too," Nan continued. "She picked a hard man, but he loved her, and she got her babies from it."

Sola opened her mouth, then closed it again, unsure how to respond to something that felt both too personal and oddly grounding at the same time.

Nan smiled at her.

"He was always a good boy," she added. "Hyder. Even when he pretended otherwise."

Sola found she couldn't be upset. Not with Nan. Not with someone who seemed to radiate something almost otherworldly.

"I've noticed."

Nan chuckled again.

"Of course you have," she replied. "You see more than most."

She kept talking, and Sola sat back and listened.

Stories of when the Kings were babies. Memories of her own childhood. Observations of how much things had changed and how much Nan missed the old ways sometimes.

Until Sola finally had to lift a hand, gently but firmly.

"Nan," she said. "I need to check your pulse."

Nan grinned.

"Yes, yes," she said. "Doctoring first, stories later."

By the time Sola made her way to the Raven that evening, to have dinner with Hyder and Charlie and Sutton, she was on edge. Not because of anything specific. Because of everything. The accumulation of all the teasing, the assumptions, the talk of...babies with a man she had only just decided she wanted to wake up to.

When she stepped inside, she immediately knew something was off that had nothing to do with her own annoyance.

The three of them were already there. So was Dutchy. And they were talking about it. Not their relationship status, of course. The boat and what happened. They were sitting there at the booth, their heads bent close, quieting just slightly when she approached.

Hyder didn't hesitate. He reached for her hand, tugging her down beside him, his thumb brushing lightly over her knuckles.

"And I'm telling you," he was saying, picking up the thread of the conversation without missing a beat, "we need to set up watches. Just like on a big boat."

Sutton nodded.

"I'll have Willow write up a schedule and ask for volunteers," Sutton added. "We'll have to keep eyes on both docks, the plane shed, everything."

· Dutchy made a face. "That sounds like a lotta work. But I 'spose with someone out there cutting cables and pokin' holes in hulls, we oughtta."

Sola stiffened and Hyder must have felt it, because he turned and explained.

"Yeah, Dutchy found that someone climbed up on top of the wheelhouse and cut through the coaxial cables for both the radio and the SAT antennae. We got lucky because the radio wasn't cut all the way. It had just enough to send out a short message before the signal bounced back and fried the radio completely. And the EPIRB, the locator beacon, must have been switched out. The batteries last for about ten years. Mine was only a few years old, and it tested fine during our checks the night before we left. The one on the boat was completely dead."

"Whoever did it had to know boats, just like they knew planes," Sutton added, frustration rolling off him.

Sola didn't speak. She just listened, understanding that there was now zero doubt that someone had done this purposely. She was also listening for what they were not saying. For the obvious next step as far as she was concerned. It didn't come.

"So," she finally cut in. "When are the cops coming?"

The table went still and Sutton met her eyes.

"I spent most of the day making calls," he admitted. "I've got a buddy who used to be in the reserves with me. He's with the troopers now. He doesn't know when, but he assured me they'll send someone as soon as possible."

"As soon as possible," she repeated. "Like in a week?"

Hyder's hand tightened slightly around hers.

"No," Sutton sighed. "Probably not that soon. But Sola, you must understand—"

"No!" she cut him off, pulling her hand from Hyder and crossing her arms over her chest. "I don't."

The table went quiet again.

"Someone cut a hole in Hyder's boat," she snapped. "And we still don't have answers about your plane. That's been hanging for too long already."

Sutton met her eyes, surprised. She could tell he was not used to people questioning him. Eventually a silent understanding passed between them. He knew she was not going to just let this go. Not now. Not ever.

"Okay." He nodded his head. "I'll push harder, call in a favor. I'll get someone here as soon as I can."

Sola continued to hold his gaze. Then nodded back, recognizing that this truly was the best he could do for now, and that it was maddening him just as much as it was her.

"Okay," she agreed. "I can work with—"

"Oh, my God."

Charlie's voice cut through everything. She was gripping the edge of the table, her face pale, her eyes wide.

Sola was moving before she even thought.

"Charlie," she said, already beside her. "What's wrong?"

"I..." Charlie gasped slightly. "I think..."

"Contraction?"

Charlie nodded slowly. Sola could tell she was scared but trying to keep it together. Whether for Sutton's sake or her own, Sola wasn't sure.

"Okay," Sola went on calmly. "Has your water broken?"

"I don't think so."

"Alright. We're going to the clinic." Sola was already turning. "Sutton."

He didn't move, his eyes staring at them as if they were speaking a different language.

"Sutton!" she repeated, sharper now.

He jerked upright, like he was coming back from somewhere far away.

"Help her," Sola told him. "Now."

He moved then. Fast. Hyder came around the table and helped too.

At the clinic, Sola took over completely. She was calm and focused. Not letting the fact that the patient before her was someone she had come to care about affect her control.

"Another one?" she asked, as Charlie's face tightened again.

Charlie nodded, breathing through it with short, practiced puffs, while Sola glanced at her watch and did the math.

Eighteen minutes.

At this spacing, they were still in early labor. With twins and no prior births, the latent phase could stretch for hours. Or accelerate without much warning.

Sutton hovered.

"Isn't it too early?" he asked, his voice tight. "We were supposed to get to Anchorage this week, three weeks before her due date."

"Yes," Sola said. "But twins don't always follow schedules, remember. And your dating was...approximate. Even Charlie said it could be a week or so off."

Charlie huffed out a breath and smiled now that the pain was gone.

"Tell me something I don't know."

Sola smiled faintly.

"Okay, let's take a look. Lie back," she told Charlie.

Sola worked quickly, attaching monitors, pulling out the sonogram machine, and getting Charlie's legs into stirrups.

The heartbeats were steady, and Charlie was barely dilated.

"It could be Braxton Hicks," she said finally. "False labor. But given everything, how close you are to delivery, we don't take chances."

Sutton was already gathering Charlie's things.

"We go. Right now."

"Yes," Sola agreed. "We go."

She turned to Hyder, whose usual grin was gone, his face white.

"Can you tell *Mamí* I won't be home for a couple days?"

He nodded, already moving, obviously grateful for something to do.

They drove to the Lodge fast, loading onto the plane while Hope and Gemma stood at the dock watching. Both quiet, seeming to sense that everything was not quite right.

Sutton helped Charlie into a seat with her feet up, while Sola sat across from her, with her medical bag on her lap. Ready, just in case.

Then, less than an hour after Charlie's first contraction, they were in the air, the town already shrinking beneath them.

Sutton glanced over at Charlie, reaching back to grab her hand. Then over his shoulder.

"Hey, Sola."

"Yeah?"

"I'm real glad you're here."

Sola looked at him, seeing the vulnerability he usually tried so hard to hide.

"Yeah," she agreed. "Me too."

THIRTY-NINE

Hyder

The message came through just after two in the morning.

Hyder wasn't asleep. He hadn't been able to sleep, not really, not since the plane had taken off. The worry was eating at him. He could only imagine what his older brother was going through.

The Lodge kitchen was dim, lit only by the low glow over the stove and a small lamp near the window. Hope and Gemma had finally fallen asleep upstairs, and Sterling, who was still up on the Slope for a few more days, was told, over the family chat, what was going on. Now, the four of them, Hyder, Willow, Tala, and Ellie, had settled into that strange, suspended state that came with waiting for news about someone you loved.

Coffee had been made. Then more coffee.

At some point, Tala had switched to something stronger and pretended it was still coffee, and Willow had pretended not to notice when Ellie leaned her head on Tala's shoulder. Or maybe she had known all along. That would track.

Hyder sat at the table, his phone in front of him, his hand resting beside it, not touching it, because touching it would not make the message come faster.

When the chime finally sounded, all four of them looked down at the same time.

Hyder swiped open the screen, reading aloud.

Hey family.
We're thrilled to announce the safe arrival of our twins!
Ahnah Primrose King, born first at 11:32 p.m.
And Charles Aksel King, born at 1:07 a.m.
Annie came into the world like her daddy, still up in the air because she clearly loves flying. Little Charlie was far more sensible, like his mama, and waited until we made it to the hospital.
Both babies are a little small, but they have some lungs on them. Especially Annie.
Annie was 4 lbs. 14 oz. Charlie was 4 lbs. 6 oz.
Mom and babies are all doing great. The twins will need to stay in the NICU for at least a week or two to grow and get stronger, but the doctor here said everything looks really good. Doc was amazing too. Marsh will probably take her home tomorrow afternoon.
We can't wait for you all to meet Little Charlie and Annie!
Sutton & Charlie

When he was done, he laughed softly, something easing in his chest, his head dropping as he let everything settle.

Ahnah and Charles. Good names.

"They're okay," he whispered.

"They're okay," Willow echoed, her voice already brightening as she leaned over to see it for herself.

"Of course they are," Tala said confidently. "Kings don't do anything halfway, not even being born."

Hyder read it again to himself, smiling, knowing his brother threw in the part about Sola for him. And he was grateful.

He missed her.

Even when they had been apart before, he had always known where to find her, always known she was just across the boardwalk, or down at the clinic. Somewhere close.

While she'd been gone, even though it had only been several hours, he spent most of the evening at her cottage, letting Lucia feed him and watching Gus draw. It was the only place in the whole town that didn't feel quite so wrong. He shook off the idea, knowing he was being ridiculous.

"Well," he yawned and pushed back his chair and stood, rolling his shoulders slightly. "I guess I'm gonna head to bed."

"Whoa, whoa, whoa," Tala blurted out, leaning forward, her eyes narrowing just slightly as she watched him. "Not so fast, puddle jumper."

Hyder froze mid-step, one foot already on the first stair, and turned back slowly.

Willow perked up instantly. "Ooh," she said, rubbing her hands together. "That's her 'I'm about to meddle' tone."

Ellie snorted and Hyder groaned.

"No," he growled, pointing at all three of them. "No meddling. Not tonight. I'm tired."

Tala leaned back in her chair, crossing her arms, looking entirely unimpressed.

"You can sleep after you answer one question," she told him.

Hyder narrowed his eyes but knew she would just follow him up the stairs if he ignored her. She'd done it before.

"What question?"

"When," Tala said slowly, savoring the moment, "are you planning to pop the question?"

Silence. Then Willow gasped.

"Oh my God!" she exclaimed, spinning toward him. "You are, aren't you? You're totally going to ask her! I mean, I knew you wanted to, but I thought you were gonna chicken out or wait for a while. You've been pretty tight-lipped about it."

Hyder looked up to the ceiling like he might find some kind of answer that didn't involve having this conversation with his sister.

"Wills—"

"When?" she pressed, bouncing slightly in her seat now, fully awake despite the hour. "How? Oh my God, is it going to be at Vår Fest? Or the docks? Or...wait...what if we string lights and flowers all the way down the boardwalk—"

"Or we get the whole town involved," Tala cut in, leaning forward again, her eyes gleaming. "Like a full setup. Music. Food. Maybe an impromptu bonfire. You walk her over blindfolded..."

Ellie laughed.

"Blindfolded?" she asked. "That's how you lead someone to a firing squad, not get engaged."

Hyder held up both hands.

"Stop," he said firmly. "All of you. Stop."

They didn't.

"If you do it at the church—" Willow started.

"I am not doing it at the church," Hyder cut her off right there.

"And why not?" she demanded. "It's so pretty in there at sunset!"

"Because," he sighed, losing patience, "believe it or not, some people like their privacy, and Sola is one of those people."

That finally stopped them.

"Oh." Willow deflated just slightly. Then, after a beat, her expression brightened again. "But still...you're gonna do it soon. Right?"

Hyder hesitated. He hadn't planned on sharing this part with his family.

Not yet. Not until he'd already asked and hopefully had a fiancée. That way, it could be just them and there was less chance of interference.

But now that Willow knew it was happening, they were all going to know soon enough.

"Yeah," he admitted. "It's gonna be soon."

Three identical looks of triumph spread across their faces.

"Called it," Tala grinned.

"Oh, this is going to be so good." Willow rubbed her hands together again. "We need another wedding. It's been too boring around here lately."

Hyder just stared at her like she was crazy, especially after the last few days, but he didn't bother to correct her.

"Go to bed," he muttered, turning back toward the stairs.

"Sleep well, future Mr. Doc," Tala called after him.

He flipped her off without looking back.

Late the next day, just as the sun was dipping below the western mountains, turning the sky into that deep blush of alpenglow that would try to hold on until it went violet in twilight, then darker as night eventually claimed it fully, Marshall brought Sola home.

Hyder was already at the dock. He'd been there longer than he wanted to admit. Long enough that Gus had gotten wiggly and eventually climbed onto his back and refused to get down, his small arms wrapped around his neck in a grip that was both affectionate and mildly suffocating.

"Buddy," Hyder winced, reaching up to pry one of those arms loose just enough to breathe, "you're trying to kill me."

Gus shifted slightly.

"No," he explained seriously. "Just holding."

Hyder chuckled.

"Yeah," he told him. "I can tell."

Lucia stood nearby, bundled in a thick coat and colorful scarf, her hands tucked into her pockets, her eyes fixed on the horizon with the same quiet patience she brought to everything.

The plane was coming in with a slow descent. Hyder could tell that Marshall was looking over the mouth of the cove, trying to decide if it was smooth enough, or if he should bank around to land by the Lodge. He must have felt confident, because the engine slowed even more.

Hyder straightened instinctively, adjusting Gus on his back as the floats skimmed the water and the plane taxied toward the dock.

The hatch opened and Sola stepped out, her hair pulled back into a high ponytail, her coat wrapped tight around her, her eyes already searching.

She found them right away, her smile breaking across her face instantly.

"Hey, GusGus!" She waved.

"Mom!" Gus shouted, nearly choking Hyder again as he tried to wave and hold on at the same time.

Hyder laughed, crouching slightly so Gus could slide down, then stepping forward as Sola reached them.

She didn't hesitate. She went straight to him. Looking up into his eyes, like she needed to see something there as much as he did.

"I've missed you," she murmured.

That was exactly what he wanted to hear before he did what he was about to do.

"Me too, *Sha'aéil*," he answered.

Marshall walked up behind her.

"Heya, Hyder. Doc here did real good," he said, nodding toward Sola. "The little Kings are loud and already bossing people around."

Sola laughed.

"They are," she agreed. "Especially Annie. I had to deliver her before we landed. You should have seen Sutton's face! But Charlie was great."

"Just wait. Now Sutton has to deal with not just two little girls comin' home with them hairy-legged ol' boys, but three," Marshall shoved his hands in his pockets and whistled.

They exchanged a few more words, easy and familiar, then Marshall moved off, talking of getting some grub and hopefully a bed for the night from Healy.

As they watched him leave, Hyder reached for Sola's hand, threading his fingers through hers, and they started up the ramp.

They didn't make it more than ten steps before the town started to close in.

"Doc!" someone called across the water. "Welcome back!"

"How're the babies?" another voice chimed in.

"Did Charlie bite Sutton?" Tala shouted from somewhere.

Sola laughed, shaking her head.

"Everyone is good," she called back. "The babies are a little small, but strong. And no biting. Not yet anyway."

"Give it time," Micah muttered from his porch.

"Did you eat?" Cheryl asked. "You look like you haven't eaten."

"I ate," Sola promised.

"Welcome home, Doc," Healy bellowed, poking his head out of the Raven, and raising a hand.

Sola smiled.

"Good to be home," she told him.

It struck Hyder that it didn't feel like something she was saying out of politeness. It felt true.

Hyder didn't take the turn to Sola's cottage. Instead, he went south, toward the square. He noticed there were more people than usual wandering around. And he knew exactly why. He only hoped they could keep it to themselves, but it was asking a lot and he knew it.

Sola slowed slightly, her brow furrowing as she seemed to notice everyone too.

"What's going on?" she asked. "Where are we going?"

"Don't worry," he said easily. "It's not far."

"It's a surprise," Lucia added.

"Surprise, Mom," Gus echoed, grabbing at Hyder's other hand now.

Sola looked between them all, then at the large crowd gathering around the square, clearly suspicious. Then she sighed.

"Fine," she shrugged. "But if this involves more people asking me about the babies, I'm going home."

Hyder laughed.

"Duly noted."

They crossed the square and Hyder found himself grateful that the only conversations were more warm welcomes and only a few more questions about the babies. He tightened his grip on Sola's hand, and they kept walking toward the clinic. Then they continued past it, down the road toward Kisa'adi.

It was almost completely dark now, except for the ice lanterns that he'd frozen the night before and lit today to mark their path. It was enough for Hyder to see a little crease forming between Sola's brows as her mind worked, trying to piece together what was happening.

He stopped when he got to a break in the snow berms, a break he'd made himself with a snowblower. He looked down at her feet, realizing that she was wearing her Kamiks for once.

Good.

"Okay," he cleared his throat, feeling a little nervous now. "From here it's a little rougher, but it should be alright. It hasn't snowed since we last cleared it."

Sola opened her mouth, then closed it when she saw the look of challenge on his face. She narrowed her eyes.

"You're enjoying this," she accused.

"Maybe a little," he admitted.

They kept walking through the narrow, snow-packed path, taking their time as the ground inclined up the rise. Hyder wasn't sure if Sola realized it, but they were almost due south of the clinic now, maybe a quarter of a mile away. They kept walking until they reached a wide clearing. Right in the middle was a hill, one of the highest points around the town except for the mountains.

Sola stopped, turning slowly, taking in the view. From where they were, they could see the town and cove just below, the lights flickering over the water, the church on the bluff.

"Wow," she breathed. "It's beautiful up here."

Hyder's chest tightened.

"Yeah?" he said quietly. "I'm glad you think so."

She looked at him then, still curious.

"Why are we here? What is this place?" she asked again.

He swallowed.

"We've been clearing it," he explained. "For a few weeks now. Me. Sutton. Tala. Whoever else I could rope into it."

"For what?"

He stepped closer.

"For a house," he told her. "For you. For Gus. For Lucia. For...us. Whatever you want it to be, *Sha'aéil*."

The only sound was soft crunching under Sola's boots as she turned full circle again.

"A house?" she asked quietly. "For us?"

"Yeah. I will build you anything. You just name it."

"Surprise, Mom," Gus said again, beaming, bouncing from one foot to the other.

They all laughed, the moment suddenly turning into something freer.

Hyder crouched, holding out his hand, letting Gus give him a high five. Then he whispered to him, "Ready?"

Gus nodded and Hyder stood, reaching into his pocket. His heart was thundering in his ears, but he finally felt certain. More certain than he had about anything else in his life.

"Sola."

She turned toward him, her eyes still big.

He held out a small bentwood box and heard her gasp.

He opened it. Inside was a delicate driftwood ring. He'd found the small piece on the beach at low tide and spent the last couple of days carving it, carefully shaping the wood into a thin, simple band, hollowing the center until it would fit her finger perfectly. He'd done it without anyone else's input, despite Ellie's offer and knowing Willow probably would have found something better.

He only hoped she would understand why. That the wood had crossed oceans, been tumbled and tested by every storm the sea could throw at it and still arrived whole and strengthened. Like them. He had shaped it into something still fragile and strong, meant to circle her finger forever, just as he hoped to circle her heart.

"I didn't know what you'd like," he admitted. "So I made this. I'll get you anything you want, though, anything. But this...this is from me."

Her mouth parted and her eyes filled with tears.

"I love it," she whispered. "It's perfect."

"Marry me," he asked simply, not having any other words that would mean as much.

"*Sí,*" she answered immediately. "Yes."

He pulled her into his arms and kissed her, and when he pulled back, he saw that Gus and Lucia were smiling too.

"Hey guys, how about we head over to the Raven? I am pretty sure Healy made up some hot cocoa and gløgg. And to be honest, I'm surprised the town was able to keep the party quiet and not come up here to drag us back already."

Everyone laughed at that, and they began walking back down. From behind them, before they made it to the road, Lucia cleared her throat.

"I think I will stay in town," she announced casually. "Maybe in one of the cottages. A small one, overlooking the water."

Sola inhaled sharply and stopped in her tracks.

"*Mamí*, why?"

Lucia smiled.

"I have never had my own space, Marisolita," she explained. "And now it is time for you to have yours."

Hyder shook his head.

"Lucia, you can always be with us. There will always be room."

"I know, *Señor* King...*Hiderito*. And I will visit every day, to cook for my family. I promise. But if I stay...," she paused for a moment, "where will you put all the babies?"

Then she walked past them, continuing down the hill like it was settled.

Gus skipped after her.

Hyder froze.

"Babies?" he echoed.

Sola laughed. Actually laughed. A joyful sound that Hyder felt in his chest. Then she shrugged.

"Babies."

Hyder grinned then too. Because now that he thought about it, babies sounded kinda perfect.

"Come on, *Sha'aéil*," he murmured, pulling her closer. "Let's go inside. It's getting cold."

As they walked back, hand in hand, the sky completely dark now, they both looked up.

Weaving across the sky, were soft ribbons of green light. They were not the brightest or the boldest. But they were there, reminding them to always look.

The story of Alpenglow will continue in:

Forget Me Not

coming soon

p.s. To everyone who made it to the final page. Some books are written because a story refuses to leave you alone. Alpenglow, and now A Northern Light, were written because Alaska never did. So truly, thank you for continuing on this journey with me.

If this story made you laugh, ache, blush, or feel a little less alone, I hope you might consider leaving a review wherever you read it. Reviews are the campfires of the book world. They help other readers find stories they might love, and for indie authors like me, they make a bigger difference than you probably realize.

Because of readers like you, I get to keep returning to Alpenglow. Which is good, because the Kings are far from finished with me.

Special Acknowledgements:

To G. Thank you for being the steady hand behind so many of these pages.

For the quiet reminders about deadlines when my thoughts drift too far ahead of themselves. For narrowing the noise when I lose my focus somewhere between imagination and chaos. For making dinner when I am too deep in a story to remember the world still expects things like food and sleep.

Thank you for being my partner in crime, in cooking, in adventures, and in all the wonderfully unpredictable moments in between. And the quiet ones too!

Again, to all my Alpha, Beta, and ARC readers, and every single person out there quietly cheering these books forward. Thank you for helping build this world alongside me, for believing in Alpenglow long before it ever had a real place on a shelf. Years from now, when these stories have traveled farther than I ever dared hope, I truly hope you will look at them and think, I helped bring that into the world.

Because you did.